CRAWFORD SMITH

Laughingstock

SWEET WEASEL WORDS
PORTLAND, OREGON, USA
sweetweaselwords.com

for Mom and Dad

Acknowledgement

Special thanks to Jess Truhan and Kim Smith who provided invaluable feedback over the years while this book was being written.

Special thanks to Pat Ferrell, who provided wonderful insight into the inner workings of Tinseltown, which I probably got wrong regardless. Also, much thanks to John Gallucci, my local comedy contact and sounding board. Extra-special thanks to Alex Falcone, a hilarious comedian and superlative comedy teacher, for his contributions and suggestions. Major kudos to Benjamin Gorman for helping break a plotting logjam at a crucial moment.

Most of all, much thanks and love to my sweet honeybee NancyAnne, whose patience and advice made this book possible.

I

Part One

REUNION

Chapter 1

July 2014

Mickey was dead, and Duckie was nervous.

Fabled comedian Mickey Gross was dead because a wicked case of pancreatic cancer had burned him up in a matter of months. He had been reduced to a husk of the dynamic man who had stormed stage and screen for decades. The only post-diagnosis photo, published by the *American Investigator*, showed a wisp of a man in a hospital bed, barely able to lift his hand to give the thumbs-up to the photographer. One week later he was gone.

Duckie Dunne was nervous because he was zooming along at three-quarters of the speed of sound, about six miles above northern Nevada. He didn't think of himself as a nervous flier, but until today his experience with air travel had been limited to a handful of flights on the East Coast. This cross-country trip from Baltimore to Portland was something else, and the longer he was in the air, the more nervous he became.

If he was being honest with himself, Duckie was more nervous about what was waiting for him at the end of the flight. He hadn't seen his childhood friend Chuck Marshall in nearly two years, and he wondered how the reunion was going to go.

Duckie and Chuck had been friends since the sixth grade in Raleigh, and it was their love of comedy that had really cemented their relationship. They were huge fans of all the greats – Carlin, Pryor, Hicks – but it was the comedy of Mickey Gross that had really brought them together. It had started the day that Chuck had showed up at school with a CD filched from his dad's collection: Mickey's *Blowing Rainbows* album.

"Hey, have you ever heard of this guy?" Chuck had asked, waving the CD under Duckie's nose.

"Quit moving your hand so I can see it," replied Duckie. "Nah, never heard of him. Is it prog?"

"No, it's comedy," said Chuck. "It makes my parents really laugh hard, but they won't let me listen to it. Wanna check it out?"

"Yeah, sure," said Duckie.

They had gone back to Chuck's house after school and waited until his mom went out, and listened to the CD on the stereo in the living room.

They laughed their asses off.

Of course, they didn't get all of the jokes – especially the title track – but there was enough that could be grasped by a pair of bright twelve-year-olds. It *was* funny.

"Man, I can't believe people get paid to do stuff like that," said Duckie.

"Yeah," replied Chuck. "I wonder what it would be like to do comedy for a living."

"Are you kidding?" Duckie had said. "I'd be scared shitless to try. What if nobody laughed?"

The seed had been planted. There was no more talk that day of trying to be comedians, but a mutual obsession had been born. Duckie and Chuck had become rabid stand-up comedy fans. They haunted cable TV, glomming on to any stand-up special they could find. They had the schedule of Comedy Central memorized. Chuck discovered that comedy LPs could be had for fire-sale prices at Schoolkids Records over by the NC State campus, and began bringing them home by the armload. He made tapes of them and traded them with Duckie.

They became adolescent comedy scholars. Their tastes weren't exactly the same. Duckie remembered a monster fight they had gotten into over Emo Philips. Duckie thought he was pretty dumb, but Chuck thought he was brilliant. The argument had escalated into a shouting match that had been broken up by Chuck's mom.

Things had continued that way until right after the beginning of their freshman year in high school. At that point, Mickey Gross's short-lived sitcom had just gone belly up. In fact, Mickey's whole *career* was in the process of going belly up, but to Duckie and Chuck he was a comedy deity who could do no wrong.

Right after Mickey's sitcom was canceled, he had appeared on Letterman. It was generally agreed that it had been a disastrous performance, but for Duckie and Chuck it had been galvanic.

Chapter 2

September 2005

It was a lovely September Saturday in Raleigh, sunny and warm, with just a hint of autumn in the breezes that wafted through the Plantation Pointe neighborhood. Duckie had his bedroom window open, even though the air conditioning was cranked up. He liked the scent of the pine straw in the sun. The houses in the neighborhood were large and tended towards Greek Revival architectural styles: a row of Taras, set well back from the street, with tasteful security fences around the perimeter. Every house had a crew of Mexican gardeners who spread fresh pine straw every month. It was really the only thing Duckie liked about the neighborhood.

Duckie saw Chuck come around the corner, pushing his ten-speed. He looked sweaty and tired. Duckie knew that he had biked nearly six miles from his house in Quail Hills, closer to the center of the city. Quail Hills was a nice neighborhood, but not nearly as fancy as Plantation Pointe. They were at opposite ends of the boundaries of the Brookmill School District. Duckie had met Chuck on the first day of middle school, three years ago.

Chuck paused in front of the walkway and leaned back on the bike seat. Duckie's mom once said that Chuck looked like a young Vince Van Patten. Duckie had had to Google the name. He could see the resemblance: tall, with all-American blond hair and pale blue eyes. Chuck's face was longer and a lot more intelligent than ol' Vince's, in Duckie's opinion.

Duckie himself was short and thick-waisted. His father said he looked "black Irish" with dark hair, pale skin and close-set brown eyes. He had full cheeks, which gave his face a pear shape. Duckie hated this, and kept his hair long to obscure it.

A coil of nervous excitement unspooled in Duckie's belly as he watched Chuck lean his bike against one of the portico columns. He'd spent a long time thinking about bringing up his idea with Chuck, and he was worried that Chuck would just laugh in his face. The thought that he might say yes was just as scary. But Duckie had seen something on TV last night that had convinced him to go ahead and take the plunge.

First, he had to get Chuck past his mom. Mrs. Dunne was old-school Scarlett O'Hara Southern gentry – or at least wanted people to think so. She interrogated anyone who came to visit with polite yet probing questions.

Duckie heard the muted *bong-bong* of the doorbell, and crept down the hallway, poking his head around the corner so he could see down the staircase to the front door. His mother opened the door, resplendent in her massively hair-sprayed blond 'do and a tasteful pantsuit.

"Charles!" she said as she opened the door. "I thought you were the caterer. You haven't seen a catering van in the neighborhood, have you?"

"No, ma'am. Sorry."

"Oh, fiddlesticks!" said Mrs. Dunne. "Oh well. How are you enjoying high school, Charles?"

"It's okay, I guess. It's a big adjustment from middle school, that's for sure."

"I'm glad you like it. Brookmill is one of the top high schools in the state. It's a magnet school, you know. People from all over the county go to great lengths to get their children enrolled there. We're very fortunate to live within the district. Wilbert seems to be having some difficulty adjusting. I can't understand why."

Duckie moved to the top of the stairs and made an impatient "hurry up" gesture. Chuck saw him and shrugged.

Duckie ducked back behind the corner and hollered, "Cripes, Mom, would you just send him up already? And stop talking about me like I'm some sort of retard!"

"Wilbert, you are being quite rude!" exclaimed Mrs. Dunne. "You should come down here and greet your guest!"

"Just send him up already!" Duckie said. He retreated to his bedroom and slammed the door. He waited a few moments and stuck his head out the door to see Chuck coming down the hall. "C'mon, c'mon," Duckie hissed, gesturing for Chuck to hurry. "Before Momzilla decides to follow you!"

Chuck sprinted the last fifteen feet and slid through the doorway. Duckie slammed the door behind him and locked it. Duckie's bedroom was a total mess, with clothes and books piled on the king-size bed and all over the Scandinavian furniture. A large entertainment center dominated the far end of the room.

"Jeez, what's all the fuss, Gus?" asked Chuck. "Your mom seemed pretty worked up about some caterer or something."

"Ah, the 'rents are throwing some sort of garden party tomorrow," said Duckie. "The caterers fucked something up and Mom is in a tizzy."

"What about your dad?" asked Chuck. Duckie's dad was a surgeon, and had a number of business enterprises, including several apartment buildings and car washes.

"Ah, Dad couldn't give the first third of a fuck about this garden party," said Duckie. "Other than the fact that Mom won't shut up about it, that is. He's got some sort of big-whoop business deal in the works. It's making him act like a bigger asshole than usual. Fortunately, he's at the office today. The only drawback is that it leaves only me to listen to Mom bitching about the caterers."

"Oh, intercourse the caterers!" said Chuck. "What about that thing with Mickey on Letterman last night? You saw it, right?"

"Of course I saw it," said Duckie. "The whole thing was staged. It's obvious."

"I don't know," said Chuck. "Letterman looked pretty pissed."

"Of course he looked pissed," countered Duckie. "He was playing along. If he'd just brushed it off, it wouldn't have had the same impact."

"Too bad we can't watch it again and say for sure," said Chuck. He unshouldered the backpack he'd been carrying.

"Who says we can't?" asked Duckie.

"Not me!" said Chuck. He pulled a videocassette from his backpack and waved it triumphantly.

"Dude, what the hell is that?" asked Duckie.

"A VCR tape," said Chuck uncertainly. "What? I taped Letterman last night so we could re-watch Mickey."

"Man, the Stone Age just called. They want their video technology back!"

"Then how the hell are we supposed to watch it?"

"With that!" said Duckie, indicating a box on top of the TV.

"Shit, when did you get a TiVo?"

"Birthday present."

"Fuckin' cool, man," said Chuck. "You always get the best gifts."

"It's a sorry substitute for real parenting," said Duckie. He snatched a pair of remotes from his desk, fired up the TV and the TiVo, and was soon fast-forwarding through the previous night's episode of Late Show with David Letterman. "Here we go," he said, and pressed play.

The show's logo appeared, accompanied by a blast of music from Paul Shaffer and his band. The camera cut to Letterman, grinning as always, sitting at his desk.

"Our next guest is a long-time friend of the show," said Letterman. "You know him as Alvin on the TV show *Star Monkey Empire*, and for his always original stand-up comedy. Please welcome … Mickey Gross!"

The band struck up a brass-heavy version of the *Star Monkey Empire* theme song, and Mickey came sauntering onto the set. He looked rough. His sandy hair was mussed up and he had a three-day growth of beard. He was wearing a tattered NYU sweatshirt with a dark stain on the left shoulder – it could've been barbecue sauce or dried blood. His jeans were faded and blown out at the knees, and he was wearing two different sneakers. He threw his lanky frame into the chair next to Letterman, and belched.

"Good to see you, too, Mickey," said Letterman.

"Jesus, he looks like shit!" commented Duckie.

"I know," said Chuck. "Like he's drunk or something."

"I thought he didn't drink," said Duckie. "Isn't he into one of those woo-woo cults that don't allow booze or drugs?"

"I dunno, he might be faking it…"

"Shh…"

On the screen, Letterman looked nonplussed. "So, Mickey, you got some bad news recently: *Star Monkey Empire* will not be back for another season. The Wolff Network has decided to cancel it, despite consistently solid ratings."

"Praise be to God!" intoned Mickey. "Best news of my life hearing that show got canceled. What a load of garbage. Mindless drivel for mindless morons."

"Whoa!" said Letterman. "You're worse than the critic for the *Post!*" This brought a rim-shot from the drummer.

"No, seriously," said Mickey. "Dave, this show is the most … just a sec…" He fished in the pocket of his jeans and dug out a squashed pack of Winstons. He pulled a bent smoke from the pack, straightened it, and lit it. "Got an ashtray?" he asked.

"Uh, no," said Letterman, stone faced. "This is a non-smoking facility. Has been for about twenty years. So, no ashtray."

"No worries," said Mickey. "I'll make do." He reached over and plucked Letterman's coffee cup from his desk and ashed into it.

"Holy shit!" said Duckie. "I still can't believe it!"

"I dunno," said Chuck. "It could all be staged. Worked it out ahead of the show."

"No way! Look at Letterman – he's pissed!"

On screen, Mickey took another puff and blew a plume over Letterman's head. Letterman just glared.

"So, anyway, Dave," said Mickey. "That monkey show was sucking my soul dry. There's no vision, no creation. It's all just hack writing and tired formulas. Just like all network television."

"Really," said Letterman dryly.

"Look, I don't want to talk about that damn show," Mickey continued. "I'd like to talk about what's next for me artistically."

"Please do," said Letterman. "Thinking of taking up macramé?"

"No," said Mickey. "I want to bring back a comedic art form, one that has been dead for decades."

"I wish you'd bring some comedy to this appearance," said Letterman. "Because there hasn't been much so far."

"Yeah, whatever," said Mickey, and he launched another plume of smoke over Letterman's head. "What I'm talking about is bringing back the comedy duo. There were Laurel and Hardy, Abbot and Costello, Nichols and May, Cheech and Chong…"

"Beavis and Butthead," said Letterman.

"That was just another dumbass TV show," snarled Mickey. "I'm talking about bringing back an underappreciated form of comedic expression, one with unlimited creative potential!"

"So you're saying that you've found a partner," said Letterman.

"You're fuckin'-A right," said Mickey. The last part was bleeped, but it was pretty obvious by how his mouth moved.

Letterman cut his eyes offstage, and then turned back to Mickey. "So, is this someone we've heard of, your new partner?" he asked.

"No, no, absolutely not," said Mickey. "My new partner is absolutely new, but he's a damn comedy genius! I met him on Houston Street, where he was busking and directing traffic. We hit it off right away. We started talking, putting some material together, and tonight is his public debut. His name's Ernie Willis, and I think you're really going to love him."

Letterman looked skeptical. "Oooo-kay," he said. "Well, let's go ahead and get this over with. Without any further ado, ladies and gentlemen … Ernie Willis!"

The camera panned over to the multi-colored curtain from where the guests usually appeared. It remained motionless. The seconds dragged out.

Finally, Letterman started to say, "Well, I guess…"

He was interrupted by a loud crash and a gasp from the audience. The camera panned jerkily over to the bandstand, where a man staggered out, knocking over a high-hat stand. He wore a black knit cap, oversized aviator sunglasses, and a stained cloth overcoat that looked so foul you could almost smell it through the television. He had a huge salt-and-pepper beard that covered his face. The small amount of skin that was visible was gray.

"Ah, here he is now," said Mickey.

The man extricated himself from the drum equipment and looked around in confusion.

"Mister, um, Ernie," said Letterman. "Over here, please." He waved his hand at the open stage area between the bandstand and the desk. "Over here. Right in the middle."

Ernie seemed to grasp this, nodded, and took a few staggering steps towards the indicated area. Then he stopped abruptly and stiffened. His hands went to his belly and his shoulders started hitching. He made a few retching sounds and abruptly spun away from the camera. The camera operator quickly turned the camera back to the desk. Still audible was a yarking sound, followed by a wet splash. The audience reaction was immediate: horrified "oohhs" and some sarcastic applause. Immediately, Paul Shaffer launched the band into a version of Aerosmith's "Sick as a Dog."

The camera stayed on a shot of the desk. Letterman gestured wildly off-camera. Mickey Gross was doubled over with laughter. The camera zoomed in on Letterman, who said, "Looks like Mr. Ernie had dinner in the CBS commissary! That's all the time we have for tonight, folks. Clean up on aisle three!" The screen went to the closing credits and Duckie stopped the TiVo.

"Man, he's done for," said Chuck. "I think we've seen Mickey's last appearance on Letterman. Or any other TV show, for that matter."

"We'll see," said Duckie. Actually he didn't care that much about the show – he was about to make his pitch to Chuck. He felt his heart racing. "Actually," he said, "I was thinking more about what Mickey said about the lost art form."

"Whaddaya mean?"

"That thing he said about comedy duos," said Duckie. "There used to be tons of them. Now there's hardly any."

"Then what is your point?" asked Chuck. "Besides the one on the top of your head?"

"I think Mickey was right about comedy duos. I think that maybe they're due for a comeback."

Chuck regarded Duckie closely. "So?" he asked.

Duckie took a deep breath. It was now or never. "Well, um, I was thinking that, y'know, maybe you and me could, like, think about doing comedy. *Real* comedy. You know, together." It felt weird saying it out loud. It was almost as if he had told Chuck that he was queer for him or something.

Chuck just stared at him, his eyes watchful, roaming across Duckie's face. The tension drew out. Finally, Duckie said, "Well? Say something! If you're gonna laugh in my face then go ahead and laugh in my face, okay?"

Another moment passed before Chuck said. "Let me show you something." He rooted around in his backpack, pulled out a spiral-bound notebook and handed it to Duckie. "No one else knows about this."

Duckie flipped it open. Page after page was covered in Chuck's chicken-scratch handwriting. They were jokes. Some short, some long – many bearing a remarkable similarity to bits by Woody Allen, George Carlin … and Mickey Gross.

"Wow," said Duckie. "How long have you, y'know, been working on this?"

"'Bout a year," said Chuck. "I started, like, last Thanksgiving. My folks were really fighting a lot, so I spent most of the break in my room. Writing jokes."

"Three by five cards," said Duckie.

"Huh?"

"I use three by five cards. I read somewhere that a lot of comedians do that when they're working up material." Duckie handed Chuck the notebook and plopped down on the bed. "Jesus!" he said. "I was so damn nervous about bringing this up with you. I was afraid that you'd, y'know, just laugh."

"Yeahhhh," said Chuck. "I'd been thinking the same thing, to tell you the truth. Ever since I started working on the notebook. I'd thought about maybe trying to perform or something, but whenever I tried to figure out, like how or where – well, I just kinda shut down."

"I know," said Duckie. "Just the thought of getting up on stage – alone – and trying to make people laugh. It kinda makes me want to piss my pants.

Metaphorically speaking."

"But if we didn't have to get up on stage alone," said Chuck, nodding vigorously. "If we did it, y'know, together, that wouldn't be so bad."

"So you up for it?" asked Duckie, his heart thumping. "You wanna try doing comedy together? For reals?"

Chuck was nodding even harder now. "Yeah!" he said. "Hell yeah! We could totally do it! Man, Mickey was right. The comedy duo is due for a comeback, and we're the ones to do it. Dig it: The comedy stylings of Chuckie and Duckie!"

"Yeah," said Duckie. "How about 'Duckie and Chuckie'? It's got a better ring to it."

"But 'Chuckie and Duckie' is alphabetical," said Chuck. "Besides, I thought of it first."

"Bullshit. We'll flip for it."

They flipped. Chuck won.

"Okay, so 'Chuckie and Duckie' it is," said Chuck.

"Best two out of three?" asked Duckie.

"Fuck, no. I won. You're not gonna be a douche about this name thing, are you?"

"Naw, it's cool," said Duckie. "It's kind of a rush, man. I've been thinking about this a long time. We're gonna fuckin' do this!"

"Hell, yes!" said Chuck. "High five, partner!" They slapped skin.

"Okay, first things first," said Duckie. "We're gonna need material. Pretty much all of the stuff I wrote was for one person, y'know? How about you?"

"Pretty much the same," admitted Chuck.

"No worries. We're a couple of funny guys – I'm sure we'll be able to come up with some good material. Now the next question. Where are we gonna perform?"

"There's always Night Yuks," said Chuck. Night Yuks was a top-tier comedy club, and got most of the A-listers touring the East Coast. "I'll bet we can get on their open mic night or something."

"Good," said Duckie. "That'll give us something to shoot for. We'll need to work out some material before we go for Night Yuks. Get some stage time."

"Where?" asked Chuck.

"I bet we can find a coffee shop or something that has an open mic," said Duckie. "We'll figure something out. First we need material, though. You got any blank pages in that notebook?"

Chuck laughed. "Plenty!" He riffled through the pages, showing that most of them were untouched.

"Let's get busy then!" said Duckie.

"Fuckin'-A right," said Chuck. "Watch out, world, here comes the amazing new comedy team of Chuckie and Duckie!"

Chapter 3

July 2014

The pilot announced that the flight was beginning its descent into Portland. Duckie lifted the shade, but beyond the wing there was nothing but clouds. He assessed the wing: It seemed to be holding up okay. He slid the window shade back down.

He thought back to that feverish fall of 2005. After he and Chuck had decided to give it a go, it had become an obsession. They spent all of their free time in either's bedroom, pitching ideas, refining ideas, discarding ideas, and writing down the good ones.

They sometimes argued about what to write about. "We need to just talk about real stuff," Chuck had said one day when they were spitballing ideas in his bedroom. "Things people can relate to. Something with a message."

"A message?" asked Duckie. "Like what? You going to spread the good news about Jesus or something?"

"I don't know," shrugged Chuck. "I just think we can do more than just make people laugh."

"Why?" asked Duckie. "That's the whole damn point. People don't go to a comedy show for politics or philosophy or any sort of fuckin' *message*. They just want to laugh!"

"Yeah, I guess so…"

"Look, let's get good at making people laugh, then we can start talking about messages and stuff," said Duckie. "That's what I want to do. I want to make them laugh so hard they crap their pants!"

"Eww!" exclaimed Chuck. "You can't be serious!"

"I dunno, I dunno," said Duckie. "I'm just talkin' shit."

"Yeah, literally."

"Or maybe like that Monty Python sketch about the funniest joke in the world," said Duckie.

"I don't know that one."

"Damn, you're lame! That's, like, one of their best sketches, in my humble opinion. I've got it on DVD. You have to see it. The gag is that this guy writes a joke so fuckin' funny that anyone who hears it laughs themselves to death."

"Damn, that's even worse! What the hell's up with you, Duckie? I just want to share something with the audience, but you want to make them shit themselves and die!"

"Okay, okay, slack, slack," said Duckie. "We'll keep it simple. No pants-crapping, no deaths, and definitely *no messages*. Agreed?"

"Agreed."

They worked up a set and rehearsed tirelessly for the Wednesday night open mic at Night Yuks. Without telling their parents, they had gotten a ride downtown from a buddy who had his learner's permit. They were almost stopped at the door – they hadn't considered that they needed to be twenty-one to get into the club. Fortunately, the doorman was very stoned, and flirting with a woman in a tube top and microskirt, so they were able to slip in unnoticed.

They managed to make the show list, which was something of a long shot. And they were on next to last, which meant they were very tired by the time they took the stage.

Their routine had gone well, but had elicited very little reaction from the audience, just as tired by then as Duckie and Chuck. Then Duckie had gone off script with a line about how they were molested as children. By some minor miracle, they had been able to win back the audience with some inspired improvisation.

As they made their way towards the exit, the woman they had seen chatting with the doorman appeared.

"That was some act," she said. "My name's Stacy. I run this joint."

"Yeah, well, it didn't really pan out like we'd planned," said Chuck, shooting an angry look at Duckie.

"That line about being sexually abused was pretty edgy," said Stacy. "You pushed it over the line, but brought it back quick enough to keep from getting in trouble. That's good. You two play well off of each other. I hope I'll see you back here again."

"Really?" said Duckie and Chuck in unison.

Stacy laughed. "Sure thing. We're always looking for new talent, and if you guys keep working at it, I think you can do well."

"Yeah, we'll definitely come back," said Duckie.

"Just do me one favor before you do," said Stacy. "Get yourselves some IDs, okay? I've got a liquor license to maintain."

Duckie had found a head shop near the NC State campus that was able to provide them with realistic fake IDs for $150 a pop. Duckie's ID had the name "George Pryor"; Chuck's was "Richard Carlin." They used them to get onstage at Night Yuks regularly. They became pets of the club's manager. This engendered some resentment from the other comics, but Chuckie and Duckie didn't care – they were getting stage time at the city's premiere comedy club.

Over the next several weeks, they were able to hone their act. It was still pretty rough, but they could tell that it was getting better. They were even getting more laughs from the jaded open-mic audience, which consisted mostly of other aspiring comics. They felt that things were going well, and that it was time to start plotting their next big move. It dawned on them that they might actually be able to make a go of the comedy business.

***

One day shortly after Christmas break ended, Duckie came home to find a "For Sale" sign on the front lawn and a moving truck in the driveway. It turned out that his dad's bigshot business deal had been a spectacular bust. Not only had he bankrupted the family, but had also incurred substantial legal liabilities. They were going to move to stay with some of his dad's relatives in Pennsylvania, in a miserable little town called Fester.

Chuckie and Duckie arranged a farewell performance at the Night Yuks open mic. They did a last-minute rehearsal in Chuck's bedroom before heading out.

"Man, we're gonna slay 'em tonight," said Chuck after they had run through the set twice. "Gonna go out there and bring the house down." Duckie could hear a hitch in his friend's voice.

"Shit, man…" Duckie started, then his words got tangled up in his throat. He knew then that he was going to cry, but he didn't care. It was more important to say what he felt rather than trying to act like some two-bit tough guy. "Shit, man," he began again. "I'm really, really gonna miss you, man. I just can't say…" The tears were coming now, but it didn't matter. "This so totally sucks. Man, you've been my best friend since Ms. Prendergast's sixth-grade homeroom. We were gonna take over the comedy scene, but more than that … more than that, I just don't know what I'm gonna do without you around. Shit."

He looked up and could see that Chuck was trying hard to keep from breaking down. His lower lip was trembling and as Duckie watched, a tear slipped out of the corner of Chuck's eye and slid down his cheek. "We're still gonna take over the comedy world, hombre," said Chuck thickly. "Ain't nothin' gonna stop that."

"Yeah, man!" said Duckie. "We can still collaborate, man. We're fucking gonna make it work, with cassette tapes, with MP3s, with the fuckin' Pony Express if we have to! Goddammit! My stupid old man, and his dumbshit greedy business bullshit!"

"Yeah, we can do it!" said Chuck. "We can keep going long-distance."

"I gotta tell you this, Chuck," said Duckie. "You're my brother, man, the brother my numbskull folks never gave me. Probably for the best in the end – one less fucked up Dunne in the world, y'know? But we're still a team, man. We're gonna kick ass in comedy *together!* We can do it, man! You know it! Because we got the balls and the brains, and we're fuckin' tough…"

He burst into tears, and so did Chuck. Chuck sat on the bed sobbing and watching Duckie across the room doing the same. He stood up, walked stiffly over to him, and wrapped his arms around him. Duckie received the hug awkwardly, but after a second he softened and wrapped his arms around Chuck's back. They stood that way for a long time, not saying anything.

There was a light tapping at the bedroom door. "Hey, guys," came Mr. Marshall's voice. "You about ready to head out?"

Chuck cleared his throat a few times. "Yeah, Dad," he managed, not quite keeping the wobble from his voice. "We're just wrapping up some rehearsal stuff. Meet you down in the garage in a sec, okay?"

They did a killer set, and even some of the more assholey comics came by to congratulate then and say goodbye to Duckie. Stacy gave them both Night Yuks sweatshirts to commemorate the occasion.

The move to Fester had been rough on Duckie. He'd always thought Raleigh was a shithole, but that was *nothing* compared to the uncivilized backwater of Fester, Pennsylvania. Duckie had trouble fitting into his new school, and frequently got into fights.

His long-distance collaboration with Chuck had worked at first. They'd worked on bits and swapped MP3 files online. Duckie was able to make it down to Raleigh twice over that first summer, and another time the following Christmas. Then things started to dry up.

One of the reasons for this was Chuck's craft was progressing much more rapidly than Duckie's. Chuck had become a regular at Night Yuks, while Duckie had to settle for the monthly "Comedy Nite" at a bar in Weaverville, twenty miles from Fester. Duckie could tell that his friend was developing much more quickly than he was. He tried not to be resentful, but only partially succeeded. By the time they were high school seniors, their career as a duo was essentially dead.

Their friendship was also strained. Their phone calls and visits became more infrequent, and dried up entirely when Chuck went to University of Colorado to study psychology. Duckie was eager to just get the hell out of Fester, but his grades precluded his admission to anywhere fancy. He opted to study business at Indiana University of Pennsylvania. The town was no metropolis, but it wasn't nearly as small and backward as Fester.

The town of Indiana had the added advantage of being close to Pittsburgh, which allowed Duckie more opportunities to work on his comedy. He did this with enthusiasm, feeling that he had to make up for the lost time spent in Fester. While his comedy improved immensely, his grades suffered. After two years of more partying than studying, Duckie decided to pack it in at IUP. Predictably, his parents howled bloody murder, but since they weren't paying for tuition, Duckie felt that they didn't have any say in the matter. He didn't see any point in racking up more student debt for a degree he didn't care about.

He bid farewell to Indiana, Pennsylvania and relocated to Baltimore. It wasn't exactly a garden spot, but rents were cheap, there were a lot more opportunities to perform along the I-95 corridor between D.C. and Philadelphia. Crummy grunt work allowed him to cover his shoestring living expenses.

Four months ago, the news of Mickey's cancer diagnosis had broken. Chuck had called Duckie, and they had fretted over the idea that their comedy idol might not be long for this world. They didn't have to fret long; less than two weeks later, Mickey was dead.

Chuck had called Duckie to share the news, and suggested that they get together to celebrate the life of Mickey Gross. He said he knew of a cool venue in rural Oregon where they could kick back and let loose. Duckie had agreed eagerly. His gigs had been sparse and his current job – working a brake press at an aboveground pool company – was horrible. Duckie felt he needed to get out of town for a while and consider his options.

When he got down to it, his only misgiving was the long flight to Portland. Fortunately, that was almost over now. The pilot came on the PA to announce that they were mere minutes away from touching down at PDX, and that people on the left side of the plane would get a good view of Mount Hood.

Duckie raised the window blind and was greeted by a breathtaking view of a grand, snow-covered mountain sliding by at eye level. The cloud cover had cleared, and the afternoon sun cast a golden glow on the peak . Duckie's breath caught in his throat, and he suddenly felt much better than he had in weeks. He was going to get together with his oldest friend and celebrate the life of their hero. With a smile, he put his seat back in its original upright position and got ready for landing.

Chapter 4

The first thing Duckie noticed when he cleared the jetway was the airport carpet. It was a funky blue-green color, with a repeating pattern of blue, pink and purple. Duckie actually reeled a little bit when he stepped off the jetway. He had never been west of St. Louis before, and the funky Portland airport carpet just underscored his worries about coming out to hippy-dippy Oregon, even if he was excited about reconnecting with Chuck.

A cluster of people lounged around the security exit, waiting to greet the new arrivals. Duckie scanned the faces for Chuck, but didn't spot him. *Figures,* thought Duckie. Ever since Chuck had moved to Colorado, he'd gotten a little flaky.

A tall blond guy wearing a tie-dyed shirt and oversized aviator shades detached himself from the wall he'd been leaning against and strolled up to Duckie, who was busy watching his phone and hadn't noticed his approach. "Excuse me, sir," said the blond guy. "Inspector Bloor, Portland Airport Uptight Patrol. I'm afraid I'm going to have to search your bag for drugs. If there are no drugs in your luggage, some will be provided to you free of charge."

"Huh?" said Duckie, looking up abruptly.

The two looked at each other momentarily. Duckie was drawing a blank on how to respond. The blond guy grinned at him crazily.

It was Chuck Marshall.

"Hey, man!" said Duckie. He held his hand out to shake, but Chuck stepped in and gave him a huge hug. After half a second, Duckie relaxed and hugged him back.

"So good to see you, Duckster," said Chuck. "It's been way too long."

"That's for sure."

"Well, this isn't the place to catch up," said Chuck. "Look, I've got my car gassed and loaded with gear. We can pick up food and beverages on the way. It's 106 miles to Eugene. We got a full tank of gas, half a pack of cigarettes, it's dark … and we're wearing sunglasses."

"Hit it," said Duckie, laughing at the *Blues Brothers* reference. It had been their favorite movie when they were kids.

They got on the interstate and cruised through Portland, zooming over an arching bridge that gave a spectacular view of downtown. The sun sparkled on the Willamette River as barges and pleasure craft cruised by. The buildings, a mélange of sturdy 19th-century buildings and gleaming new high-rises, looked like something from a near-future movie set.

"Wow," said Duckie, peering out the window. "This place is something else. It just seems so … I dunno … bright. Not what I expected at all."

"What were you expecting?" asked Chuck.

"Rain. Perpetual downpour, like Seattle. Or at least a solid gray overcast."

"Nah, summers here are pretty sweet. Hardly rains at all."

"You come out here a lot?"

"Yeah, they've got a pretty solid comedy scene here. Couple of good clubs and improv places. It's like a farm team for L.A. comedy, y'know? People work out their chops here and move up to the big league in L.A. or San Francisco."

Duckie sighed. "I can't believe Mickey's dead," he said. "It's like it's … unreal. *Surreal*."

"I know," said Chuck. "That pancreatic cancer's a stone bastard. Eats you up in no time flat. Did you see that picture of him in the hospital bed? You could barely recognize him."

"Yeah, it was pretty awful," said Duckie. Awkward silence filled the car like cheap cigar smoke. "But let's not dwell on that, huh?" he continued. "The whole point of this excursion is to celebrate Mickey's life, not wallow in the ugly details of his death."

"Amen, brother," said Chuck. "And I'm really glad to be doing it with you, man. Nobody I've met has ever gotten Mickey's comedy the way you do, Duckster. I'm really glad you could make it out."

"Wouldn't have missed it," said Duckie. "It's been too long since we've had a chance to just, y'know, hang."

"Fuckin'-A. We'll celebrate the legend," said Chuck. "So, what's new in Baltimore? Getting any decent gigs?"

"No, but plenty of indecent ones," said Duckie. "Seriously, it's not too bad. Between Baltimore and D.C., there are some pretty cool venues within an hour's drive. How about you?"

"Doin' all right, doin' all right. I'm getting some pretty decent gigs around Denver and Boulder. Making connections in L.A., too, which is huge. Good to get your foot in the door there, y'know?"

"I bet," said Duckie, feeling a pang of jealousy. Truth be told, he wanted to get away from Baltimore and the East Coast, and try and strike out in some more promising spot out west. Los Angeles would be the logical choice, but the thought of going to L.A. was scary. It was too big, too foreign, with too many picture-perfect hardbodies who would look down on his fireplug physique. Baltimore was like a well-worn sneaker: dirty and smelly, but comfortable.

"You got a decent day job?" asked Chuck.

"Nope. I stamp out parts for aboveground pools. It's a shitty gig, but it beats working fast food or something godawful like that. Fortunately, Baltimore's a pretty cheap place to live. How about you? Comedy paying the bills?"

Chuck snorted. "Hell, no," he said. "I got my psych degree, which is almost worth the paper it's printed on. Got a job as a 'floater,' helping out with different therapeutic programs around Denver. The pay's shit but I can pick and choose when I want to work. Makes it easy to work around those out-of-town gigs."

"Sounds like you're doing okay," said Duckie. "Flexible job, starting to make a name for yourself in La-La Land. You're gonna go big-time, Chuck. I can tell."

"You will, too, brother," said Chuck. "You're a funny fucking guy. We'll have the comedy world by the nuts." He turned on the radio and punched buttons until he scared up some Led Zeppelin. Duckie grinned and nodded along with "Kashmir." For the first time since he had gotten up at zero-dark-hundred this morning, he started to relax. He was with his oldest friend in the world, listening to some righteous tunes and on his way to a cool camp-out. Life was good.

Chapter 5

Almost there," said Chuck. "We'll be in Eugene in about fifteen minutes. We can pick up some food and supplies there. Then it's about another twenty minutes to get to the campsite by the Country Fair."

"Country fair?" said Duckie. "Seriously? Sounds rustic as fuck. What are we gonna do, look at livestock and watch a butter-churning competition?"

"Nope, this is the *Oregon* Country Fair," said Chuck. "The name can be a little misleading."

"So what's the dealio?"

"Well," said Chuck, "the way I heard it, the Grateful Dead used to come through Eugene every summer, but they played at a venue kinda out in the country, rather than in town. Ken Kesey had something to do with it, although I'm a little hazy on the details."

"Yeah, if it involved the Dead and Ken Kesey, it sounds like it would be a hazy-details sort of thing."

"Indeed," said Chuck. "Anyway, since it was a Kesey-inspired Dead show out of town – and away from authority figures – things were a little, um, looser as far as behavior went. Anyway, it ended up being so much fun that a bunch of local folks pooled their money and bought some land nearby so they could do it every year. It became an institution, y'know? I came out for the first time my sophomore year at CU, and have tried to make it out whenever I could ever since."

They turned off the interstate and stopped at a Fred Meyer grocery store to buy beer and food. Duckie insisted on stopping at a nearby liquor store to grab a bottle of Yukon Jack. Pretty soon they were past the suburbs and zooming along farms and stretches of woodland.

They turned off the main highway and down a rural road. On either side, Duckie saw cars and clusters of tents lined up by the fields. It was just as he'd feared: just tents and grody hippies crammed cheek to cheek.

Chuck must have sensed Duckie's unease. "Don't worry, bro, those are the budget campgrounds. We're staying at a place that's a little better equipped. And … here we are!" He swung the car off the road onto a gravel track that passed under a large wooden arch. On the arch, Groovy Grove Campground was painted in orange Day-Glo.

The gravel track wound through the trees. They passed two young women who were wearing nothing but diaphanous tie-dyed skirts. They smiled and waved as Chuck and Duckie cruised slowly by.

"Holy cow!" said Duckie. "Those chicks were, um, lettin' it all hang out!" Suddenly, he thought that this might not be so bad after all.

"This is a 'clothing-optional' campground," said Chuck. "You ain't seen nothing yet."

They came out of the trees and into an open area that buzzed with activity. A big barn had been subdivided into a number of spaces, with a small store selling food, bagged ice and beer. Another space had a sign that said Showers. In the large space in front of the barn was a covered wooden stage, where a band was noodling with their instruments. It was like a small town.

Chuck pulled the car to a stop by a corner of the barn and hopped out. "Just need to check in and get directions to our campsite," he said. "Be right back."

"No prob," said Duckie. He got out of the car to stretch his legs and take in the scene. It was amazing. People wandered all over the campground, many in various states of undress. Tie-dye was the predominant color scheme. Everyone seemed relaxed and happy. People chatted, laughed, hugged and danced to music that only they could hear.

Chuck emerged from the barn, smiling widely. "Hey, we got a great spot," he said. "I'm almost a regular now, and they saved a good one for me this year. Relatively isolated, so we'll have privacy, but not too far from a Porta Potty."

"An important consideration," said Duckie. "Sounds good."

"Let's make camp," said Chuck with a grin.

They climbed back into the car and drove beyond the open area around the barn. Behind a screen of trees, there was another field with cars and clusters of tents. Between each of these groups was a Porta Potty.

"They really got this place figured out," observed Duckie.

"It can be a little confusing, but they have this," said Chuck, waving a printed map of the campground. "Here we are!"

They began setting up camp under Chuck's directions. When Duckie had been camping before, the setup had pretty much been a pup tent, a Boy Scout sleeping bag and a fire from scavenged wood. Chuck had assembled a much more comfortable campsite: a frame tent large enough to stand up in, a couple of thick air mattresses, down sleeping bags with a pile of microfiber blankets. There were two lightweight but surprisingly comfortable folding chairs. Over the entrance to the tent, Chuck hung a large Coleman lantern. As a finishing touch, he strung a length of battery-powered lights that looked like honeybees all around the site. "This will look great later," he said.

"I think it's well past beer-thirty," said Duckie, fishing a couple of brews from the cooler. They took their seats, cracked open the beers and clinked bottles.

"To Mickey!" said Duckie.

"To Mickey!" agreed Chuck. "And to old friends!"

"Hear, hear!" said Duckie. They both turned up their beers, drank deeply and belched loudly.

"Oh, wow," came a voice from the edge of the campsite. "There *is* someone back here." A small man with long hair and a pointed beard wandered into the camp. He wore a pair of ragged cut-off cargo pants. He was shirtless, but there were dozens of colorful plastic tubes looped around his neck. Duckie was nonplussed that the guy had just wandered into their campsite uninvited, but Chuck was unfazed. Chuck negotiated with the guy for a handful of glow-in-the-dark necklaces and a bag of weed called Golden Pineapple.

When the vendor left, Chuck fished a pack of rolling papers out of his backpack. He deftly pasted several of the papers together and used them to roll a large joint. "You still partake, right?" he asked, waggling the joint in front of Duckie's face.

"Yeah, sure," said Duckie. "I have been known to take a hit or three in social situations."

"Fantastic," said Chuck. "Remember, we're here to honor the memory of Mickey Gross, who, as you know, was a lifelong proponent of mind-expanding substances."

"Fire it up, man."

Chuck sparked the joint, took a large hit and held it out to Duckie as he exhaled a huge plume of fragrant smoke. Duckie snagged it and took a big hit. He blew out a tremendous smoke cloud and launched into a coughing fit.

"Easy there, hard charger," said Chuck as he relieved Duckie of the joint and hit it again. "This stuff's pretty potent."

"Okay, just one more," said Duckie. He took a moderate hit, blew it out without coughing and handed it off. "That'll do it for me, I think."

Chuck nodded and butted out the joint on the heel of his shoe. Duckie lifted his bottle of beer to his mouth and was surprised to see that it was almost empty. That would never do; his mouth had suddenly become very dry. "I need another beer, bro. How 'bout you?"

"Hell, yes," said Chuck. "Hey, while you're in the car, how 'bout some tunes? Just pop the hatchback; there's a box of CDs in the backseat."

Duckie stood up and his head swam. The weed definitely had a kick to it. "Whoa!" he said. "You weren't kidding about that Grape Ape or whatever that shit's called."

"Golden Pineapple," said Chuck. "Yeah, kinda grabs you by the boo-boo, don't it?"

"Consider my boo-boo grabbed," said Duckie, and they both cracked up.

Duckie managed to get the hatchback popped open. He fished out a couple of beers and carefully walked back to where Chuck was sitting, holding out the cold brew like it was the Holy Grail. Chuck took it gratefully and twisted off the cap.

Duckie was lowering himself into his own chair when he remembered the music. "Oh, shit!" he exclaimed. "I forgot the tuneage!"

"I'll get it," said Chuck. "Got any requests?"

"How 'bout Chelsea's Birthday Monkey?"

"Coming up."

Chuck leaned into the car and fumbled around with the stereo. Finally, the opening lyrics of "I Love You, But You Kinda Suck" pumped from the stereo:

> *I love you but you kinda suck*
> *I love you but you kinda suck*
> *Should hope to smile and kiss a duck*
> *But I love you and you kinda suck.*

"Good choice," said Duckie. The album, *In A Nearaway Land*, wasn't their most popular, but it was Duckie's favorite. He leaned back in his chair, sipping his cold beer and grooving to some of his favorite music.

"This is all right," Duckie said.

"Right on," said Chuck.

They sat in companionable silence for a few minutes, then Chuck said, "Hey, man, you getting hungry? I'm gonna set up the grill."

"Oh, hell yes!" said Duckie. The mere mention of food set his stomach growling. He hadn't eaten all day, and the weed had made him ravenously hungry.

Chuck set up the grill with brisk efficiency. "So, what sounds good, Duckster?" he asked when the grill was fired up.

"Whatever's gonna cook the quickest."

"That would be the hot dogs."

Chuck served up the hot dogs, with the standard trimmings. Duckie slathered his in ketchup and tucked in. It tasted heavenly. He took a second bite without bothering to swallow the first. "Holy shit," he said through a mouthful of animal by-products. "This is the best fuckin' hot dog I've ever eaten, bar none. How many more we got?"

"There's half a dozen left."

Duckie ended up eating five more of them. His belly bulged with the load of six weenies and a couple of pawfuls of chips, washed down with two beers.

"Holy mother of God!" said Duckie. "I can't believe I ate the whole thing." He belched like a battleship foghorn.

"Color me impressed," said Chuck. "Hey, how about some Mickey? Let's give the master a listen. I've got pretty much all of the albums, plus a bunch of bootlegs. Any requests?"

"How about *Rainbows?*" asked Duckie.

"Ah, the one that started it all," said Chuck. *Blowing Rainbows* was Mickey Gross's second album released on the Little David label. Most fans considered it his best. It was the CD that Chuck had filched from his dad's collection, the one he and Duckie had bonded over.

They settled back into their chairs and listened to their muse. Chuck produced the remains of the joint, and they both took a couple of postprandial tokes to get their heads straight. By the time they got to the third track, they were laughing uproariously.

"Wow-o, sounds like you guys are having a good time." A young lady with frizzy brown hair and a bright yellow sundress stood at the edge of the campsite, sipping from a huge wine glass. "Whatcha listening to?"

"Mickey Gross," said Duckie. "You ever listen to his stuff?"

The girl scrunched up her face. "No," she said. "Isn't he a horrible sexist? I mean, he uses 'cocksucker' as a pejorative."

"I wouldn't say he's sexist," said Chuck. "He's offensive on an equal-opportunity basis. He could be kinda edgy, but he always had a good point to make. What's your name?"

"Daffodil," said the girl.

"Nice to meet you, Daffodil. I'm Chuck and this is Duckie."

"Duckie?" said Daffodil. "You must be a U of O fan, right?"

"Oh, hell yes," said Duckie. "Go Ducks, or whatever."

"Would you like to hang out and give Mickey a chance?" asked Chuck. "He's actually pretty insightful."

"No, thanks," said Daffodil. "I'd rather hear some tunes. Uncle John's Band is getting ready to play on the main stage. See ya!" She gave them a wave and disappeared.

Duckie watched her go. "So, people just wander into your camp to sell drugs and criticize your listening choices?"

"Pretty much," said Chuck with a shrug. "We're all just one big happy family here. Now that the fair's shut down and everyone's getting a good swerve on, it'll probably happen more often."

"Swell."

"Don't worry about it, man. It's all part of the fun."

The CD rolled on to its next track – the 20-minute title track. It chronicled in hilarious detail an LSD trip Mickey had taken when he was eighteen. It was funny, warm and insightful, and when he got to the punchline ("I spent the next eight hours blowing rainbows out my ass"), Chuck and Duckie were convulsing with laughter.

When the laughing subsided, Chuck said, "You want to give it a try?"

"What?"

"LSD, man," said Chuck. "Wait, I'll show you."

Chuck stood up, and after some effort got the lantern above the tent going. He pulled a backpack out of the tent and rooted around in one of its myriad pockets. Eventually, he came up with a piece of tinfoil about two inches square. He carefully unfolded it and held it up in the lamplight. "Take a look," he said.

Duckie peered into the open foil. Sitting inside were two small squares of a translucent blue-green substance. They looked like tiny pieces of the gel filters used for stage lighting. "What is it?" he asked.

"Windowpane LSD," said Chuck. "Just like Mickey was talking about. Five-hundred micrograms of high-purity LSD-25. It just doesn't get any better than this. Whaddaya say? Ready for an adventure?"

"I don't know," said Duckie. "I mean, I've always been interested, especially after hearing *Blowing Rainbows*. But I've never, uh, really done it before."

"You've never tripped?"

"Not on acid. I tried mushrooms once, but I didn't really get off on 'em. I only ate a few – they tasted fuckin' awful."

Chuck laughed. "Yeah, not the tastiest treat," he agreed. "I always eat them with Beer Nuts – helps cover up the taste and the texture. Well, no bad taste with this stuff, that's for sure. Wanna give it a go, Duckie? I think you'll really dig it."

"Yeah, sure," said Duckie. He actually wasn't sure about this. He'd never really tripped before, and it made him nervous. Still, he'd always wanted to try it, and here he was with his best friend. There wouldn't be a better opportunity. "Count me in," he said. "I'm on the bus, or whatever."

Chuck beamed broadly. "My man!" he said. "All right! This will be so cool!" He levered one of the squares of windowpane onto his index finger and held it out to Duckie.

"What do I do?" asked Duckie. "Just eat it?"

"Well, you can just swallow it, but since you have a full belly it'll take longer to kick in. You could also just let the windowpane dissolve under your tongue. It'll kick in faster that way."

Duckie plucked the windowpane from his friend's finger, popped it in his mouth, and swallowed it immediately. Chuck did likewise, then licked the tinfoil for good measure.

"Now what?" asked Duckie.

"We wait. Did you swallow yours or let it dissolve?"

"Swallow."

"Me too. I tried this stuff out at home a few weeks ago. Took about an hour to kick in. Might be a little longer for you, since you got a belly full of weenies."

"Ugh," said Duckie. "Please don't say that again. Ever."

"Duly noted," said Chuck. "I say we load up a couple of beers and take a walk; see what we can see."

"Sounds good," said Duckie.

"Here, better take these," said Chuck, holding out some of the glow-light necklaces.

"Right on." Duckie held them up. They were actually glowing, just as advertised. It was nearly nine now, but there was still light in the sky. It was a mellow purple color, shading to gold in the west. It was warm and comfortable, and around them were the sounds of the entire campground really getting cranked up for the evening's fun. They snagged a couple of beers and headed out.

Chapter 6

Duckie and Chuck wandered through the campground, sipping their beer and taking in the atmosphere. Tents and cars sprawled in semi-random profusion. At campsites, people were getting their fires stoked up and their dinners cooked. At others, people were dancing around the fires in various stages of undress.

"Far out," said Duckie.

"Yeah, pretty pagan, isn't it?" said Chuck. "And things are just getting started. Just wait 'til everything people have imbibed really kicks in."

A pair of attractive young women danced by them on the path. They were wearing nothing but feathered headdresses. They danced a circle around Chuck and Duckie, then went on their way.

"Peace and love!" said one from over her shoulder.

"And understanding!" replied Chuck with a laugh.

"Wow," said Duckie. "So, like, what are the chances of hooking up at this thing?"

"That's up to you, I guess. But overall, pretty good – at least as good as any other place with naked, intoxicated hotties dancing around."

"You ever meet a short-term soulmate here?" asked Duckie. It was a couple of months since he had been on a date. The thought of finding a special friend here had a strong appeal.

"Yeah, I hooked up here two – no, three – years ago," said Chuck with a smile. "Her name was Shalimar."

"Think you'll get lucky this time?"

"I wasn't planning on it," said Chuck. "I'm seeing someone back home.

Her name's Gretchen, and she's pretty cool. How about you? Anyone special in your life?"

"Nope," said Duckie. "Broke up with my last girlfriend about a year ago."

Chuck must have noticed Duckie's hangdog expression. "Look, don't get too hung up on it," he said. "Remember, we're here to relax and have a good time. If you try too hard to make something happen, you're just setting yourself up for a bummer. Just chill and let things flow, and whatever happens, happens."

"Sounds like advice to me," said Duckie. "Where are we going, anyway?"

"I thought we'd go check out the action by the stage," said Chuck. The sound of a band echoed through the trees. "But first I just want to cruise around, see if I can spot anyone I know."

"Sounds good," said Duckie. "You feeling anything yet?"

"Yeah, a little, I think," said Chuck. He held his hand up in front of his face and twiddled his fingers. "Yep, some slight tracers. I think it's starting to kick in."

"Man, I don't think I'm getting anything off this."

"Just be patient," said Chuck. "You ate a Babe Ruth-sized serving of hot dogs; it's gonna a take a while for the acid to fight its way through all that grub."

From the woods off to their right came a strange sound, an explosive exhalation, like someone had pressed the button on the world's largest can of shaving cream. In the campsites around them, a number of people prairie-dogged at the sound. About a dozen began walking quickly in that direction.

"Hot damn!" said Chuck. "Whippets! That'll turbo charge our trip. Let's grab a few before they run out." He began quick-stepping in the direction of the sound, with Duckie behind him.

"What's this shit now?" asked Duckie.

"Whippets. Hippie crack. You know … nitrous oxide. Don't tell me you've never had nitrous."

"Yeah, I took a few huffs off a whipped-cream can once," said Duckie. "It made me slightly dizzy for about fifteen seconds. I couldn't see what the big deal was."

"Just wait," said Chuck. He pushed through a stand of bushes and into a clearing. In the middle of the clearing was a large industrial tank, painted bright blue. Two guys in tie-dyes manned the tank. Chuck handed over a ten-dollar bill and received two large balloons.

"Let's go find a place to sit down before we do these," he said. They went a few yards into the woods and sat down on a fallen log. The throbbing beat of the band pulsed over the regular bursts of whippet-dispensation.

"Salud!" said Chuck, and inhaled from his balloon. Duckie shrugged and did likewise. The whippet had a slightly sweet flavor, and the gas was cold. He held it as long as he could and breathed out, wondering what the fuss was about. As he sucked in some regular air, his vision narrowed down to the size of a saucer held at arm's length. Fascinating colored patterns twisted and writhed around the periphery. The bass line from the band and the staccato industrial plosives from the whippet tank seemed to form the rhythm section for the music of the spheres that was all around everything, everywhere. Duckie felt a deep sense of peace and relaxation, and the certainty that regardless of how bad things seemed in the world, everything would be all right in the end.

Then he was just sitting on a log in the woods.

He looked over and Chuck was sitting next to him with a half-inflated balloon, staring at him expectantly. "Holy moly," said Duckie in a strangely deep voice. They stared at each other for a half-second more, then burst into gales of hysterical laughter. Duckie laughed so hard that he fell off the log, but managed to keep the neck of his balloon pinched shut. He clambered back up and took another hit, and soon they were laughing like loons again.

Before long, the nitrous was gone. Duckie stood up and wobbled alarmingly. Chuck jumped up and grabbed his arm before he could topple over. "Which way to the stage?" asked Duckie.

"I don't know," said Chuck somberly. "I believe I've become disoriented." They looked at each other for a moment and fell out laughing again.

"Okay, okay," said Duckie when he was able to catch his breath. "We can at least still hear the band. We'll just follow the sound, okay?"

"Roger dodger."

They pushed their way through the bushes with no small difficulty and emerged on the main pathway between the barn and the camping area, then homed in on the sound of the band.

Duckie looked down at the glowing necklaces on his chest. There were five of them: two reds, a yellow, a green and a purple. The purple one seemed to be glowing with a particularly rich intensity. As he watched, the purple glow faded and the green one grew in strength. Then all of them began waxing and waning, seemingly in time with the music coming from the stage.

"Duckie?" said Chuck. "Duckster? Everything cool, man?"

"Huh?" Duckie looked up. He had come to a dead stop while he was contemplating the dancing glow lights. "Oh, yeah, man," he said. "These glow necklace thingies are just lookin' a little funky."

"Oh, right on. It's probably the acid starting to kick in."

"Oh, yeah," said Duckie. "Cool. How about you? Anything happening?"

"Dude," said Chuck. "I'm tripping balls!"

This was the most hilarious thing either of them had heard all night, and once again they were carried away on gales of laughter. Other campers passed by and couldn't help but start laughing themselves. Chuck and Duckie were oblivious to the others; they were in their own world.

"Oh, holy shit," said Duckie. "This is a fine time." He saw Chuck grinning, and he'd never felt closer to him. They'd always been like brothers, but now there was something stronger between them – a bond that hadn't been there before.

"That's so awesome to hear, man," said Chuck. "I was really worried you wouldn't … y'know … dig it. I'm glad to be back with you." He stepped up and gave Duckie a big hug; Duckie hugged right back.

Suddenly, Chuck stood back with an alarmed look on his face.

"What's wrong?" asked Duckie.

"The beers! What happened to the beers?"

"Oh, shit. We musta left 'em in the woods."

"No sweatsky," said Chuck. "They sell beer at the Barn. We can grab a couple brews to hold us until we get back to the tent."

They managed to negotiate the vending of two draft Budweisers and wandered over to the stage, slurping suds. Uncle John's Band was tearing into an up-tempo version of "Casey Jones." All around them people were leaping about and dancing with abandon. There were no dance steps, no rules – just move your body in time to the music.

Chuck drained his beer, threw the cup decisively to the ground, and began cavorting like a baby goat in springtime. Duckie shrugged, chugged the rest of his beer, and lost himself to the music.

Chapter 7

Duckie danced like a dervish. He had never felt so free. He didn't care how he looked. He didn't care what anyone else thought about him – he just moved. The word "ecstatic" popped into his mind, and was quickly overwhelmed by the music.

He danced like a fool.

He didn't care.

The band shifted gears, and launched into a version of "Play That Funky Music." Some Dead purists scowled and moved away, but Duckie bopped along with the beat and threw his limbs about. He glanced over, and Chuck was doing the same. It was a blast.

Soon, the song came to an end, and the band moved to a slower number called "Althea." Duckie slowed down but kept dancing. Next to him, Chuck was bent over with his hands on his thighs, breathing hard.

"Hey, man," said Duckie. "You okay, bro?"

Chuck held up his hand and continued wheezing. "Okay, okay," he said at last. "That last one really took the wind out of me. I think I need to go back to the camp for a little bit."

"Okay by me," said Duckie. "Let's go."

Chuck shook his head. "Man, I don't think I can find it right now," he said. "I'm really trippin' hard."

Duckie peered into his face. Chuck's pupils were so dilated that he could hardly see the blue of his eyes. Duckie was almost there himself. He was definitely tripping, but it was nothing he couldn't handle … at least for now. On the other hand, there was no way he'd be able to get back to their campsite. He supposed that they could just wander around until they saw something familiar, but that could lead to them walking in circles all night.

"Hey, man," said Duckie. "Do you still have that map?"

"Huh? Map? What do you mean?"

"That map they gave you when you checked in. The one that shows where the campsite is."

"Oh, yeah – that." Chuck felt around in his pockets, shaking his head. Just when Duckie had resigned himself to wandering at random, Chuck pulled a folded-up piece of paper from his back pocket. He carefully looked at it, frowning, and thrust it out towards Duckie, who jumped back from the sudden movement. "Is this it?" asked Chuck.

Duckie took the paper. "Yeah, that's it," he said. Now he just had to interpret it. It was not going to be easy. The edges of the page kept blurring into nothingness, and the lines and colors ran together. Duckie led Chuck over towards the Barn, in the hope that the lights there would help him figure out the map.

It didn't help much. The lines were a bunch of squiggles that kept squiggling. Duckie kept turning the page in his hand, trying to orient the map to the barn, so they could at least start walking in the right direction.

"Are you guys doing okay?"

Duckie looked up at a familiar figure, a short girl in a bright yellow sundress. Where had he seen her before? "Oh, uh, hi there … Daffodil."

"You're lookin' a little … y'know … turned around," said Daffodil.

"We're a little … um … messed-up," said Chuck. "We dropped some windowpane earlier, and it just got right on top of us, y'know? We just wanna find our campsite."

"Oh, sure!" chirped Daffodil. "I can take you there."

"We've got this," said Duckie, thrusting out the map.

Daffodil laughed. "I don't need a map, silly. I know this campground like the back of my hand. C'mon, I'll take you right there."

For some reason, this bothered Duckie. He was just trying to be helpful, and she had laughed at him. He wasn't sure he liked being called "silly," either. He sort of hung back and let Daffodil and Chuck walk a few paces ahead. They chattered together as Duckie regarded their surroundings.

He didn't like what he saw. Primitive fires glowed menacingly all around them. Strange people wearing strange clothes were doing strange things. It reminded Duckie of some freaky Hieronymus Bosch painting. He looked forward to getting back to their own campsite. He'd get the fire going again. But it wouldn't be a menacing fire; it would be a friendly fire.

The phrase "friendly fire" circled around his head, and it occurred to him that it had another meaning. He thought about Vietnam and all the movies he had seen about that war. Friendly fire had killed a lot of American soldiers. A lot of kids who would never come home.

And neither would Mickey Gross, thought Duckie. Mickey was dead. Dead and gone, never to return. That was the whole reason he'd come out here on this perilous adventure. How macabre was that? The thought sent him even further into a funk.

He'd always wanted to see Mickey perform live, and he'd never had the opportunity. Mickey had radically cut back his touring after the notorious appearance on Letterman. By the time Duckie had the means to go to a show like that, Mickey had become a recluse. Regardless, Duckie had derived no small amount of comfort in knowing that his idol and intellectual template was still out there. And maybe one day he'd tour again.

But not now. Not ever again.

Duckie trudged behind Chuck and Daffodil. The trip to the campsite seemed to take forever.

"Well, here we are!" said Daffodil brightly.

"Oh, wow, thanks," said Chuck. "You're a real lifesaver!"

"I'm glad to help," said Daffodil. "I've been there before."

Duckie said nothing. He went to one of the camp chairs and slumped into it. There were still embers glowing in the firepit, but he didn't really feel like getting the fire started again. He'd rather just sit in the dark.

Chuck and Daffodil were still chatting away; flirting, really. Duckie regarded them darkly. It figured. Chuck always got the breaks, always got the girls. He was the fair-haired boy, and Duckie had always felt a little insecure about his own social skills and lack of luck with the ladies.

"So, do you wanna … y'know … hang out for a bit?" asked Chuck.

No, no, not now, thought Duckie. He didn't want Daffodil complicating things.

"Well, I'm supposed to meet my friends," she said. "Tell you what," she said, reaching out to touch Chuck's hand. "I'll come back in a little bit to check up on you. You gonna be okay?"

"Oh, yeah, sure," said Chuck. "We're just gonna chill out a little bit, listen to some music. See you later, Daffodil."

"See you soon, Chuck." She looked over at Duckie and gave him a small wave. "You too, Donny." Then she was off.

"Donny?" said Chuck, and started laughing.

Duckie didn't think it was that funny. Typical situation with Chuck: the girls were pawing him, but couldn't be bothered to remember Duckie's name.

"Hey, you're not laughing," said Chuck. "You doin' okay, bro?"

Duckie briefly considered expressing his frustrations, but decided not to bother. Instead, he said, "Eh, this acid is just getting on top of me. I just need to chill."

"No worries," said Chuck. "I'll take good care of you." He stood up and lit the Coleman lantern.

"Ewww, too bright!" said Duckie, shielding his eyes.

"Sorry, man." He turned the lantern down to a low, orange glow. "That better?"

Duckie nodded. "Thanks, man."

"Look," said Chuck. "I know what you need: some good tuneage and some more of that Golden Pineapple."

"Yeah," said Duckie. "That sounds good. Play something mellow, y'know?"

"Yeah, I got just the thing."

Chuck opened the car door, and sat sidesaddle on the driver's seat while he thumbed through the box of CDs. He found the one he wanted, popped it into the car's CD player, and rolled a joint on the center console. He sparked it as laidback, jazzy music came from the speakers. "Here you go," he said, holding out the joint.

Duckie took a small hit and passed it back. "What is this music?" he asked.

"The band's called Blue Nietzsche," said Chuck. "You like it?"

"Not really. The guitar's too jangly."

"Oh, wow," said Chuck. "You're really in a rough spot, aren't you, man?"

"Yeah, kinda feels like it," Duckie said. He was starting to feel the effects of the weed. It had taken a bit of the edge off the trip, but not much.

"I got just the thing," announced Chuck. He went back to the car and switched CDs. Low, slow-tempo tones came from the stereo. It sounded like a recording of church bells played at half speed, but it was oddly soothing.

"I know I'm bein' a bummer," said Duckie. "I don't wanna bring you down."

"It's okay; I've been there before, and it's no fun. Wait, maybe this will help." He went back to the car, rummaged around in the backseat, and waved the bottle of Yukon Jack.

Duckie snatched it and took a long drink.

"Whoa!" said Chuck. "You might wanna take it easy with that."

Duckie waved him off. The huge slug of sweet booze rocketed down into his stomach, hitched once and settled. He took another.

"You gonna be okay?" asked Chuck.

"Yeah, I think so," said Duckie. "This stuff is like soda pop."

"Yeah, you can pound booze like a mad bastard when you're tripping," said Chuck. "You gotta take it easy, though. You won't feel a thing for hours, then all of a sudden, the alcohol overtakes the acid and hits you really hard."

"I can handle it," said Duckie. He took another drink.

"Whoa, *Music For Airports*," said Daffodil, who had materialized by the car. "Someone having a bad trip?"

Duckie glared at her. She was the last person he wanted to see. Chuck must have caught the look, because he jumped up and fast-walked over to her. Duckie could overhear snippets of the hushed conversation: "bad trip" and "chill out" and "antisocial" and "maybe later." After some more whispers, Daffodil left.

"Who's 'antisocial'?" demanded Duckie. "You tellin' that Daffodil chick that I'm some sort of psycho or something?"

"No, man, no. I was just saying that we just needed to chill until the trip levels out, and that until then, we are gonna be a little antisocial."

"Yeah, well, don't let me stop you from getting laid," said Duckie. "Not that it ever has before."

"Hey, I'm not here to get laid," said Chuck. "I'm here to spend time with my old friend, and to celebrate the life of Mickey Gross."

"Don't you see?" cried Duckie. "There is no more life of Mickey Gross! He's dead, Chuck! Dead! And soon enough we will be, too! And nothing to show for it!"

"Jesus, what are you talking about? We've got decades ahead of us. There's no telling what we'll be able to achieve. Don't be such a downer, man!"

"Yeah, it's easy for you to say. You'll do okay, sure. You always got the breaks. You've got the looks; you've got gigs in the big cities; you've got the good parents; you always get the pretty girls … and everything!"

"Good parents?" said Chuck in disbelief. "Your parents were loaded compared to mine."

"For a while, until Doctor Dumbass blew it all on a shady real estate deal, and we had to go live in Fester Fuckin' Pennsylvania! You got to stay in Raleigh and work out your chops at Night Yuks while I had to settle for Comedy Nite once a month at the Sharpe Turn. Besides, you're the one that broke up our act!"

"Whaddaya mean? I didn't 'break up our act'!"

"Sure you did! You quit sending the tapes and files. You said that you thought we should both work on our solo acts!"

"Well, what the hell else were we supposed to do? We were living three hundred miles apart! We couldn't perform together like that! What were we supposed to do? Put on shows over Skype?"

"I dunno," pouted Duckie. "You've just always gotten the breaks. You're cooler, more outgoing … and you're funnier!" He couldn't believe this last statement had come out of his mouth. He'd never thought it before, at least not consciously. But having said it, it felt true.

Chuck goggled at him. "I can't believe you're saying this, Duckie! Funnier? What the hell does that even mean? It's so subjective! You're just as funny as me! Funnier! But you're just having a bad trip and wallowing in self-pity!"

"This acid bullshit was your idea, man. It's your fault!"

"I didn't force it down your throat, dude. Don't lay your bad trip on me!"

"Aw, fuck you!"

"You're pissing me off right now," said Chuck. "Big time!"

Duckie jutted out his chin. "So what are you gonna do about it, huh?"

Chuck took a slow, deep breath. "I'm going to take a walk," he said, "before one of us says something we'll regret."

"Oh, bullshit! You're just gonna leave me and boink that goofy hippie chick!"

"No, I just need to clear my head. I'll be back in ten minutes." Chuck got up and walked quickly away from the campsite, leaving Duckie alone in the dark.

What the fuck? he thought. Just a few minutes ago, he'd felt closer to Chuck than he ever had with anyone. Now they were pissed at each other. What had happened? *It was you,* he thought. *You brought this bummer. You always fuck up everything good.*

Duckie plopped back in his camp chair and started taking long pulls from the Yukon Jack bottle. He waited and drank alone in the dark. It seemed like Chuck had been away much longer than ten minutes, but he couldn't tell for sure. Time had become very elastic. He took another swig from the bottle and held it up to the faint light from the lantern. He was surprised to see that two-thirds of it was gone.

He began to wonder about the effects of dumping a large quantity of sugary booze on top of a half-dozen hot dogs and a hit of LSD. There was a liquid rumbling in his guts, and he realized that he was about to find out. He lurched to his feet, swaying. His guts gave another alarming rumble. It was time to get to the Porta Potty, and fast.

He took a few tentative steps, and finding that he was not going to fall over, began to quick-step, then run. By the time he reached the Porta Potty, he knew that he only had seconds. He skidded around the front of the crapper and ripped open the door, hoping that no one was inside. Fortunately, it was unoccupied. Duckie yanked down his pants and squatted just in time for a terrible torrent to rush out.

Spasm after spasm wracked him, and he moaned piteously. Just as the action downstairs seemed to be subsiding, his stomach hitched. He leaned over and threw up into the plastic urinal trough.

Eventually (Duckie had no idea how long) the outflow subsided. He sat slumped over sideways, breathing heavily in the awful miasma inside the john. This was, without a doubt, the absolute low point of his life so far. The walls of the Porta John seemed to bulge in and out rhythmically, like it was breathing. Despite the horrible atmosphere, Duckie didn't want to leave. At least he was protected in here from all of the weird goings-on in the campground.

He stared up at the door of the Porta Potty. Embossed on the back was the manufacturer's info: P-Rite Corp., Baltimore, MD. It figured that such a foul contraption had been made in Baltimore. For Duckie, it perfectly encapsulated his personal situation: stuck in a horrible place, but too scared to leave. He had to get out of this Porta Potty. He had to get out of Baltimore.

Above the embossed logo was a sticker of the company that had rented the unit. Sunshine Sanitation, Portland. There was a cartoon logo of a sun rising above a humorously rustic outhouse. For some reason, Duckie found this comforting. Perhaps it was a sign.

There was a light tapping at the Porta Potty door. "Fuck off!" yelled Duckie. "I'm getting enlightened in here, you damn hippies!"

"Duckie?" came Chuck's voice. "Are you in there, buddy? Everything okay?"

Duckie had recovered enough equanimity to respond with a Rodney Dangerfield line: "I'm okay now, but last week I was in rough shape."

"Are you coming out?"

"Depends," said Duckie. "Is that Daffodil with you?"

"Yes."

"Tell her to buzz off!"

Muffled whispering from outside the door, then, "Okay, she's gone now."

Duckie stood up shakily, and managed to pull up his pants. By some blue-eyed miracle, he hadn't gotten any of the mess on his clothes. He fumbled with the door latch and stumbled outside. He almost fell over, but Chuck caught him before he could tumble. Duckie's legs were shaking hard.

"You okay to walk?" asked Chuck.

"I think so." Duckie took a few tentative steps. His knees were a little weak, but they would hold … at least until they could cover the twenty yards to the campsite. As he wobbled away, a dude with long gray dreadlocks approached the Porta Potty. "Yo, Jerry Garcia," said Duckie. "You'll want to find another john. This one's *bad*."

He made it back to the campsite, with Chuck following close behind in case he started to falter. Duckie collapsed back into his chair, breathing heavily. He felt spongy and weak.

"Dude, are you sure you're gonna be okay?" asked Chuck. "They got some EMTs on duty at the Barn. Do you want me to go fetch one?"

Duckie shook his head. "The worst has passed, I think," he said. "Jesus, what a rotten deal this turned out to be."

"Dude," said Chuck. "I am *so* sorry. This was meant to be a fun time, not this king-hell bad trip. Man, if there's anything I can do…"

Duckie was about to say something biting, but he saw the genuine anguish in his friend's face. Hell, his good time was being spoiled, too. "Water?" asked Duckie. "Is there any water?"

Chuck's face crumpled. "No!" he said. "Shit, I forgot! What the hell was I thinking?"

"It's okay, brother," said Duckie wearily. "Don't beat yourself up. I'll just scoop out some of the melted ice from the cooler."

"No, no," said Chuck. "I'll go get a bottle from the Barn. Will you be okay if I leave you alone for a few minutes?"

"Yeah, I just survived an hour locked in a plastic shitter. I think I can manage a few more minutes here."

"Okay, I'll be right back. Don't worry." Chuck hustled off, casting concerned looks over his shoulder.

Duckie sat in the darkness, just breathing. *Made it through,* he thought. He had passed through the eye of the psychic (and gastric) hurricane, and had come out on the other side. He was emotionally battered and physically wrung out, but he had emerged grasping something of value: a plan. He resolved to get the hell out of Baltimore and move to Portland at the earliest opportunity. It seemed so much brighter than Baltimore, so full of possibility.

This thought cheered him up, and by the time Chuck returned with the water, Duckie had gotten the campfire going and had put Pink Floyd's "Wish You Were Here" on the stereo.

"Sorry it took so long," said Chuck. "The store was closed, but I managed to snag a few bottles from one of Daffodil's friends. I'm sorry you guys aren't getting along. She's really very cool."

"These things happen. I'm sure she's really awesome."

"Yeah!" said Chuck brightly. "She said she has friends in L.A. who are looking for a roommate. I might just make that big move to Tinseltown."

"Gonna bust a move for the Left Coast, huh?" said Duckie. "Interesting idea." Actually, he was a bit miffed. He had been excited to share his idea of moving to Portland with Chuck, but here he had gone and one-upped him. Again.

"Sorry you're not having much fun," said Chuck. "It'll be better tomorrow, I'm sure."

"Tomorrow?" said Duckie. "Hell, no! I've had enough of this cut-rate Woodstock. I'm going home, ASA-fucking-P."

"What?" said Chuck. "You gotta be kidding! C'mon, man, give it another chance."

"I don't think so," said Duckie. He'd had enough. Maybe things would be better tomorrow, but at this point he didn't care. The place held bad psychic ju-ju for him now. It was best to just go home and recuperate.

"You don't really want to leave, do you? We haven't even seen the fair!"

"I sure as hell ain't staying, after all this shit. If the fair's anything like this freak show, I wouldn't be interested, anyway."

"I can't believe you want to bail after just one night!" said Chuck.

"Look, you don't have to drive me back to Portland. Didn't I see a sign for an airport in Eugene? Just drop me off there and I'll catch a crop-duster or something."

Chuck's shoulders slumped. "No, I'll drive you up to PDX in the morning," he said slowly. "We'd better get some rest. I'd like to get going early so I get back in time to catch some of the fair."

"Okay."

They climbed into the tent but neither one of them could sleep. When the sun came up, Chuck buttoned up the campsite and drove them blearily back to Portland. They hardly talked for the entire two-and-a-half-hour drive. When Duckie got out at the curb of the airport, he looked at his old friend, trying to think of something to say. "Well," he said at last. "See ya."

Chuck looked despondent. "Yeah," he said. "Safe travels."

Duckie turned and walked into the terminal without looking back.

II

Part Two

RISE

Chapter 8

June 2015

It all started at the hardware store.

Chuck didn't know why a hardware store would host an open mic. All he knew was that it was stage time, and that's what he was after. He'd written some new material that he wanted to try out in a low-key setting before honing it and performing it at a comedy club open mic.

He'd been in L.A. for about a year, sharing an apartment in Los Feliz with three other showbiz wannabes. He'd landed a day job at a company that distributed small aircraft components. The pay wasn't great, but it was enough to cover his share of the rent, keep himself reasonably fed, and put gas in the tank.

The latter was crucial, as he spent most of his free time driving all over L.A. and trying out material at any venue that would grant him stage time. He'd developed a core of friends with similar aspirations; young stand-ups who'd come from all over the country to try and grab the brass ring.

Some of his friends were picky about where they performed, opting to only get on stage at high-profile venues. Chuck wasn't as discerning. He wasn't trying to get noticed; he was trying to get *good.* He figured that as he was able to hone his craft, he would get noticed eventually. Besides, the competition for stage time was fierce, so there was no point in limiting himself.

Even if it meant hauling butt up to Encino and performing in a fer-Chrissakes hardware store on a Sunday afternoon. All he knew was they were going to give him ten minutes of stage time. If he could get a laugh out of people shopping for roofing nails and window blinds, his material was solid. And he *had* gotten a few laughs from the gig. He'd found it encouraging, but hadn't thought more about it.

The next day, he got a phone call from someone who had been at the show. Her name was Michelle, and she was an assistant to a producer at Comedy Central. She'd liked his set and wanted her boss to see him. She asked when he would be performing next. It just so happened that he was booked later in the week for a comedy showcase at a new place called Giggles in Culver City. Michelle said she'd see about having her boss come out and see the show.

He spent a lot of time that week polishing his act. He was so amped up that he may have over-trained. He was certainly overthinking it, and by the time he hit the stage he was almost out of his mind with worry. What if this was his one big chance, and he blew it? He hadn't been this nervous since he and Duckie had first weaseled their way into Night Yuks in Raleigh.

He'd *almost* blown it. When he was introduced, he hustled out on stage and tripped over the mic stand. He went down hard, did a complete somersault and had managed to smoothly regain his feet. He held his arms up like a gymnast and improvised: "Wow, that's the worst trip I've had since I took the brown acid at Burning Man. But at least I stuck the landing!" This got a hearty laugh, and all of the tension and nervousness of the week washed away. Chuck relaxed and did his set flawlessly.

After the show, a guy who looked like a surf shop employee approached and handed Chuck his card. His name was Joel, and sure enough he was Michelle's boss at Comedy Central. He said he had loved Chuck's set. He had a half-hour slot for *Comedy Central Stand-Up Presents*, and thought Chuck would be perfect for the show. Chuck agreed, and before he knew it, he was on a plane to New Orleans, where the show was taped.

He had a blast in New Orleans, and his set went well enough – good but not really great. He went back to the hotel that night feeling he'd accomplished something, but with a nagging doubt that he could've done better.

Chuck had a big viewing party when the show aired, and all his friends were secretly jealous … or not so secretly, in Farrah's case. Danny and Arthur were a little more subdued, but Chuck couldn't help wondering if they thought, *It should have been me, not him.* Their jealousy was short-lived, as it soon became apparent that a half-hour on Comedy Central wasn't a golden ticket to stardom. Not that many people watched the network.

Still, Chuck was able to add "as seen on Comedy Central" to his promo material, which led to an easier time getting booked at some of the nicer clubs in the area. He needed to put some of the Comedy Central bits on his demo DVD. He spent one slow Sunday learning a video editing program, and chopping up the entire special into internet-attention-span-sized pieces. The best two went on the DVD, and just for laughs he started uploading all of them to his YouTube channel.

To his surprise, one of them went viral. It was one of his newer, less-polished bits, one he had debuted at the hardware store gig. It was about a little kid experiencing his first day of kindergarten. Chuck liked it – not for what it was, but for what it could be. He could sense the pure humor and pathos in the bit; he just had to dig it out. He didn't want to rush it, but was happy to try out slight variations from show to show. The variation he'd done in New Orleans must have been the right recipe.

Two days after the kindergarten video had blown up, he'd received a call from a manager named Philo Spinoza. This was a good sign, but Chuck knew to be careful. There were a legion of talent reps hungry to find the next big star. Many of them were sleazebags. Chuck asked around and apparently Philo was the real deal.

Philo took Chuck out to lunch. The manager was in his early thirties, pale and balding, with a mouse-brown comb over. Despite his horrible hairstyle, he dressed conservatively and tastefully. His demeanor was laid back and confident, and he told Chuck that he could help him get better gigs and maybe some entry-level TV exposure. Chuck liked what Philo had to say, and by the end of the meal, Philo was Chuck's manager.

Chapter 9

S o you got yourself a manajah, huh?" said Danny. "Well, ain't you
just King Shit of Turd Mountain?"

"Turd Mountain?" said Arthur. "Isn't that the part of Ireland
your people are from, Danny? Of course, it's bound to have some
unpronounceable Gaelic name with too many vowels, apostrophes and
phlegm-gurgling 'gh' sounds. But the meaning's the same, I'm sure."

"Aw, knock it off, you two," said Chuck. Danny Boyle and Arthur Watson
liked to swap insults, but sometimes one would go too far and a real spat
would erupt.

"Yes," said Farrah Ortega. "You little boys quit squabbling. We should be
pleased for Chuck's break. He deserves it."

"Indeed," said Arthur. "He has parlayed a chance encounter at an obscure
open-mic to a spot on *Stand-Up Presents*, then of course someone would
seek him out to represent him. It's a causal relationship, facilitated by an
adroit personality. Well-played, sir!"

"Thanks," said Chuck. "I think."

They were sitting at a back booth in Simi's, a small comedy club in East
Hollywood that Chuck thought of as his home base. It wasn't as big or
as popular as some of the famous clubs on Sunset, but it was much more
comfortable. It didn't frequently get A-list comics, and it was small and
a little dingy. However, Simi Cohen, the owner, was a mother hen who
supported all of the novice stand-ups that frequented her place.

Chuck was sitting with the people that made up the core of his L.A.
comedy crew. They were stand-ups who were all relatively recent arrivals

to L.A., and had come to know each other through the various comedy workshops and open mics. They tried to get together every Wednesday for Simi's open mic.

Danny was from South Boston, and looked and talked the part. He had pale skin, mischievous blue eyes and thinning red hair that he wore in a flat-top. Arthur was from Davenport, Iowa. He was a Black man, thin and elegant, and very well spoken. He sounded like he had graduated from an Ivy League school, but had actually studied English at Southeast Iowa State before moving to Los Angeles to pursue acting and comedy.

Farrah had been born Miguel Ortega in Lubbock, Texas. She was pre-operative, but had been undergoing hormone therapy for several years. The effects were pretty stunning, in Chuck's opinion. She was smart and wickedly funny.

"Besides," continued Farrah. "I've been in L.A. longer than any of you *pendejos*. If anyone here should have gotten a break, it's me."

"Jeez, jealous much?" asked Chuck. "I know two of you are persons of color, but I didn't know that color was *green!*"

"Whaddaya mean, I'm not a person of color?" asked Danny. "My Irish blood runs green!"

"Are you sure you're not a Vulcan, then?" asked Chuck.

"No," said Arthur. "Vulcans are intelligent and logical. I'm afraid our Danny-boy here goes oh for two on that account."

"Yeah," said Farrah. "You got about as much color as a Wonderbread sandwich with the crusts cut off."

"I guess you'd know about having things cut off, huh?" said Danny.

"*Vete a la mierda,*" said Farrah. "Besides, until I save up enough money for the surgery, I'm still doing the tuck and roll. Hell, you wouldn't have that problem – you'd simply have to wait for that tiny Southie pee-pee to shrivel up and drop off from embarrassment!"

"Enough, enough," said Chuck. "To show that I am generous in my good fortune, I'll get the next round." That brought cheers from the table, and Chuck went to the bar to get another Ballantine ale for himself, a Sam Adams for Danny, a Manhattan for Arthur and an appletini for Farrah.

"It's just so difficult for a new comic to get broad exposure these days," lamented Arthur when the drinks had been distributed.

"Yeah," said Danny. "Back in the days when Carson was king, gettin' on his show was a real leg up. *Especially* if he called you ovah to the desk after your set."

"Still, there are stand-ups who make big moves," said Chuck. "Like Seth Meyers or Jason Sudeikis."

"Both those guys came up through *Saturday Night Live*," Farrah pointed out. "Shit, you make it on that show as a writer or cast member, you already got it made."

"Yeah, if you can make it past the Guardian of the Gate," said Danny. "Othahwise known as Lorne Michaels."

"Still, sketch comedy is a good place to showcase your versatility," said Arthur. "Help you land a big-time gig."

"Shit," said Farrah. "I don' like sketch comedy. Too formulaic."

"Ah, bullshit," said Danny. "You tellin' us that if Michaels rolled up and offered you a slot on *SNL*, you'd turn him down?"

"Yes," sniffed Farrah. She turned up her nose and sipped her appletini. "I gots standards to maintain, *ese*."

Everyone laughed and rolled their eyes.

"Danny's got a point, though," said Chuck.

"Yeah, and that cheap haircut doesn't do much to conceal it," said Arthur.

"Spearchucker," said Danny.

"Bogtotter," said Arthur.

"You two shut up before I slap you both," said Farrah. "Chuck, you were saying?"

"I was just thinking that it would be great if there was a show that combined the two, right?" said Chuck.

"Whaddaya mean?" asked Danny.

"I'm thinking like a sketch-based show that also featured up-and-coming stand-ups," said Chuck. "You know, like every episode would start with a showcase for a little-known stand-up, then the rest of the show could be sketches."

Surprisingly, this idea was met with considerate silence – an unusual response for a table full of comedians.

"I think you may be onto something there," said Arthur. "Clearly, this is an idea that deserves more consideration."

"That's a *great* idea, Chuck," said Farrah. "Start writing it down. Work up a treatment, eh?"

"Yeah, well my manager's been bugging me about developing a sitcom idea," said Chuck. "Says it could really help raise my profile. Maybe he'd go for this."

"Ah, theah he goes bringin' up his damn manajah again!" said Danny. "Rub it in, why dontcha, Mr. Hotshot?"

"Don' listen to him," said Farrah. "Just put together a couple of pages and show your manager. What's the worst that could happen?"

"Yeah, hell yeah," said Chuck. He was warming to the idea. It could really work out. And also provide an avenue for his friends and other ambitious comics to get a leg up. "You're right, Farrah. Couldn't hurt to give it a try."

"Great," said Arthur. "You can get started tonight. As for me, I must be on my way. Early shift tomorrow."

"Yeah, me too," said Danny. "Can I get a ride with you, Arthur?"

"Okay, but no stupid jokes about Cadillacs, okay?"

"Okay, I promise … at least until we're within walking distance of my apartment."

"Me three," said Farrah. "A girl's gotta get her beauty rest. Good luck with your show idea, Chuck. And remember us if it actually goes anywhere."

"I thought you hated sketch shows," said Chuck.

"Ah, don' listen to me," said Farrah. "I'm just on the rag. It's that time of the month."

"What?" said Danny. "How can you…"

"I'm always pissy around the beginning of the month. It's called commitment to a bit." She snapped her fingers in Danny's face, stood up and sashayed to the door.

"Damn, but that *person* gets undah my skin sometimes," said Danny.

"Get over yourself," said Arthur. "Let's go."

They got up to leave, but Chuck stayed for a few minutes more, scribbling notes on the back of a Simi's cocktail napkin. Then he hurried home and began fleshing out his idea in earnest.

Chapter 10

Chuck's phone rang. It was his manager.

"Chuck, it's Philo. Are you sitting down?"

"Yes, Philo. I always sit down when I see I'm getting a call from you." He was actually standing at the kitchen counter, making coffee. Philo led off any conversation by asking Chuck whether he was sitting. It was cute at first, but now it was skewing annoying.

"Good," said Philo. "I'm glad you're sitting down, because I got some big news, babes. I got a producer who just loves your TV show idea. What are you calling it again?"

"*Hot Mic*," said Chuck.

"Great!" said Philo. "This producer loves *Hot Mic*. Absolutely *loves* it, really! He wants to take a meeting on Monday. He also wants to see the first draft of a script."

"What?" said Chuck. "By Monday? I only have a seven-page treatment!"

"Then you better get writing," said Philo. "Don't worry, it doesn't have to be good. It doesn't have to be anything other than twenty-two pages long. Trust me, the final product will bear no resemblance to the first draft."

"What's the deal with this producer?" asked Chuck.

"His name's Simon Apriori, and he's a good one to know. He's bagged a couple of shows for Wolff, CBS, even a few for Netflix. He helped develop *Chimp Patrol*, *The Shakes* and *Pardon My Hard-On*."

"A real renaissance man, eh?"

"Look, babes, don't be negative," said Philo. "Simon's good people, he's connected and he can make your show a reality, okay? Be nice."

"Sorry," said Chuck. "Haven't had my morning coffee yet."

"Okay, we're meeting Simon at 10 am on Monday," said Philo. "Make sure you're well-rested, well-caffeinated, and have twenty-two pages of *something* by then. Don't knock yourself out over the script, though. It's gonna change, babes, believe me."

Chuck spent all weekend fussing over the script. When they got to the meeting, Chuck found Simon to fit the image of a Hollywood producer: aviator shades, slicked-back hair, and a dress shirt with the top three buttons undone. Simon spent about twelve seconds flipping through the script. "Looks, good," he said. "Looks *real* good. We can work with this."

Chuck cut a quick glance Philo, who just nodded and smiled sagely.

"Look, stand-up is due to make a comeback," explained Simon. "I know studios are looking for more comedies and more comedians. This show is right on target. I should have no trouble interesting a studio in this. Hell, maybe even get a bidding war going. This has a lot of potential." He thumbed through the script again. "I just have one or two *minor* suggestions."

"No problem," said Chuck. "Just let me know what you think should be changed."

Actually, Chuck wasn't that keen on taking notes from the producer, but he knew that he was going to have to be flexible if he ever wanted *Hot Mic* to go anywhere. Philo had told him that the whole process was going to involve many, many meetings and many, many suggestions from producers, studio executives and network bigwigs.

So Chuck went home and rewrote the entire script. Then they had another meeting with Simon. Then he went home and rewrote the script again.

After that, Simon began arranging meetings with studios who might be interested in producing a pilot. Their first meeting had been with CBS Studios. They said they loved it, and then passed. Same with the next two independent studios.

Simon may have been feeling a little desperate when he approached an old frenemy who had worked his way up the ladder at Wolff Studios. To

Simon's surprise, the frenemy, one Balthazar Smoak, had called them in for a meeting immediately.

Balthazar was tall, deeply tanned and had a huge mound of hair that could rightfully be called a pompadour. His colleague, Francesca McLaren, looked like the girl-next-door with her blonde bob and simple sundress, but according to Simon, she was ruthless.

Balthazar led off the meeting with, "We love *Hot Mic* – we really do. And, unlike all of the other studios who've said that, we *really* mean it."

"Yes," said Francesca. "The Wolff Network is keen to get into more comedy, both sketch-based shows and stand-up. This show has both. It's a home run!"

The meeting went well, and the next one went even better. Balthazar and Francesca wanted to be part of *Hot Mic,* and they seemed pretty confident that they could get the Wolff Network to back it.

Which meant more meetings, this time with Simon, Balthazar and Francesca, as well as Maraquita Putan and Hans Spaagfelt from the Wolff Network. Maraquita and Hans looked like Nordstrom's catalog models. Despite Balthazar and Francesca's optimism, Maraquita and Hans had seemed unenthusiastic. Chuck came away from the meeting feeling down, but Simon told him to buck up, because there would be another meeting.

He was right, and the six of them got together again. Chuck delivered what was essentially the same pitch, and Maraquita and Hans were enthusiastically receptive. "Told ya," said Simon.

Two days later, Philo called Chuck again. "Are you sitting down?" he asked. Chuck assured him that he was. "It's a go!" Simon crowed. "The network loves it! They've promised complete creative control!"

"Really?" Chuck asked.

"Yes, they actually said that," said Simon. "However, you shouldn't believe it for a second. In this business, there's no such thing as complete creative control. Still, the fact that they even lied about it is a good sign."

The next thing Chuck knew he had some things that he hadn't had in a long time. One was a guaranteed income, at least for the next year. He would have to write a script for the pilot, but he would be paid according to Writers' Guild guidelines. The other thing was a deadline. He had a year to develop an acceptable script and turn it into a pilot episode.

He wondered what things were going to be like when *Hot Mic* really got cranking. He was going to have to start busting heavies getting the script written and the guest act booked. He had already developed detailed outlines for five shows, and had some good ideas for several others. Fortunately, the scripts didn't have to be too long. Since the show featured relatively unknown stand-ups, that was six minutes of programming that he didn't have to provide.

Chuck felt even more nervous now about the project than he had when he'd first pitched the idea to Philo. He'd put a lot of work into the script, and felt that now he had more to lose. Yet the path forward was unclear, and strewn with all sorts of entertainment pitfalls and showbiz dangers. Chuck sighed, pushed these worries aside, and sat down to re-write the pilot. Again.

Chapter 11

The next nine months were insane. Meeting after meeting, rewrite after rewrite, trying to field the suggestions from the studio and network execs – some legit, some ludicrous. It had been exhausting. After what seemed like several ice ages, Chuck had finally produced a script that satisfied all of the suits.

Then it was off to the races filming the pilot episode. Casting hadn't been a problem – Chuck had talked the studio into casting Farrah, Danny and Arthur, as well as a handful of his peripheral stand-up crew for lesser parts. It had been fun, at least at first. After the initial buzz of pretending to be a Hollywood hotshot wore off, it was all down to hard work. The editing process had quickly grown tedious, and Chuck had been dismayed with the final product.

Simon had talked Chuck off the ledge after they watched the final cut. "Don't worry about it, man," he'd said. "Happens every time. The gritty reality never matches the auteur's vision. But you've got a good product, Chuck. It has a good chance of getting picked up."

Chuck hoped so. He had made a number of lifestyle changes over the last couple of months. With the money he was making writing and producing the pilot, he'd bid *adios* to his roomies in Los Feliz and gotten a small (but expensive) one-bedroom apartment in Silver Lake. He'd also traded his old Corolla for a new Prius. All of that was now on the line.

Chuck's phone rang. It was Philo. He had been waiting for this call ever since they'd submitted the finished pilot for *Hot Mic* to the Wolff Network. He was about to find out whether the show would be picked up.

"Chuck, it's Philo. How you doing?"

Uh-oh, thought Chuck. *He didn't ask if I was sitting down.* Not a good sign. "I'm okay, Philo. What's up?"

"Got some good news and some bad news, babes. Which do you want first?"

"Better give me the bad news first," said Chuck.

"Good," said Philo. "It makes more sense that way. Okay, the bad news: *Hot Mic* was not picked up for the next season."

"Oh." Chuck deflated. All of the crazy hard work he had put in over the last year or so was all for naught. It was crushing, but there was also a tiny sense of relief in that disappointment. "What's the good news?" he asked.

"You came really close. From what I heard, it came down to your show and a sitcom called *Washington Street.* They opted for that one. But it was close."

"So what?" said Chuck. "Close only counts in horseshoes and grenades."

"Not so, babes. There's a good chance that your show will be tabbed for a mid-season replacement. Those things don't just pop up out of thin air when another show bites the big one. The timing's just a little different. Early summer, they'll start thinking about lining up a potential mid-season replacement. If that happens, *Hot Mic* has a good shot at getting the nod."

"Okay," said Chuck. "I guess we'll see. In the meantime, I've got rent to pay. You need to start getting me some good-paying gigs, Philo. I don't want to go back to selling propellers."

"Yes, and you need to start working up some fresh material. Get me some good video, babes. I've been talking you up to a guy at Netflix. I showed him some bits from your Comedy Central set. He liked it, but we're going to have to kick things up a notch to get him to make us an offer. Think about it."

"Yeah, I will."

"What are you going to do now?"

"Ah, I think I need to blow town for a while," said Chuck. "Think I'll head back east, visit my family. Maybe spend some time on the Outer Banks."

"The what? You're going to hang out at a bank?"

"The beach, Philo, the beach. Say what you will about the East Cost – at least you can go swimming at the beach there."

"I prefer the Mediterranean," said Philo. "But I support your idea one thousand percent. Go relax, babes. Start thinking about some new material. I'll see about setting up some gigs for you so you can work it out. We'll get you on Netflix, babes – it's almost a done deal. And don't give up on *Hot Mic*. I think you still got a shot. Hang in there."

"I will, Philo. I'll give you a call when I get back."

***

Chuck's family was glad to have him back home, and Chuck was glad to be able to slow down and relax. However, he soon tired of knocking around his hometown haunts. A lot of his friends had fled, and he had trouble relating to those that were still around.

After a few days, he rented a house on Hatteras Island, in a town called Buxton. The house was cozy, isolated and right on the beach. Chuck spent most of the time sitting on the porch with a beer or a joint, reading or just staring out at the Atlantic. Occasionally, he had an idea for a joke, and would scribble it down in his spiral-bound notebook. He'd work on punching up the jokes later. Right now, he was content to just let his mind slide along in neutral. He knew that deep down, jokes were coalescing. There was no point in trying to force it. He just had to jot down a few quick notes when one of these nascent gags bubbled up to the top.

By the time Chuck boarded his return flight, he had about fifteen pages of notes. He felt pretty good; his intuition told him that there were some really good bits in there. He only had to tease them out. He'd also had some ideas about how to punch up his kindergarten bit. He started reworking his ideas on the flight to L.A.

When he got back home, he got some interesting news. The show that had beaten him out, *Washington Street*, had had a few new characters written in. Based on their performance on the *Hot Mic* pilot, Danny and Arthur had been invited to audition. They had both gotten parts, and were gearing up for a hectic production schedule.

Chuck felt conflicted at the news. He was glad for his friends, but he also felt a little cheated. He tried to suppress these feelings, especially when he was around Danny and Arthur. Unfortunately, this didn't happen too often, as they were so busy with *Washington Street* that they had precious little time to hang out with friends.

Instead, he worked on material, hit as many open mics as he could and started to feel confident about the strength of the bits that had grown from his notes on the beach. Philo got him some fairly decent gigs, and he was able to bag a number of smaller ones on his own. He still had a few bucks in the bank from his work on the pilot, and was able to keep the rent paid and the car payments covered. He didn't have a whole lot left over at the end of the month, but comedy was actually paying the bills.

***

One Thursday in early July, Chuck was nursing an unaccustomed hangover. The day before had been the Fourth of July. Chuck had gone to a party in Venice, and had imbibed quite a few tequila sunrises. He had ended up getting a ride home, which meant he had to get back to Venice to pick up his car. First, he had to get out of bed, something he was in no rush to do.

The phone rang, and Chuck cursed. He opened one eye and saw that it was Philo. Maybe he had good news. Chuck had gotten some good video from a showcase he'd done at a club called Flappers. He'd put portions of it on his YouTube channel, and they were getting a lot of hits. Chuck felt that it was better than the material from his Comedy Central show. Maybe Netflix had taken notice.

"Hey Chuck, it's Philo. Are you sitting down?"

"I'll do you one better than that," said Chuck. "I'm *lying* down. There's no way that the momentous news you're no doubt about to impart will result in my physical injury."

"Good," said Philo. "Because this *is* momentous. They want your show."

Chuck's heart sped up. "What? Netflix wants me for *The Standups?*"

"No, babes … I said *your* show. Wolff wants it as a potential mid-season replacement. They've ordered six episodes, and want full scripts for seven more!"

70

"Holy shit, Philo! Are you serious?"

"As a heart attack, babes. You're back in the TV biz."

"Six episodes?" asked Chuck. "But there's no guarantee that they'll actually air, right?"

"Yes, that is true," said Philo. "But if I had to make odds, I'd say that the network thinks there's a pretty good chance that they'll find a slot for the show. Six episodes is a good chunk of money. These cheap bastards wouldn't spend it if they didn't think they were going to need it."

"Okay, that's good," said Chuck. "When do we start?"

"Yesterday, babes, yesterday. There's a pre-production meeting tomorrow at 10 am."

"But tomorrow's Saturday. I was going up to Pismo Beach this weekend."

"Pismo Beach is going to have to wait. We're already behind schedule. That's the way it is with these mid-season replacements: periods of insane activity followed by periods of insane waiting. You just gotta cowboy up and work through it. You can do it. You did it with the pilot."

"Yeah, okay," said Chuck. "What's this production meeting about?"

"They want to see the scripts and need to talk about casting, since Arthur and Danny aren't available any longer."

"Oh, yeah," said Chuck. "I hadn't thought of that." His mood sank a little. It was going to be different doing the show without his friends. "Farrah's going to stay, though, right?"

"Most likely," said Philo. "First things first, they need six scripts, in good condition. Developed."

"No worries," said Chuck. "I have about ten scripts' worth of material written."

"Okay, great, babes. Bring everything you got to the meeting. I'm sending the deets right now. Call me if you need anything."

"Will do, Philo. Thanks."

Chuck hung up. He thought that he ought to get up and get to work on those scripts. It was tempting to just roll over and go back to sleep. Instead, he dragged himself out of bed and got a large pot of coffee going.

It occurred to him that Duckie could be a good fit for the cast. At the very least, he could get Duckie down here for an audition, and they could spend some time hanging out. He hadn't spoken to his old friend in many months; now seemed like a good time. He called Duckie's number in Portland, but it rang twice then went to voicemail. "Hey buddy," Chuck said. "Got some big news today, and there may be an opportunity for you to get your foot in the door here in L.A. Could be pretty big if it works out. Call me as soon as you can. I hope to hear from you soon."

He was bummed that Duckie hadn't picked up, but what the hell – hardly *anyone* picked up anymore. Still, *Hot Mic* was going to move forward, at least a little bit. Even if it didn't get broadcast, he'd be able to count on a regular income for a bit. Plus, his head was starting to clear and his gut wasn't griping as loudly. Things were looking up. Chuck whistled a jaunty tune as he poured his coffee.

Chapter 12

The summer went by in a blur. From the first production meeting following Philo's phone call until they wrapped the filming in late August, Chuck was busy, busy, busy. As Philo had warned, the production of a mid-season replacement was insane. On one hand, there was an overwhelming sense of urgency. In effect, the project was behind schedule from the very beginning. On the other hand, since there was no guarantee that the show would actually be aired, the studio and the network were unwilling to part with a lot of money for production.

It was hectic, but that was okay with Chuck; he got lost in the pure pleasure of creation. It didn't even bother him to know that the show might never be aired. At least it didn't bother him very much. He knew that they were making something good, and that gave him a sense of accomplishment.

By the time summer ended, the six episodes of *Hot Mic* were in the can. There was still work to do. Chuck continued to rewrite and revise the additional seven scripts that the Wolff Network had ordered. Then there was the seemingly endless editing of the material that they had already taped. Chuck didn't mind, especially since it kept a steady influx of money going into his bank account.

Eventually, even the post-production activities tailed off. *Hot Mic* receded somewhat into Chuck's rear-view mirror. There were other things going on in his life. Most importantly, Philo actually came through with a slot on Netflix's *The Standups.* For four months, it completely consumed Chuck's life. He wasn't entirely happy with his final segment, but he wasn't upset, either. He had good material, and his performance was solid – so what if the editing wasn't so hot? At the viewing party in March, all of his comedy buddies who had downplayed his appearance on *Comedy Central Stand-Up Presents* were forced to eat a bit of crow.

Philo and Chuck were able to leverage the Netflix exposure into more lucrative gigs for him. He was playing better clubs around L.A., occasionally headlining shows at smaller places, and getting more stage time at big-name venues like the Comedy Shoppe and the Giggle Factory. He was also touring more, frequently acting as the feature – or warm-up – act for A-list comics.

Chuck got a gig touring the West Coast with Sebastian Maniscalco as the feature comic. The itinerary included Portland, so Chuck made it a point to give Duckie a heads-up and ask about getting together while he was in town. Duckie didn't respond until they had already started the tour. They made plans to meet at a faux English pub called the Moon & Sixpence.

The place was dark, furnished in heavily stained wood paneling. It took Chuck a few moments for his eyes to adjust, and he couldn't find Duckie in any of the place's nooks and alcoves. He slid into a booth, spent some time studying the extensive beer list, and ordered a Samuel Smith's Oatmeal Stout.

In truth, he was a little uncomfortable. His communications with Duckie over the last few years had been brief to the point of abruptness. It had taken Duckie nearly a month to get back to him about the offer to audition for *Hot Mic,* and by then the roles had already been cast. Chuck was actually a little surprised that Duckie had agreed to meet him at all, strange as that seemed.

He had nearly finished the beer when Duckie wandered in, nearly forty minutes late. It looked like he had just woken up: his hair was mussed up and his eyes half shut. He spotted Chuck in the booth and came over, a grin spreading across his puffy face.

"Sorry I'm late, man," said Duckie. "I've just started a graveyard shift job, and I'm still getting used to the schedule."

"No problem, Duckster," said Chuck "Good to see you again. It's been too long. How do you like living in Portland?"

"Beats the ever-loving shit out of living in Baltimore."

"That's a pretty low bar, I imagine."

"That it is. I'm sure it's not like living in Hollywood, though," said Duckie. A waitress came by and he ordered a Pabst Blue Ribbon draft.

"Actually, I don't live in Hollywood," Chuck pointed out. "I've got an apartment in Silver Lake."

Duckie shrugged. It was all the same to him, Chuck supposed. Still, it irked him for some reason. He smiled widely and tried to forget about it.

"So you're middling for Sebastian," said Duckie. "That must be cool."

"Ah, not as cool as you'd think," said Chuck. "The only time I see him is in the green room before the show. He's not the most sociable of people, y'know? He'll do a meet 'n' greet before the show if he has to, but as soon as he's off the stage, he's gone. Doesn't even stay in the same place as me."

"You're at Hydrogen tonight, right?"

"Yeah."

"You staying in the condo?" Many prominent comedy clubs maintained a condo where they put up touring comedians.

"Yeah, I'm in the condo, but Sebastian's staying at a fancy hotel downtown. The Heathman."

"Wow, that's pretty sweet," said Duckie.

"You coming to the show?" asked Chuck. "I can get you on the guest list."

"Man, I'm sorry, but I can't," said Duckie. "Have to pull an early shift tonight. Covering for someone who's on vacation. Being the new guy sucks."

"Yeah, that's too bad."

Duckie must have heard the disappointment in his voice. "I *did* catch your show on Netflix, though," he said. "Fucking funny stuff, man. I always knew you'd make it big. I'm glad at least one of us did."

"Hey, man, don't count yourself out of the running, okay? It's a shame we couldn't get you to audition for *Hot Mic*. But you're still doing gigs, right? I see some of your stuff on YouTube. You've got the chops, Duckie. Keep doing what you're doing."

"Thanks, man." He took an enormous swig from his mug. "Making the move to Portland was definitely a boost. A *lot* more comedy here than where I was hanging out back east."

"You should move to L.A.," said Chuck. "Opportunities out the wazoo. Open mics everywhere, every night."

"Sounds pretty cool," said Duckie. He polished off his beer, checked his cell phone, and said. "Hey, gotta bounce. Need to make it out to Beaverton by eight. It was good seeing you, man." He pulled out his wallet.

"Hey, I got this," protested Chuck.

Duckie made a sour face, and dropped a fiver on the table. "Break a leg tonight, man. If you ever get to talk to Sebastian, tell him I said 'hi.'"

And with that, he was out the door. Chuck checked his cell phone; his reunion with his old friend had lasted nineteen minutes. He was disappointed, but not surprised. It hurt to think that he and Duckie had drifted this far apart. Hell, in a year or two they might have stopped communicating altogether. It made Chuck's soul ache.

He finished his beer, paid the tab and left. His set that night was flat, just because of the aftertaste of the meeting with Duckie. He recovered the next night in Seattle, however, and the rest of the tour went well.

***

In the fall, *Washington Street* premiered, and Danny and Arthur hosted a viewing party. Chuck actually thought that the show was pretty sucky, but he wasn't going to say anything to dampen the spirit of the occasion. Besides, it was a blast to see his friends on a TV show.

Philo pulled off another win by landing Chuck a bit part on *Better Call Saul.* Technically, it was a speaking part, even if the entirety of Chuck's dialogue was one word. In the show, Chuck would play an EMT. The ambulance he's riding in pulls up next to a car. In it is one of the main characters having a freak-out. Chuck's character notices this, taps the ambulance driver on the shoulder and says, "Hey." They both turn to look, then the main character drives off, still sobbing. That was it. Chuck was on the screen for a total of twelve seconds. He got flown out to Albuquerque, got to rub elbows with comedy heavyweights Bob Odenkirk and Michael McKean, and banked a decent chunk of cash for his monosyllabic performance.

He had another viewing party, to celebrate his one-fifth of a minute on an immensely popular TV show. Most of the partygoers spent the rest of the evening whapping each other on the shoulder and saying, "Hey." It was fun.

***

Just before Halloween, he received a call from Philo.

"Hey, Philo," Chuck said. "What's up? I'm sitting down. Sock it to me."

"I don't know if that's gonna cut it, babes," said Philo. "You need to be *lying* down for this news. Ideally in a hospital, with a resuscitation crew on standby. It's *that* big."

Chuck laughed. In the realm of Philo Spinoza's hyperbole, this had to be a record. "Sounds pretty big, with that build-up," he said. "Don't keep me hanging."

"Okay, babes, here it is: Your show's a go."

Chuck was momentarily unsure what Philo was talking about. "Huh? You mean *Hot Mic?*"

"Yes, of course I mean *Hot Mic.* The Wolff Network wants it as a mid-season replacement. There are a couple of new shows that aren't going to make the cut. They want *Hot Mic* to premiere on…" – Chuck heard papers shuffling in the background – "on January 24. A Thursday. A great slot! Ready to be a TV star, babes?"

Chuck was speechless. His mind raced and went nowhere.

"Chuck?" said Philo. "Charles? You still there, babes?"

"Yeah, I'm here, man. I'm just totally blown away. I never expected this to happen."

"Well, *I* did," said Philo. "I told you that they wouldn't have ordered six episodes if they didn't think they'd air. Now they want seven more, and they want them *yesterday.* I hope you don't have extensive plans for the holidays, because you're gonna be spending a lot of time at the studio for the foreseeable future."

"Uh, okay." Chuck had made plans to go back to North Carolina for Christmas, but it would actually be a relief to cancel. Going back to Raleigh wasn't as fun as it used to be. "No plans that I can't change."

"Good. That's very good, babes. You're about to be extraordinarily busy. Think about how hectic it was getting those six episodes made? Well, that's gonna a be a day at Disneyland compared to what comes next. Think you're up for it?"

"Hell, yes!" said Chuck. "I guess the first production meeting's Monday, huh?"

"Nope, it's Saturday. Tomorrow. I'll send you the deets *immediamente*."

After some further congratulatory small talk, Chuck hung up. He was dizzy from this incredible news. He decided that he needed to get some perspective on the situation, so he rolled a joint and put some Hendrix on the stereo.

Twenty minutes later he was feeling much more low-key. The whole thing was ludicrous. Who would be so foolish as to allow *him* to make a TV show? He giggled at the ridiculousness of the whole mind-roasting scenario. It wasn't until much later that he stopped to wonder which show was going to be canceled to make room for his.

Chapter 13

Halfway through "The Wind Cries Mary," Chuck realized that he had a date that night.

"Holy shit!" he exclaimed. He sat up and stubbed out the joint. Fortunately, he still had an hour before he had to leave. Plenty of time to get his head straight and get ready.

Chuck was slightly apprehensive about his date with Caroline. His friend Brian had introduced them over a year ago when they had been out bar-hopping one Saturday night. Caroline Swenson was an attractive all-American girl who had moved to L.A. from Iowa to Make It in Showbiz. She and Chuck had gone out two or three times, but nothing much had come of it. Chuck hadn't been especially disappointed, and he suspected that Caroline felt the same way.

Last week, he had run into Brian at a Quizno's in Little Armenia, and in the course of their chit-chat, he'd mentioned to Chuck that Caroline had asked about him. Chuck had given a noncommittal reply, but two nights later Caroline called him up. Chuck had just returned from the shoot in Albuquerque, and was gearing up for some gigs around L.A. He had time on his hands. Otherwise, he might not have even taken her call.

But he had, and they had ended up chatting for nearly an hour. At the end, he'd asked her out again without really thinking about it. It seemed like a good idea. He really hadn't had time for a social life over the past several months, and he was ready for some R & R.

Chuck checked his phone. Time had slipped away; he had to put on his boogie shoes. He took a quick shower and shucked into a clean pair of jeans and a sweatshirt. At the last minute, he swapped the sweatshirt for a moderately fashionable dress shirt and was soon cruising towards his old stomping grounds in Los Feliz.

Baron's was a middle-of-the road steak and seafood place on Hillhurst Avenue. Parking was a bastard, but Chuck managed to find a place for his Prius and strolled up to the restaurant right on time.

He almost didn't recognize Caroline. She was dressed in a snazzy little black cocktail dress with a high hem and plunging neckline that showed off her corn-fed assets to maximum advantage. A pair of six-inch stiletto heels rounded out her ensemble.

"Hey, pretty lady," said Chuck. "Are you a famous movie star?"

"Not yet," said Caroline. "But soon, just you see." She leaned in and gave him a hug – a long one.

"Holy moly, Caroline! Did you just come from an audition or something? I mean, you look great – awesome, in fact – but this isn't any sort of fancy place. Just, y'know, some serviceable steaks and seafood. Not exactly the place to see and be seen."

"I know that, silly," she said, grabbing his bicep. "Sometimes a girl just likes to get a little dressed up. There's nothing wrong with that."

"You are absolutely correct. And might I say that you look quite fine."

"Thank you. I'm really glad you think so."

"Well, I don't know about you, but I'm getting hungry," said Chuck. "Shall we?" He opened up the door and bowed slightly.

"Yes, I've got a bit of an appetite myself," she said in a sultry voice.

Baron's wasn't high end, but it wasn't McDonald's, either. There was a *maître d'* dressed in a simple white dress shirt and black slacks at a stand just inside the front door. Caroline leaned into Chuck and whispered, "Get us something out of the way. Intimate." Her warm breath tickled his ear, and he could feel the first stirrings of desire south of the beltline.

"Uh, yeah," Chuck told the *maître d'*. "Do you perhaps have a booth in the back? Low lighting?"

"I don't know, sir," said the *maître d'*. "Let me have a look." He made a show of looking over the seating chart and flipping through the reservation book.

Caroline dug her elbow into Chuck's ribs, and he took the hint. He dug a twenty out of his wallet, folded it lengthways, and used it to point at a booth on the seating chart. "How about something around here?" he asked.

The *maître d'* made the twenty disappear. "Ah, yes, sir," he said. "I think I have just the spot. Please follow me." He led them to a small horseshoe-shaped booth in a dark corner of the restaurant.

"So, what have you been up to?" Chuck asked as they perused the menu.

"Well, I'm still working at the Sephora on Sunset," Caroline said. "And I've been taking acting classes."

"How's that going?"

"Well, Sephora's just okay. We get a lot of tourists in there, and they can really be a pain in the ass. I like the acting class, though. The teacher says I'm a natural. Maybe with some one-on-one coaching, I could really get somewhere."

Chuck eyed the low-cut neckline of Caroline's dress and figured he knew what sort of one-on-one coaching the teacher was talking about.

"I know what you're thinking," she said. "And it's not that. Julio – my instructor – is as gay as old Dad's hat band. He really thinks I have talent." She took a long drink from her cocktail.

"Hmm," said Chuck. "Well, what sort of role would you like? Like, what would be your dream part?"

"Oh, I'd want to be the lead in a musical. I just adore musicals! I was Laurey in my senior class production of *Oklahoma!* The local newspaper said I brought the house down."

"Wow, that's pretty cool. I mean, if you can act and sing, then you're a double threat. I have to admit that the idea of getting in front of a crowd and singing scares the crap out of me."

"Yes, but you get up in front of strangers and tell jokes. That's got to be ten times worse."

"Well, I've been doing that for years, so I'm used to it. I'd like to think I've gotten good at it, at least a little. But I can't sing at all. Couldn't carry a tune in a bucket."

"Oh, that's too bad! I love to sing! Wanna hear?"

Before he could answer, she tossed back the rest of her drink and began belting out "People Will Say We're In Love."

Chuck listened in amazement. She was *terrible*. He tried to keep a neutral expression on his face as her tone-deaf rendition continued. He hoped she'd quit after the first verse, but she just kept going. People at nearby tables cast annoyed looks in their direction. Finally, it was over.

"Well?" she said. "What did you think?"

"Words fail me," said Chuck. "I can see how you brought the house down in Des Moines."

"I'll do it again, here, too, given half a chance. What about you? What have you been working on?"

"I was mostly working on a pilot for Wolff. Until today, I didn't think it was going anywhere."

"Pilot?" asked Caroline. "For a TV show? Really?"

"Yes, really," said Chuck. "Didn't I mention that on the phone?"

"Well, I think Brian might have said something about it. But you know how it is in this town. Everybody's got some big, exciting project in the works. Most of it is exaggeration and bullshit, y'know?"

"Yeah, I do," said Chuck. "But in the words of George Carlin, It's. No. Bullshit!"

"Wow, really? "Caroline said. "So have you finished filming it yet? What's it called?"

"It's called *Hot Mic*. Wolff actually ordered six episodes as a potential mid-season replacement. We didn't even know if they were going to use them."

"Omigod, omigod! You can't be serious! Do you know if it's going to air?"

"Well, as a matter of fact, I heard something just today…"

She reached over and squeezed his forearm. "Oh, don't tease me, Chuck. What did you hear?"

"They went for it," said Chuck. "Wolff wants it as a mid-season replacement. I'm going to be on network TV starting next January."

"*Squeeeee!*" shrieked Caroline. Everyone in the restaurant turned and looked.

"That's so great, Chuck! Congratulations! I always knew you had star potential. This calls for a celebration!" She waved over a passing waiter.

"Yes, ma'am," said the waiter. "Are you ready to order?"

"No, we're celebrating," said Caroline. "We need champagne!"

"Yes, ma'am." The waiter immediately produced a wine list. Chuck snagged it before Caroline could order something extravagant.

"Uh, let's go with this, um, Laurent-Perrier Brut," he said quickly. It was the second-cheapest sparkling wine on the list. Still, it was 85 bucks a bottle – and Chuck didn't even really like champagne.

The waiter brought the bottle and two flutes, popped the cork and poured. "To *Hot Mic*," said Caroline. They clinked glasses and drank.

"So, tell me," she said. "How did you go from new-kid-in-town comic to TV showrunner?"

"I'm not going to be the showrunner," said Chuck. "Just not enough bandwidth if I'm actually in the show. I will be the head writer, though."

"And the star, right?"

"Yeah, I guess so." Chuck had never thought of the show in terms of stars. It was originally just him and a couple of friends having fun. He suddenly realized how much had changed, and it made him feel a little sad – and a little scared.

"Top me off," said Caroline, hoisting her glass. "These flutes are so tiny, barely more than a shot glass." Chuck filled her glass, and they drank to stardom.

After their third toast, Chuck put the flute down. He could feel the beginnings of a headache behind his eyes. Caroline was evidently not having the same problem. He kept topping her off and she kept throwing them back.

"Sho, tell me," she said fuzzily. "Tell me all of your shecrets of shuccess."

"I had a YouTube video go viral," he said. "After that, it was mostly just good luck." He went through the whole story of signing with Philo, then the idea for *Hot Mic* and shopping it around to different studios. Caroline kept proposing toasts. Chuck pretty much just backwashed the champagne so he wouldn't get more headachy, but Caroline kept downing the Brut. She slid around the horseshoe-shaped bench until she was snuggled up against him.

Chuck felt conflicted. Caroline was cute, and she felt good pressed up against him. He hadn't been with anyone since a one-nighter on the road about two months ago. On the other hand, she seemed pretty starstruck and very drunk. Chuck didn't like the idea of taking advantage of her.

Caroline had no such misgivings. "Wow, Chuck shweetie, I have to say that you've done really well for yourshelf. Here's to you!" She gestured grandly with the champagne flute, and some of the bubbly slopped out onto the table and Chuck's trousers. "Oh no!" she squealed. "I got some on your pants. Let me get that!"

She snatched up a napkin and began rubbing his crotch.

"It's okay," said Chuck. "It's only a little drop…"

"Oh, no," said Caroline. "I'm gonna take care of you, baby." She began rubbing more vigorously, and Chuck's manhood was soon at full alert.

"O-ho!" she said. "What have we here? I think I'd better investigate!" She disappeared beneath the table, and before Chuck could fathom what was going on, she had undone his fly, pulled out his cock and slipped it into her mouth.

What the hell? thought Chuck. Was this really happening? He looked around to see if anyone else had noticed. In the dim light, the other diners were blithely enjoying their meals. Underneath the table, Caroline continued her oral ministrations. For a few moments, Chuck enjoyed a surreal sense of zen-like calm. His hands rested lightly on the linen tablecloth and he gazed around with equanimity at his fellow restaurant patrons as he received a world-class blowjob.

But it was also all wrong.

A tarantula of guilt began creeping up his spine. A few years ago, he would have crowed about an escapade like this to the hills and back. Now, it just felt greasy and exploitive. The show hadn't even aired yet, and here he was living a horrible Hollywood cliché. Chuck felt his ardor beginning to wane.

"Excuse me sir," said the waiter, who had materialized in front of the table. "Are you ready to order n…" His eyes cut down, where he could obviously see a pair of stiletto pumps sticking out from beneath the tablecloth. "Um, I'll come back later," he said, and vanished.

This threw a bucket of ice-water on what remained of Chuck's enjoyment. He could feel his dick starting to wilt. Caroline must have felt it as well, and she began pumping more vigorously to avoid a total meltdown. The back of her head began hitting the underside of the table, making the silverware rattle rhythmically. Now people at nearby tables were beginning to notice.

Chuck lifted the edge of the tablecloth. "Caroline!" he hissed. "Knock it off! People are watching." *Holy shit*, he thought. *Did I really just tell a beautiful woman to stop sucking my cock?*

Caroline slithered up from beneath the table. She looked around with a dazed expression on her face. Chuck took her hand. "Hey," he said quietly. "It's not like I don't really appreciate the … um … sentiment. You just kinda caught me by surprise there. The … uh … waiter also seemed pretty surprised when he came by with the menus and saw your feet sticking out from under the tablecloth."

Caroline held her head in her hands. "Oh, holy shit," she said. "That damn bubbly always goes straight to my head. Oh!" Her shoulders hitched once, twice, then she stumbled to her feet and zig-zagged towards the restrooms.

Everyone was definitely watching now. At the far end of the room, the waiter regarded him with a mixture or contempt and amusement. *What the hell,* thought Chuck. He raised his hand and called out, "Check, please!"

It got a laugh.

Ideally, he would have thrown a fistful of bills on the table and walked out with his back straight and his head held high. But he had blown the last of his folding money on the *maître d'.* So he had to wait for the smirking waiter to charge his credit card, and Chuck added on an enormous tip out of embarrassment. Then he waited some more. There was no sign of Caroline. After ten minutes, he got up to look for her.

He walked up to the door of the women's restroom and rapped gently with one knuckle. "Caroline?" he asked. "You in there?"

After a pause, she said "Yes," in a small voice. "I've never done anything like that before. I'm so embarrassed."

"It's okay," said Chuck. "I've already paid up. We can just quick-step to the door and be gone like a cool breeze."

"Okay."

They took their leave of Baron's and stopped at In-n-Out for burgers on their way back to his apartment, where Caroline ended up spending the night.

Chapter 14

Don Bundy was about to take his shot.

He was getting ready to step into a high-powered executive leadership meeting of the Wolff Network. Normally, his boss would be the one going to the meeting, to report on the activity in the Engineering group. However, the boss had suddenly become very sick, throwing up uncontrollably, so Don had been tapped to go in his place.

The reason Don's boss had gotten very sick was because Don had put a large dollop of dish soap in his coffee. Don's boss took his coffee with a lot of sugar, which had masked the taste of the soap. He had drunk the entire cup without batting an eye.

Don had another reason to be nervous: he had fucked up. Sort of. Actually, he had *solved* a fuck-up. The problem was that Don's solution wasn't entirely legal. However, he was convinced that overall his actions were a plus for the corporation, and he was eager to make that argument to the head of the network, Malachi Wolff.

Hence the soap in his boss's coffee.

Don was an ambitious guy in a competitive organization. He had been in Engineering limbo for three years. It was not a good starting point for corporate climbing, but it was a great place to gather intel. Don had gathered as much as he thought advisable. Now it was time to make a bold move. He had been looking for an opening, and the Australasia incident had presented an unparalleled opportunity for Don to show his mettle.

He rode up to the C-suites in an elevator full of other network suits. His own suit was a high-end off-the-rack number. It clearly separated him from the de la Renta dames and Armani zombies, but also said "good taste on a budget." At least Don hoped so. He had a subscription to *GQ* and a tailor who knew how to make a $300 suit look like a $3000 one. That was good enough for Don Bundy.

The elevator opened and Don followed the group confidently to the conference room on the corner of the 20th floor of the Wolff Network tower. The tower wasn't big, but it was famous, having originally been the headquarters of a now-defunct record company; the building was shaped like a pile of records on a turntable. It was an L.A. landmark, and Malachi Wolff had paid top dollar for it, knowing that its history gave it more of a cachet than the rival networks' glass-box high-rises further downtown.

Don took a seat and began reviewing his notes. He already knew what he was going to say, but he wanted to look prepared and he didn't really want to engage in any chit-chat with the other suits. He checked his watch. It was one minute to the hour. That was good. Malachi Wolff was a stickler for punctuality. His meetings started exactly on time, and woe to anyone who was so much as a minute late.

At ten o'clock on the dot, Wolff's entourage swept into the room. It was preceded by Reese, Wolff's factotum and all-around gofer. Reese was short, shapeless and ruthlessly unremarkable. She rarely said a word.

Malachi Wolff came next, looking splendid in a bespoke suit with a brightly colored tie and pocket square set contrasting with the somber gray of the jacket. His hair was glossy black streaked with silver, and swept back in a cut so expensive that it would have covered Don's mortgage payment. Malachi Wolff looked to be in his late thirties, but Don knew that he was actually fifty-eight.

Behind Wolff came his immediate toadies, a trio of senior vice presidents. One of the toadies took a look at Bundy and leaned over and whispered to Wolff.

"Okay, it's the top of the hour," said Malachi. "Let's get this show on the road. First order of business: who the hell are you?" He looked directly at Don.

"Don Bundy, sir," he replied. "Engineering."

"Engineering?" said Malachi. "Where the hell is McClellan?"

"Sick, sir," said Bundy. "He sent me in his place, sir."

"Good," said Malachi. "I've got some questions about that fuck-up in Australasia."

"I am prepared to address those questions, sir," said Bundy.

"I should certainly hope so," said Malachi. "But you'll have to wait your turn. I'm not going to bugger my agenda because McClellan has a tummy ache." Don nodded, saying nothing. His experience in the Marines had taught him how to deal with psychotic superiors.

Don listened intently. He always did when he was in these C-suite meetings. He wasn't so much interested in the topics of the meeting as he was in the participants. He liked to try and gauge their character, their strengths and weaknesses. Such information could be quite useful.

"Okay," said Malachi. "January is coming, people! We just ordered mid-season replacements, and we need to get things moving on them. Fast! I want all of the paperwork and contracts on these new shows tied up by the end of the week. I want them in production *next* week. Especially that new sketch show with that kid Marshall. What's the name of that one again?"

"*Hot Mic*," said Reese into Malachi's ear.

"Ugh," said Malachi. "We'll have to do something about that name. First things first, contracts signed and production scheduled. Got it?"

There was a general obsequious nodding of heads. There was further talk of schedules, time slots, promos and budgets. Don listened attentively, feeling a little nervous knot blooming in his stomach.

Don had been a sniper in the Marines, and he knew about the importance of setting up a shot. He was used to the knot in his gut. It helped keep him focused. It was almost time.

Finally, Malachi said, "Okay, last and possibly least: engineering. Mr. Barton, since you're representing Engineering, perhaps you can tell us about this little fuck-up in Australasia."

"Yes, sir," said Don. He knew that Malachi had gotten his name wrong on purpose, as a show of dominance. No point in responding to a provocation like that; it just showed weakness. "Last Saturday night, there was a series of cascading failures in our broadcast feed to the SoroTel 1 satellite that covers Australia, New Zealand and the western portion of the South Pacific. It was an unprecedented failure that crashed the primary and backup servers, and tripped the transmitters uplinking to the satellite."

"Jesus!" said Malachi. "What the hell, Ballmer? Don't we pay you engineering weenies to make sure shit like this doesn't happen?"

"Sir, yes, sir!" barked Don. "That is our mission, and we failed it, sir!"

Malachi paused. This wasn't the sort of groveling he expected after a high-profile fuck-up. "Explain yourself!" he demanded.

"Sir, our resources for error detection and redundancy are finite," said Don. "Naturally, most of our attention is focused on the big markets: North America and Europe. Other parts of the world get the older systems and less attention. This most likely wouldn't have happened if we had better equipment and a bigger budget—"

"Shit!" said Malachi. "Don't start with that! You fucked up and you've got the nerve to ask me for more money? You must have brass balls, Beatty!"

"Sir, yes, sir," said Don.

"Okay, okay," said Malachi. "Shit, as they say, happens. How long did it take to get back up and running?"

"Sir, it took exactly fifty-two minutes to get the servers rebooted and the antennas back online."

"Jesus H. Tapdancing Christ!" exclaimed Malachi. "We were down for almost an hour?! That's a non-trivial portion of the English-speaking world! And we weren't broadcasting there for nearly an hour on a Saturday night? Why the fuck didn't I hear about this?"

Don suppressed a small smile. His shot was now lined up; it was just time to squeeze the trigger. "Actually, sir, our broadcasting was able to resume after just forty-two seconds."

"What the fuck are you talking about, Burton?" demanded Malachi. "You just said that our equipment was out for fifty-two minutes. Now you're saying it was only forty-two seconds? Well, man, which is it?"

"Both, sir," said Don. "Allow me to explain."

Malachi narrowed his eyes. "I await your explanation with bated breath," he said.

"Sir, yes, sir! I've always been concerned about the performance of the older systems. I knew there was a chance, however small, of a cascading failure like we experienced, so I developed a contingency plan."

"Jesus, don't keep me in suspense," said Malachi. "Just spill it, Bartly!"

"Sir, yes, sir! Basically, we switched to another satellite until we could reestablish the link to the SoroSat."

"Holy shit!" said Malachi. "You rented time on another satellite? That must have cost an arm and a leg! And how did you manage that in less than a minute?"

"As I said, it was a contingency for which I had been planning. And it didn't cost the network a dime."

"Bullshit! How is that possible?"

"We sort of hitched a ride on the Vitalcom 7 satellite. Didn't even have to pay for gas. So to speak."

Around the huge mahogany table, the suits looked at him in amazement. They'd never seen anyone admit to something like this in front of Malachi Wolff. Some were aghast, and others watched in morbid fascination, certain that they were watching this engineering rando commit professional suicide.

"What do you mean you 'hitched a ride'?" asked Malachi. "This better be good, Bullfinch."

"Sir, the Vitalcom 7 carries signals for ABC, HBO and Netflix. We just sort of stowed away on the carrier signal. Of course, it degraded the signal of all three networks, but not so much as to be especially noticeable."

"Especially ABC," snickered one of the SVPs.

"Wasn't our signal also degraded?" asked Malachi.

"No sir," said Don. "We were able to maintain our full signal quality. At the expense of the others, of course."

Malachi narrowed his eyes. "So you basically stole their satellite time, is that what you're saying? Surely you know that you've opened up the network to an enormous legal liability? They must have ways of detecting an intrusion like that! Holy Christ, this is going to be a PR nightmare!"

Don took a deep breath. "Under normal circumstances, that would be a legitimate concern, sir."

"And why aren't these 'normal circumstances'?"

"We took care to cover our tracks, sir. As soon as we had linked up with Vitalcom, I had a trusted team of IT specialists making sure that no one would be able to catch us out after the fact. I've got some real hacker all-stars. They can do anything with – or to – a computer.

"They hacked the comm logs. If anyone bothered to look, the degraded signal would appear to be due to slightly above-average background disruption. Sunspots, cosmic rays, random radio noise like that. So far, I don't believe they bothered to check. Basically, their signal was slightly shittier than usual for fifty-two minutes, then it went back to its normal level once we'd re-established our uplink. No harm, no foul."

Malachi narrowed his eyes and tented his fingers. He looked quickly at the EVP toadies at the head of the table, all of whom were trying to keep a neutral look on their faces. "Welllll…" said Malachi. "I suppose you're right. Indeed: no harm, no foul. Very good. Yes." He leaned over to Reese and asked a question. Reese tapped on the ever-present iPad and whispered something back to Malachi.

"Mr. Don Bundy of Engineering," said Malachi. "I'd like to see you in my office at ten thirty tomorrow morning to discuss a budget increase. We should upgrade our equipment, and make sure we don't have any more of these unfortunate incidents."

"Sir, yes, sir!" said Don.

"Super," said Malachi. "Great job, everybody. Meeting adjourned."

Chapter 15

At 10:25 the next morning, Don Bundy presented himself in the anteroom to Malachi Wolff's office. He was dressed in his apex-predator outfit, an Armani suit he'd gotten on eBay. He'd had his wizard tailor do some alterations, and now it fit like he'd worn it out the door of the shop on Rodeo Drive.

"Don Bundy for Mr. Wolff," he told Reese, who sat at a desk in front of the massive carved doors that led to Malachi Wolff's inner sanctum.

"One moment, please," she said, and pressed a button on her phone.

"What the hell do you want?" came Malachi's voice. "Didn't I tell you not to disturb me? Christ, Reese! I'm trying to keep this pig's anus of a network afloat, and I need total concentration! I can't have you pestering me every goddamn minute of every fucking day with petty interruptions and minor bullshit. This is serious, man! What the fuck do you want now?"

"Mr. Bundy to see you, sir," said Reese.

There was a long pause, then a heavy sigh over the intercom. "Oh, well," said Malachi. "Go ahead and send the bastard in."

Reese stood up and opened the huge cocobolo doors. "You may go on in," she told Don.

Don gave her a curt nod, then stepped through the door. Malachi Wolff's office was massive, at least the size of two tennis courts. The far end of the office was a window-wall with a perfectly framed view of the Hollywood sign. Malachi's desk was right in front of it – but facing away from the window. A visitor only saw Malachi in silhouette as they advanced through the huge space with the glare in their eyes.

Don suppressed a grin. He had to hand it to Wolff: The way in which he had arranged his office was intimidating. He knew this meeting was going to be a challenge. Just like in the boardroom the day before, he felt a coil of tension in his gut, but knew that he was up to the task.

He marched resolutely across the office, his feet sinking into the deep plush of the maroon carpet. It took a while to cover the distance, and Malachi sat unmoving behind his desk the entire time. Finally, Don arrived at the massive desk and stood at attention. "You wished to speak with me, sir?" he said.

Malachi sat unmoving for a moment, then said, "So, uh, Bundy, was it? Have a seat."

"Sir, yes, sir." Don sat at attention on the straight-backed wooden chair in front of the enormous desk, spine yardstick-straight, hands on his thighs.

Malachi gave him the hairy eyeball for another fifteen seconds, then said, "You really fucked up, Bunsen. You exposed this network to a massive legal liability. The fact that you managed to cover your tracks is of little consequence. You're a loose cannon, and loose cannons cause damage."

"Sir, yes, sir!" said Bundy. He reached into his briefcase and pulled out a sheet of paper. "I understand, and am prepared to tender my resignation." He slid the paper across the desk.

Don's eyes had adjusted to the glare from the window, and he could now read Malachi's face. He was gratified to see Malachi's eyes widen momentarily as he picked up the paper. He knew that this was all play-acting; if Malachi had wanted him fired for his transmitter stunt, he would have been escorted out of the building before yesterday's meeting was over.

Malachi made a show of reading the letter, then crumpled it up. "I've had a change of heart," he said. "Under normal circumstances, I would have expected some groveling and maybe even tears from an ambitious junior peon who had fucked up. You're made of sterner stuff, I see."

"I'm a Marine, sir," Don pointed out. "We're not very good at groveling, and as for tears – fuckin' forget it. Pardon my French, sir."

Malachi looked at him sternly for a moment, then burst into laughter. "Oh, I like you, Bundy!" he said. "I've got a real good feeling about you."

"Thank you, sir."

"Do you know why I took time out of my schedule to meet with you today?" asked Malachi.

"Sir, yes, sir," said Don. "You wanted to discuss how we could avoid such mishaps that resulted in my putting the network at such great legal peril."

Malachi made a spinning motion with his index finger.

Don pulled another sheet from his briefcase and said, "I've prepared an upgrade plan so that our systems will be more error-proof. It will bring the transmitters up to—"

"What's the bottom line?" interrupted Malachi.

"Eight point seven five million, sir."

"Let's call it ten million and be done with it, then," said Malachi.

"Very good, sir. Is there anything else?"

"Of course," said Malachi. "I didn't bring you up here to discuss transmitter upgrades."

Don said nothing, but smiled inwardly. His risk had paid off; his shot was true. He'd stuck his neck out to get noticed, and it had worked.

"What do you know about creating a television show?" asked Malachi.

"Well, sir, one of the things I enjoy about working in Engineering is that I am afforded exposure to many aspects of the network's business. I feel I have a decent grounding in the basics of how we create and broadcast."

"Oh, wow," said Malachi. "You are an absolute font of sweet-smelling bullshit, aren't you?"

"If you say so, sir," said Don.

"You're an engineer, right?" said Malachi. "What the hell's that good for?"

"Pretty much everything," said Don. "Engineering is all about problem-solving. No shortage of problems, here at Wolff or anywhere else in the world."

"Okay, good," said Malachi. "Here's one for you, Mr. Problem Solver. Suppose I have a new talent, an actor that I'm interested in, shall we say, cultivating. Like all new artists, they want a mythical something called 'complete creative control.' How would you manage a talent like that?"

"I would offer them complete creative control, sir."

Malachi scowled. "Like I said, it's mythical. It doesn't exist."

"Sir, yes, sir," said Malachi. "I said I'd offer it them. That doesn't mean they would actually get it. The best way to manage that would be with the contract. Offer the mythical control, but provide a contract stuffed full of exceptions and loopholes. Make it so convoluted and recursive that even the most experienced manager wouldn't know what to make of it. We'd need a really good lawyer, one that's very experienced and completely amoral."

"Ha! Is there any other kind?" Malachi laughed. "I've got an entire floor full of amoral lawyers. Yes, there's one in particular who would fit the job. He could put together a contract that would make Lead Belly's look equitable."

"Sir, yes, sir."

"Okay, you're off to a good start," said Malachi. "We get him in the door with the contract. Now, how would we keep him there?"

Don felt that he was in the clear; that Malachi was just messing with his head now. Not a problem; he was like many of his commanding officers in the Corps. Besides, he was now enjoying tackling a new and interesting challenge.

"Welllll…" said Don. "I suppose that you would need someone associated with the show, someone who can call the shots and make them stick. Producer? Nah. Anybody with a flush checkbook can be a producer. Director? Yeah, maybe if it was a movie, but with TV shows, the director changes episode to episode. So you'd want someone who was going to be around, someone with some juice to control the show, someone who's got their fingers in most if not all aspects of production."

Malachi nodded. "Yes," he said. "Sounds to me like you're describing the showrunner."

Don snapped his fingers. "Yes, sir," he said. "That's it. Right on the tip of my tongue."

"Great," said Malachi. "How would you like to be the showrunner for a new show? A comedy show featuring a hot new stand-up comic."

"You must be talking about *Hot Mic,*" said Don. "I saw the pilot. Pretty funny."

"Fantastic. The show's got potential. I need someone with a, say, special temperament to be showrunner for this show. Someone who can problem-solve, think outside the box, and not be afraid to be a little bit ruthless. Or a lot. I think you'll fit the bill, Don Bundy."

"I'm honored, sir. I do have to point out that I have no experience as showrunner. Won't there be, ah, political friction if I'm promoted over the heads of others with more experience?"

"I'll handle the political friction," said Malachi. "Anybody who has a problem with my decision can take it up with me. As for experience: Fuck it. I don't need someone with a master's from Showrunner University, I need a good – and ruthless – problem-solver. Can I count on you?"

"Sir, yes, sir!" said Don loudly. He had to restrain himself from standing to attention and saluting.

"Great," said Malachi. "Welcome aboard, Don. If this goes well, there are other special projects with which you may be of assistance. I'm in need of a good man."

"Sir, yes, sir! I will not let you down."

Chapter 16

Chuck eased his Prius into the parking lot of The Dancers and scoped for a spot. It was early afternoon, but he still had to go to the far corner of the lot to find a space.

The Dancers was a Hollywood institution: a well-known restaurant and night spot that went through cycles of popularity. Now, it was on a down-cycle, which was the only reason why Chuck was able to find parking at all. Four years ago, you had to make reservations a week in advance just to get sneered at by the *maître d'.* Four years hence, it might be the same.

It took Chuck three passes to get the car lined up in the parking stall properly. He always drove poorly when he was nervous, and he was nervous now.

The main source of his current nervousness was the new showrunner, Don Bundy. For the original six episodes, the studio had used a grizzled vet named William de Groot, who specialized in managing short-term projects and moving on quickly. Now, the network had made Bundy the showrunner. Word was that this was his first show in that position, and that it had royally pissed off a lot of people with more experience who'd wanted the job.

Chuck had only met him once before, when the contracts had been signed. He'd called Chuck the day before and suggested that they get together for lunch, just to get to know each other a little better, since they would be working so closely in the future. Bundy seemed nice enough, but he gave off a scary vibe. Something about his eyes, like they had never really smiled.

Chuck finally parked the car and locked it, then hiked his way to the entrance. The Dancers fronted Sunset Boulevard with a solid wall of chrome-trimmed glass, sitting on a slight rise that gave a great view of the west end of the Strip. It looked like it had been built in the '40s, but it may have been built in the '80s to look like it had been built in the '40s.

At the front desk, a severe-looking young lady with a tux top and leather miniskirt raised an eyebrow. "Yes, sir?"

"Yes, I'm meeting a … an associate. His name's Don Bundy."

"Yes, sir," she said crisply. "Mr. Bundy has just arrived. Please follow me." She led Chuck through the restaurant, which had a few empty tables – but not many. In the far corner, she stopped at a large booth with an impressive view of Sunset. Bundy was lounging there with aviator shades and a sweater wrapped around his shoulders, sipping a mimosa.

"Charles! Chuck-O! So glad to see you!" He half-stood up and reached out with a meaty paw. Chuck gave it a perfunctory shake and plopped down in the booth opposite him. "How are you feeling? You look a little rough around the edges. Out late last night?"

"Sort of. I hit up some open mics last night, trying out some new material. I was thinking of lining up some road dates for later next month."

"Hmm, no can do, pardner," said Bundy. "We need to make sure you are well-rested and healthy. Shooting for the new episodes starts next week, and we'll need you in tip-top shape, okay?"

"Yeah, of course, I'll be ready," said Chuck. "I wouldn't tour for another six weeks."

"Oh, no, that's not going to work," said Bundy. "Our production schedule is going to go balls-to-the-wall for three months at least. We're going to need you close by. You are a very important asset to the Wolff Network, Chuck!"

"But I *need* to tour," said Chuck. "I've got to keep trying out new material, and refining the stuff I already have. Especially material for the show. Besides, I've got it all worked out. I've just got a few short hops scheduled – it won't affect the production schedule at all."

"No can do, Chuck-O," said Bundy. "Touring takes a lot out of a comic – even short tours. Can't have you coming in to work all burned out and sleep-deprived. Besides, it's all settled. I've already spoken with your manager."

"You talked to Philo? He hasn't said anything to me!" He couldn't believe that Philo would agree to anything like that without consulting him.

"Oh, I spoke to him just a few minutes ago," said Bundy. "Just before you walked in."

"And he agreed to cancel those shows?"

"Not in so many words," said Bundy. "But he will." He whipped off his mirrored shades and leaned into Chuck's face. "I can be very persuasive."

Chuck looked into Don Bundy's gray eyes. They looked like chips from a glacier. He did not like what he saw there: quiet contempt with a thin veneer of humor. Like he could tell you a joke and then slit your throat without changing expression.

"Man," said Chuck, "are you threatening me?"

For a split second, the veil of humor fell away from those eyes and the only thing left was steely contempt. Then Bundy's golf-tanned face widened into a 200-watt smile. "Threatening?" he repeated. "Of course not! Wouldn't dream of it! Look, I think we may have gotten a little cross-wired here. Let's back up and examine this situation so there's no misunderstanding. We need to have good communication, right? We want the show to be a success, don't we?"

"Yes, of course —"

"Well, we're all going to have to be a little more flexible in order for that to happen. One of the things we have to be concerned with is you, our prime attraction."

"Your 'asset,'" said Chuck with a grimace.

"Exactly!" exclaimed Bundy. "We know that for shows of this sort, it is absolutely necessary for the creative talent to be in tip-top condition. Mentally, physically, spiritually – you name it. And that means cutting back on the touring when we're in production. Don't try to tell me that being on the road doesn't take a lot out of you. We need you in town and in good shape while we're in production – we know this from experience."

"Experience?" asked Chuck. "I thought you said this was your first show."

Bundy put his shades back on and leaned back. Somehow, this was even more unsettling than looking into those cold eyes. "You're right, Chuck," he said. "This is my first gig as showrunner. However, the network has a lot of institutional knowledge. Hell, we've got one guy on the team who was a PA for Ed Fuckin' Sullivan. We know how to make a successful show. Don't you want a successful show? The show that has your name on it?"

"Yeah, I guess so," said Chuck. He had an uncomfortable feeling in the pit of his stomach.

"Hey, I understand – I really do. This is a big change for you. Me too. Let's work together to make it work right, whaddaya say? We just need to focus really hard to get this season in the can. Once we've got that done, and the show's a hit – which I'm sure it will be – then we can relax a little. You can go back to touring your ass off, if you like. In the meantime, Gomer's Laugh Bag in Walla Walla will just have to get by without you. It'll still be there when you get back on the road."

"I don't know," said Chuck. "Last time I was there, Gomer was looking pretty sick."

Bundy stared at him for a second, then threw his head back and bellowed laughter. Even in the lunchtime din of The Dancers, it was loud enough for half of the restaurant to stop what they were doing and look. "Oh, Christ!" he exclaimed. "Gomer's looking sick! That's hilarious! *You're* hilarious, Chuck. Oh, man, this show is going to kill them! Look, man, I'm getting hungry. I feel like steak. You like steak?"

"Yeah, sure," said Chuck, who at this moment couldn't care less about steak. The small knot in his stomach was growing by the minute.

Bundy raised his hand and snapped his fingers. Almost immediately, a waitress was there with oversized menus. The front was an image of The Dancers logo: silhouettes of a man in a zoot suit doing the lindy hop with a woman in a poodle skirt.

"Don't need those, darling," Bundy told the waitress. "Just bring us two T-bones, medium, baked potatoes, Caesar salad. And make it snappy, huh?"

"Absolutely, Mr. Bundy," said the waitress. "And to drink?"

"I'll have a double Macallan's, one rock."

"And for you, sir?" the waitress asked Chuck.

"Huh? To drink? Oh, water's fine."

"Very good, sir." She hustled off.

"Um," said Chuck. "What are your thoughts about the show?"

"We should be done casting by the end of the week," said Don. "We lost a few people from the pilot to attrition."

"Well, that might not be a problem," said Chuck. "I've got a buddy in Portland who'd be perfect for one of the second-tier cast members." Chuck had been feeling a little weird about Duckie ever since their meeting in Portland. He hoped that if he could get his friend some work in L.A., it would be a big boost for him – and it might help knock out some of the dents in their relationship.

"Don't worry about it," said Bundy. "Casting's pretty much got the new people sewed up. Just need to get the t's crossed and i's dotted."

"Don't I get a say in this?" asked Chuck.

Bundy removed his shades and gave Chuck a piercing stare. "I know that, as a stand-up, you made all the decisions, wrote all the material, took all the risks and reaped all the rewards – or the failures. It's not like that anymore, Chuck. The sooner you internalize that fact, the better off we're all going to be. The network is putting a lot of money into this project, and they want to make sure that it pays off. That means you have to be willing to make compromises."

"But my contract—"

"Contract, schmontract," said Bundy. "You can't start whining about contracts every time you don't get your way. As showrunner, I'm content to let you – as head writer – make all of the writing decisions. It *is* your show in that regard. However, there is a pretty large hunk of the org chart above me who don't see it that way, and they can do whatever the hell they want, including making the decisions about casting." He leaned in and gave Chuck a toothy, humorless grin. "Learn to fucking deal with it, Charles."

Before Chuck could formulate a response, the waitress swooped in with huge platters bearing sizzling steaks. Both Chuck and Bundy relaxed as this *deus ex machina* cut the tension. They both dug into their meals. The steaks were good, and Chuck was surprised to find that he was hungry. He filled up quickly, though, and about halfway through the baked potato he had to throw in the napkin.

He looked up and Bundy was grinning back at him. Bundy's plate was spotless and shiny, as if it had just come from the dishwasher. Chuck wondered if he had licked it clean.

"Hey, you gonna eat that?" Bundy asked. He leaned over and pointed at the remainder of Chuck's T-bone with a thick, blocky finger.

"Uh, no."

"Great!" Bundy reached over with an overhand stab and speared the meat with his knife. He returned it to his plate, sectioned it and consumed it in a matter of seconds.

When he was done he uttered a mild belch, pushed his sleeve up and glanced at his wristwatch. It was a solid gold Patek Phillippe, and it looked chunky enough to stop an artillery round. "Sorry, Chuck, gotta run. Big meeting with the money people, y'know?" He fished a fat calfskin wallet from his slacks, threw two C-notes on the table and got up. "Hey, man, it was great getting to know you better. Really looking forward to working with you. See ya tomorrow."

And he left.

Chuck felt like he had just been hit by a bus made out of jelly. The whole meeting had been unsettling. Don Bundy was like a human bulldozer, just plowing into whatever was in his path. This was the person who was going to be running his show?

Then there were some of the things Bundy had mentioned during the meal. Bundy said he was now a Wolff Network asset. Fucking creepy. It made him sound like he was a piece of equipment or a bank account.

"Is there anything I can get you, sir?" The waitress was back, and she kept cutting her eyes at the pair of hundreds sitting on the table.

"No, I was just leaving," he said. He got up and wandered back to his car. The steak sat in his gut like a lump of lead. He took a few deep breaths, trying to regain some composure. Just what the hell had he gotten himself into?

Chapter 17

Even though he was nervous about the way things were shaping up, Chuck threw himself into the new work with zeal. After his lunch with Don Bundy, he had called Philo Spinoza to bitch. Philo had listened patiently, and had soothed Chuck's concerns to the best of his abilities. That was, after all, a large part of his job and he was pretty good at it. *For fifteen percent, he'd better be good at it,* thought Chuck. As his manager, Philo also got a producer credit for the show, which seemed to Chuck like double-dipping.

After the first week of production, Chuck and Farrah Ortega – now the only veterans from the pilot – went out to have a celebratory drink. The Best Western hotel bar wasn't the most glamorous watering hole, but it was conveniently close to the studio and the drinks were cheap. Farrah was, as usual, dressed to the nines. She wore a tight, red silk blouse and a black slit miniskirt. Her hair was straight and shoulder-length, framing a face with high cheekbones and obsidian eyes. She attracted a lot of attention in the bar.

"Well, that was an interesting week," said Chuck. "It's just not the same without Danny and Arthur, though."

"Shit, honey," said Farrah. "I thought that they were going to give *me* the axe. I'm surprised they even accepted the pilot at all with me in it. The Wolff Network isn't exactly a welcoming home for trans folks."

"Well, maybe they didn't know," suggested Chuck. "Those people at Wolff aren't the most observant. Besides, you present as very feminine; hell, you're a total hottie!"

Farrah laughed and threw back her head, "Oh, Chuck," she said. "I just love you to pieces! You're so refreshingly innocent and kind-hearted. Ignorant as the people at the network might be, there's no way they gonna miss this." She pointed at the sizable bulge on her neck. "No, people in this town are aware of stuff like this, believe me, *cuate*."

"I know," said Chuck. "Don told me that the network wanted more diversity. That they had been fielding a lot of criticism about the makeup of their programs. Said they were all too white."

"Or totally pandering to the Black folks," said Farrah. "Like that dumbass *Washington Street*. I mean, I feel bad for Danny and Arthur, having their show canceled midseason, but *damn*. That show was *puro pedo*."

It turned out that the show Danny and Arthur had been working on was the one that *Hot Mic* was going to replace. It tempered some of the exuberance Chuck had felt at learning that his own show was going to air. "It's a shame they can't rejoin *Hot Mic*," said Chuck. "They're not giving me much say in casting, it turns out."

"Aw. It's all about the money, honey."

"What do you think of the new kids?" asked Chuck. Two new cast members had been chosen to replace Arthur and Danny.

"Eh, they okay," said Farrah. "Not as good as Danny and Arthur – not as funny. Honestly, I don't mind it too bad that Danny's gone. He was always kinda mean to me. He could be a real dick, especially when he started drinking the hard stuff."

"Really?" asked Chuck. "I don't recall him saying anything, y'know, overtly bad or sexist or anything."

"Oh yeah, he's one of the sly ones," said Farrah. "He's like our Dear Leader. Blows the dog whistle hard as hell, but always leaves enough leeway to cover his ass. Deniability, y'know? Shit." She took a hefty slug of her appletini.

"I'm surprised you didn't just, y'know, tear him a new one."

"Well, I knew I was going to have to work with him, so I let a lot of shit slide. He tries any of that shit now, though…" She drew her thumb across her Adam's apple.

"Hope it doesn't come to that," said Chuck. "Hold the fort, hot stuff. Gotta pee."

He went to the can, and when he came back there was a long-haired guy with a jean jacket macking on Farrah. He looked like he might work on the stage crew at one of the nearby studios. "Sorry, babe," Farrah told him. "My date's back."

The guy gave Chuck a quick glance and turned back to Farrah. "Well, will I get a chance to see you later?" he asked.

"Who knows?" she said. "I'm pretty busy right now, choo know? Still, anything's possible. Now be a good boy and *vete.* I got business to discuss."

The guy gave Chuck a dark look and slid off the barstool to rejoin his buddies sitting at a table across the room.

"The thing that bugs me now is how different it is," said Farrah. "Back when we were doin' the pilot it was so much fun. Now it's all so fuckin' serious."

"Yeah, I feel ya," said Chuck. During the pilot, the project had had a much more relaxed feel about it. On the other hand, Chuck had been busier than a one-armed fiddler with a case of crabs. Now, at least he had some help taking care of the details. "What do you think of our new showrunner?" he asked.

Farrah shrugged theatrically. "Eh, just another cisgender *gabacho* in a corporate suit. I try not to think of him too much."

Across the room, the jean jacket guy who had been chatting up Farrah looked pissed. His two buddies were laughing, which seemed to make Jean Jacket even madder. One of his buddies said something and rubbed his hand across his own Adam's apple, which caused Jean Jacket to say "Fuck you!" loud enough to be heard across the bar.

"Uh-oh," said Chuck. "I think your admirer over there has just been informed that you're not, um, sporting factory-original equipment."

Farrah looked over at Jean Jacket's table, shrugged, and went back to her 'tini. Jean Jacket and his friends stood up. "Uh-oh," said Chuck. "Him and his buddies are getting up."

"So what?" said Farrah. "They probably leaving. Good riddance."

Chuck watched nervously as the men walked towards the exit. All three were looking daggers at Chuck and Farrah. He started to relax as they approached the door, but then Jean Jacket peeled off and stalked over to where Chuck and Farrah sat.

"Oh, shit," muttered Chuck.

"*De nada,*" said Farrah. "Not my first rodeo."

Jean Jacket walked up, shouldered Chuck out of the way. "You're a guy!" he said in an aggrieved voice.

"I'm all woman, honey," said Farrah. "Not that you'll ever find out."

"You fooled me!"

"Look, lover boy, you the one came up and started talkin' to me. Not my fault you don't know what an Adam's apple is."

Jean Jacket stood there huffing, not sure what to do. Chuck's heart was in his throat – he hated confrontations like this. He said, "Look, man, just let it go, okay? Sorry about the mix-up and all, but there's no point in making a big deal about it, is there?"

Jean Jacket looked from Farrah to Chuck and back, still huffing. "Okay," he said to Chuck. "I'll just leave you with your boyfriend!"

"Thanks," said Chuck. Farrah just dismissed him with a backwards flip of her hand.

Chuck watched him go, and when he was sure that Jean Jacket was actually leaving, he turned back to Farrah and said, "Jeez, sorry about that."

"Not your fault," said Farrah.

"I shouldn't have left you alone…"

"Hey, I don't need you to look after me," said Farrah. "I can take care of myself."

"No doubt," said Chuck. "Does that sort of shit happen a lot?"

"Eh, less than you'd think," said Farrah. "But more than it should." She rubbed her throat. "This damn thing causes me too much trouble. I already got an appointment to get it shaved down. Used the money from the pilot to put down a deposit on the procedure. This series takes off, I'm gonna do some major construction downtown, know what I mean?"

"I hope you do, Farrah," said Chuck. "You deserve to be happy. You're good people."

"Seriously, Carlos," said Farrah. "Thank you. Thank you for putting me in your show, and thank you for being my friend. You a good guy. Maybe too good."

"Whaddaya mean?"

"You need to watch out for yourself, *ese*. You a kind person. People in this town mistake kindness for weakness." She tossed back the rest of her drink with a snap of her head. "Shit, I wish you *was* my boyfriend. A good man is hard to find. And a hard man is good to find. That reminds me, how things going with that *chica* of yours. Wassername? Karlene?"

"It's Caroline," said Chuck. "And things are going really well, actually. She's going to move in with me, week after next."

"*¡Guau!*" said Farrah. "That's a big step. You ready for it?"

"Yeah, I think so. Never had a live-in girlfriend before."

"Oh, man, this is big. She moving in with you, or are you two getting a new place?"

"She's moving into my place."

"Let me give you a bit of advice: don't have her sign the lease. You keep everything in your name. If you two still together in a year, then go out and find a place together. 'Til then, protect your territory."

"Sounds like the voice of experience," said Chuck.

"Bitter experience, yeah," said Farrah. She pulled her phone from her purse and looked at the time. "Gotta bounce now. Meeting a friend for dinner."

"Yeah, I better get going too," said Chuck. "Gotta be back on the set bright and fuckin' early. Look, you want me to walk you to your car?"

"Nah, I got it. It's sweet of you to offer."

"Aren't you worried that that douchebag is outside waiting for you or something?"

"No, I ain't worried. Like I said, this ain't my first rodeo. That guy is probably at the nearest strip club, buying lap dances for his buddies to prove he's not queer. I know the type."

"But what if you're wrong?"

"Like I said, I can handle myself." She turned and hiked her skirt up, revealing a small automatic pistol strapped to her thigh just above the top of her stocking. It was smaller than Chuck's hand, and the frame was a vivid lavender color.

"Wow," said Chuck. "Cute. Is that a pistol in your skirt, or are you just glad to see me?"

"Little of both, honey," said Farrah. "This is a Ruger LC9. Shoots nine millimeter. Can't hit shit at a distance, but up close it will ruin somebody's day. Any asshole fucks with me, I gon' blow their guts out their back."

"Reason number 7,423 not to fuck with Farrah Ortega," said Chuck.

"You know it. See you tomorrow, Carlos."

Chuck watched her sashay out the door, then quickly drained his beer. He thought it would be a good idea to head out to the parking lot, just in case. When he got out the door, Farrah's Miata breezed by him with a blip of the horn, then turned and disappeared into the night.

Chapter 18

The holidays flashed by. Chuck completely absorbed himself in making the new episodes. The days were long, and the time he didn't spend rehearsing and taping was spent in the writers' room, endlessly rehashing the scripts for the new shows. The studio had nominated a number of staff writers of varying quality. Overall, they were pretty good to work with, although Chuck would have preferred to have his original pilot crew doing all of the writing.

One afternoon just after New Year's, Don made a rare appearance in the writers' room for the daily writing jam. He sat in the corner, and said little during the session. After it broke for dinner, he asked Chuck to stay behind.

"Everything okay?" asked Chuck.

"Oh, absolutely fine," said Don. "Couldn't be better. I'm really impressed with how the show's coming together. You're doing a hell of a job. The folks upstairs know that, too."

"That's great," said Chuck. "Uh, is there anything I can help you with?"

"Just wanted to put a bug in your ear," said Don. "I was talking with Maraquita about the show. She's really excited about how it's shaping up. She suggested that we might think about developing a recurring character, y'know? Could do wonders for the ratings – and the merch sales."

Chuck immediately hated the idea. Maybe because it came from on high and was geared towards making more money for Wolff. "I dunno," he said.

"No, no, *no*," said Don. "Don't seize up on me, Chuck-O. There have been lots of good recurring sketch characters. Eddie Murphy's Gumby. The

Church Lady. Ed Grimes."

"You mean Ed Grimley?" asked Chuck.

"Yeah, him," said Don. "Give me a good recurring character. It'll be great for the show."

Chuck didn't give the first third of a fuck what Don Bundy thought would be great for the show. However, the man was tenacious as a pit bull. Chuck knew he was going to have to throw him a bone, or he'd never let go of it.

"C'mon, Chuck-O," coaxed Don. "I know you got something for me."

"Well…" Last fall, he'd been up late, smoking weed and trying to come up with a Halloween costume. As he'd been drifting off to sleep, the phrase "crotchless clown pants" floated through his consciousness. The idea was weird enough for him to sit up and scrawl it in his notebook before lying back down and giggling himself to sleep. The next morning, he looked at the note, and discovered that it wasn't as funny as he remembered.

Maybe he could use it to come up with a character so godawful that it would immediately get vetoed. Then there would be no more bad noise about manufacturing a recurring character.

"You got something," said Don. "I knew it! Now give."

"I dunno," said Chuck. "It's a little, um, raunchy."

"No problem there," said Don. "This is the Wolff Network, after all. If viewers want highbrow, they'll go to PBS. Now what's your idea?"

"Okay," said Chuck. "It's called, uh, Dangles the Crotchless Christmas Clown."

"Okay, okay," said Don. "Tell me more."

Chuck scanned his face, looking for a sign of disgust or refusal. Instead, Don just looked thoughtful and curious.

"Well, uh, he's this guy who's a clown," said Chuck. He was grabbing at straws. "So, he's got, like, a Santa hat and a pair of crotchless clown pants."

"Go on," said Don, nodding.

Clearly, Don wasn't turned off by the concept. Chuck knew he had to turn the awfulness up to eleven. He said, "Yeah, so, anyway, he's got this huge schlong hanging out, and it's clown-white. We'd have to pixilate that, of course. But we'd make it so that it would swing and bob all around whenever he moved. Which he'd do a lot. He's a clown – lotsa physical humor, you know?" He looked for any sign of rejection on Don's face, but there was none. The guy actually *liked* the idea.

Don frowned. "Hmm," he said. "There's one problem with that concept."

"Oh?" Chuck breathed a small sigh of relief; Don would now finally see the idea as being totally unacceptable.

"Yeah. We're looking for a recurring character. Christmas was a couple of weeks ago. If this guy is a Christmas clown, we'd have to wait until next year to do it – provided we get picked up for a second season. I mean, he'd really only be relevant once a year."

"Uh," said Chuck. He hadn't given the matter much thought. His mind had just spit out "crotchless Christmas clown," partly for the alliteration, and partly because it seemed like a crotchless *Christmas* clown was an order of magnitude worse than a regular crotchless clown.

"Hm, well," said Chuck. "We can sorta retool him for other holidays, right? Dangles the Crotchless New Year's Clown, Dangles the Crotchless Arbor Day Clown, stuff like that. A clown for all seasons." *Jesus, why am I trying to sell this?* thought Chuck. Perhaps his inner thirteen-year-old really thought it was funny.

So did Don. "Perfect!" he said. "What a great idea! Truly, I am in the presence of a fuckin' comedy genius." He gave Chuck a painful slap on the shoulder. "Look, I want to see a script for a Dangles sketch by the end of the week. It's too late for Easter – maybe Dangles the Crotchless Mother's Day Clown? We still have some time to fill in the last episode – that would be perfect. I'll check the schedule."

"Yeah, swell," said Chuck. He just wanted to get away from Don before things could deteriorate further.

"Great, perfect, Chuck-O!" said Don. "You've done it again!"

"Yeah, great," said Chuck. He turned and headed for the exit.

***

When Chuck got home, he found Caroline curled up on the couch watching TV. She had on a large t-shirt that had the words "Frankie Say Relax" in huge block letters; she wore it as a night shirt. Her long legs were folded beneath her, and she looked very cozy.

"Hey, babe," she said. "How are you?"

"Whew," said Chuck. "It was a long day. Again. I'm glad to be back here with you."

"And I'm glad you're back." She patted the couch next to her. "Come sit with me. I'm watching *Entertainment Blast!*" Celebrity gossip was pretty much the only current events that interested her. She gave him an inquiring look. "Problems with the show, sweetie?"

"Yeah. No. Not really."

"Aw, c'mon," she said. "You can tell me." She leaned into him and wrapped her arm around his shoulders. She was warm and soft, and smelled like lilacs.

"Well," he said. "Don Bundy wants a recurring character. Says it would be marketable, and help the show's ratings."

"He's probably right," said Caroline. "What's the matter with that?"

"I don't have an objection to having a recurring character. It's just that I'd rather it happened organically, rather than manufacturing one for the marketing department."

"Did you tell him that?"

"No, but maybe I should have. Then again, he's not a guy who takes 'no' for an answer."

"So what did you say?"

"I agreed," Chuck said. "Then I proceeded to think up the most repulsive character I could think of: a clown with crotchless pants."

She wrinkled her nose. "Sounds gross. What did he say?"

"He liked it! I tried piling it on, y'know, making it even grosser, but the more I did, the more he went for it. Now I have to come up with a script for 'Dangles the Crotchless Mother's Day Clown' by Friday."

"You have so many good ideas," she said, stoking his shoulder. "Why don't you just think of a better character instead?"

He sighed. "Yeah, I guess that might work. Thanks, babe."

"You're welcome, honey." She leaned over and gave him a peck on the cheek. "You know, this is just like that old movie with Gene Wilder. You know, where that guy pretends to be Hitler, and everyone likes it?"

"You mean *The Producers?*"

"Yeah, that's it!"

"Hell, you're right," he said. "That movie doesn't seem quite as funny now."

"I never thought it was funny," she said. "It was just mean."

Chuck gave her the side-eye. Caroline had a very dull sense of humor. She hated Monty Python but laughed out loud at the Sunday funnies. In fact, she had stuck three Garfield comic strips to the fridge. Chuck thought they were idiotic, but knew better than to say so.

Opposites attract, I guess, thought Chuck. How had someone who had devoted years to an almost monkish study of the comedic art ended up with someone with no discernible sense of humor? He sighed. Chuck sometimes wondered why he stuck with Caroline.

He looked over at her. She smiled an orthodontist's-daughter smile and stretched her arms up. Her half-erect nipples poked through the thin cotton of her Frankie t-shirt.

Is it just for the sex? thought Chuck. A hot feeling in the back of his head told him that it was, mostly. He genuinely enjoyed her company – at least when they were alone at home. When they went out, Caroline was constantly preening and trying to attract attention. It had started to be a contentious issue between them, as Chuck typically just wanted to nest after putting in a long day at the studio.

Tonight, however, everything was fine; they were just chilling at home.

"Aww, you seem tense, baby," she purred in his ear. "What you need is to relax."

Chuck arched his back as her tongue slid into his ear. Her hand rubbed slowly up and down his pants leg, then slid up and gave his stiffening member a light squeeze. "Oh, wow…" said Chuck.

Abruptly, she stood up and faced him. She pulled her oversized Frankie t-shirt over her head. She was naked underneath. She let the shirt drop behind her but kept her arms raised, showing off her round, tanned breasts. She lifted her long blond hair and let it drop.

Chuck was transfixed. She looked just like the centerfold in the Playboy magazine that he'd found in seventh grade and hid under his mattress. She held her golden goddess pose a few moments longer, then dropped to her knees.

She deftly undid his buckle, then pulled belt, pants and drawers down to his ankles in one sure motion. With one hand, she began untying his sneakers while the other hand slowly stroked his hard-on. Once the shoes were out of the way, the pants quickly followed. She smiled, tossed her hair back and slid his cock into her mouth.

After a few moments, she pulled her head back and said, "My, you are a hard boy, aren't you? Can't waste this with just a BJ."

She stood up and climbed onto the couch and straddled him, reaching down to guide him into her. She held on to the back of the couch and slowly rode him, grinding on the downstroke. Chuck closed his eyes. *Goddamn* but this was good. He raised his chin, needing to kiss her. She had her eyes closed, head thrown back, high-pitched gasps coming from her slightly parted lips.

"Kiss me," said Chuck, but she didn't seem to hear.

She moved faster now, riding him in long, smooth strokes. His own breath was coming in audible pants now. They'd been together long enough to know each other's rhythms. She slowly worked her way up through Chuck's gears, drawing it out but keeping the pleasure mounting. By the end they were both gasping as Caroline bopped up and down like a monkey on a stick.

Chuck felt the pressure behind his eyeballs suddenly rise and then he came explosively. His back arched violently and Caroline had to hang onto the couch to keep from being bucked off. Three long, intense squeezes pumped out what felt like a quart of hot oil. He froze, back arched, then relaxed back into the couch, with Caroline slumped on top of him, his cock still inside her.

For a few moments, the only sound was heavy breathing.

"Oh, huh-holy shit!" wheezed Chuck. "That was superlative! Damn, but you're good, baby! Wow!"

"Put me in your show," she said.

"What?"

"Put me in your show."

Chuck was flummoxed by this *non sequitur*. He was trying to square this with what had just happened; his nervous system was still a little fried.

She rolled off of him, his cock coming out with an audible *pop*. "You should put me in your show, baby," she repeated. "You just said I was good."

Chuck considered putting up resistance, but he was too drained. "I'll see what I can do," he said.

She squealed and gave him a tight hug, then slid her hand down to stroke his relaxing penis. "Oh, thank you, baby, thank you!"

Chuck relaxed and enjoyed the afterglow for a few moments before spoiling it. "Full disclosure," he said. "I don't make the final call. Irma the casting director does."

"What?" she said, letting go of him and sliding to the end of the couch. "I thought it was your show!"

So did I, thought Chuck. "I'm sure it'll be fine. We've maybe got some small parts for later in the season that we're still casting. I'll give Irma a call tomorrow."

"You'd better not be getting my hopes up for nothing," said Caroline. She pulled the t-shirt back on. "I don't understand why you can't just say who will be on your show," she pouted.

"It's not my call. It's the studio's," said Chuck. "If it was my choice, Danny and Arthur would be back."

Caroline poked her lower lip out. Under other circumstances, it would be sexy, but now it was just childish and irritating.

"I'll do what I can, I promise," said Chuck. "You can't ask any more of me, can you?"

"No, I guess not," she said. "I'm getting ready for bed." She disappeared into the bathroom.

"Damn," said Chuck. He knew he should be pissed at Caroline's transparent Lucy Ricardo move to get into his act. He was still too buzzed from that mind-bending orgasm to be too worried about it. He'd do what he said. Maybe Irma could find a small role for Caroline, a non-speaking part, just to be on the safe side.

It occurred to Chuck that while he was asking favors of Irma, he might as well see if there was a small part for Duckie. Maybe a small part in a show would help him get a start in L.A.

Chuck pulled on his pants and wandered into the kitchen. Behind him, Caroline flitted from the bathroom to the bedroom, closing the door behind her. Chuck didn't notice. He yanked the milk out of the fridge, spun the cap off and drank directly from the jug – with a little look over his shoulder first, to make sure Caroline wasn't watching. He then gobbled a few stale Oreos, belched loudly, and picked up his phone.

Duckie's number went to voicemail on the first ring. "Hey, hi, Duckie," said Chuck. "Hope everything's going okay up in Portland. Things have been pretty crazy down here, with the show and all. I think we've got some uncast parts for later in the season, and I just wanted to see if you'd be interested in something like that. Nothing major, just a line or two, if that. Even if you're not interested, give me a call, man. I'd love to catch up – it's been too long. Peace, brother."

He hung up, now at a loss for what to do. After a moment, he grabbed another fistful of Oreos and plopped down in front of the TV.

Chapter 19

Okay, I think we've got this script in the bag," said Chuck to the rest of the writers. "Good job, people." He looked at his phone – he wasn't needed on set for another twenty minutes. "Everybody take a break. I'm going to start filling out some of the sketches for Episode Twelve, starting with the 'Community College Commercial' bit. Remember, that's going to be filmed on location, so we need to get it nailed down by tomorrow at the latest."

The rest of the writing team got up and headed out to get a bite or some coffee. Chuck stayed in the writers' room. It seemed like he'd been spending a lot of time in there. Not too surprising; he was, after all, the head writer. However, he had to work with a team of other TV writers, which meant taking a more organized approach than he was used to.

It's not as if the writers' room was a great place in which to spend a lot of time. It was a windowless corporate conference room with whiteboards on all of the walls. The whiteboards were covered with chicken scratch from the various writers, and each had the admonishment "DO NOT ERASE!" in large red letters on an 8 ½ x 11 sheet taped to the bottom of each one. There was a mini-fridge filled with Red Bulls, a balky coffee maker, and a broken Galaga console in the corner.

Chuck tried to ignore the buzzing of the wonky fluorescent light, and pulled out a battered spiral-bound notebook where he had jotted down a few ideas. He was coming up with blanks on this community college bit; hopefully, the rest of the writing team would help get him past the roadblocks.

He heard someone come into the room behind him. Without looking up, he said, "I'm definitely gonna need some help with this community college thing. You got any ideas?"

"Not a single one," said Don Bundy. "That's your area, not mine."

"Oh," said Chuck. "I didn't know it was you. What's up?"

"Emergency production meeting in ten," said Don. "We both need to be there."

"What's it about?" asked Chuck.

Don shrugged. Chuck knew he was hiding something.

"All right, I'll be there," said Chuck.

"Good," said Don. "How's everything else going?"

"Look, uh, Don, I've been thinking about that recurring character idea we talked about last week. I've got a better idea: a hippie called Al Tiedye. I've already got some good material worked up."

"Good" was a bit of an exaggeration; the character was more of an homage to George Carlin's Al Sleet, the Hippy-Dippy Weatherman. Still, Chuck thought that with a little work it could be a good character in its own right, and not too derivative.

"Hippie?" said Don. "What is this, 1969? What about the one we were talking about last week. You know, the clown with the schlong?"

"Dangles the Crotchless Clown?" said Chuck with a sigh.

"Yeah, that's it!" said Don. "I gotta admit, I wasn't too keen on the idea at first, but it kind of grew on me. I ran it up the food chain, too; the network loves it! The demographics hit right where we shooting for: males aged 18 to 34."

With IQs 18 to 34, thought Chuck. "Swell," he said. "If the network loves it, we might as well run it off the end of the Earth. They know their demographics."

"Fuckin'-A right, they do," said Don. "Well, I gotta take a leak. The production meeting's in the Rosewood Room. See you in a few." He left.

Chuck finished up a few notes for the community college bit, then headed upstairs for the production meeting. There was a bad feeling in the pit of his stomach. Anything Wolff execs rolled out on short notice tended to be very problematic.

***

"You want to call it *what?*" Chuck asked.

"*Chuck Marshall's Chucklefest,*" said Hans.

"Are you kidding me?" asked Chuck. "Jesus, that's terrible. Who came up with that name?"

"Marketing," said Mariquita.

"Marketing?" said Chuck. "Christ on a crutch! I was promised creative control of this show, and now you're telling me I can't even pick the name?"

There were uneasy looks around the conference room. In addition to Hans and Mariquita, Balthazar and Francesca from the studio were there, as well as Simon Apriori, the producer. They didn't seem to be interested in what the show was called. Don Bundy just looked bored. Chuck's manager, Philo Spinoza, was also there, but he wasn't providing the backup Chuck had hoped for.

"Philo!" said Chuck. "You're supposed to be my manager. How about you help me out here?"

"I'm sorry, babes, I really am," said Philo. He opened up his Gucci messenger bag and pulled out a thick sheaf of papers. "I called the lawyer and had him look over the contract. There's really nothing we can do."

"Jesus," said Chuck. He looked around at the other people at the table; none of them would meet his eye. "I don't get it," he said. "The name of the show is *Hot Mic.* That's always been the name. If that was a problem, why am I just hearing about it now?"

"We understand that you're upset," said Mariquita. "It's just that the name *Hot Mic* didn't test well."

"What do you mean it didn't 'test well'?" demanded Chuck.

"Well, we tried out a number of names on members of the target demographic. They didn't like it. They thought it sounded like the name of a political talk show."

"Shit," said Chuck. He'd never felt this angry ... or betrayed. "So *Chuck Marshall's Chucklefest* tested okay? Your test audience liked it?"

"Yes," said Hans. "It really improved the incrementality of the reach."

"What?" said Chuck. "Are you even speaking English?"

"He means that it demonstrably increased positive response," said Mariquita. "I can see that you're not enthusiastic, Chuck. Mind telling us what your objections are?"

Chuck's mouth worked soundlessly for a moment as he tried to articulate the problem. "It's just so fucking lame!" he said. "The word 'chuckle,' particularly. It's weak. I don't want the audience to just chuckle – I want them to laugh. And to think!"

"Whoa, hold on there!" said Hans. "The last thing that the Wolff Network wants is for its audience members to *think*. We want them to *feel*. It's so much easier to get them to buy our advertisers' products when we play on their emotions. We don't want them thinking, or they might quit watching TV altogether. It would completely fuck up our business model."

"I know it's difficult to take in at first," said Balthazar. "I also know that you are pretty new to the TV biz, and some things may take some getting used to."

"Right," said Mariquita. "We all want this show to succeed, Chuck. Don't you?"

"Of course, I do," said Chuck. "It's what I've been focused on for well over a year."

"Good, good," said Mariquita. "We all want the show to succeed. Nobody's trying to undermine you here. We're trying to help."

"By giving it a shitty name?" demanded Chuck.

"'Shitty' is a pretty subjective term," Simon pointed out.

"Look," said Hans. "Mariquita's right. We want the show to succeed. What does that mean? We want it be broadcast for as many episodes as possible. For that to happen, people have to watch the show. For that to happen, they have to *want* to watch the show. No one will want to watch the show if the name is confusing. Marketing felt that *Chuck Marshall's Chucklefest* lets potential viewers know what they're getting. And it tested well with the target demo."

Frustrated, Chuck ran his hands through his hair. He looked over at Philo, who just shrugged and looked sheepish. *Figures,* thought Chuck. It was in Philo's financial interest not to rock the boat.

"Okay, we're all grown-ups here," said Hans. "Surely we can come up with an acceptable compromise, right? Sure, nobody's gonna get exactly what they want, but we ought to be able to keep everyone's feathers from being ruffled."

"How about this," said Philo. "How about *Chuck Marshall's Laughfest?* That eliminates the objectionable 'chuckle.'"

The Wolff execs looked at each other with pained expressions. "Well, I dunno," said Hans. "If we do that, then we don't get the wordplay between 'Chuck' and 'chuckle.'"

"Why use my name at all?" asked Chuck. "I'm an unknown. I can't see how using my name is going to be a big draw."

Francesca grinned widely. "We're going to change all that," she said. "Once people see how awesome this show is, Chuck Marshall will be a household name."

"Look," said Hans, "when people hear the name *Chuck Marshall's Chucklefest,* they're going to wonder who the heck Chuck Marshall is. Then they're going to tune into the show just so they can be in on this hot new name."

"It's a proven strategy," added Mariquita. "FOMO."

"Huh?" said Chuck. "Who's a mofo?"

"No, no," said Balthazar. "FOMO. It stands for Fear Of Missing Out. You can really leverage people's buying habits by playing on their fear of missing out on trends."

Chuck felt sick to his stomach. He didn't want to manipulate people's emotions or leverage their buying habits; he just wanted to connect with them and make them laugh. "No," he said finally. "Absolutely not. I'm putting my foot down."

Everybody around the table exchanged pained expressions except Don, who continued looking bored. Simon led the Wolff executives into a corner, were they had an intense whispered conversation. After a minute, they broke and returned to the table.

"Okay, Chuck," said Hans. "What's it going to take to bring you around? Gotta be honest: *Hot Mic* is pretty much off the table. Also, remember that

Chuck Marshall's Chucklefest tested really high. Marketing is really keen on it."

"Also," said Mariquita. "We need to line up the promotional materials, like, last month. This show premieres three weeks from yesterday. We need a name *now*."

Chuck slumped. He wasn't sure what to say. He felt on the spot, and couldn't think of a new name right now. "I don't know," he said. "Sounds like you've already made up my mind for me. Call it what you want, just don't tack my name on the result of your corporate decision-making process."

This announcement elicited another round of worried looks around the table. "So," said Hans, "you'd be okay if it were just called *Chucklefest?*"

"Yeah," said Chuck. "Sure. Whatever."

"Perfect!" chirped Mariquita. "We will only have to make some minor changes to the existing promotional material. I'll call the art department right away."

"Yeah, yeah!" said Hans. "Tell them to make 'Chuck' and 'lefest' different colors or a different font so we can still work the Chuck angle. How's that sound?"

"We've already chosen the font," said Mariquita. "We'll just adjust the color palette."

"Is there anything else?" sighed Chuck.

"No, no," said Hans. "This is perfect! Thanks so much, all of you. We'll let you know when the media kit is ready to go."

There was meaningless chatter as the meeting broke up. Philo approached Chuck as he as walking out the door. "Hey, Chuck," he said. "I'm sorry that it came down to this. I was hoping we could work something out. If you'd like to talk about this a little more…"

"Not now," said Chuck. "I'll call you tomorrow."

"Uh, no can do, babes," said Philo. "I'm heading off to Cannes tomorrow morning. On vacay for two weeks. If you need anything, you can call my assistant."

"Thanks a pantload, Philo," said Chuck. "Enjoy your trip."

"Hey, don't be that way, babes, I can—" began Philo.

Chuck cut him off with a hand flip. He just wanted to get away from these Hollywood creeps. He went back to the writers' room, shooed the other writers out and locked the door.

Chapter 20

Chuck spent an hour trying to flesh out the community college bit. He was too pissed about the name change, and the way he had been hoodwinked. *Fuck it,* he thought. He crammed all of his stuff into his messenger bag and took off.

Against his better judgment, he swung by the office of Irma Schmidt, the casting director.

"Sorry, Chuck," she said. "Pretty much got all the roles cast." She flipped through a stack of papers on the corner of her desk. "Nope, we're all full up, unless you come up with some new material. Even then, things would be pretty tight. Maybe next season. If there is a next season, that is."

"Yeah, great," said Chuck. "Thanks a bunch, Irma."

"Just doing my job, kid. Don't let the door hit you in the ass on your way out."

This was the capper to an already crummy day. Even worse was that there was nothing for Duckie. He had really been hoping that he could lure Duckie down to L.A., and that he would end up staying. He thought Duckie would help ground him, help him reconnect with the fun, exciting part of comedy that had been lacking in Chuck's life for the last few months. It didn't look like that was going to happen.

Chuck was wiped, but wasn't really interested in going home. Now that he knew that he wouldn't be able to get Caroline on the show – at least not this season – he was worried about how she was going to react. He was certain that it wouldn't be good. She might even leave him. He was glad he had taken Farrah's advice and kept her name off the apartment lease.

He decided to swing by Simi's. Tonight was open mic night, so he was sure to get as much stage time as he wanted. Not that he had a surfeit of energy at this point in the day. The doorman greeted him warmly, and as soon as he walked into the main room, the bartender slid him a Ballantine ale.

Simi Cohen, the owner, appeared from her office behind the bar. "Sir Charles!" she said. "So good to see you! It's been too long, bubbie, way too long since you've graced us with your presence." Simi was of indeterminate age, and had a nimbus of frizzy hair dyed a shade of red not found in nature. She wore huge tortoiseshell glasses on a gold chain, and typically sported about fifteen pounds of chunky costume jewelry.

Everybody loved Simi. She had been involved in the L.A. comedy scene since the mid-sixties. In that cut-throat world, she was a genuinely nice person. She had carved out a small but comfortable niche in the local comedy scene and was content to dwell there.

Chuck took a healthy swig of his drink and gave Simi a hug. "Oh, Christ, you don't know how much I've missed this place. Sorry I haven't been here in a while but things have been absolutely batshit crazy."

"I can only imagine," said Simi. "We're all looking forward to the premiere of your show. How is that going for you, sweetheart?"

Chuck rolled his eyes and polished off the rest of his drink.

"That's what I thought," said Simi. She moved close and grabbed Chuck by his sleeve. "Look, bubbie, you need to be careful, very careful. Those networks will chew you up and spit you out if you don't watch your ass. Everyone thinks that having your own TV show is the best thing that can come out of comedy, but it's not." She gestured at the stage, where a woman of about twenty was complaining about her girlfriend. "Every damn comic in here wants to be the next Jerry Seinfeld or Jason Sudeikis, to have their own popular TV show and make a zillion bucks. Well, those two schlubs were the exception, not the rule. Look at what happened to Dave Chapelle or Chris Titus – their TV shows nearly broke them. And Andy Kaufman! He hated that character from *Taxi*, even though it was *his* character! It had been his signature bit, and that TV show ruined it for him."

"Yeah," Chuck laughed, "but Kaufman doled out as much damage as he took, way I heard it."

"It still fucked with him hard, honey," said Simi. "He could never shake that Foreign Man character once it became Latka Gravas."

"Yeah," said Chuck. "I can see now why Kaufman always talked about faking his own death."

"Don't you say that!" exclaimed Simi. "Don't you ever say that!"

"Why not?" asked Chuck. "It's kinda funny."

"It's morbid," said Simi. "And poor Andy's dead, just the same."

"What about Mickey Gross? You've been around awhile. Surely you've heard the rumors that Mickey faked his death, right?"

"Oh, honey, he's dead too. Comics have morbid senses of humor, all of you. You spend too much damn time thinking about death."

"It's because a lot of the time, life doesn't seem to be, y'know, all that and a bag of chips."

Simi sighed. "Everybody feels that way, honey. Just seems that comics feel it a little too much. You need to be careful."

"Ah, shit, Simi, I'm tryin' to, but this show … it's not what I hoped it would be. Hell, I don't even *remember* what I hoped it would be. Sometimes I just want to get in my car and start driving. Just pick a direction and head off."

"Always an option," said Simi. "Beats killing yourself, or pretending you're dead. You just gotta make sure you get far enough away. Like Canada, maybe."

"What?" Chuck started to ask, but Simi waved the question away.

"Shh … not now," she said. "Lola's getting the red light. If you want stage time, you should go on now."

The woman with girlfriend problems departed from the stage and Simi bounced up and grabbed the mic. "Now, ladies and gentlemen, I am very pleased to present a special friend of Simi's. He's got his own TV show on Wolff, please welcome to the stage – Chuck Marshall!"

The crowd of about two dozen people clapped with surprising vigor. Most of them were comics waiting for their turn at the mic, although there were some civilians who had wandered in for the free entertainment.

Open-mic audiences could be tough, but they gave it up for him, hard.

Unfortunately, his set was flat. He tried some improv about the trials and tribulations of doing a network show, but it came out sounding whiny. He caught the flat-eyed looks from some of the other comics: *Oh, poor baby. It must be so hard having your own TV show and getting paid with sacks of cash. Glad I'm here sitting through three hours of bad comedy to get my four minutes of stage time.*

Finally, he did a couple of quick, reliable laugh-getters and cleared off.

"Headin' home?" asked Simi.

"Yeah, I'm done in," said Chuck. "Wasn't at my best tonight. Sorry."

Simi shrugged. "Don't worry, hon, happens to the best of 'em. You just take care of yourself, Charles. You ever feel like the alligators are closing in, you can always talk to me, okay? If you need a place to get away, to just entirely unplug, let me know. I got a place in Azusa that's unoccupied right now. If Azusa's not far enough away, there are other options."

"Thanks, Simi. You're the best."

"Don't you forget it, bubbie."

Chuck was introspective on the drive back to his apartment. It had been an exhausting day, and his detour to Simi's hadn't provided the pick-me-up he had hoped for. Well, too bad. Now it was time to man up and face whatever bullshit Caroline was going to throw his way.

She was asleep when Chuck let himself into the apartment. Good. He'd probably be in a better place to break the bad news to her after a good night's sleep.

Just the same, he made it a point to be very quiet when he slipped into the bedroom and undressed. Fortunately, Caroline was deeply asleep and didn't notice when he climbed carefully into bed. Despite the exhaustion and stress of the day, he found it difficult to drop off. He lay there for a long time, listening to Caroline snore, before he was able to sleep.

Chapter 21

Chuck's phone went off at 5:00 the following morning. He grabbed it off the nightstand, and groaned when he saw that it was from Don Bundy. He looked over at Caroline, who was still snoozing away as soundly as when he'd come home the night before. Being careful not to wake her, he silenced the phone, slid out of bed and padded into the living room.

He swiped right and said, "Yeah, Don, what's going on at the asscrack of dawn?"

"Whaddaya mean?" snorted Don. "I've been up an hour and a half already."

"That makes one of us," he said. "What's up?"

"It's Ortega," said Don. "That bastard's ghosting me. I've been trying to get hold of him since Friday and haven't heard anything. You guys are old butt buddies; maybe you can find him."

Chuck was grumpy. He didn't like being woken early, especially with this sort of bullshit. It was bad enough that he had to be on set by 7am – earlier if there was any makeup or wardrobe to deal with – but having Don Bundy gripe in his ear this early definitely sucked. "Well, Don," he said, trying to inject plenty of sarcasm in his voice, "maybe if you called her *her* instead of *him*, and quit throwing around terms like 'butt buddies,' Farrah would be more responsive to your calls."

There was a long silence on the end of the line. Chuck grimaced, expecting Don to blow a gasket, but when he spoke again, it was in a calm and reasonable tone. "You know, Chuck, you're absolutely right," he said. "I've been pretty insensitive with my language, and I really need to work on that. Sometimes, when I get stressed out, I talk like I'm still serving in the Corps. I know that's not an excuse; it's just an explanation. The next time I talk to *Ms.* Ortega, I will apologize to *her*. And if I've offended *you*, please accept my sincere apology as well."

"No need," said Chuck. "I wasn't offended. I just didn't like being blasted out of bed with a phone call so early." Behind him, Caroline emerged from the bedroom and padded into the bathroom.

"Okay, well," said Don. "I'm just a little worried about Farrah. If she doesn't turn up this morning, I'm going to be *really* worried. I was just hoping that you two had talked, and I could stop my worrying early."

"Yeah, okay," said Chuck. "I'll call her, just to make sure everything's okay. If I get hold of her, I'll ask her to call you. Is that okay?"

"Yeah, that'll be fine."

"Don't worry," said Chuck. "She'll probably wander on set half an hour late with a huge Starbucks in hand."

"As usual," said Don. "Okay, guess I'll see you soon enough. Later." He hung up.

There was no point in going back to bed now. Chuck went into the kitchen and got some coffee going. In the bathroom, he heard the shower start up. Caroline was up for the day, as well.

He poured two cups of coffee, black for him, and extra cream and sugar for Caroline. He thought it might cushion the blow of the bad news. He stationed himself outside of the bathroom door, and when Caroline stepped out in her fuzzy pink robe he said, "Coffee, babe? Good and hot. Sorry if I woke you earlier."

"Huh?" she said. Her hair hung in wet chunks in front of her half-closed eyes. "No, uh, it's okay. I have to go into work early today. Some sales training thing."

"Oh, great. Glad I didn't disturb you too much." He took a sip of his coffee. "Afraid I got some bad news, babe. I talked with the casting director, and they have everything cast for this season. Even the crowd extras. Sorry, sweetheart." He braced himself for impact.

"Wha?" she said. "Oh, that. Bummer. Maybe next season, then? You just be sure to make it good enough so there *is* a next season. Thanks for the coffee, honey." She gave him a peck on the cheek and went into the bedroom.

That was easy, thought Chuck. He figured that he might as well call Duckie and give him the news. It was still pretty early, but he didn't really expect Duckie to answer, anyway. Chuck had called him three times in the last three months, and had only gotten text messages in reply. Chuck picked up his phone and dialed Duckie's number.

Astoundingly, Duckie picked up. "Holy shit," he said. "Is that you, Chuck?"

"Uh, yeah, wow, man," said Chuck, surprised that Duckie had actually answered.

"As articulate as ever, I see," said Duckie. "You're gonna knock 'em dead in Hollywood with lines like that."

"Actually, I wasn't expecting you to pick up," said Chuck.

"Then why'd you call?" asked Duckie.

"Just wanted to leave you a message while I was thinking of it," said Chuck. "Since you haven't answered the last couple of times I called and all."

"Huh, yeah. Sorry about that," said Duckie. "Late shift. Just got home from work when you called."

"Ugh, sounds awful," said Chuck.

"It's not so bad, now that I've gotten my sleep schedule adjusted. I can do gigs and open mics at night and still be able to work. Plus, my boss is pretty good about letting me take time off when I have out-of-town gigs."

"You getting many of those?"

"Not as many as I'd like," said Duckie.

"Well, I was hoping to be able to help you with that," said Chuck. "But it doesn't look like I'm going to be able to … at least not until next year."

"Huh? Oh. Yeah, getting a part on your show. Shit, and here I'd put a down payment on a Maserati."

"Yeah, sorry if I got your hopes up, man," said Chuck.

"Don't worry," said Duckie. "They weren't up very high. Much as I would like to be Coffee Shop Customer #3 in one of your sketches, I'll probably get over it."

"I had hoped I could get you a showcase stand-up spot, too," said Chuck. "You know, that's part of the format. We have a stand-up do six minutes at the beginning of each show, then we go into the sketches. You could do both. So six minutes of Duckie Dunne, then a bit as Coffee Shop Customer #3."

"Sounds like I'm not doing either," Duckie observed.

"Not right now," admitted Chuck. "It's been a little more complicated than I'd thought. The network is making a lot of decisions that I have little influence over. Especially casting."

"That blows," said Duckie. "I guess being a Hollywood hotshot isn't all it's cracked up to be."

"Look, why don't you come down anyway?" Chuck asked. "I can't get you on the show, but you can hang out on set, meet a few people. We could hit a few mics. Get your name and face out there."

"Man, I don't have the time right now," said Duckie. "Besides, didn't you say you'd be coming through Portland pretty soon? We could hang out then."

"Yeah, I thought I would be able to do a mini-tour, but things are just too hectic right now. I can't really tour until we're done with this first season. After that, it might be a different story. For now, I've got to stick close to home."

"Yeah, me too," said Duckie. "In fact, I'd better hit the hay. I'm emceeing a show tonight at Hydrogen. Nate Bargatze's headlining."

"Well, say 'hi' to him for me," said Chuck.

"Hell, you can do it yourself when he opens for you at the Hollywood Bowl."

"Jesus, Duckie, why're you being such a pill?"

Duckie sighed. "Yeah, sorry, man," he said. "Just fatigued, I guess. Look, I'd better hit it. I'll talk to you soon." And he hung up.

"Shit," said Chuck to himself. He thought Caroline would be the one to flip him shit, and instead it was Duckie being a jerk. Maybe Duckie really *had* gotten his hopes up, and didn't want to admit it. Well, there was nothing Chuck could do about it right now. He polished off his coffee and started to get ready for another day as a Hollywood hotshot.

***

He had just plopped down in a chair in the writers' room when Don Bundy barged in. "You heard from Ortega yet?" he demanded.

"No," said Chuck. "I take it you haven't been able to get in touch with her, either."

"Where'd you park your squad car, Dick Tracy?" said Don. "No, obviously I haven't, and as best as I can tell, neither has anyone else for the last three days."

"Shit," said Chuck. This was worrisome. Farrah was perpetually late, but she was mostly reliable. If she said she was going to be somewhere, she would be there … just not on time. "Let me try again." He pulled out his phone and called Farrah's number. It went immediately to voicemail, with a robotic voice informing him that he couldn't leave a message because the mailbox was full.

He tried calling Arthur and Danny. Arthur's went to voicemail immediately, but Danny picked up. "What's up, Chuck?" he asked.

"I've got a problem," said Chuck. "Have you heard from Farrah lately? Like, this weekend?"

"Naw, not for a couple of weeks," said Danny. "Is there a problem?"

"Yeah, as far as I can tell, she's kinda disappeared," said Chuck. It startled him to hear it put that way, but it was true. "She can be a little tardy sometimes, but she's not answering calls, nobody knows where she is and her phone goes straight to a full mailbox."

"That doesn't sound good," said Danny. "Is there anything I can do?"

"Start calling around," said Chuck. "If you know anyone who knows Farrah, give them a call. Put the word out, starting with Arthur. Do you know what her address is?"

"I gave her a ride home once or twice," said Danny. "Give me a minute, I can figure it out." There was a pause. "Yes, here in Koreatown. Five-oh-three South New Hampshire."

"Maybe I'll ride over there and see if she's home," said Chuck.

"I'm not sure it will do you much good," said Danny. "It's a pretty big apartment building, and I have no idea what unit she's in. I just dropped her off and she zipped in the front door."

"Okay," said Chuck. "I'm gonna try, anyway. You call around. If you hear anything, please let me know right away."

"Okay, good luck," said Danny. "I'll start making some calls."

"Right," said Chuck, and he hustled back to the set to grab his coat. He drove over to the address Danny had given him, but couldn't even find the apartment. The woman at the rental office refused to give him any information. Frustrated and increasingly worried, he went back to the studio. When he got back to the writers' room, Don was there, pacing.

"No luck so far," said Chuck. "I made some calls, checked with some friends, even went to her apartment building. Nothing."

"I don't think it matters," said Don. "We won't find Ortega because he doesn't want to be found." He held out his phone. On the screen was a text message. The header at the top read "Ortega." Below it, in larger letters, the message said simply "IM OUT".

Chuck pulled out his phone. He had an identical message. "Maybe she just means she's out sick for the day, or something."

Don shook his head. "I don't think so," he said. "I think our little bird has flown the coop. For good."

"That doesn't make sense," said Chuck. "Why would she just take off like that?"

"Why would he want to get his wiener cut off?" asked Don. "Sense doesn't enter into it, if you ask me."

"But that's just it," said Chuck. "She was going to use the money from the show for sex reassignment surgery. She wouldn't just walk away from this job."

Don grimaced. "Too much information, Marshall," he said. "Look, maybe you're right. I *hope* you're right. If Ortega shows up later, great. But I don't think that will happen. In the meantime, I've got a show to run. We've got just a few weeks to finish up. Christ, do you realize that this show premieres in less than three weeks?"

Chuck felt a sinking in the pit of his stomach. "The show must go on," he said weakly.

"Fuckin'-A right," said Don. "And I have to proceed as though Ortega's history. Shit. I'm going to have to juggle the shooting schedule and see about finding a replacement. Maybe Lorraine."

Lorraine Oldman was one of the supporting cast who had shown a lot of promise. Chuck thought she was smart, a good actor, and had great timing. "Yes, I think Lorraine would work well," he said.

"Plus, I'm pretty sure she's a dyke," said Don. "Not as good as a tranny, but it'll do for diversity in a pinch." He tucked his clipboard under his arm and strode out of the room, leaving Chuck speechless.

Chapter 22

Don hurried back to his office. He had been offered one in the junior-executive suite, but he had declined that in favor of a larger-but-dingier one lower in the building by the studios. It wasn't as high profile as the junior-executive suite, but it wasn't as exposed, either.

He felt exposed right now. Reluctantly, he thumbed on his phone and dialed Malachi's number. He had never called before, only received calls from Malachi requesting updates about the show. He honestly didn't expect Malachi to pick up. After all, he was busier than a one-legged man in an ass-kicking contest. Don was surprised when Malachi picked up after the first ring.

"Don," said Malachi. "It's good to hear from you. Do you have news for me?"

"Sir, yes, sir!"

"Everything okay with our little show?"

"Not exactly, sir. We're having a bit of a personnel issue. Ortega has taken off."

"Oh, really?"

"Sir, yes, sir," said Don. "Ortega hasn't showed up for the last few days. Nobody's been able to reach him. I've had people calling all over, but no luck. I got the emergency contact number from HR, but that just goes to a disconnected number in San Antonio. Marshall and his friends have been trying to reach him as well. Nothing."

"Anything else?"

"Both myself and Marshall got a text from Ortega this morning. It just said 'I'm out.'"

"Short and to the point," said Malachi. "Sounds like a letter of resignation to me."

"Really? You don't want me to keep looking for him?"

"Doesn't seem like there's much point, does it?" said Malachi. "Trust me, I've got experience with stand-up comics. Did you know that I once worked with Mickey Gross? Utter pain in the ass. I was glad when we parted ways, believe me. Overall, we're probably better off without this Ortega person."

"I see," said Don.

"I doubt it," said Malachi. "But you will soon. Tell you what, Don. Why don't you come up to my office tomorrow evening around seven? I'd like to share a drink with you and discuss some plans for the future. Think you can make that?"

Don was surprised that he wasn't getting chewed out. Instead, he was being invited to the boss's office for drinks. "Sir, yes, sir," said Don. "I will be there at nineteen hundred hours, sharp. In the meantime, what do you want me to do with this Ortega business?"

"Nothing. I'll handle it at my end. How is Mr. Marshall taking the situation?"

"He's upset, as you can imagine. He and Ortega are pretty close. He's surprised and upset that Ortega just left without saying anything."

"I understand," said Malachi. "Do what you can to keep him from becoming too upset. We still have a show to produce, after all. Besides, he was the one I was interested in the most. Ortega was just a backup, you might say."

"Sorry, sir," said Don. "I don't follow."

"Not to worry," said Malachi. "All will become clear in time. Starting tomorrow night. See you then."

Malachi hung up and Don spent several moments just staring at his phone. He was glad that he wasn't chewed out. However, he was surprised that Malachi was so sanguine, especially given his legendary impatience.

Then there was the cryptic invitation for Don to join him for a drink.

Don shrugged. These things would sort themselves out. Or they wouldn't. In the meantime, there was no point in worrying about them – he still had a show to run.

Chapter 23

The next night, Don Bundy wound his way through the upper echelons of the building, passing through higher and higher layers of security on his way to the very top. His key card got him through most of the doors and checkpoints. Just outside the C-level suite, a security guard was on duty around the clock. The guard saw Bundy approaching, held up his hand in greeting and buzzed him through. Then he stood up and followed Don through the mahogany-rich trappings to the big door that led to Malachi Wolff's office suite. The guard unlocked the brass-bound door with a large metal key and held it open as Bundy passed through.

"Have a good evening, Mr. Bundy," said the guard.

"As you were," said Don.

He went through the anteroom, past the dozen or so desks used by Malachi Wolff's harem of secretaries and personal assistants, and stopped in front of the enormous double door that led to Wolff's inner sanctum. He thought about just barging in – a show of dominance – but decided that it would be premature. Instead, he knocked firmly on the heavy cocobolo door.

"Come in already!" came the response from the office.

Don pushed through the door, and strode across the half-acre of plush wine-red carpet to where Malachi Wolff sat at his massive desk.

"Ah, Don!" said Malachi. "So glad you could make it. Please, have a seat." Don did as requested.

"Any word on our itinerant Ms. Ortega?" asked Malachi.

"I'm afraid not, sir," said Don. "Still no contact. I very humbly beg your forgiveness, sir. I have failed my mission."

"Oh, spare me the bowing and scraping," said Malachi. "This isn't the damn Marines. Not that I don't respect your service, Don – I respect that a great deal. However, as I mentioned before, Ortega was of secondary importance. Things didn't really work out with her, anyway. Losing her is no great blow, so long as Mr. Marshall is still on the reservation."

"That he is, sir – and I will endeavor to keep him so."

"I'm certain that you will, Don. Drink?"

"Sure."

Malachi took out two small glasses and a dark green bottle with foreign writing on the label. He produced what looked like an ornate serving-fork and a box of sugar cubes. He put one of the cubes on the fork and poured the contents of the bottle through the cube. The glass filled with a milky green liquid. "Absinthe," said Malachi. "The best possible, direct from the Czech Republic. This is the real deal, Don, not some cheap imitation. Ever had it?"

"No," said Don, squinting at the bottle. "Can't say that I have."

Malachi laughed. "I think you'll like it," he said. "You seem like a man of discriminating taste." He poured out a second glass, and handed it to Don. "*Prosit!*" said Malachi, and downed his glass in one gulp.

Don wasn't about to be out-drank by his boss, and tossed his glass down just as quickly as Malachi. It roared down his gullet like a rocket. It was strong. The stuff had to have been at least 120 proof, with a bitter licorice flavor. His eyes teared up, and it took all of his effort to keep from coughing. He swallowed hard, twice, then held out his glass for more.

"Good stuff, eh?" said Malachi. "It's a personal favorite of mine, and there are very, very few people with whom I share it. You should be flattered."

Don nodded, still not quite sure of his ability to speak. His throat was spasming a little, but an intense warm glow spread from his belly, making him feel quite relaxed. It was like a super-high-quality scotch or tequila, but better.

Malachi returned the nod. "You're a good man, Don Bundy. I need a good man, someone I can trust. What I'm looking for is a person who shares my outlook, who is my intellectual equal, or at least can play in the same league. You seem to fall into that category."

Don smiled and nodded. Of course, someone with an ego like that of Malachi Wolff would never admit that *anyone* was their intellectual equal. The fact that he would suggest that Don was even in the same league was pretty impressive. "Thank you, sir," said Don with sincerity.

Malachi chuckled lightly and poured himself another absinthe. He knocked down the drink in one go. "Ah, good stuff, this absinthe. Another?"

Before he could answer, Malachi snatched Don's glass and lined it up with his own, filling both nearly to the rim. "Here's mud in your eye!" he exclaimed jovially as he shoved one of the glasses back across the desk.

Don regarded the glass dubiously. He hadn't eaten much over the course of the day, and the liquor he had already consumed had gone straight to his head. Also, there was something funny going on at the periphery of his vision. Back in the Corps, Don had the reputation of being able to out-drink anyone. Yet here was Malachi Wolff, outpacing him and showing no signs of intoxication. Incensed, Don tossed back half of his new drink and immediately regretted it. His stomach took a hitch – a small one, for sure – but still a sign of weakness. He grimaced.

"Don," said Malachi, "there are some things we need to discuss. One of them is the situation with the Chuck Marshall show, but that's really just a small part of a larger picture. Much larger."

Don considered this for a moment. When superiors started talking about the "big picture," he had found that it was best to just let them talk. A lot of the time, that big picture existed only in their heads, and usually as a means of justifying really shitty behavior.

"Things with Marshall are under control, chief," Don reported. "Although he's still showing some reluctance to be a team player."

"Absolutely not surprising," agreed Malachi. "These comedians show up thinking they can just do things their way. It's usually a shock for them to realize they're not running the show."

"Indeed," said Don. "I think it will all work out, though. Marshall still tries to think for himself, but as time goes on we'll break him out of that habit."

"Oh yes, we will!" said Malachi. "Most excellent! Don, you've been doing a bang-up job on this show. Things are running smoothly … or at least as smoothly as possible given the personalities involved. I am impressed with your work." He hoisted his glass. Don did likewise and they clinked and drank.

Don had to suppress a shudder; the absinthe was starting to get on top of him. "Th-thank you, sir," he said. "I appreciate you taking a chance on me, given that my background was more, um, technical."

"Of course," said Malachi. "And I *was* taking a chance. There were dozens of people more qualified than you who really wanted that showrunner position."

"Then why in the hell did you pick me?" Whoops – he was getting a little too informal with his superior. Never a good idea. "Sir," he added.

"Because I am a good judge of character," said Malachi. "I needed a special person for a special job, and I thought you were that person. I went with my gut. It's what got me to where I am today."

"Of course, sir."

"Look," said Malachi. "The Wolff Network is big – *huge.* I took a third-rate bunch of tabloid newspapers and radio stations and turned them into the biggest media empire in the world. I'm proud of that. If only my rotten old man could see me now!"

"Indeed, sir. I'm sure he'd be proud."

"Bullshit," said Malachi. "That old buzzard was incapable of feeling anything even remotely positive. If he could see me now, he'd be *jealous.* Jealous as hell that I took his idea and made it so much bigger than he could even conceive."

"I'm sure he would, sir."

"I've achieved what I wanted to achieve with this network," said Malachi. "Of course, there's more I could do – there's always more. Bigger market share, greater income streams, yadda yadda yadda. Just ask the Board of Directors; those bastards are never satisfied. Fuck 'em."

"Fuck them indeed, sir."

"I've got much bigger concerns now, Don. I feel like I've done what I need to do regarding my job. Now I need to focus on my avocation. Does that make sense?"

It didn't. Don was having a little trouble focusing at this point. "I don't know if I'm entirely certain, sir," he said. "Are you talking about a hobby?"

"NO!" roared Malachi. "I am absolutely NOT talking about a mere hobby. Hobbies are for stupid schmoes, building model airplanes and playing bridge. Ways for the peons to pass the time before they punch back in to their slave-wage drudgery. What I'm talking about is my *raison d'etre*. Are you familiar with that phrase, Don?"

"Yes, sir. The literal meaning is 'reason to exist' or 'reason for being.'"

"That's good, Don, real good. Now, I'm going to let you in on a secret; something I've never told another living soul. Are you listening?"

"Yes, sir."

"My *raison d'etre*, my avocation, my goal in life is simple: I want to live forever."

Don sat back, trying to process this information. He was aware that Malachi was watching him closely, waiting to see how he would respond. It was a pretty audacious statement, and he wasn't entirely certain what to say. Was Malachi Wolff yanking his chain? Was he talking metaphorically? Or was he just the latest in a series of filthy-rich, egomaniacal douchebags who thought that their ability to amass material wealth entitled them to eternal life?

"Well, sir," said Don, "I believe that you are well set up for that. You've made quite a name for yourself. This network – this empire – bears your name ..."

"No, no, no!" shouted Malachi. "You don't get it. This isn't some bullshit about a legacy. Especially in this industry. Does the name Mary Pickford mean anything to you?"

"Well, sir, I have to say that the name sounds familiar, but can't actually place it."

"One hundred years ago, Mary Pickford was the hottest ticket in this town. She was arguably the first superstar in the entertainment industry. She was 'America's Sweetheart.' She was 'Queen of the Movies.' She was the first entertainer to sign a million-dollar contract. Now, no one remembers her.

"The point I'm trying to make, Don, is that this is a fickle industry. Corporations can be bought out; networks can be renamed. I can spend millions of dollars to fund a building at a university, but that building will last, what? Sixty, seventy years, tops. All of that stuff is bullshit. What I'm talking about is *literal* immortality. I want my metabolic processes to go on forever. And to be healthy enough to enjoy them. I don't want to end up as some sort of vegetable, hooked up to dozens of machines, trying to eke out another day of so-called life. I want to keep on living exactly the way I'm living now, world without end, forever and ever."

"Amen," said Don.

Malachi stared at him for a moment, then burst out laughing. "Yes! Yes!" he said. "You do get it! I knew you would!"

Don was nonplussed. Was this guy serious? For Don, the thought of living forever didn't have a great deal of attraction. He wasn't afraid of dying, he thought. He figured that most of the people who pursued immortality throughout history were just cowards who were afraid of death. It wasn't much of an issue for him. He had been critically wounded twice in Afghanistan, and had managed to pull through.

He looked across the expansive desk. Malachi watched him sharply, his eyes narrowed and a thin, wolfish grin appeared on his lips. Don knew that what he said next would make or break this conversation – and maybe his entire career with the Wolff Network. He took a long slow sip from his drink to buy some time.

And immediately regretted it. The absinthe hit his gut like a burst from a flamethrower. For a worrying moment he thought that he might actually puke. He stuffed that impulse down, hard. He was not going to let this soft trust-fund weenie out-drink him. He coughed mildly, and blinked away tears. His vision swam, settled, swam again. He was, for lack of a better word, wasted.

"You doing okay, Don?" asked Malachi. He seemed like he was enjoying watching Don's struggle.

"Yeah, sure," said Don in what he hoped was a normal-sounding voice. "Never better."

"Good, good. It's somewhat of an acquired taste."

"What is?"

"The absinthe, of course. A strange drink, for a strange life. Life *is* strange, don't you think, Don?"

"Pretty strange right now."

"Exactly!" exclaimed Malachi. "That's why I want to live forever – so I can plumb all of the myriad strangeness that life has to offer. So what do you want, Don?"

Without thinking, Don said, "I want your job."

Holy shit! Had he just said that out loud? He looked at Malachi Wolff, expecting a look of horror or anger. Instead, Malachi just looked amused.

"Really?" asked Malachi. "That's it? You disappoint me, Don. I had thought you a man of grander vision than that."

Don's mouth now seemed to be running of its own accord. "Well, actually, sir, I want to rule the whole fuckin' world. And from where I'm sitting now, that line runs straight through where *you're* sitting now." This struck him as being fabulously funny and he laughed loudly.

"That's more like it!" said Malachi. "I appreciate your honesty Don, I really do."

"Thank you, sir. I, uh, hope you're not mad about me saying that I wanted your job."

"What? Oh, hell, no! That's not a problem at all. Do you think I really give that much of a fuck about this job? It's a bore, to be perfectly honest. I have no idea why you would want to rule the world. Running an entertainment network is a big enough burden; ruling the whole damn world must be significantly worse."

Don felt himself start to relax. He said, "Well, if you don't mind me asking … if running the network is such a pain in the ass, why do you keep doing it?"

Malachi laughed. "Hell, Don, that's simple. Once I figure out how to live forever, then I'm going to work on how to resurrect the dead. Then I'll bring my piece of shit old man back and show him how much better than him I was at this job!"

Don squinted across the desk. There were two slightly different images of Malachi Wolff staring at him intently. Then they broke into a wide grin and began laughing again. "Oh, my goodness, that would be wonderful. I hope you're not taking me too seriously, though. Resurrect the dead! The very thought! No, Don, I don't want to be God. I just want to live forever."

"Well, I hope you don't think I want to be God, with wanting to rule the world and all."

"Goodness, no! The idea is absurd. God doesn't rule the world. The Devil does."

"Then I think I'm qualified for the job," snorted Don.

"No doubt," said Malachi. "I've been looking for a like-minded scoundrel like you, Don Bundy. I think we can help each other out. I've got to warn you, though: it may get a little weird."

"I can handle weird."

"Good," said Malachi. "I figured as much. Don, I know it's late, but we still have much to discuss. We need to go back to my place. I have something in the basement that I want to show you."

Chapter 24

They took a private elevator to a special section of the parking garage, where a chauffeured Bentley Flying Spur waited. They wended their way through the tangle of streets around the Wolff HQ, and cruised east down Sunset Boulevard. Malachi had the driver crank down the windows, even though the January evening was chilly.

"Hope you don't mind," said Malachi. "I really love Sunset at night. The lights, the sounds. I just need to *connect*. Do you understand me, Don?"

"I think so, sir."

"Ah, bullshit you do," said Malachi. "So I'll tell you." He gestured at the people on the crowded sidewalk. They wore expansive pants and brightly colored shirts. Most were gawking at mundane storefronts; many were taking pictures with their cellphones. Their skin tones came in one of two colors: pasty white or sunburned red. "These are my people!" Malachi exclaimed. "They're the tourists, the so-called deplorables, the middle American mouth-breathers that make the Wolff Network and its affiliated enterprises such a roaring success. How I love them! Fans of fart jokes and conspiracy theories – I bask in their simplicity and credulity. They are *my* people: I understand them and use that understanding to get rich off of them."

"Sounds like a great business model, sir," said Don.

Malachi leaned up and tapped the driver on the shoulder. "Remember to turn up here, Joseph," he said. The car took a quick right and then another quick left-right that put them back on Sunset.

"Excuse the detour," said Malachi. "There are some bad memories

147

associated with that block."

Don looked over his shoulder. "The Comedy Shoppe?" he asked.

"Yes!" spat Malachi. "And I will thank you to never mention that name again. I had a very traumatic experience there once. Damn comedians."

They cruised past the commercial part of Sunset and into the residential area. The buildings became larger and further away from the street until all that was visible were tall hedges and ornate security gates. One of these swung open and the Bentley wound its way up a long curving driveway depositing them at the foot of a grand marble staircase.

"Come, now," said Malachi. "You're getting the grand tour that few people ever do. *Very* few."

They entered through a three-story atrium with an immense crystal chandelier that hung down nearly to the floor. The house was richly furnished, but as they continued deeper into the estate, things began to look … weird.

Don rubbed his eyes, wondering if that damned absinthe was doing something to his perception. Once past the main wing of the house, the rooms were like a funhouse designed by a detoxing psychotic. Beautiful salons opened on raw wall framing with pipes and electrical stubs sticking out at random. Staircases ended halfway up the run. Doors opened onto blank walls. One corridor had a dozen functioning urinals installed over the antique silk wallpaper.

It was well known that Malachi Wolff was forever redesigning and altering his house. There were contractors and work crews year-round. In the land of Tinseltown excess, this was just one more minor quirk of the entertainment industry's ultra-wealthy.

Don and Malachi navigated nearly a quarter mile of convoluted hallways, corridors and rooms in various states of construction or demolition. They wound up at a dead end in a long corridor. It looked to be a semi-demolished wall with scraps of drywall and corroded copper pipe protruding. Malachi reached up and pulled on the stub of a pipe. The wall swung out to reveal an elevator door with no buttons. There was a square metal pad installed to the side. Malachi held his right hand to the pad, and somewhere far below Don could feel the hum of the elevator motor.

The whole experience was messing with Don's head. *Psy-ops,* he thought. That had to be it: Malachi Wolff was trying to keep him mentally unbalanced. He seemed to be succeeding. Loading him up with that absinthe and bringing him through his crazy house had definitely knocked Don's perception into a cocked hat. He growled.

"Is everything okay, Don?" asked Malachi.

"No, sir, it is not," barked Don. "I feel somewhat disoriented and I don't care for it, sir. Respectfully, sir, did you doctor my drink?"

Malachi laughed again, no girly titter this time, but a deep, manly guffaw. "Haw, haw, haw! No, Don, you drank the exact same thing as I did, out of the same bottle. You saw me pour it, didn't you?"

"Yes, sir."

"So what's the problem? Maybe your tolerance isn't as high as you thought, eh? Certainly, your tolerance for the active ingredients in the absinthe is pretty low. Especially that particular brand. It's known for high thujone content. They use a specially cultivated type of sage to augment the artemisia – the wormwood."

"Reckon I'll be more careful next time, sir," said Don.

"Good man!" cried Malachi, and gave him a hearty whack on the back.

Don nearly belted him. Despite the intoxicant, his reflexes were still as sharp as ever, and he stopped himself at the last second from turning and using the heel of his hand to fracture Malachi's nose.

There was a mild chime. "Elevator's here," said Malachi.

They stepped into the elevator, which looked just like a normal office elevator. There were only two buttons on the control panel. Malachi pressed the down button and the doors closed. A speaker in the ceiling played a saccharine instrumental version of "The Girl from Ipanema."

The elevator descended for a long time. There was another mild chime and the doors opened to reveal a small anteroom. There was a closet with a shoe rack against one wall, but nothing else.

"Please remove your shoes," instructed Malachi. Don did as ordered, placing them neatly on the shoe rack.

"Ready?" asked Malachi, waggling his eyebrows like Groucho Marx. The doors swung open to reveal a pleasant room, wide and warm, with saffron-colored walls. In one corner was a life-size Buddha statue, in the other a stone water feature burbled amongst a nest of potted ferns and orchids.

Around the floor were small mounds of tasseled pillows. Malachi waved at a nearby pile. "Have a seat, Don," said Malachi, and he plopped down onto one of the pillow piles.

As soon as they were seated, the Buddha statue in the corner stood up and smiled. Don twitched; how had he missed that? A threat right there in the corner of the room and his eyes had slid right off of it. Must have been that damn absinthe.

"Hello, Malachi," said the Buddha. He pressed his hands together and made a slight bow to Malachi. He turned and repeated the gesture to Don. "And hello to you, new friend."

"Don, this is Gordie," said Malachi. "You could say that he's my guru. Gordie, this is Don Bundy. The one I told you about."

Gordie smiled widely. "So nice to meet you, Mr. Bundy."

Don eyed him skeptically. "Gordie the Guru?" he asked.

Gordie's eyes widened and then he laughed long and loud, joined by Malachi. "Oh, yes, yes!" said Gordie. "That's exactly right! You are a perceptive sort, aren't you?"

"That I am," said Don flatly. He didn't like Gordie the Guru. Part of it was that he didn't like being startled, and was embarrassed that he hadn't realized that he was a real person and not a statue. Also, there was something just off about the guy. Don couldn't put his finger on it; it was very subtle. It reminded him of the sensation of chewing on a foil gum wrapper. There was the sweet taste on top, but an unpleasant metallic bite underneath.

"Well, I certainly hope we can be friends," said Gordie.

"Sure thing," said Don. He stuck out his hand. "Put 'er there, pal."

Gordie shoved his hand into Bundy's outstretched paw. Don squeezed with all his might, but Gordie didn't flinch. Gordie had pushed his hand so far into Don's hand that he couldn't get the bone-crushing leverage to really make it hurt. Don looked straight into Gordie's eyes, looking for a sign of submission. Gordie just stared back with a bland, open expression, like he was standing in line at the post office.

"My, you sure have quite a handshake there," said Gordie. "You're just like G.I. Joe with Kung-Fu Grip!"

Pissed that he wasn't causing Gordie any pain, Bundy gave Gordie's hand one final squeeze, then dropped it. "Well, sir," said Don. "If you don't mind me asking, why did you bring me down here?"

"Oh, I just wanted you to meet Gordie," said Malachi. "Since we're sharing our deepest desires and goals, I thought I'd show you some of what I was doing to achieve mine. And perhaps we can discuss what we can do to achieve yours, eh?"

"With all due respect, sir, I'd prefer to discuss that privately," said Don.

"Oh, c'mon, Don," said Malachi. "Anything you can discuss with me you can discuss in front of Gordie. He has my absolute trust."

Gordie beamed and Don scowled.

"Very well," said Malachi. "I understand. It's still very early. I'm sure you'll come to trust him soon."

"Actually, sir, it's rather late," said Don. "If you don't mind, I should be on my way. I have an early meeting."

"You're going to leave so soon?" asked Gordie, sounding genuinely disappointed. "Are you sure you can't stay for a little guided meditation?"

"I'm afraid I'll have to take a rain check, Gordie," said Don. Right now, he had a strong urge to vacate the premises, drink about a gallon of water and sleep until noon.

"That's too bad," said Gordie. "Maybe next time?"

Don shrugged. He wasn't sure there was going to be a next time.

"Well, in that case," said Gordie, "let's skip the guided meditation and spend some time in the chamber, shall we?"

"Oh, yes!" said Malachi, his eyes lighting up like a child's at Christmas. "Don, you really have to see this before you go. C'mon!"

He walked over to what appeared to be an empty wall. He pressed his hand in the middle of the wall, and a section swung away, revealing a long, well-lit corridor with doors spaced on either side. On one side of the hall, a door was marked "Chapel of Thoth," with hieroglyphics running around the frame. Malachi hurried to the one across from it, which was marked "Hyperbaric Therapy."

"It's a hyperbaric oxygen chamber," said Malachi. "Does wonderful things for the tissues, especially the nervous system. Quite invigorating."

"Absolutely," said Gordie. "This is just one of the many therapies we have for Mr. Wolff's longevity program."

The room looked like a doctor's examining room. At the far end was a long, transparent chamber on a raised plinth. It looked like a Plexiglas coffin. Malachi walked over and lifted the lid. "Want to give it a try, Don?" he asked.

Don shook his head. The box reminded him too much of the metal box they used to shove prisoners into back at the firebase in Afghanistan. "Ah, I'm afraid I'll have to take a pass, sir. I have a meeting in the morning—"

"Very well," said Malachi. "Perhaps later. I'll walk you back to the elevator. Joseph will meet you at the top, and give you a ride to wherever you need to go."

"Thank you, sir," said Don. "I look forward to learning more about your … ah … program very soon."

"And we look forward to having you do so," said Gordie with a broad smile. "I enjoyed meeting you, Don."

That makes one of us, thought Don. To Gordie, he smiled and nodded.

"Be back in a jiff, Gordie," said Malachi. He held open the door for Don and followed him out.

"So, what do you think of Gordie, Don?" asked Malachi.

"Um, how well do you know him, sir?" Don responded.

"Well enough," said Malachi. His kid-at-the-carnival demeanor was gone, replaced by his usual ruthless-business-oligarch mode. "I trust him as much as I trust anyone in the world. I hope that I will be able to trust you that way, Don. Someday."

"Yes, sir."

Malachi led them back through the meditation room and into the anteroom.

"The elevator will be here momentarily," said Malachi. He touched Don on the shoulder. "Look, Don, I know it's been an unusual evening for you. I can understand that it may have been a bit unsettling."

Don shrugged. "Nothing I can't handle, sir."

"Well, that's good!" said Malachi. "I know that you are the stalwart sort. That's what I like about you. I know Gordie can be an acquired taste, but trust me when I tell you that the man's a genius. With his help and his program, I know I will be able to live forever. And what does a man who has eternal life need with a meager media conglomerate? I'll look for some able hands to hand off this business to. Your able hands, Don. Can I count on you for that?"

"You can count on me, sir."

"I knew I could!" beamed Malachi. "Things might seem a little … unconventional at first, but I trust that you are a man of intelligence and vision who can see past the surface appearance through to what really matters. To see the big picture. Be true, Don, and we'll both get what we want. Think you can do that?"

"Sir, yes, sir!"

"Excellent!" There was a mellow *bong* and the elevator doors slid open noiselessly. "Here you go, Don," said Malachi. "Thank you for indulging me. We'll be discussing this more in detail soon. Have a good night!"

As the elevator doors slid close, Don saw Malachi hurrying back through the meditation room – almost running – to keep his date with the hyperbaric chamber.

Chapter 25

Chuck's worries about the direction of the show were eclipsed by his worries about Farrah's disappearance. Why had she just left without saying a word? Surely she would have said something if she were considering quitting. He was glad that the studio had filed a missing persons report with the police, but it did little to alleviate the worry.

In the meantime, he worked harder than ever on the show. He hadn't realized how much he had relied on Farrah for the writing. She wasn't officially on the writing staff, but Chuck always bounced new ideas off of her, and she always came up with ways to improve them, or convince him that they weren't worth pursuing.

Four days after Farrah's *IM OUT* text, Chuck rolled into work early. There were two short scenes that needed to be re-shot, and he had some more writing to do.

When he got there, he was surprised to see that the set was dark. The normal bustle of the crew setting up was absent. Instead, a handful of people were milling around looking upset. There were also a number of strange men, wearing cheap suits. A dark vibe hung over the set, and Chuck's stomach contracted. This had to be bad news.

Don Bundy was talking with two of the cheap-suits when Chuck walked in. When Don noticed him, he nodded in his direction. One of the cheap-suits peeled off and walked over to Chuck. He was a man in his late forties, with short iron-gray hair and a 70s porn 'stache.

"Are you Charles Marshall?" he asked.

"Yes," said Chuck. "Who are you?"

"Detective Vincent Barknight." He flipped open a leather folder containing a badge and an ID card, then quickly closed it. "LASD Homicide Bureau."

"Homicide?" exclaimed Chuck. "What the hell do you want here?"

"You were acquainted with one Miguel Ortega, aka Farrah Ortega?"

"Yes," said Chuck. "I've known her about two years. We work together here. What's this about?"

"I'm afraid he's dead, sir," said Barknight.

"Jesus!" said Chuck. His head swum and his coffee threatened to come back up. He wobbled towards a folding chair on the other side of the studio.

"Hey!" said Barknight. "Where are you going?"

"Here," said Chuck as he plopped down in the seat. "What the hell happened?"

"I'm afraid that Mr. Ortega's remains were discovered yesterday evening in the Angeles National Forest. Well, most of them."

"What the fuck?" said Chuck. "What do you mean, 'most of them?'"

"We're still looking for the head," said Barknight.

"Don't take this the wrong way, Detective Barknight," said Chuck. "But your bedside manner sucks."

"Sorry," said Barknight. "I've been doing this job a long time. It desensitizes you. Mind if I ask a few questions?"

He pulled out a notebook and asked Chuck about the last time he saw Farrah. Chuck recounted his visit with her at the hotel bar. Barknight was especially interested in the guy in the jean jacket who'd gotten upset when he figured out that Farrah wasn't born a woman.

"Do you think you could recognize the guy again?" asked Barknight. "Maybe provide information for a sketch artist?"

"Yeah, sure," said Chuck. "Do you think he might have had something to do with it?"

"It's possible," said Barknight. "This could be a hate crime, related to Ortega's gender identity."

"Well, Farrah didn't seem too worried about the guy in the bar. I offered to walk her to her car, but she just laughed. Said she could take care of herself. She had a gun, actually."

"Oh, really?" said Barknight.

"Yeah, she showed it to me. Had a holster strapped to her thigh."

"Do you know what kind it was?"

"Um, no, not really," said Chuck. "I'm not really a gun guy. It was small and purple – smaller than my hand. She told me the name, but I don't remember it. Ruger? Remington? Something that started with an R. It was a nine-millimeter, though – I remember that."

"Why do you remember that?"

"Because Farrah said that it had more stopping power. Said it could blow a guy's guts out his back."

"That's useful information," said Barknight. "Thanks." He handed Chuck his card and asked him to call if he remembered anything else. Chuck nodded and got up to leave.

As he was heading for the exit, Don Bundy stepped up to him. "Are you okay?" he asked.

"I'm still on my feet," said Chuck. "That's something, after having some horrific news dumped in your lap first thing in the morning."

"Look, the show's doing okay," said Don. "We've got just about everything we need in the can, at least for now. We can start shooting the rest tomorrow, I guess. I'll have to tell Mr. Wolff about this, too. He's not going to be too happy."

"About what?" demanded Chuck. "That his damn show is going to lose a day of shooting, or that one of his actors had her fucking head chopped off?"

"Whoa! Easy there," said Don. "Just go on home and get some rest. This is very upsetting for everyone."

Don seemed about as disturbed as if he'd been told that a restaurant was out of the dessert he wanted. Maybe in the Marines he'd seen people with their heads chopped off all the time. No wonder he was so cold-blooded.

Chuck turned to leave, but Don stopped him. "One more thing. I'm still waiting for the script for that sketch we discussed."

"What sketch?"

"That Dangle Clown thing," said Don. "Marketing loves the idea. Says it hits the 18-34 douche-bro demographic right square in the nuts. They think the merch possibilities are limitless: T-shirts, beer cozies, coffee mugs, you name it. Maybe even a movie deal, if the stars align. Haven't you ever wanted to be in the movies, Chuck?"

Not as a crotchless clown, thought Chuck. He cursed himself. He'd spat the idea out without thinking, hoping it would be a nonstarter for the network, and instead they loved it. The terrible thing was that they were probably right. The Wolff Network audience would probably go ape for a clown brandishing an oversized, pixelated dick.

"We'll talk about it later, Don," he said. "I'm going the fuck home."

Chapter 26

The next two weeks dragged by in a numb slog. At the studio, things reached a fever pitch as the finishing touches were put on the early episodes. Farrah was greatly missed. On the set, Lorraine moved up to a leading role with style, filling in admirably for Farrah. It still felt weird to Chuck, and he sometimes found himself watching the door to the studio, as if Farrah might come strolling in like she owned the place, saying that it was all a silly mistake.

Of course that didn't happen.

Detective Barknight and some of the other cops came by the studio another time or two, but soon disappeared. Chuck knew that they had recovered the rest of Farrah's remains; he'd seen a lurid headline on the *American Investigator* at a grocery store checkout line. It made him feel sick to his stomach, and he had no interest in perusing the details. He knew what he needed to know: his friend was gone forever. He hoped she hadn't suffered much.

He also hoped that her murderer would be caught and face harsh justice. He suspected that wouldn't happen, especially now that Barknight & Co. had stopped asking questions around the studio. Maybe they had leads elsewhere, but Chuck suspected that the unsolved case would end up crammed into a dusty filing cabinet sooner rather than later.

Similarly, the news of Farrah's gruesome death was headline news in the local papers and trade dailies for a while. But after a week or two with no new information, the story disappeared, replaced by a fresher titillating atrocity.

Chucklefest premiered on Thursday, January 24th. Rather than make a big affair of it, Chuck opted to have a small viewing party at his apartment. Arthur and Danny brought dates, and there were a few other members of their comedy crew in attendance, but it only totaled about a dozen people. Caroline had been disappointed about that at first, but when Chuck let her know that there was going to be a full-blown Hollywood extravaganza the following Saturday, she perked back up.

Chuck was surprised at how nervous he felt about watching the premiere, even with his closest friends. He knew that his family was watching, and he'd certainly blown the trumpet far and wide on social media about the show. Chuck wondered if Duckie would watch. He hoped so.

His stomach was in knots as they sat down and tuned in to Wolff. He hadn't seen the final cut of the opening credits yet, and he stared in amazement as the show started. It was loose-looking CGI animation of Chuck and the cast, bouncing around to an upbeat soundtrack.

The first act was his own inaugural stand-up bit. It was six minutes of his best bits, practiced over and over again. Chuck could do those six minutes, word perfect, in his sleep. On the screen, Chuck felt that it was flat. It seemed very polished, but lacking something fundamental. *All technique, no passion,* he thought.

The first sketch featured Chuck as a head cook at a fancy restaurant and Farrah as a sous chef. As soon as Farrah's face took the screen, the mood in the room immediately dampened. Chuck knew right away that he probably wouldn't watch any of the other shows with Farrah. It was just too sad.

After the credits, a picture of Farrah flashed on the screen with the caption "Dedicated to the memory of Farrah Ortega." Chuck had never seen the picture before; it was stunning. She was in a red sequined dress, turned three-quarters profile to the camera. She looked like Rita Moreno in her prime, but much sexier. Her dark eyes radiated heat.

Danny Boylan amazed everyone by bursting into tears, his Boston tough-guy demeanor dissolving into a series of deep, braying sobs. "I guh-guh-guess I ruh-really loved her," he huffed, eyes red and teary. "Maybe that muh-makes me a queeah, I don't care. Go ahead and laugh if you want to."

"No, man," said Chuck. "Nobody's gonna laugh."

Arthur patted him on the arm. "Make no mistake, Daniel," he said. "Farrah was all woman. Just a work in progress. But what a work! What progress!"

The party broke up shortly after that. Caroline was disappointed, but Chuck was deeply relieved. "Are you guys coming to the big shindig on Saturday?" he asked as the guests began making for the door. "It's at Gazpacho's. You're all invited."

"Ah, I think I'm gonna take a pass," said Danny. "Hope you don't mind, but just don't think I can huh-handle it."

"I'm kind of on the fence about this, myself," said Arthur. "If I weren't out of a job, I'd probably say 'no.' It seems like a good opportunity to network, though."

"Network?" said Caroline, who had been sulking on the couch. "What do you mean?"

"Ah, these sorts of parties are total schmooze-fests," said Arthur. "I'm going to brush up my résumé, maybe get some new headshots made."

"You're kidding, right?" said Chuck.

"Maybe about the headshots," said Arthur. "But I think it would be foolish to pass up the opportunity. I really liked working on a TV show. I'd like to do it again, preferably on a show that actually lasts an entire season. See you Saturday."

"Yeah, see you, man," said Chuck.

He was relieved when the last of the guests left fifteen minutes later. Caroline was immediately on her phone, checking out the ModCloth website for a new dress. Chuck rolled a joint, but after two hits he just felt depressed so he stubbed it out.

He really wanted to talk to Duckie, but Duckie's phone went straight to voicemail. Chuck declined to leave a message and went to bed instead.

Chapter 27

The official premiere party for *Chucklefest* was at a trendy restaurant/nightspot that had started life as the flagship restaurant for an inexplicably popular Austrian chef. It had changed ownership a half-dozen times in as many years, falling in and out of fashion. It was now called Gazpacho's, featured California fusion cuisine, and was very popular this month.

Chuck liked Gazpacho's because it was dark. The decor looked like they had ripped the previous interior down to the studs, spray painted everything flat black, and removed every other light bulb. Chuck had already spotted a dark booth way in the back that looked good for hiding out.

First, there was the obligatory schmoozing. Caroline was on cloud nine. She was in a sky-blue knit go-go dress that she'd had overnighted. It wound up fitting well, and Chuck told her that it really accentuated her Nordic features. She blushed and simpered as Chuck made the rounds of the assembled cast, network big shots, and various hangers-on. Chuck had snagged a bottle of Ballantine ale from the bar while Caroline had opted for champagne. This made Chuck nervous, remembering how she'd been at Baron's, but she seemed content to sip her drink and goggle at the assembled multitude of mid-level Hollywood chic.

He was about to head over to the dark booth he'd spotted, when there was a commotion near the front door. "Who is it? Who is it?" said Caroline as she craned to get a look at the newcomer who was the object of such attention. A sub-vocal wave spread throughout the room: *Malachi. It's*

Malachi. Malachi Wolff is here!

Ah, shit, thought Chuck. He'd only met Malachi once for about thirty seconds towards the start of production. They'd exchanged some superficial pleasantries, but Chuck had come away feeling like a missionary who'd just been sized up by a hungry cannibal.

"Might as well get this out of the way," he muttered as he touched Caroline's elbow.

"What?" she asked "We're going to meet Malachi Wolff? Really?"

"Yes, really."

"Oh, I should have brought one of my pictures with me," said Caroline. "Why did you make me leave them in the car?"

"Because it would have been gauche, darling," said Chuck. "Let's go." He ignored her pout, and began pushing through the crowd towards the commotion at the front door.

Malachi Wolff was dressed in a sharp tux with a blinding-white bow tie that matched the blinding-white shirt and cummerbund. On his arm was a stunning six-foot-tall woman with straight dark hair and a tiny dress. Behind Malachi was Reese, in a shapeless black frock that still managed to look like it cost two grand. She carried her ever-present iPad and was tapping furiously on a scheduling app. Behind her were lesser toadies and members of Malachi's entourage.

Malachi spotted Chuck and turned away from the man who was talking to him. "Ah, here's our star, Mister Chuck Marshall!" he exclaimed. The crowd parted as Malachi graced Chuck by identifying him by name. Moses by the Red Sea couldn't have done better.

"Hello, Mr. Wolff," said Chuck, shaking hands. "So glad you could make it out."

"It's my pleasure," said Malachi. "I've a busy night, but I just couldn't miss this. And by the way, you should call me Malachi."

"Yes, sir … Malachi. May I introduce my girlfriend, Caroline Swensen."

"Please to meet you, my dear," said Malachi. He ran a slow, appraising gaze up and down Caroline's body. She smiled and preened as Malachi's date stared blankly into the distance.

"I'm an actress!" piped Caroline.

"I'm sure you are, my dear," said Malachi, patting her on the forearm. Caroline beamed.

"I'm glad you made it out," repeated Chuck, even though it was the furthest thing from the truth.

"I wouldn't have missed it," said Malachi. "I'm very interested in your program. I'm told that the ratings and reviews for the first episode were quite good."

"Third-highest premiere ratings ever for a mid-season replacement," offered a toady who had been standing off to the side. Malachi waved him off.

"Yes, I'm glad that the reviews were good," said Chuck. Actually, he was more relieved than anything else. Except for one obnoxious reviewer for the *Boston Globe,* the reviews had been generally positive. Good but not great, but Chuck could happily live with that.

"Oh, fuck the reviews," said Malachi. "The important thing was that the ratings were better than expected. Good reviews don't sell ad time, Chuck; eyeballs do."

"Certainly, um, Malachi," said Chuck.

"Of course, it's not all about money," said Malachi. "After all, if it were only about making money, we would be selling office supplies or used cars, right, Chuck?"

"Right you are, Malachi," said Chuck. He eyed the empty booth in the back corner. It looked invitingly anonymous.

"No, there's more to it than making money," continued Malachi. "It's about making a *connection.* It's about touching something inside all of us, sharing a common part of our very humanity."

"Uh, yeah," said Chuck, unsure of what else to say.

"That's why I'm so keen on comedians," said Malachi. "The right comedian can bring a transcendent perspective, something that can change our lives forever, given the right circumstances. I think you are one of those unique voices, Chuck. I'm very much looking forward to getting inside your head."

"Oh, yes," said Chuck. What the hell was Wolff talking about? Maybe he was drunk. "I'm looking forward to … uh … sharing what's inside my head, too." *Did that come out sounding as stupid as I think it did?* he thought.

"Fantastic!" said Malachi, giving Chuck a hardy whap on the back. Reese stole up and whispered in his ear. "Oh dear," said Malachi. "I'm afraid I'm late for a gala to benefit – what was it again? Glaucoma? Houselessness? Hatlessness? Whatever – I must be off." He raised his hand in the air, snapped and turned on his heel. Reese and the rest of the entourage fell in line behind him and followed him out the door.

"Omigod! Omigod! Omigod!" enthused Caroline. "I can't believe I just met Malachi Wolff! It's a shame he had to leave so soon."

Whew, thought Chuck. "Let's grab a seat," he said, leading Caroline away by the wrist. He led her to the table in the corner he'd been eyeing and plopped down.

"Ah, that's better," said Chuck. Relieved, he took a sip of his beer.

"It's too dark here," said Caroline. "I can't see what's going on. There are celebrities here!"

"You mean besides the one you're sitting with?"

"No, I mean *real* celebrities!"

Chuck sighed. He never wanted to be a celebrity *per se*, but Caroline's comment stung just the same. Instead, he said, "Tell you what. Why don't you go get us a couple of drinks, then go mingle. I'm just going to hang out here for a bit."

She took off like a shot, and returned a few minutes later with fresh drinks. "Here you go," she said, plopping down a bottle of Budweiser. It foamed up and spilled over on the table. "There's so many people here. Some of them have to be celebrities. I don't know why you want hang out in a dark corner when we could be meeting famous people!"

"I'm just waiting for Arthur to show up," he said. "Go ahead and circulate. I'll catch up in a little bit."

"Okay, I'll just… Omigod, is that *Will Ferrell*?" Without waiting for a response, she was off into the crowd. Chuck looked after her. He was pretty sure that the person Caroline had spotted was a busboy and not Will

Ferrell.

The party flowed and ebbed around him. People came by to say hi, and Chuck greeted them amiably. He just didn't feel like getting up and doing anything.

"Hey, aren't you a famous TV star?" said a familiar voice.

Chuck looked up to see Arthur Watson grinning down at him. "Not according to my girlfriend," said Chuck. "Man, am I glad to see you. I wasn't sure you'd make it." He indicated the chair across from him.

"I wasn't sure I was going to make it," said Arthur as he took a seat. "To be honest, I really didn't want to come out. But the fact that I'm still out of a job somewhat compelled my attendance."

"And after what you've been through, you still want to stick around for more abuse?" asked Chuck. "*Washington Street* seemed like a pretty crummy experience. I'm surprised you're not licking your wounds like Danny."

"Danny's got other concerns now," said Arthur. "This thing with Farrah really hit our Danny-boy hard. Especially after he lost it at your place the other night."

"I couldn't believe it," said Chuck. "I didn't know his feelings for her were so deep."

"I'm pretty sure he didn't, either," said Arthur. "And in addition to processing the loss of someone he felt very close to, he's also struggling with his own self-image."

"Oh, man," said Chuck. "I can't imagine what that must be like. After that Southie upbringing, the realization that he was attracted to a guy must be hard to internalize."

"But Farrah wasn't a guy," said Arthur. "As I said before, she was all woman, even though she didn't come with all of the original equipment."

"You speak truth," said Chuck. He sighed. "To be honest, I'm not digging this scene too much, y'know?" He gestured at the crowd with his beer bottle, causing more suds to slop out onto his hand.

"Looks like Caroline is enjoying it, though," said Arthur. He nodded towards a table across the room where Caroline was talking to a number of men in expensive-looking casual outfits. She was chattering away, striking little poses as she did so.

"Ah, she's telling her joke," said Chuck.

"Her joke?"

"Yes, the *one* joke she knows how to tell. It's a traveling salesman joke that was old when Henny Youngman was just starting out. Until I met you, I thought that people from Iowa had no sense of humor."

Across the room, Caroline thrust out her hip and put her fist on it.

"Okay," said Chuck. "Next comes the cleavage reveal…"

Caroline put her arms behind her back and leaned way over, giving her shoulders a little shake, just in case someone wasn't paying attention.

"Annnd … the punchline," said Chuck.

Caroline held her arms out and straightened her back. The guys around the table erupted in laughter.

"Looks like she can tell a joke to me," said Arthur.

"She's had a lot of practice with that one," said Chuck. "Besides, she was giving the audience what they really wanted."

"Can't go wrong with tits," said Arthur. "Tits and exploding robots – all you need for a successful show in this town."

"I think you've just come up with the name for my next project," said Chuck.

"At least it has some originality," said Arthur. "*Washington Street* was just a lot of formulaic plot points. Just like every other sitcom. And especially like every Black Wolff sitcom. Basically, it featured a lot of Black people playing the fool. For some reason, the Black audience eats it up, especially if there are enough raunchy jokes. I think Wolff knows that white audiences eat it up, too, because it reinforces their favorite stereotypes."

"And after all that, you still want to work in TV?" asked Chuck.

Arthur sighed heavily. "Yeah, but not as an actor. At least not on this network. I want to get behind the scenes in the creative process. I want to make good TV shows for Black audiences, not just drivel that leans on tropes that were tired when *Diff'rent Strokes* premiered."

"Oh, Christ, no!" exclaimed Chuck. "Please don't tell me you 'want to direct.'"

Arthur looked sheepish. "Yeah, kinda," he said. "Not that I've got near enough experience to do so right now. But someday, maybe."

"Well, man, hang in there," said Chuck. "Just keep beating the bushes."

"Kinda looks like your girlfriend is already disturbing the underbrush herself." Arthur nodded towards the table that Caroline was working. She had a manila envelope, and removed a photograph and handed it to one of the guys at the table.

"Aw, jeez," said Chuck. "I told her to leave those in the car."

"Well, you might want to keep an eye on her," said Arthur. "I know the guy she gave the photo to. His name's Tucker Pratt. He was an assistant director on *Washington Street.*"

Chuck stared at him. Tucker was in his late twenties and working the SoCal surfer look hard. His sun-blond mullet cascaded to the shoulders of the slightly tight polo shirt that showed off his pecs. "What's there to look out for?" asked Chuck.

"The guy's a hound," said Arthur. "There were a lot of stories about him on set. He banged most of the female PAs, according to the rumor mill."

"Sounds like a good enough excuse to get the hell out of here," said Chuck.

"Yeah, I think I've pretty much maxed out my patience with this scene myself."

"Look," said Chuck. "I need you to do me a small favor."

"Sure thing, my man. What do you need?"

"Wait about forty-five minutes and give me a call. I just need you to call me, that's all."

"Why?"

"Because I know I'm not going to be able to drag Caroline away right now," said Chuck. "The only way to crowbar her away from this scene is to promise her an even better party somewhere else."

"Pretty underhanded, guy," said Arthur. "Still, if it gets her away from Tucker the Fucker, more the better."

"Yeah, I don't like it," said Chuck. "But I also don't like the idea of spending the rest of the evening watching her flirt with every two-bit player in the room. And I know she'll make a scene if I try to get her away now."

"Okay, I got your back," said Arthur. "Let's do this. I'll talk to you later, man."

They bumped fists, and Arthur hopped up from the table. He made his way towards the door, stopping on the way to talk with Caroline.

Chuck shrugged, polished off his beer and got up from his dark vantage point. He arrived at the table Caroline was working just as Tucker came back with two champagne cocktails."

"Are those for me?" said Chuck quickly. "Thanks!" He grabbed both drinks and gave Caroline a long, loud smack on the lips.

"Hey, babe," he whispered to Caroline. "Ready for the real party?"

"What do you mean?" she asked. She was flushed – a sure sign that she was well on her way to being whammed. It might make her stubborn, but it might also make her easier to bamboozle.

"Look," said Chuck. "This is the fake party, okay? This is the party for the posers and wannabes." He leaned back and gave Tucker a long stare. "We're gonna go make the *real* party, where the A-listers are. I heard Adam Driver's gonna be there."

"Ooooh!" squealed Caroline. "Let's go. Right now!"

"Be cool, be cool," whispered Chuck. "We don't want a bunch of bozos following us there. Arthur's going to meet us there. Let's go."

Chuck said some abbreviated goodbyes on his way out the door. They got back in his car and headed back home.

"Is the real party in Silver Lake?" asked Caroline.

"Nope," said Chuck. "I just want to swing by the apartment to get another shirt. I spilled beer on this one. Don't want to meet Adam Driver in a dirty shirt."

Arthur's timing was perfect; Chuck's phone rang as soon as they walked in the door."

"Yo," said Chuck. "Uh-huh. Uh-huh. What? No shit! Wow, that's too bad! Yeah, okay. Thanks for the heads-up. See you later."

He hung up.

"What's up, babe?" asked Caroline. "Are we leaving soon?"

"Sorry, sweetheart," said Chuck. "Party's off. Adam Driver had an attack of diarrhea."

"Well, can't we go anyway?" asked Caroline.

"Nope. He had the attack in the middle of the dance floor. Kinda killed the vibe. Arthur says everyone's bailing, fast."

"Well, can we go back to the first party?"

"No, by the time we get there, it'll be over. I think that's it for the night. Hell, we might as well go to bed."

"I'm not sleepy."

"Who said anything about sleeping," said Chuck with a grin.

"I just wanna watch TV," pouted Caroline.

They watched TV for nearly two hours, hardly saying a word. When *Entertainment Blast!* came on, Chuck gave up and went to bed alone.

Chapter 28

The second episode of *Chucklefest* dropped, and it garnered better reviews – and ratings – than the first show. It now seemed like Wolff had a *bona fide* hit on their hands, and the top brass started taking a closer interest in the show.

The reviews had also been very positive for Chuck personally. *Entertainment Blast!* had described him as "a charismatic comic." *Variety* had called him a "very funny and personable rising star." All of these adjectives had made Chuck a little uncomfortable. Well, all except "funny," which is something he'd been working on for years. "Charismatic" was something else entirely, and Chuck didn't really know what to make of it.

The Wolff Network did. As soon as the positive reviews had started rolling in, they had Chuck in the studio shooting twenty-second promos. There had also been a session with a photographer who looked like he had been beamed directly from the set of a '60s comedy. He had shot hundreds of pictures of Chuck, some with ridiculous props like rubber chickens and Groucho Marx glasses.

Fortunately, none of those pictures had shown up on the billboards that went up just a few days later. Chuck had seen the first while driving down Sepulveda Boulevard, and it had unnerved him enough that he'd pulled into the parking lot of a Jack-in-the-Box to gather his wits. It was freaky to see himself pictured nine times the size of Jesus on a major thoroughfare in L.A. The caption "He puts the Chuck in *Chucklefest*" was pretty lame, but at least they had chosen a decent headshot.

A week later, Chuck's phone rang. It was Philo.

"Chuck, babes! You sitting down?"

"As soon as I saw your number," said Chuck. "What gives?"

"Good news, babes – *great* news. The network really likes the show. They want another season. Twenty-two episodes."

"Whoa," said Chuck, who actually had to sit down when he heard this.

***

The weeks flew by. By early May, they had put the finishing touches on the final episodes of the half-season, and began working on new episodes for fall. *Chucklefest* continued to pull good ratings and decent reviews. Since the show was a mid-season replacement, Chuck and the rest of the cast and crew always felt like they were behind. Everything seemed like a crisis.

Chuck was stressed, but keeping his focus entirely on his work helped keep him from thinking too much about Farrah. He still felt sick and horrible whenever he thought of her. Of course, there was no more information from the cops, and after a while, Chuck quit expecting anything.

On the first Monday in May, Chuck was called into a last-minute production meeting, with a few more of the network bigwigs in attendance than usual. They were discussing the work that needed to be done on the show to round out the season and build hype for the next season.

"We need a good bit for the fall season," said Hans. "Something that will make a big splash with the fans. Something seasonal. Halloween, Thanksgiving, Christmas – whatever."

"I've already got a Christmas skit," said Chuck. "What's the problem?"

"Yes, well, it's a great skit, Chuck," said Hans, who was point man for the network. "We love it. We really do!"

"Again, what's the problem?" asked Chuck.

"Well, it's just not the sort of thing that our target audience would go for," said Mariquita.

"What do you mean?" asked Chuck. "It's a great Christmas message. It's called 'How to Be Happy.' What could be better for the holidays?"

Hans scrunched up his face. Chuck wanted to punch it. "It's just … well, we don't think the audience will go for it."

"It's a great bit," said Chuck. "I know it's a little experimental, but it's good stuff. It's basically a take on the Sermon on the Mount."

"Really?" said Hans, arching an eyebrow. "That's the problem right there. Too preachy. Our viewers don't like that sort of thing."

"What do you mean?" asked Chuck. "The network's always going on about the Christian demographic is such an important part of our audience. This is straight from the Bible!"

"Yes," said Mariquita. "But our viewers are more into the parts of the Bible about smiting one's enemies. The parts about forgiveness and being nice to people just don't test that well."

"Jesus Christ!" said Chuck. "I thought this was supposed to be my show! Now you cut something that's directly from the Bible!"

Mariquita sighed. "Look," she said, "in some ways, we're victims of our own success here." "Now that the show's doing well, getting good ratings, and selling more expensive ad time, well, there's a lot more attention being paid towards us."

"So what?" said Chuck. "That doesn't give you the right to just run me over!"

"Nobody's running anyone over," said Don Bundy. "We love the show, Chuck, and we love your writing. We also love this 'Happy' bit, and maybe we can use it in season three. But we've got to finish the second season, first. Fortunately, you've *already* come up with a perfect Christmas skit."

"Oh, no," said Chuck. "Not 'Dangles the Crotchless Christmas Clown!'"

At the name, everyone around the table burst into laughter – except Chuck.

"See?" said Don. "Just the name is hilarious. People are gonna love it."

That's what Chuck was afraid of. "I wasn't serious when I came up with the idea," he said. "It was a joke."

"Joke or no joke, it's funny," said Hans. "We've been testing the idea, and it's polling well. Marketing has been playing with concepts, and they're really enthused. This is Annette Burnside, associate director of Marketing. Annette?"

"Um, yes," said Annette. "We've been playing around with some marketing and promo paradigms. It's testing super-high with eighteen- to thirty-four-year-old males without a college degree."

"That's our strongest market," added Mariquita.

"We've even got some merch prototypes," said Annette.

"How the hell can you have merch prototypes?" asked Chuck. "I haven't even written the bit yet!"

"Well, no," said Hans. "But the name's pretty much self-explanatory."

"Take a look," said Annette. "We've had the art department take a whack at some character concepts. Here's the one that's tested the best." She held up a piece of cardstock that featured a colorful clown. He had frizzy green hair and oversized Santa hat, and wore a goofy cereal-box-character grin on his painted face. He seemed to be dancing a hornpipe, and between the legs of his oversized clown pants was a pixelated white blur that was obviously an enormous penis. Chuck groaned. It was awful.

"And there's more," enthused Annette. "Chuck's idea was that Dangles could be, um, reconfigured for other holidays. What was the phrase he used?"

"'A clown for all seasons,'" said Don. Chuck gave him a dark look.

"For example," continued Annette, "there's Dangles the Crotchless Easter Clown." She flipped a card to show the clown with floppy pink bunny ears.

"Dangles the Crotchless Independence Day Clown." A picture of the clown in a tri-cornered hat and crotchless breeches.

"And it doesn't have to be just holidays, either," said Annette. "How about Disco Dangles?" A picture of the clown in a Saturday Night Fever outfit with huge lapels and collar.

"Ah, jeez," said Chuck. "You're really sold on the idea, aren't you?"

Nods of affirmation all around the table. "You bet!" chirped Annette. "The merchandising will be epic. Look!" She produced a large paper bag and began pulling sample items from them. "T-shirts, beer cozies, frisbees, cell phone cases, baby onesies!"

"Baby onesies?" said Chuck. "Seriously? People out there would want to dress their baby up in an outfit featuring a clown with his dick hanging out?"

"Sure, why not?" asked Mariquita. "The … um, member is pixilated, and the baby would be too young to know, anyway."

"I've been thinking," said Chuck. "Maybe we should lose the crotchless aspect of this character. I didn't really think that was such a good idea in the first place."

"Are you kidding?" said Hans. "That's what makes it *funny!* It doesn't work without the crotchless part. Hell, even the name doesn't work! How can we call him Dangles if nothing's dangling?"

Something inside Chuck snapped. This had gone way too far. They had taken his dumb-ass idea too seriously, and it was time to shut it down, hard. He was tired of Wolff walking all over his ideas.

"Nothing's going to dangle, because we are not doing this skit," said Chuck. "We're not going to do it because I'm not going to write it. Is that clear?"

"We can just get someone else to write it," said Mariquita.

"No fucking way!" shouted Chuck. "I'm head writer of the show. I have the final say. And I say *no!*"

The network executives exchanged conspiratorial glances. Chuck felt his heart sink. They were about to shaft him. Again.

Hans turned to Annette and said, "Thanks, Annette, those are great ideas. We really love what you've come up with. Could you please give us the room?"

Oh, this doesn't look good, thought Chuck. "What now?" he asked. "What do you vipers want?"

"Well, Chuck," began Don. "We all really appreciate all of the hard work you've put into this show. Your dedication and talent have put us in a great position. We all want to thank you for that." Around the table, there were insincere murmurs of gratitude and praise.

"We've put a lot of faith in your project," said Hans. "And it has paid off – handsomely. The network has a hot new show, and your own stock, Chuck, is going through the roof."

"Okay, get to the point," said Chuck wearily. All this buttering up could only mean that they were really going to bring the hammer down.

"Like we were saying," said Don. "We appreciate all of your hard work, but we're also a little worried. We don't want you to burn yourself out."

"We're concerned that you might be spreading yourself too thin," said Mariquita. "Being the star of the show *and* the head writer is a lot of responsibility, a lot of time."

"We're thinking of moving someone else into the head writer position," said Hans. "You would get an executive producer credit. It would be a promotion, really. A bigger paycheck and less responsibility. What's not to like about that?"

"But I *like* being the head writer," objected Chuck. His stomach had tightened into a hard knot.

"We *love* your writing!" said Mariquita. "We really do! And it's not like you wouldn't be writing anymore. It's just that Cyril would be taking on the burden of head writer, allowing you more time to focus on your performance."

Cyril Dienst was one of the staff writers he'd been working with, a long-term fixture at Wolff Studios. He was a skinny, awkward guy from Brooklyn. His social skills were poor, but he could write funny material.

"I guess I really don't have any choice in the matter," said Chuck, looking from face to face around the conference table.

"Now, we don't want you to look at it like that," said Don. "We want everyone to be satisfied with the decision."

"However," intoned Hans, "your contract stipulates that we have the option of promoting you to executive producer and going with a new head writer. We've decided to exercise that option."

"In other words," said Chuck, "I'm fucked." He looked around the room again. All of the network bigwigs had remarkably insincere looks of concern on their faces. The bastards. Well, he'd give them something to be concerned about.

"No," he said. "Just fucking no! If you replace me with Cyril as head writer, I walk. I'm done with this shit. You've gutted the show. You wouldn't even let me choose the fucking *name*, and now I can't even write it. Fuck that noise! No, I'm done!"

He stood up abruptly. Hans started to say something about how he sympathized, but Chuck gave him the finger, spun on his heel, and practically sprinted out of the conference room.

He walked quickly down the hall. His only thought was getting out of this building, getting into his car, and going home. Caroline should be home; she wasn't working today. He just wanted to go home to a sympathetic ear and a warm lap he could lay his head in while he spilled out his woes.

"Chuck! Wait up!" Don pounded down the hall behind him. Chuck kept going. He didn't want to talk to anyone right now, especially Don.

He felt Don's hand clamped down on his shoulder, pulling him roughly and spinning him around so they were face-to-face. Suddenly, Chuck was angrier than he had ever been in his life. For a flickering moment, he thought about throwing a punch at Don Bundy. Don must have caught the look, for there was a look of feral anticipation in his ice-gray eyes. *Go ahead, punk,* Chuck imagined him thinking. *Give it a shot. I'd enjoy pounding you into hamburger.*

Instead, Chuck shook Don's hand off his shoulder. "You sold me out, you son of a bitch!" Chuck hissed.

"No, I didn't," said Don. "In fact, I tried to talk them out of it. They didn't listen. I know how you must feel."

"I doubt it," said Chuck. He was breathing heavily, and his stomach took a sudden lurch. He felt like he was going to puke.

"Look," said Don. "Take a couple of days off, give it some thought, talk to your manager. It's not as bad as it seems. Trust me."

I don't trust you any further than I can throw your ass, thought Chuck. He didn't know what to say, so he just shook his head, turned away from Don, and headed towards the parking garage.

Chapter 29

The traffic downtown was a total bastard. Chuck got angrier with every red light and slowpoke tourist. He just wanted to get home, talk to Caroline and smoke a joint.

Beyond unburdening himself to Caroline and catching a buzz, he really had no plans. Would he go back to work on *Chucklefest*? He wasn't sure. They had done him up one side and down the other. The fact that they had yanked the head writer position out from under him stung hard.

His mind raced, trying to find a way out of the conundrum. He was sure that he could hang on to the head writer position if he agreed to move forward with that rotten clown sketch. Chuck cursed himself. He'd been foolish to think that he could out-crass the Wolff Network.

Maybe he could go ahead, write the sketch and perform as Dangles, and just do such a shitty job that it would only air once. The idea did not sit well. Sure, Dangles the Crotchless Clown was a shitty idea, but it was *his* shitty idea. He couldn't bring himself to sabotage his own creation, even if it really deserved it.

At the core of his worry was the certainty that the network was right: Dangles would be a huge hit. Christ, what if that became the thing that he was known for, perhaps the *only* thing he was known for. The thought of spending the rest of his career fending off requests to "do Dangles" made him sick to his stomach. He understood why John Cleese *hated* the Ministry of Silly Walks guy. After a long and storied career, to be constantly pestered to perform a goofy, irritating character would have made anyone angry.

Shit, thought Chuck. Can't go forward, can't go back. Right now, he didn't care about going anywhere but home. Fortunately, he was past the abysmally horrible downtown traffic and into the regularly horrible Silver Lake traffic. He was almost there.

He sensed something was wrong as soon as he opened the apartment door. It took him a moment to realize exactly what was wrong: the place was too orderly. Caroline kept the apartment in a state of organized anarchy. Now, the apartment was clean: no clothes draped over every horizontal surface, no random piles of cosmetics, no dirty dishes on the counter, no discarded magazines on the floor.

"Oh shit," said Chuck. Just when he thought the day couldn't get any worse, it absolutely had.

He fast-walked to the bedroom. The bed was made, something that hadn't happened since Caroline moved in. He threw open the closet. The only items there were his. Ditto the dresser.

Caroline had left him.

He found the note on the otherwise-spotless kitchen table. It read:

> *Dear Chuck,*
>
> *Im sorry it has to be this way, but I think youll agree that its for the best in the long run. Your a great guy and I no youll go far, but you dont have what I need right now. I might as well tell you now before you find out on your own – I've moved in with Tucker. Hes got what I need and he cares about my career unlike some hotshot comedians I know. Im sorry its come to this but its the way its got to be. Hope you understand one day.*
>
> *-Caroline*

He couldn't believe it.

Actually, he could believe it quite well; it was just that the timing couldn't have been worse. That was Caroline, no sense of timing at all.

He crumpled the note and slumped down at the kitchen table. "You picked a fine time to leave me, Lucille," he muttered bitterly.

That bitch, he thought. Was that fair? Probably not. Caroline could be kind and nurturing when she wanted to. Unfortunately, she was convinced that she was chock-full of talent. What might have passed for talent in Des Moines wasn't going to cut it in Los Angeles. There was just no way to get her to understand that. Oh well, she was Tucker the Fucker's problem now.

What to do? Earlier, he thought that he couldn't go forward and couldn't go back. Now he couldn't stay put, either.

Without thinking, he reached for his phone and thumbed in Duckie's number. Duckie would be able to talk him through this. Maybe Chuck could boogie up to Portland for a few days and stay with him, get his head straight and some perspective away from the madness of La-La Land.

It rang a few times and went to voicemail. "Hello, you have reached the number for Duckie Dunne, comedian extraordinaire. Words cannot express the regret I feel for not being able to answer your call. However, you may rest assured that should you see fit to leave a message, I will return it with the utmost alacrity."

Chuck almost hung up, and he waited a long time after the beep to say anything. "Whoa," he said finally. "Duckie. This is Chuck. Holy shit, man, I don't know where to begin. It feels like the bottom has fallen out. Jesus." He could feel himself starting to tear up, and he took a few deep breaths to regain his composure. He didn't want to melt down on Duckie's voicemail. "Look, man, just give me a call. I was thinking I might come up and spend some time with you in Portland. Just give me a call. *Please.*"

He hung up, put the phone down and put his head in his arms.

He stayed that way for a long time.

Finally, he stood up. He left his phone on the table and walked out the front door, not bothering to lock it behind him.

Chapter 30

H e's *WHAT?*" yelled Malachi Wolff.

Don winced. "Gone, sir," he said. "No one seems to know where."

At first, Don hadn't been too worried – he thought Chuck had just been sulking. However, after Chuck had failed to show up for a second day, he realized that he might have a problem.

"Get your ass in my office, immediately!" yelled Malachi.

Once Don's ass was appropriately relocated, Malachi began grilling him. "What the fuck's going on, Bundy? Where the fuck has Chuck Marshall gone?"

"Sir, I don't know, sir!" said Don. "He's not answering his phone, not returning messages. I went by his apartment, but no one answered the door, and I couldn't spot his car anywhere in the vicinity."

"Shit!" said Malachi. "Shit, shit, *shit!* You were supposed to keep an eye on him and now he's disappeared. This will not do, not at all!"

"Sir, yes, sir!" barked Don. He was surprised that Malachi was so upset. Marshall may have just gone to the beach or something. Malachi certainly hadn't been this concerned when Ortega had disappeared.

"Okay, okay," said Malachi. "We need to think about this logically. Has Marshall been acting erratically or out of sorts lately?"

"If you ask me, he always acts that way," said Don. "At least since the production for the show really got into gear. First, he was upset about the name change. Then, when Ortega turned up dead, he really went into a funk."

"Yes," said Malachi. "That was an unfortunate incident. Have you heard anything about how the investigation is going?"

"Sir, yes, sir. I talked with the detective in charge of the case, Barknight. He said that they're treating it as a hate crime, that Ortega was killed because of his sexual orientation, or whatever you call it. Frankly, I don't think they're pursuing the case very hard."

"That's just fine," said Malachi. "It was a shame that Ortega wound up that way, but that's the way things go sometimes. Ortega's dead. Marshall is not, hopefully. We need to find him. And we also need to get in front of the story, right fucking now." He pressed a button on his desk. "Reese, get in here, pronto!"

Reese materialized in a matter of seconds, iPad in hand.

"Reese, we've got a little problem," said Malachi. "Chuck Marshall has apparently gone AWOL. Coming on the heels of the mishap with Ortega, this could look pretty bad for us. We need to get the story out that Marshall's exhausted from putting together a new hit show, and is taking a few weeks of R & R to recharge. Go to Morey in PR; she's the best spin doctor we have. I want this in all the dailies by tomorrow morning, understand?"

Reese nodded, made a note on the iPad, and disappeared.

"What a fuck-up," said Malachi. "The timing couldn't be worse."

"Sir, I failed you," said Don. "I am more than willing to offer my resignation, effective immediately."

"Oh, no," said Malachi. "No fucking way you're getting off that easily. You made this mess; you're going to clean it up. Find Chuck Marshall, NOW!"

"Sir, I understand the urgency of the mission," said Don. "I don't know if I'm the proper person for the job.

"Don't give me a load of horseshit about not being the right man for the job," said Malachi. "You're a Marine, aren't you? A sniper? A *hunter*? Then hunt down Chuck Marshall!"

"Sir, yes—"

"Yeah, yeah, yeah," interrupted Malachi. "You're a devious fuck, Don. I wouldn't have taken you into my confidence otherwise. So shut up and listen. You've got your dream, and I've got mine. And we can both get what we want, but only if you find Chuck Marshall."

"But sir—"

"No buts. It's simple. Find Marshall, and then call me and tell me where he is. That's all. I don't want you to talk to him or try and bring him back. Just find him and let me know where he is. Got it?"

"Sir, yes, sir!"

"Good. Now get going."

Don got going.

Chapter 31

Chuck peered between the window blinds. A car had just pulled up in front of the house. He relaxed when he saw it was Simi's old Mercedes. She got out and stood on the sidewalk with her hands on her hips, surveying the property.

C'mon, c'mon, thought Chuck.

Simi marched up the front walk. Chuck swung open the door just as she approached, and she breezed right in without breaking stride. She dropped her purse on the coffee table and lowered herself onto the couch. "You're keeping the place nice, Charles," she said. "Very respectful. I appreciate that."

"I'm trying to keep a minimal footprint," said Chuck. "A low profile. So, did you talk to your cop friend?"

"Indeed I did," said Simi. "You don't have a club in L.A. for so long without getting to know a few cops – the good, the bad and the ugly. He put me in touch with the sergeant in charge of your missing persons case. I told him the story, and he seems okay with it."

Chuck exhaled slowly. This was a *huge* relief. "So I'm off the hook, then?" he asked.

"Not quite," said Simi. "He wants to talk with you before he closes the case." She fished in her enormous purse and came up with a scrap of paper with a phone number. "His name's Sergeant Alex Julius."

"Might as well get this over with," said Chuck. His hand was shaking as he punched in the number.

"Missing Persons Unit, Julius speaking."

"Uh … yeah, hi. Um … my name's Chuck … Charles Marshall. You guys think I'm missing, but I'm not. Everything's … uh, cool."

"Oh, yeah," said Julius. "Your manager talked to me. She said you were stressed out at your TV show, took a hike."

"Yes, that's right."

"Whew, must be tough," said Julius. "Well, you don't sound like you're under duress, so I'll just assume you're another Hollywood crybaby, and close the damn case."

"I'd appreciate it," said Chuck. He didn't like being called a crybaby, but was too relieved to say anything about it. "Uh … you're not going to tell anyone about it, are you?"

"Hey, I'm not your publicity agent, pal," said Julius. "Anybody asks, only thing I'll say is that the case is closed."

"Is that it, then?"

"Yeah. I assume I can reach you at this number," said Julius.

"That's right," said Chuck.

"Okay," said Julius, and hung up.

"So that's that," said Simi. "Now what?"

"I think I'm in the clear, at least for a little," said Chuck. "I went back and emptied out the apartment. The lease is up soon, anyway. I'd like to just stay here for a little while, think of what I'm going to do next."

"Well, I expect the network is going to keep looking for you," said Simi. "Even if the cops aren't. Have you told anyone else where you are?"

"Only my folks," said Chuck. "I really don't want to bother with anyone else. I got my old phone, but I leave it turned off. Maybe I should get a new burner, since that cop has this number."

"Well, look, bubbie, you can stay here for as long as you want. You know I'll run interference wherever I can."

"Thanks, Simi. I appreciate it so much. You're a lifesaver."

"I'm glad to help, Charles. You know, this isn't the first time I've helped one of my comics take a little French leave. So what are you going to do next?"

Chuck sighed. "I don't really know, Simi," he said. "I'm just trying to get

some perspective on my career and my life. The last six months have been
… draining."

"I bet, bubbie. You've been through the wringer, that's for sure. You need
to think really hard about what comes next. You realize that you're turning
your back on a lot of money, right?"

"Money's not everything, Simi."

"I'm glad to hear you say that. Still, you don't want to be cast into the outer
darkness. You get a bad rep, you'll have trouble finding work anywhere.
Give it a lot of thought, Charles. Feel free to call me if you want to talk."

"I will, Simi," said Chuck. "Thank you. Right now, I'm good just
unwinding. I hike up in the mountains, or just sit on the back porch and
read. I try not to go out much during the day – I want to avoid dealing with
the neighbors. I *have* been thinking of going to some nearby open mics."

"Ah, you'll blow your cover for sure," said Simi. "If one of the tabloids
finds out about it, the story will be all over the place by morning."

"I know," said Chuck. "I'm developing a new persona to stay incognito.
Check it out." He indicated a pile of shopping bags on the end of the couch.

Simi got up and poked around in the bags. "Well, well," she said. "Tie-dye
t-shirt, love beads… Holy Moses, where'd you get these bell-bottom jeans?
Did the Flying Burrito Brothers have a yard sale?"

Chuck laughed. "I've been combing thrift stores and costume shops. I'm
going to go by 'Al Tiedye.'"

"I look forward to seeing the act."

"I'd be glad to come by your club and do a mic," said Chuck.

"No, no," said Simi. "Too close to the heat. Hell, I'd say don't do mics any
closer than Berdoo, Cucamonga at the closest."

"Good advice, Simi. I just need some stage time. It doesn't have to be a
top-tier venue."

"Good, good," she said. "Look, bubbie, I have to run. Call me if you need
anything. And let me know if you get a new phone number."

"Will do, Simi. And thanks for everything. You're a saint."

Simi got in her car and headed off. Chuck picked up the copy of *Sometimes
A Great Notion* that he'd been meaning to read for two years, and dove in.

III

Part Three

THE SEARCH

Chapter 32

May 2019

Duckie sat bolt upright in bed, face covered in sweat. He'd had the dream again. This was the third time this week. He grabbed his phone from the bedside table and checked the time: 3:13 am. *Shit,* he thought. He knew he wasn't going back to sleep. He was usually awake this time of the night, anyway. The shift work at the print shop saw to that. On his days off – like today – he usually attempted to keep a normal sleep schedule so that he might be able to socialize with some of his normal friends.

He stumbled out of bed, went to the bathroom to take a leak and toweled the sweat off his forehead. His mouth was dry. He checked in the fridge: a quart of milk and two bottles of beer. He twisted off the cap of one of the beers and plopped down on the futon in the living room.

A couple of sips of beer helped exorcise the uncomfortable remnants of the dream. The first time he'd had the dream, it had been preceded by a strange incident at work. It had been late at night and he'd been running a boring job: cranking out a huge corporate training manual from a copier the size of a sub-compact. It was supremely dull. Duckie's main responsibility was to make sure the copier didn't run out of paper, and to pack the 500-page documents into cartons as they came out.

As the copier's rhythmic, somnolent hum washed over him, he began to feel spacy. It was an *active* spaciness. He felt energized but also weird and a little nervous. His vision began to cloud over, and it seemed that the

189

room was dark, that there were people all around him and that there was something going on in front of him and above him. The thump and hum of the copier became a Grateful Dead song, "Touch of Grey." He felt a warm presence close to him in the dark. It made him feel happy and safe. The area in front of and above him came into focus: it was a band. Then Duckie noticed that the band were all skeletons and that they had no skulls. A bolt of terror shot through him, but he felt that warm presence reassuring him, telling him not to be scared.

Then the copier buzzed, and Duckie snapped back to the here and now. He shook his head. "What the fuck was that?" he said out loud. He began loading more paper into the copier, but the strangeness of the episode stayed with him. Had he just had some sort of psychic experience? Fortunately, there was a co-worker who could shed some light on the subject.

"Yo, Fruit Stripe!" hollered Duckie.

"In the break room, man," came the reply.

Duckie got the copier running and went into the break room. Fruit Stripe Smythe was lounging with his feet up on the table, reading a book called *Principia Discordia.* His lank gray hair was pulled back in a ponytail that descended halfway down the back of an ancient Allman Brothers t-shirt. A pair of tiny wire-rimmed glasses rounded out the ensemble. "What's shaking, man?" he asked, putting down the book.

"I just had a … I dunno, an otherworldly experience," said Duckie. He felt like a dope saying it, but since it was only Fruit Stripe, it didn't matter as much.

"Tell me all about it," said Fruit Stripe, with an avid gleam in his eye.

Duckie gave him a rundown on what had happened at the copier.

"Wow, man," said Fruit Stripe. "This sorta thing ever happened to you before?"

"No."

"Ever do acid, man?"

"Well, only once."

"Was it, like, pretty intense?"

"Yeah. It was cool at first, but then it got weird."

"Been there," said Fruit Stripe. "Sounds like you may have had a flashback from that trip, brother. I hear they can be kinda scary."

"You *hear*?" said Duckie. "You don't know? Don't tell me you've never done acid, man."

"Oh, I've done plenty," said Fruit Stripe with a wistful smile. "I've never had a flashback, though. Go figure."

"So, what the fuck just happened to me, anyway?"

"Well," said Fruit Stripe, drawing himself into full hippie pedagogue mode. "The deal with LSD is that it basically rewires your brain. Opens neural pathways that were previously blocked, or didn't exist at all. If you had a really intense trip, it might've, y'know, really blasted a new tunnel in your mind. Where does that tunnel go, huh? Maybe you're starting to find out. Or maybe it was nothing."

"Well, that just about covers the fuckin' waterfront. Thanks, Fruit Stripe."

"Any time, brother."

That morning, when Duckie had got home from his shift, he'd had the dream for the first time. In it, he was back at the Oregon Country Fair, riding out his bad trip in the Porta Potty. He had a copy of the *American Investigator* on his lap. The headline read "Gorilla Girl to Get Own TV Show!" Gorilla Girl was the unofficial mascot of the tabloid, first introduced in the mid-'90s with the cover story "Bill Clinton Loses Fist Fight with Gorilla Girl!" That issue had been the highest-selling in the tabloid's history, and ever since then the poorly Photoshopped image of the hirsute young lady had appeared on the cover of *American Investigator* at least four times a year.

In the dream, Duckie had attempted to open the tabloid to the cover story, but every page he turned to just had the same image as the cover: Gorilla Girl in a pink bikini posing on a TV talk show set. For some reason, this really disturbed him. In the dream, as he sat there flipping through the same page of the *American Investigator*, he became aware of voices from outside the Porta Potty. He could hear Chuck's voice, and could tell he was talking to someone else. Somehow, he knew that it wasn't that Daffodil chick, though. It was Mickey Gross who was with Chuck.

"Come on in, Duckie," said Chuck. "Come on in!"

"Whaddaya mean?" cried Duckie, who suddenly felt very upset. "I'm the one who's in. *You* come in."

"No, no," said Chuck. "You need to come in, Duckie."

There was a sharp rap on the Porta Potty door, and Duckie sat bolt upright in bed, half a breath away from a scream.

Now, Duckie sat on his futon, swigging his beer. The first few gulps helped banish the weirdness of the dream, then he put it down and got a pot of coffee going.

When the coffee was ready, he went to his computer to look for news about Chuck. It had been over two weeks since Chuck had left the last message for Duckie. Despite Chuck's plaintive "please" at the end of the message, Duckie had not bothered even attempting to return the call for several days. He felt guilty now, knowing that it was resentment and jealousy that had kept him from reaching out.

Soon, word began to get out that the star of Wolff's hottest new program had apparently walked away from his own show. Then it came out that Chuck had not just had a hissy fit and split, but was now the subject of a missing persons report.

The tabloids had gone nuts at the news. The murder of Farrah Ortega had immediately been rehashed, and there was no end of wild speculation connecting Chuck's disappearance with Farrah's murder. Was someone stalking the cast of *Chucklefest?* Did Chuck have something to do with Farrah's demise? Had he run away to escape prosecution? Nobody knew, but that didn't stop the rampant speculation and rumor-mongering that was the bread and butter of the sleazetainment press.

The crazy stories about Chuck and Farrah had raged for about a week. Then, a young pop music star had flashed her freshly shaved crotch during a meet-and-greet at a petting zoo, and subsequently checked into a high-end rehab in Santa Barbara. Since then, there had been a half-dozen other celebrity scandals to suck up the tabloid oxygen.

Duckie took a sip of coffee and fired up his laptop. He did a search for "chuck marshall disappearance." It turned up a bunch of hits, but most of them were old; he had read them all before. The only relatively recent one was a week-old article from the *American Investigator* website, titled "Comedian Tragedy: Was It a Bigfoot Love Triangle?"

Duckie read the article, which didn't take long; articles in the *American Investigator* were rarely more than two hundred words. The article was as scuzzy as the headline suggested: Chuck was romantically involved with both Farrah Ortega and a female bigfoot living in the San Gabriel Mountains. The bigfoot had killed Farrah in a fit of jealous rage and was now living with Chuck in a cave not far from Mt. Baldy.

Duckie slammed his laptop shut in disgust. He hated *American Investigator.* There was something unsettling about it right now, much more than the insipid story about his friend. The part of his dream where he was flipping through the tabloid and seeing the same goofy picture of Gorilla Girl in her bikini, that part of the dream always made him feel weird. That and the idea that Chuck was outside with Mickey Gross.

He felt like he was overlooking something important, some connection that wasn't being made. He remembered Fruit Stripe talking about LSD forging new connections in the mind, and felt like he was on the verge of completing an important mental circuit. What could it be?

He took another sip of coffee, willing his mind to be blank. It was a technique he'd used when getting ready to go onstage for a particularly intimidating gig. He sipped his coffee and stared blankly at the closed window blind, letting ideas coalesce and dissolve without grasping at them. Chuck. LSD. Porta Potty. *American Investigator.* Mickey Gross. Gorilla Girl.

He started. There *was* a connection between the *American Investigator* and Mickey Gross that he had forgotten about: The tabloid had been the first to break the story about Mickey's illegitimate daughter. What was her name? Sharlene? Cheryl?

The more he thought about it, the stronger the sensation of connection became. Mickey Gross had a daughter. Mickey had died. Chuck had disappeared. Like John Dillinger and Jim Morrison, rumors swirled that

Mickey had faked his own death. Certainly, he'd talked about it onstage.

Maybe Mickey really was still alive. If so, he would be able to provide some insight into finding Chuck. It seemed crazy, but it was worth a shot. Duckie kept thinking back to the message Chuck had left, especially the plaintive "please" at the very end. It made Duckie's stomach sink to think that his friend had reached out for help, and Duckie had ghosted him. Maybe if he hadn't been such a self-pitying snotrag, he could have helped Chuck before things had gotten too bad.

Duckie decided that he should try to get in touch with Mickey's daughter. If Mickey was still alive, she was his best bet to track him down. The problem was that he had no idea how to contact her.

But he knew someone who did.

Chapter 33

The headquarters of the Official Mickey Gross Fan Club was in the basement of a rundown ranch house northeast of Topeka, Kansas. Doobie Collins had run the club since he'd founded it in 1988. It was a fulltime job, or at least that's what he told his Ma whenever she asked him when he was going to get out of the basement and find a job and an apartment and a girlfriend.

Duckie had been a member of the fan club since he was twelve. Over the years, Duckie had been actively involved with the group enough to have a personal relationship of sorts with Doobie Collins.

He'd emailed Doobie saying that he wanted to talk in person about a highly sensitive matter. He'd hoped to pique Doobie's interest without giving too much away. It had taken several days for Doobie to respond to the email, and further cajoling to get him to agree to a phone call.

"What do you want?" asked Doobie when Duckie finally got him on the phone.

"Well, I'll tell ya," said Duckie. "I'm looking to buy some Mickey memorabilia. Got a lucky scratch-off lottery ticket and I'm looking to splurge."

"Well, you can't have any of mine," said Doobie. "It's not for sale!"

Duckie figured as much. Doobie had a contrarian streak. Duckie knew that he was going to have to finesse Doobie to get what he wanted. Normally, that wasn't really Duckie's strong suit, but with Doobie, he was dealing with someone even more socially awkward than he was. "Hey, Doobie," he said. "I'm not trying to bite your style or anything. I know that

I'll never be able match your collection, man. Hell, *that* stuff should be in a museum."

"Then what are you bugging me for?" asked Doobie. "Why dontcha just go to eBay or something."

"Ah, all they got on eBay is garbage," said Duckie. "You know that. Nothing there worth a shit, all just cheap junk. I'm looking for some high-end stuff, know what I mean?"

"So you got the money for some high-end stuff?"

"I told you, I got some money from a lottery scratcher. I'm good."

"How much are we talking about here?" asked Doobie.

"That's on a need-to-know basis, bro," said Duckie. "I'm sure you understand my position."

"Y'know," said Doobie. "I could just hang up on you right now. I've got a lot of important things to do."

Duckie doubted it. "Look, you know me, Doobie," he said. "I've been a member of the fan club for, like, fifteen years. You know I'm a true believer, and I know that you got the juice to hook me up with some premium merch."

"Whaddaya have in mind?"

"I want the tie he was wearing at the Apollo show," he said. "The one in '89." Mickey Gross had played an infamous show at the Apollo Theater in New York. He'd done a lot of amazing riffing, but some of what he said had riled the notoriously raucous Apollo audience. The show had to be stopped, and the cops were called in to restore order.

"You want the tie from the '89 Apollo show? The one that looks like a piano keyboard?"

"That's right," said Duckie. "Like I said, I'm after quality memorabilia, not some thrift-store LP with a fake autograph."

There was a long pause. Duckie knew that Mickey's daughter Cheryl owned that tie. In one of the few TV interviews she'd given after the news of her paternity had come out, she'd been wearing it.

"Okay, Mr. True Believer," said Doobie. "We both know who owns that tie. And, yes, I can get in touch with the owner of that tie. But it's gonna cost you."

Here it comes, thought Duckie. "Yeah, sure," he said. "What's the deal?"

"First, I want any bootlegs you have that I don't. I don't suspect that you have much that's not already in my collection, but you never know."

"Done," said Duckie. "Anything else?"

"Of course," said Doobie. "Additionally, I will require you to purchase a super-diamond-platinum membership in the club."

"'Super-diamond-platinum membership'?" asked Duckie. "What's that get me?"

"Me not hanging up right now."

"Yeah, okay, and how much is a super-diamond-platinum membership gonna cost me?"

"Five hundred bucks."

"Five *hundred?*" said Duckie. "Jesus, you gotta be kidding!"

"You said you got the big bucks," said Doobie.

"I said I won a scratch-off, not the fuckin' Powerball," said Duckie. "One hundred."

"No way," said Doobie. "This is a very special request. Hell, she might not even be willing to talk to you."

"I know," said Duckie. "And I sure as hell ain't gonna give you a wad of money if she's not even gonna talk to me."

"Okay, okay. I get the bootlegs either way, but you don't have to buy the membership unless she agrees to talk with you."

"Yeah, okay, but not for five hundred. One fifty."

"Three fifty."

"One seventy-five," said Duckie. "Final offer."

"Okay, fine," said Doobie. "You're robbing me blind."

He was getting nearly two hundred bucks for making a phone call, but Duckie knew better than to complain. "Good deal," he said. "Thanks, Doobie. I'll email you a list of bootlegs."

"Yeah, okay," grumbled Doobie.

Duckie sent Doobie a list of the Mickey Gross bootlegs he had. Doobie replied almost immediately, saying that he had all but three. Duckie suspected that he already had all of them, but was just being a pain in the ass about it. Still, a deal was a deal, and Duckie dutifully went out and bought a pack of blank CDs.

Soon after he sent the CDs out, he got an email from Doobie reading, "Client agrees to discuss merch. Send money for email addy."

Duckie went to his PayPal account and sent the money for the "super-diamond-platinum" membership. Doobie responded by forwarding an AOL email address.

Duckie started to feel optimistic. He sent a thoughtfully worded email to the AOL address and wondered if he'd even get a reply. He didn't have to wait long. The next day, he got a reply from Cheryl. It said, *Need to discuss transaction face-to-face.*

Cool, thought Duckie. Finally he was getting somewhere. He replied, *No problem. FaceTime or Skype?*

No, came the reply. *In person. I need to make sure you're serious.*

"Jesus!" said Duckie This was turning into a real pain in the ass. Well, it was too late to bail now – he had too much invested, both emotionally and financially. He wrote back, *Where?*

L.A.

That wasn't so bad – at least it wasn't New York, or Miami, or Kathmandu. *Works for me,* he wrote.

Chapter 34

A week later, Duckie got off his cheap flight, picked up his cheap rental car and drove it to his cheap motel. Once he'd settled in, he entered the address for the diner in Northridge where he was to meet Cheryl. It didn't look like it was too far away, but he decided to get going so he could get there early. It was a good call, as the traffic was crazy. *How can people live like this?* he thought as he battled the road warriors on the 405. The trip took him three times longer than he'd expected, and he ended up pulling into the diner parking lot ten minutes late.

Stepping through the front door of the Friendly Family Diner was like stepping back sixty years in time. It was as if someone had dismantled an all-American diner around the time when Kennedy had been elected, carefully packed and stored it, then reassembled it in a tedious strip mall.

It wasn't all New Frontier chic, though. A modern whiteboard behind the cash register showed the specials of the day. The prices were definitely twenty-first century Southern California. And the retro jukebox was cranking out Don Henley's "Boys of Summer."

"Hssst," came a voice from a booth near the door. "You looking for me, funny boy?"

Duckie whipped his head around to see a dark-haired woman giving him the eye. She looked to be in her early thirties. She had an oval face with a small nose and high cheekbones, and straight black hair pulled back in a rough ponytail. She was wearing an oversized Cal State sweatshirt and no makeup, although it looked like she could really rock her looks once she got her warpaint on. In fact, she was pretty cute. Duckie felt a little tuggle in his lower belly. He could probably go for this woman, under the right circumstances.

"I've been looking for someone like you my entire life," said Duckie. He was surprised to hear the words coming out of his mouth. He was pretty damn nervous about this meeting, and wasn't even sure how to get it started. This situation was going to require finesse, something that he knew damn well he had in short supply. His mouth had a mind of its own. It got him in trouble plenty of times, but sometimes it did him a solid. He knew how to read an audience, and he could see that his wisecrack had landed favorably. He tried on his most charming grin and slipped into the booth.

"Ooh, funny and romantic," said Cheryl. "This must be my lucky day."

"Hey, maybe we'll both get lucky," said Duckie.

"Don't hold your breath, Slick."

He widened his best promo headshot smile and stuck out his hand. "Duckie Dunne, comedian at large."

She grabbed his hand, gave it a listless pump, and took a sip from her coffee mug. "I'm Cheryl," she said. Duckie looked at her, hard. Was there a family resemblance with Mickey? Maybe. It was hard to say; Mickey had a pretty average-looking face. The only thing that bore a close resemblance were her sparkling blue eyes.

"You didn't bring anyone with you, huh?" asked Cheryl. "No press? No paparazzi?"

"No, just me." Duckie could understand her caution. Cheryl Watson had been a nine-days wonder in the tabloid press five years ago. Word got out that she was the illegitimate kid of a dead celebrity, and the tabloids went nuts. It was front page material in the celebrity-stalker rags for about a week, then had been mostly forgotten.

"Good," said Cheryl. "I hate those fuckin' creeps, y'know?"

"I dunno," said Duckie. "I feel lucky if the local arts rag spells my name right. I'm not exactly an A-lister, you know?"

"Oh, yeah, I know," said Cheryl. "I've seen your YouTube videos. Not exactly Netflix special material. Still, you've got good timing – really good. You can't learn that, although you could use an improv workshop or two.

Couldn't hurt."

"Shit," said Duckie. "What the hell would you know about it?"

Cheryl took a long sip of coffee and stared at him over the rim of the sky-blue mug. There were clumps of old mascara around her eyes. "Yeah, I know comedy, Duckie-boy. You might say it's in my blood."

"Okay, you got a point there," conceded Duckie. "Look, I'm just a little blown out, y'know, actually meeting you. Maybe it's your natural charm, or maybe it's because I haven't eaten in a while. I'm definitely gonna need some fuel to keep going."

A waitress wandered by and Duckie asked for a cup of black coffee and a menu. She nodded absently and wandered off.

"So, Mr. Funnyman," said Cheryl. "We've got something to discuss, huh?"

"Mickey Gross was your dad?" asked Duckie, still trying to wrap his head around the fact that he was talking with the daughter of his hero. "Really?"

Cheryl put her mug down, slopping coffee onto the sparkling Formica tabletop. "No, asshole," she spat. "I just made that up so I could waste time with tenth-rate comedy wannabes!"

Duckie held up his hands. "Sorry," he said. "I don't mean any disrespect. It's just that … I dunno … he's kinda like my idol. I know that sounds cheesy as hell, but it's true. If it weren't for him, I wouldn't have gone into comedy."

"Hell, I hope you don't hold that against him," said Cheryl. "It's a shitty way to live."

"You ain't tellin' me anything I don't already know," said Duckie. "It sucks, but I love it. Don't ask me why."

Cheryl took a sip of her coffee and muttered something about the stupidity of comics. The Don Henley song ended and the juke followed it with "Ultimate Recursion" by Chelsea's Birthday Monkey. Duckie grunted.

"What?" said Cheryl.

"Oh, it's just that I haven't heard this song in a while. I was a huge CBM fan when I was in high school. Guess I still am. A CBM fan, not in high school."

"I could believe either one," said Cheryl.

"You're funny," said Duckie. "You should work up an act."

"Hell, no. I'm not enough of a masochist for that," said Cheryl. "You know, Mickey opened up for them once."

"What, CBM? No way! When?"

"It was a long time ago, back when both of their careers were just getting going. Eighty-seven, eighty-eight, maybe. Anyway, Mickey had met CBM's David Starr at one of their gigs, or one of his. They hit it off, and Starr asked him to open for a festival they were headlining in Detroit."

"No shit," said Duckie. He was fascinated. He was a huge geek about Mickey Gross and Chelsea's Birthday Monkey, but he had never heard that they'd performed together. "That's fuckin' amazing. I thought I would have heard about this. Is there a tape?"

"No, and it's probably just as well. Mickey bombed, big time. The crowd turned ugly, and ended up throwing beer bottles. I guess it set the tone for the rest of the show, because it was a bad scene for everyone who played. There was a thunderstorm in the middle of Toto's set, and by the time CBM went out the crowd was fuckin' hostile. Then, to cap it all off, the cops busted the show afterwards, and hauled half of the bands off to jail."

"Oh yeah!" said Duckie, fascinated. "I heard about *that*. I had no idea that Mickey opened that night."

"Yeah, well, even a knucklehead like you should understand that it wasn't something he was particularly proud of."

"What about Mickey? Did he get busted, too?"

"Almost. A cop put the arm on him, but just then his girlfriend flashed her tits, and Mickey was able to slip off."

"That's awesome," said Duckie. "I never heard that story."

"Then I guess you don't know everything then, do you?"

"Why didn't you tell the *American Investigator* that story? It's got everything a tabloid story needs: violence, celebrities behaving badly, tits."

"You really are dumber than you look," said Cheryl. "What, you think I'm going to tell that rag anything other than the absolute bare minimum?"

"Hell, no. Why'd you talk to them at all?"

"For the money, honey. Look at it from my point of view. I grew up in Binghamton, totally normal life. Mom, Dad, little brother, a dog named

Rover. No shit, his name was *Rover*. Then, on my eighteenth birthday, Mom and Dad sat me down and told me I was adopted. How bad d'you think that fucked me up?"

"Pretty bad, apparently."

Cheryl flipped him the bird. "You know how all that happened, right? Michael Gross, the black sheep son of a well-to-do Long Island dentist, knocks up Margaret McGuire, the daughter of an equally well-to-do banker. They're both seventeen years old. The black sheep son is a good kid, but has no ambition, wants to be a fer-Chrissakes comedian. His family is Jewish and wants an abortion; her family is Catholic and says absolutely not. Michael gets shuffled off to the Big Apple to try his hand at the yuk-yuk business. Margaret gets shuffled off to a convent upstate until the baby comes and gets adopted out. And that's how I wound up as the daughter of Brent and Madge Watson of Binghamton, New York."

"Yeah, that part I know. How did you find out that Mickey was your dad?"

"Some asshole from the *American Investigator* called me. It was a couple of months after Mickey died. Someone had spilled the beans. I dunno who. I heard that one of Margaret's sisters kinda let it slip to someone on the *Investigator*, probably for a couple hundred bucks. The paper put their sleaziest investigators on it and managed to dredge up a birth certificate and some adoption records. The *Investigator* broke the story, and after that it was off to the races with the other tabloids. A mad whirlwind for a few weeks, then nothing. I'm not proud about it, but I was between jobs and needed the money. What would you have done?"

"Same damn thing, probably," admitted Duckie. He flipped open the menu. "Breakfast served all day" was printed in bold letters across the top. Perfect. He ordered a tall stack of sourdough pancakes and a side of bacon.

"Okay," said Cheryl. "Enough of the pleasant chit-chit. Let's get down to business." She reached into her purse and pulled out a Ziploc baggie with a folded piece of black and white cloth in it.

"What's that?" asked Duckie.

"Dumbass, it's the tie you were asking about," said Cheryl. "The one you wanna buy? The infamous Apollo show? Hello?"

"Oh, yeah," said Duckie. "Can I see it?"

"Sure," said Cheryl, holding up the bag. Duckie held out his hand, but Cheryl shook her head. "Not until you cross my palm with silver."

"How much?"

"Two grand, firm."

Duckie held up his hands. "Wow, that's pretty steep," he said. "Where did you get it?"

"What do you mean, 'Where did I get it'?" asked Cheryl. "Mickey Gross is my father, doofus!"

"Yeah," said Duckie. "But you didn't find out about that until he was dead. So how did you get it?"

Cheryl looked flustered, and glanced around the diner. "Well, uh, a lawyer contacted me. Said he had a bunch of Mickey's stuff and the family didn't want it. So he sent it to me. So are you gonna buy it or what?"

Duckie ignored the question. "You ever heard of Chuck Marshall?" he asked.

"Huh? Yeah. Why?" said Cheryl. "I saw the first couple episodes of his new show. Funny guy. Wasn't there some weird shit with someone from the show getting killed, and then he took off. What happened with that?"

"Nothing," said Duckie. "He's still gone. No one knows where. He's just disappeared."

"And why would you care?"

"Because he's my best friend," said Duckie. "We grew up together, started doing comedy together back in high school. Then my family moved, so I didn't see him as much, but we still were close – sort of. But now he's disappeared. I'm trying to find him."

"Ah, the old best friends bit," said Cheryl. "One makes it big and one languishes in the sticks. Jealous much, Duckie?"

"No – shit, no!" said Duckie hotly. That wasn't entirely truthful, but Duckie didn't feel the need to go into detail. "Why are you being such an asshole?"

"I'm about two seconds away from walking out on you, fan boy."

"Okay, look, I'm sorry," said Duckie. "I'm just a little keyed, right? He's my friend, and I think he might be in trouble. Yeah, he's funnier than me. He's funnier than practically *everybody*. He could be the next Carlin, the next Pryor … or the next Mickey Gross."

"Yeah, okay," said Cheryl. "Sorry I'm being a little bitchy. I've had a couple of rough days. Anyway, why do you want to bother me about your buddy?"

Duckie paused. This was the make-or-break moment. Things with Cheryl hadn't developed well up to this point, but he had come too far to back out now. He just had to pick his words carefully. "It's just that, well … I guess I figured that you might know a thing or two about what comedians do when they want to disappear."

Cheryl froze. Her mouth hardened into a steel-straight line; her blue eyes glittered. Finally, she said, "What the fuck are you talking about?"

Duckie resisted the impulse to roll his eyes. "I'm talking about the rumors that Mickey Gross faked his own death. I figured there might be some truth there."

"Yeah," said Cheryl, biting off the words. "So what?"

"I figure that if he is still alive, there have to be at least one or two people who know about it. One of them would most likely be you."

"Did Doobie tell you something? That son of a bitch! I'll castrate him! I swear to God, I'll fly out there to Omaha and cut off his goolies with a butter knife!"

"Doobie didn't tell me jack shit," said Duckie. "And it's Topeka, not Omaha."

"Topeka, Omaha, who cares? I'm gonna cut his balls off."

"All I told Doobie was that I had heard that you had a piece of memorabilia that I wanted," said Duckie. "That's it. The bastard charged me an arm and a leg to put me in touch with you, but he didn't say anything about you knowing Mickey's whereabouts. On the other hand, you've pretty much just told me yourself."

"Oh, bullshit!" said Cheryl loudly. Duckie could hear a quaver in her voice.

She knew.

"Oh, c'mon," said Duckie. "First, you know a salacious story about Mickey and CBM that nobody's ever heard. Also, the story about how you got the tie is utter crap. No lawyer sent you a box of memorabilia. Mickey gave that to you himself. Furthermore, you said earlier that 'Mickey Gross *is* my father,' not *was*."

"Fuck," said Cheryl. "You bastard. Are you even interested in buying the tie, or was that a ruse so you could destroy my life?"

"Cheryl, I'm a struggling comic that lives in Portland," said Duckie. "I work third shift in a print shop to pay the rent. Just the flight here and the car rental is gonna drain my bank account. Sorry."

"Shit," said Cheryl. "I really could've used that money. Fuck. So what do you want, jerk-off?"

Duckie looked at the plate of pancakes that had materialized. Then back up at Cheryl. "Cheryl, when was the last time you talked to your dad? To Mickey, I mean."

She stared at him, wide-eyed. "Fuck, no," she muttered. "No, you gotta be fuckin' kiddin' me."

"Aw, c'mon, Cheryl," said Duckie, leaning in, still striving for the sincere-and-harmless effect. "I just want to talk to him. I've got a gut feeling that he could help me find Chuck."

Cheryl shook her head.

"Mickey Gross started talking – on stage – about faking his own death at least ten years before he supposedly died of pancreatic cancer. I think he liked the idea of getting out from under the burden of his own fame."

Cheryl's mouth had hardened into a nearly nonexistent line. "Fuck you," she said through clenched teeth. "I'm outta here."

She grabbed her purse and made to get up. Duckie's hand shot out and grabbed her wrist. "Let go of me," she said in the same clipped tone.

"Cheryl, please," said Duckie. "Please just listen to me."

She didn't say anything, but made no further moved to leave.

"You gotta understand," said Duckie. "Chuck Marshall was like a brother to me. We pretty much grew up together. We psyched each other up to try doing comedy. He ended being a helluva lot more successful than me.

Was I jealous? Sure, a little, not a lot. Because he's better than me, funnier. And because he's my brother. Now he's in trouble. Don't ask me how I know; I just do. I'd do anything to find him. See?" He gestured around at the suspiciously homey interior of the Friendly Family Diner. "Why do you think I came down here to talk to you? Not to buy some damn collectable! If you need money, put that tie on eBay. I guarantee you'll get more for it than I could ever pay. I came down here to try to help my friend. You know what it's like to have someone taken away from you. Can't you help me out?"

Cheryl just stared at Duckie for a long time. The moment drew out, cold and slow as a glacier. Just as Duckie figured she was going to bail, Cheryl slapped her purse down on the table. "I can't believe I'm doing this," she muttered. She fished out a pen and snatched a napkin from the chrome dispenser on the tabletop. She checked her cell phone, scrawled something on the napkin, and thrust it across to him.

"There, you sonofabitch!" she said, and stood up. "I hope your friend's okay. You, on the other hand, can drop fucking dead." She turned and marched out the front door without looking back.

Duckie looked at the napkin. It had an address in Tucson. He looked up to see Cheryl's car peeling out of the strip mall parking lot. Oh well, she wasn't exactly a candidate for the Duckie Dunne Fan Club, but she had come through with the goods. Duckie shrugged and finished eating his pancakes.

He then retreated to his plastic room at the airport Motel 6 to consider his next move. He was a little surprised that things had gone as well as they had. He had pretty much solved a mystery that had been bedeviling comedy fans for years, and he felt a flush of excitement. On the other hand, he wasn't surprised at all. Somehow, he had known that Mickey was still alive, and that Cheryl Watson was in contact with him. The amazing part was that he had been able to convince her to share his address.

Duckie examined the napkin and looked up the address on his phone. It appeared to be a small apartment complex on the south side of Tucson. He was scheduled to fly back to Portland tomorrow morning. It seemed foolish to go back to Portland, then turn around and get back down to Tucson. It made more sense to push on and make it to Tucson now. Besides, he was on a roll.

He made a few calls. Work wasn't a problem – he wasn't scheduled to go in for another three days. The rental car company was happy to let him keep the car for as long as he wanted. The airline was, of course, the real bastard. After nearly two hours of waiting on hold, and being shuffled from one customer service agent to another, he finally determined that the least painful option would be to drive to Tucson and back, then fly home from L.A. on standby.

According to Google, it was about five hundred miles to Tucson, maybe an eight-hour drive. He was tired and had already paid for the room. He decided to stay overnight, and head out first thing in the morning.

He then made a reservation at a cheap motel in Tucson, got a sandwich from a nearby Subway and watched a Clint Eastwood movie on the hotel room TV. It was still pretty early, but he dug a dusty Ambien out of the bottom of his kit bag. He kept a couple stashed for his infrequent out-of-town gigs. Despite the food, it hit him pretty quickly, and he was conked out before the sun went down.

The next morning, he got up before the day was old, wolfed down the rest of his turkey club, and was booming down the highway before 4 am, headed into the desert.

Chapter 35

About fifty miles east of Indio, Duckie decided that he hated the desert. Everything was too jagged. The sky was weird and too bright. His eyes hurt. It got worse as he entered Tucson. He checked into his cheapo motel and drove to the address that Cheryl had given him.

It was a faded wood-framed apartment building with washed-out walls, a gray and rickety-looking exterior walkway servicing the units. He backed the rental into the corner of the parking lot with the nose pointed towards the entrance. He watched the door to apartment 203. Mickey Gross – or whatever he was calling himself now – was inside, or would be. It was just a matter of time until he showed.

Duckie had bought a foldable windshield screen at a Circle K just as soon as he'd gotten off the interstate. It was cardboard, and had a picture of a pair of sunglasses printed on it. It was a good investment, as the sun blazed brutally on the crushed-gravel parking lot. He arranged it so that he could watch the door to unit 203 through the notch in the middle. It would be difficult for anyone to see inside Duckie's car, but he could keep an easy eye on his target.

Not that it mattered – most of the people who emerged from the cracker-box apartment building walked out with their heads down, and climbed into one of the beaters scattered around the parking lot, or trudged to the bus stop a quarter mile away.

Duckie was prepared for a long wait. He'd loaded up on stakeout supplies at the Circle K: couple of Clud Bars, a liter of water, two boxes of Pop Tarts, a fistful of beef jerky, and a 32-ounce cup of black coffee.

A few scraggly bushes clung to the dirt around the periphery of the gravel parking lot. This was littered with crushed beer cans, empty burrito wrappers and broken glass that kicked back wicked reflections of the desert sun.

Beyond the apartment were miles of nothing, just flat dirt and rocks, baked a sterile gray-brown. In the distance, Interstate 10 sliced through the wasteland like a scalpel incision. Duckie could see the sun heliographing off the passing cars. Far to the south, a mountain range rose up like fangs erupting from a broken jaw. From this distance, they appeared to be a uniform dust-gray color, a cheap painted backdrop to a Z-grade cowboy movie.

There was some motion in the front of the apartment, and Duckie slid down in his seat. A woman came out of the door of 204. She shuffled to a battered Datsun pickup, started it up and drove off.

The vicious sun rose higher. Duckie rolled down the windows and slumped in his seat. He was starting to doze off when he noticed motion at 203. The door opened. A man came out.

Duckie slid down in his seat, grabbed the door handle, and prepared to make his move. The man turned and locked the six separate locks on the door. He wore a loose-fitting red robe. A pair of heavy glasses gripped his closely shorn head like a spider grappling a tennis ball.

Duckie hadn't anticipated this amorphous creature. In his mind, he figured that Mickey would look pretty much like he had on that final Letterman show, albeit a little grayer and scragglier. Duckie squinted. The gray color of the head-stubble indicated that the age was in the ballpark. Beyond that, no resemblance. The man descended the stairs and walked across the parking lot towards the distant bus stop. Duckie could feel his pulse hammering in his throat. Could this person really be his comedy hero?

Duckie remained momentarily frozen, uncertain of what to do. He had not been expecting a Dalai Lama wannabe. Maybe Cheryl had just been fucking with him, had given him a random address or something. A voice in his head yelled, *Go, idiot!* Duckie jumped out of the car and slammed the door.

The man in the robe looked around at the sound, then disappeared behind a bushy clump of cholla cactus. Duckie quick-walked to catch up, his Chuck Taylors crunching loudly on the gravel. By the time Duckie made the sidewalk, the man in the robe was already halfway to the bus stop, lightly jogging. Duckie picked up the pace. Ahead of him, the man in the robe looked over his shoulder, and began moving even faster. Duckie broke into a fast trot. The man in the robe went for a full sprint, then pulled up by the bus stop. He looked frantically up and down the street, but there was hardly any traffic, and no bus in sight. Duckie closed the gap.

When he was about twenty feet away, the man in the robe spun to face him, held his hands palms together in front of his face and made a slight bow. "Namaste, brother," he said. "I carry no cash."

"Huh?" said Duckie. "Who's nasty?" His head spun. He squinted at the face behind the RPG eyewear. It *could* be Mickey; it was hard to tell with no hair. The sparkling blue eyes did look familiar, though.

"Seriously," said the man, "I carry no cash. No wallet or anything." He lowered his hands and tucked them into the folds of his robe. "I want no trouble, friend."

"I know, I know, it's not that." said Duckie, unsure how to proceed. "I need to talk to you ... I need ..."

"You need your fix, I understand. I wish I could help you, but as I said, I have no cash with which to purchase narcotics."

"Narcotics?" asked Duckie, now thoroughly confused. What the hell was this guy talking about?

"No!" shouted the man. "I have no drugs! Please step away from me!"

"C'mon, man," said Duckie. How could he get through to this guy? Maybe he wasn't Mickey Gross after all. He held his hands out, reaching for him, supplicating. "Look. It's not what you think! I just gotta know. Look, man, are you Mickey Gross?"

The man winced. "My name is Karma Zhimay," he said.

"What? Bullshit! C'mon, man, I been bustin' my ass trying to find you!

I need your help finding my friend. Your name ain't Chimichanga or whatever. You're Mickey Gross. I know. I'm your biggest fan!"

"All right, motherfucker," said the man in the robe. His bland accent was now replaced with the New York sneer that had graced many hours of recordings. "You fuckin' asked for this!"

Of course, Duckie knew that voice – he had listened repeatedly, obsessively to hundreds of hours of recordings. He broke into a huge, sunny smile as his childhood hero yanked a can of pepper spray out of his robe and blasted him square in the face.

"Ggahhhh!" said Duckie. He doubled over, wheezing and trying not to puke. "You … asshole!" he gasped. Then he puked.

"I'm sorry, I'm so sorry!" said Karma Zhimay. "I despise violence, but … that name. You had to use that name."

"Jesus … Christ," wheezed Duckie. "What? Why?"

"You don't understand. You … you just took me by surprise," said Karma Zhimay. Behind him, a bus pulled to the curb with a mighty diesel fart, and the doors flapped open. Karma Zhimay looked to the bus, then back at Duckie, then back to the bus again.

Duckie retched.

Karma Zhimay's shoulders slumped. He turned and waved the bus on. The bus driver gave him a sour look and pulled away.

"There goes my last chance outta here," said Karma Zhimay. "Shit, I knew this would happen sooner or later. Hoped it would be later. It was Cheryl, wasn't it?"

Duckie, still doubled over, nodded.

"Well, I can't blame her. She's been through a lot because of me. Okay, chief, let's go get you cleaned up." He took the spasming Duckie gently by the shoulder and began leading him back to the apartment.

Chapter 36

"Almost there," said Karma Zhimay. He led the blind and gasping Duckie up the stairs to his apartment door. He reached under his robe and pulled out a wad of keys on a shoelace, opened the door, and propelled Duckie inside.

"Jesus … burns …" sputtered Duckie. "Still can't see. What was that shit? Nerve gas?"

"I am so, so sorry," said Karma Zhimay. "It was a can of pepper spray. I've never had to use it on anyone before."

"Well, you didn't have to use it on *me!*"

"Again, my apologies are boundless. You startled me, especially when you used my old name. And then you wouldn't back off." He seemed to think about it, and get more perturbed as he did so. "Yeah, you were kind of an a-hole, kid," he said. "You're lucky a face full of pepper spray was all you got. You hassle some people in this neighborhood like that, man, and you go home with a nine-millimeter trepanation." He closed his eyes, took a deep breath, and began muttering to himself.

"Oh shit," said Duckie. "You're not having a psychotic episode or something are you?" It occurred to him that he was alone and concealed from the world with a weirdo who had just attacked him. But it wasn't just any weirdo; it was Mickey Gross, *the* Mickey Gross. Wasn't it?

"Just saying a little prayer," said Karma Zhimay. "Trying to get my head together, okay? This is not how I foresaw this day unfolding."

"Yeah, me neither," said Duckie.

"If you don't mind me asking, just what did you think was going to happen?" asked Karma Zhimay. "You say you've spent much effort trying to track down this comedian, a person who clearly did not want to be found. So you decide to just show up in this person's life without warning, and do what exactly? Sing him a song? Present him with an award? What were you going to do, huh, smart guy?"

"I was going to ask him for help," said Duckie.

"So you said," said Karma Zhimay. "And you could certainly use it. First things first, I suppose. Let's wash out your eyes."

Karma Zhimay pulled a chair over to the studio apartment sink, and arranged Duckie so his head was hanging back over the sink. His eyes were still almost swollen shut.

"Well, they say that milk is good for washing out pepper spray," said Karma Zhimay. Duckie heard him rummaging around in the fridge. "Okay, this'll do," he said to himself. "Okay, I'm going to flush out your eyes with this milk."

Duckie felt the cool liquid pour onto his swollen painful eyelids. It felt okay, but it wasn't the relief he'd been hoping for.

"There?" asked Karma Zhimay. "Is that better?"

"Not really. Kinda burns, too."

"Really? That's too bad. I would have thought that this almond milk would be just as good as regular milk."

"What?" asked Duckie. "That was ALMOND MILK? But I have a severe NUT ALLERGY! Oh my God, it burns!"

He fell to the ground with his hands clutched to his eyes, wailing piteously and trying not to laugh. Through the gap in his swollen eyelids, he could see Karma Zhimay gaping in horror. Duckie let him wallow in it for another five seconds, then bounded to his feet. "Wait, did I say *nut* allergy?" he asked. "I meant *penicillin* allergy. I always get those two mixed up. Sorry."

"Oh, Jesus!" said Karma Zhimay. "Oh, Jesus Christ! You scared the crap out of me! Why would you do that?"

"Why would I act like you loaded my eyes with a chemical irritant?" said Duckie. "Because you loaded my eyes with a chemical irritant!"

"Okay, you got me there. Let's just get your eyes rinsed with water and call it good."

"Yeah, great," said Duckie. "I think I can handle it from here." He lurched over to the sink and began splashing water in his face. After a few minutes, he was able to open his eyes almost the entire way.

He looked around the apartment. It was a cramped studio. The walls were beige cinder block. The only natural light came from a small window in the front wall. Directly back from the door was the kitchenette. A small card table was shoved up to the wall by the kitchenette, with a couple of mismatched folding chairs. In the far corner was a twin bed, with a rusty air-conditioning unit penetrating the wall just above it. In the center of the mud-brown carpet was a shrine with a dark wooden Buddha statue on top. On the steps below were an assortment of incense burners, beads, cloths and photographs of Asian men with shaved heads and robes. A small, square cushion sat in front of the shrine.

Karma Zhimay retreated to the corner of the room. He sat cross-legged on the bed, breathing deeply and eyeing Duckie intently. "So you found out where I was – who I was – through Cheryl Watson, huh?"

"Yeah, but don't be mad at her. I kinda weaseled the information out of her. I haven't told anyone else. Hell, I didn't believe it myself until ten minutes ago."

"Well, I'd appreciate it if you kept it to yourself, although you probably won't. I don't blame Cheryl, either. I knew it was a risk getting in touch with her. There wasn't any way I couldn't, though. I never really stopped thinking about her, after her mother was bundled off to the convent. An embarrassing family problem swept away in the classic Long Island upper-middle-class way.

"But I can't blame Cheryl for anything. I put her through hell, I know. I put myself through hell, too, once that article came out and I found out who my daughter was. I had to weigh the benefits of getting in touch with her with the possible exposure that I wasn't really dead."

"About that," said Duckie. "What really happened, man?"

Karma Zhimay held up his hand. "You were smart enough to find me, so I guess you're smart enough to figure that out. All I'll say is that fame isn't all it's cracked up to be. Your personal life, your privacy, all go down the crapper. I'd had enough of show business, and I knew that I wouldn't be able to leave on my own terms. I really wanted to do a deep-dive in my study of Eastern religions. Buddhism and Bön." He plucked at his robe.

"What's Bön?"

"It's the religion that Tibetans practiced before Buddhism showed up. Very similar, but Bön is more … um, mystical." He sighed. "If I could do everything all over again, I'd make my exit differently. Hope that's answer enough for you, because that's all I'm saying."

"Yeah, okay, man," muttered Duckie.

"But you saw Cheryl, right?" asked Karma Zhimay. "How's she doing? Is she okay? Last time I saw her, she looked a little skinny."

"She seemed fine, I guess," said Duckie. "It was kind of a weird meeting. We didn't spend a lot of time discussing our health or respective outlooks on life."

"Well, speaking of health, you look a little better. We're going to have to wash those clothes, though."

Duckie eyed him critically. Was he coming on to him or something? It didn't seem likely, but you never knew. Besides, his shirt reeked of pepper spray, and there was some on his jeans as well. "Okay," said Duckie. "But I'm keeping my undies on."

"That is good," said Karma Zhimay. He hauled a battered plastic laundry hamper from the tiny closet and presented it to Duckie. The two stared at each other. "Well?" asked Karma Zhimay.

"I'm not stripping down with you watching," said Duckie.

"Oh, for goodness sake!" said Karmay Zhimay. "Look, I'll find you something to wear, then I'll go in the bathroom while you change, okay?" Without waiting for an answer, he went to the closet and pulled out a chewed-up white plastic trash bag. He opened it up and tossed Duckie a tie-dyed t-shirt and a pair of worn sweatpants.

"Holy moly!" said Duckie, holding up the shirt. "This thing looks ancient! Didja pick this up at Woodstock?"

Karma Zhimay laughed. "No, not quite that old," he said. "But I'm pretty sure I wore that thing to a couple of Dead shows in the '80s. Look, I'm going to take a leak. You can get changed."

"So, are you really Mickey Gross?" Duckie asked him when he emerged from the bathroom.

Karma Zhimay stared at him for a long, long time before replying. "If I thought there was even a miniscule chance of successfully denying it, I would. I think it's a little late for that now. To answer your question, I am Karma Zhimay. The man who went by the name of Mickey Gross is gone now. Yet that man had a profound influence on my life, and shaped me into the person I am now. I have no doubt that I could say the same for you."

"Huh? What do you mean?"

"Back there on the sidewalk, you said that you were Mickey Gross's 'number one fan,' right?"

"Yeah."

"So what do you do for a living?"

"Well, I normally work graveyard shift in a print shop, but I actually do stand-up. Mostly local stuff around Portland, maybe some out of town gigs on the weekend."

Karma Zhimay began laughing uproariously. "Oh, that's just perfect! A stand-up comic! Yes, yes, clearly Mickey Gross has had a profound influence on who you are today. Heck, I'm not doing any stand-up. Maybe *you're* really Mickey Gross!"

"Don't I wish!" gushed Duckie. "I'd give my left nut to be one-tenth as funny and talented as you!"

"You still don't get it," sighed Karma Zhimay. "I'm not a funny and talented stand-up comedian, man. Maybe I was once, but I'm not that person anymore."

"Sure you are! Just because you shaved your head, put on a bedsheet, and gave yourself a goofy name doesn't mean you're not the same person."

"Those are all superficialities. Tell me…" He paused. "Hold on, you haven't even told me your name. Maybe it's Mickey Gross, eh?"

"Maybe it's Fucknuts McFarland," said Duckie sourly. He was now pretty certain of two things: That this was actually Mickey Gross and that he was messing with his head.

"If you say so," said Karmay Zhimay. "Tell me, Fucknuts, are you the same person you were ten years ago?"

"Well, duh," said Duckie. "Of course I am. And you can call me Duckie."

"Is that your real name?"

"No, but it's what I answer to. And it's better than Fucknuts."

"Ah, something we have in common: We've given ourselves new names. Interesting. Anyway, you say you're the same person you were ten years ago. Science tells us that the human body replaces all of its cells every seven to ten years. Dig it? All of the cells, the molecules and atoms that made up your body of a decade ago are long gone. The Ducknuts of ten years ago is dispersed to the four winds."

"Ducknuts?"

"First you tell me that you're called Fucknuts. Then you say you answer to Duckie. I thought I'd split the difference."

"Swell. I guess I had that coming. Look, I didn't go to all this effort to get a philosophy lesson. I need your help."

"So you said," said Karma Zhimay. "Why should I help you?"

Duckie was about to whip out a smart-ass answer, but his jaw just hung open. Why *should* this guy help him? Because he was his hero. Well, that didn't mean jack shit. Mickey Gross could be a real dick – just ask David Letterman. Plus, Duckie had just stalked the guy and scared the shit out of him. "I dunno," he admitted. "I mean, it's not really for me, anyway. It's my friend. He's missing, and I thought you could help me find him."

"And why would I be able to help find your friend?" he asked flatly.

"Because he's Chuck Marshall."

"Is that name supposed to mean something to me?"

"He's a stand-up. He's famous. Well, not Mickey Gross famous, but on his way. Headlining big clubs, has his own TV show and everything. Then he just disappeared."

"Again, why would I be able to help you find your friend?"

Duckie was starting to get pissed. He hadn't come all this way and actually found Mickey Gross to get stonewalled now. "I think we've established that you are an expert in stand-up comedians pulling a disappearing act."

"I guess you've got a point there," Karma Zhimay sighed. "And I think I may have heard the name Chuck Marshall. Can't say I'm that familiar with his work, though. I don't really keep up with the comedy scene anymore."

Duckie nodded. He could understand. There were some nights when he wondered why he bothered going out of his way in order to make a bunch of asshole strangers laugh. On other nights, when the room was good and the jokes were landing, Duckie wouldn't have traded it for the world. All of the dud sets, the awful open-mics, and cheap beer were absolutely worth it when you were in the groove and getting laughs.

"When was the last time you heard from him?" asked Karma Zhimay.

"About a month ago," said Duckie.

"How did he sound?"

"Pretty stressed. He was trying to get this new TV show ready for Wolff."

"Ugh," said Karma Zhimay. "The Wolff Network. I've had some experience with that outfit. None of it good. Best to just stick with fart jokes for Wolff."

"Actually, I'm more of a fart-joke guy than Chuck. He's more, y'know, cerebral."

"I can understand the pressures that go along with that," said Karma Zhimay. "Anything else? Any girl problems?"

Now it was Duckie's turn to laugh. "What do you think? He's a fuckin' comic, man. With all of the relationship problems that go along with it."

Karma Zhimay rubbed a hand over his stubbly head. It made a soft rasping sound. "Yeah, that sounds like a lot of pressure all at once. I can understand the urge to just bolt. Y'know, the twelve-steppers have a saying: *Fear* stands for Fuck Everything And Run."

"I think that's what happened. But why not contact someone? Why not contact *me?* And where would he have gone?"

"Why are you asking me?" asked Karma Zhimay. "It's a damn big world out there. You've known this guy since you were kids, huh? You should know where to look for him. Why spend a buncha time looking for some washed-up comic who isn't even supposed to be alive?"

"I dunno," said Duckie helplessly. "I called all over the place. No one knows where he is. None of our comic friends, none of our high school friends, none of his family. All zippo. I thought you might have an idea, or some insight or something. It feels like I'm out of options."

"What, so you think there's some sort of Village for exiled comedians? Where they give you a number and spend all day asking why you retired?"

"Village?" asked Duckie. "What the hell are you talking about?"

"Haven't you ever seen *The Prisoner?*" asked Karma Zhimay. "That old British TV show? Not the crappy reboot."

"Oh, yeah, yeah!" said Duckie. "I remember that show! It was on PBS when I was a kid."

Karma Zhimay thought for a moment, then said, "Look, I'd better put your clothes in the washer. They're starting to smell up the apartment." He got up from the bed, pulled a jelly jar full of change from the top of the refrigerator and dumped it on the counter. He spent quite a long time sifting through the change.

"You got enough?" asked Duckie. "I think I have some quarters in the car."

"No, no," said Karma Zhimay. "I made this mess; I'll clean it up. Aha!" He fished out two more quarters and held them up triumphantly. "Be back in a sec." He snagged the laundry basket and zipped out the front door.

Duckie plopped down in one of the folding chairs by the card table and contemplated his situation. Here he was, in borrowed clothes, sitting in the dingy studio apartment of a man who was – or had been – a superstar comic. Duckie was sure that he had found his man. But now what?

The door opened, admitting Karma Zhimay and a blast of Tucson heat. "I'll go back down and check on your clothes in a few minutes," said Karma Zhimay. "Sometimes clothes walk away from the laundry room."

He went back to the bed and sat down cross-legged, and seemed to be mulling something over. Finally, he said, "It's more like the Bohemian Grove than the Village."

"What?" asked Duckie.

"The place we were talking about earlier. It exists. But it's more like a retreat than a prison."

"What? You mean there's really a place where comics go to hide out? Really?"

"Hell, yes," said Karma Zhimay. "As I'm sure you well know, there are pressures in being a stand-up that few other entertainers have to deal with. Touring, performing alone, in-your-face interaction with the audience night after night. It can really wear a person down, physically and spiritually."

Duckie thought back to some of his uglier gigs and nodded.

"Well, back in the '70s, a comic named Murray Langford bought some property in British Columbia – an island off the coast of Vancouver. It was originally a fishing camp, with a few cabins and stuff – pretty rough. Murray used it as a get-away where he and some of his stand-up buddies could go and blow off steam when they weren't touring. Word started to get around, and it became … oh, I don't really want to say a 'secret society,' but that's as good a description as any. Anyway, once you were in, you could use the place when you wanted. There were fees, which went towards upkeep. Actually, it ended up growing pretty big. Jerry Seinfeld donated some big-time cash to the place. It got pretty fancy."

"Holy shit!" said Duckie, amazed. "I had no idea. I mean, I thought I was a major comedy nerd, but I've never heard of this place. Not even a dumb-ass rumor. Have you been there?"

"Yeah, I went a few times in the '90s, but I wasn't what you'd call a regular."

"How do you get there?"

"Honestly, I don't know," said Karma Zhimay. "First, it's deliberately difficult to get to. Second, the handful of times that I was there, I was totally wasted the whole time. My memories are hazy at best. I'd fly into the airport at Victoria, and someone would meet me there. Then it was a three-hour ride in the car, then finally we'd get into a boat to get ferried to the island."

"Amazing," said Duckie, who was already mentally figuring how he could get up to Victoria to explore. "Does this place have a name?"

"Yes," said Karma Zhimay. "It's called 'Laughingstock.'"

Chapter 37

Duckie woke up and squinted. The motel curtains and blackout shade were drawn, but the harsh desert light managed to sneak around the edges and make his eyes ache. He had spent the previous evening hanging out with Mickey Gross/Karma Zhimay at his apartment. Sitting, literally, at the feet of the master, listening to the amazing adventures of his lifelong hero. It had been an epiphany, everything he had hoped for.

He had tried asking more about Laughingstock, and how he might be able to find it, but Mickey/Karma had been reluctant to discuss it. "We can talk about that later," he'd said, and then had launched into a story about getting into a drinking contest with Robin Williams at a club in New York.

Duckie hadn't minded. Once the effect of the pepper spray had lessened and he was able to get back into some clean clothes, the weirdness of his initial encounter with Mickey had subsided. He was just happy to have found him, and to have gotten a lead on his missing friend. Man, Chuck was just going to *fucking die* when Duckie told him about locating Mickey in a shitbox apartment in Tucson.

Now it was time for him to vacate his own shitbox motel room. He turned in his key at the front desk, charged the room to his nearing-maxed-out credit card and threw his meager luggage back into the rental.

The Rodeway Inn was right by an onramp to the interstate. A few miles later, another ramp dropped him onto the sterile street that led to the Mickey/Karma's apartment. Duckie slewed into the gravel lot and parked with a great deal less care than he had the day before. He sprang from the car, bounded up the stairs to apartment 203 and rapped on the door.

He stood back to wait. Nothing happened. He knocked and waited some more. Nothing.

After a few more minutes, he gave it a couple good hearty belts with his fist. "Yo!" he hollered. "Lama Chimichanga! It's me, Duckie! C'mon, open up!" He unloaded a few more whacks to the door.

The door to the next unit opened a sliver. A sleepy red eye peeked out of the crack. "Choo doon, mang?" inquired a voice from within. "I chust got home from work, okay? Trine to sleep!"

"Oh, hey, sorry, man," said Duckie. "I was supposed to meet Karma Hoo-ha this morning, but he's not answering the door."

"He gone, mang."

"What? Where? Did he say when he'd be back?"

"No – he *gone*. Moved out this morning. Saw him loadin' up a Ryder truck chust as I was comin' home."

"Shit! Did he say where he was going? Damn!"

"He don't say nothin'. Now go 'way. Trine to sleep." The door slammed.

Reluctantly, Duckie trudged down the stairs and got into the rental. *Well, at least it wasn't a total loss,* he thought. He'd found out about Laughingstock on Vancouver Island. Unless Mickey had been bullshitting about that, too. Shit, what a mess.

He keyed the ignition and pulled out of the parking lot, heading towards the interstate. He turned on the stereo to the classic rock station he had found when he'd arrived. It was playing CBM's "(The) Parenthetical (Song)." It reminded him of his meeting with Cheryl.

Without really thinking about it, he pulled into the parking lot of a Circle K. In Tucson, it seemed like there was one every three blocks or so. He pulled out his phone, thumbed the power button, and dialed Cheryl's number.

The phone rang. And rang. Six times … seven. He was on the verge of hanging up when there was a click. A sleepy voice said, "Hello? If it's you, Nigel, just fuck off."

"Uh, no, it's me, Duckie. We met at that diner the other day, remember?"

"Ah, yes, the funnyman," said Cheryl. "Have any luck finding my dad?"

"Oh, yeah, I found him all right. He sprayed me with pepper spray, then ran out on me."

Cheryl laughed. Duckie liked the sound, even if she was laughing at him. "Guess you got what you came for, huh?"

"Well, I was kinda asking for the pepper spray to be honest. I was a little wound up when I met him. I guess I came on kinda strong."

"Well, I don't know you all that well, but it doesn't seem like subtlety is really your thing, y'know."

Uncharacteristically, Duckie didn't have a reply to that. Instead, he said, "So, uh, who's Nigel?"

"Nobody," said Cheryl quickly. "Less than nobody. Forget about him – I have. So Mickey split on you, huh?"

"Totally," said Duckie. "And I mean totally. When I came back by his place this morning he had fuckin' moved out."

Cheryl laughed again. It sounded to Duckie like a crystal windchime in a strong breeze. "Well, you should have seen that coming, I guess," she said. "You knew he's had some big-league experience with pulling a vanishing act!"

"Yeah, I guess so. I mean, I've had people ditch me before, but none of 'em went to the bother of changing addresses."

"Guess it's part of your natural charm. Look, Duckie, why are you laying this on me? It's not like he's gonna come here or anything."

"I know, but he did tell me some stuff. Stuff that might help me find Chuck. I just kinda, y'know, wanted to talk it over with someone. Get a fresh perspective and all. You seem to have a pretty good head on your shoulders."

"If I did, I would hang up right now," muttered Cheryl.

"What?"

"Nothing. Just clearing my throat. So, what, you wanna talk about this shit right now?"

"Uh, no, I'm still in Tucson. Look, I'm gonna have to come back to L.A. to catch my flight home. Wanna get together and talk?"

"Really?" She paused. "Yeah, sure, okay. When?"

"Uh, today, actually. If I hustle, I can be there by dinnertime."

"Then you hustle, Duckie Dunne. Think you can find your way back to the diner?"

"No prob. I've got an impeccable sense of direction."

She laughed again. "Yeah, you're Mr. Impeccable, all right."

"You sure have a lot of nicknames for me," observed Duckie, with a strange feeling of lightness in his belly. She'd also remembered his last name.

"Take it as a compliment," said Cheryl. "All right, call me once you get into town. I can be there in, like, five minutes."

"Will do," said Duckie.

"Okay, Mr. Funnyman, I'll wait for your call. Drive safe." Then she hung up.

Duckie paused for a moment, scratching his head. Were they actually flirting? Hard to say. Did he want them to be? Also hard to say, but he thought: *yeah, maybe I do.* She seemed okay, seemed to have a good sense of humor. Not surprising, given who her father is. Pretty cute, too, in a not-quite-put-together way. Well, he could speculate about Cheryl on the road; he had to make tracks if he wanted to get to Los Angeles in time for dinner.

Chapter 38

The sun was sinking into the Pacific as Duckie wheeled the rental into Los Angeles on I-10. Leaving Tucson, he'd hoped that he could time his arrival in order to miss the bad traffic. As he passed through Pomona and saw the sea of taillights and headlights on the highway stretching before him, he realized that there was *never* a time to avoid bad traffic in L.A.

He slid into the L.A. basin right around dinnertime, and called Cheryl's number and left a message telling her to meet him at 7:30. However, it took him almost two more hours to make it up to Northridge. By the time he got to the diner, it was quarter to nine.

He got out of the rental and stretched. He'd pretty much driven nonstop for the last 10 hours, and he was tired, hungry and grumpy. He looked up at the diner, wondering if Cheryl was even there. He'd spent most of the trip thinking about her, until he'd gotten to El Monte, at which point all of his attention was focused on surviving the L.A. death race.

Now he just felt numb and wanted nothing more than a meal. He scanned the windows on the diner, looking for Cheryl. No luck. He took a few steps closer to the front door, then stopped and looked through the windows again. He could see every booth in the joint, but no Cheryl. *Shit,* he thought. She had ditched him.

"Fuck," he muttered. He might as well grab a burger and start calling around to find a place to crash.

"Hey, big boy," came a sultry voice from the darkness. "Lookin' for a good time?"

Duckie snapped his head around to see Cheryl, half-hidden in the shadow of a jacaranda tree, smoking a cigarette. "Sheeee-it, sister," he said. "I haven't had a good time in so long, I wouldn't know what to do with one."

"Whoa," said Cheryl. "You really are a smoothie, aintcha?" She flicked the cigarette into the parking lot, where it died a tiny Viking funeral.

"Uh, that didn't come out quite the way I thought it would," said Duckie. "Low blood sugar, probably."

"Well, c'mon then, let's get some nourishment in you."

They went into the diner and slid into the same booth they had sat in before. The jukebox played Blue Öyster Cult's "This Ain't the Summer of Love." The neo-retro color scheme seemed extra garish under the heavy fluorescent lighting. Duckie rubbed his eyes, then took a good look at Cheryl.

She was definitely better put together than the last time they'd met. She had make-up on for one thing, and it looked like she'd spent some time attending to her hair, which was done up in a modified '70s flip. Duckie kind of liked it. She was wearing a dark-red silk blouse and a pair of plain black jeans. Both were moderately tight. "You're looking pretty sharp tonight, Cheryl. Big plans for later?"

"Not anymore," she said, taking an exaggerated look at the slim gold watch on her wrist. "You're lucky you showed up when you did. I was gonna bolt right after that cigarette."

Duckie shrugged. "Sorry, Cheryl," he said. "I got here as fast as I could. I spent the day thrashing through the Great American West. On an adventure like that, impediments and surprises are bound to occur." He flagged down the waitress and ordered a Sam Adams. Cheryl ordered a margarita.

They made small talk until the drinks arrived, then made slightly louder small talk as the booze began to kick in. Food was ordered, delivered, consumed. Duckie had two more beers. Cheryl kept pace with her margaritas. The food, the booze and the company helped Duckie shake the dust of the day's drive from his psyche, and he was able to relax.

Cheryl looked at him with glittering eyes. "So…" she said. "So you actually met my father." She wore a small gold ring on her left hand that she twisted nervously.

"Yep. Met and got pepper sprayed, thank you."

She laughed her wind-chime laugh. "What were you doing to get a face full of mace?"

"Well, it maybe wasn't the best neighborhood to be runnin' up to a stranger and start talking crazy. Also, I wasn't really sure it was him. He didn't really look like I expected."

"What? Why?"

"Well, he was bald, for one thing."

"What, he's lost all his hair?"

"Nah, pretty sure he shaved it. Also, he had these awful glasses and was wearing robes."

"Like a bathrobe?" She continued to twist her ring. Duckie was drawn to it, but tried not to make his interest too obvious.

"No, like a monk. He looked like the Dalai Lama. Said his name was Karma something. Karma Zhimay, something like that."

"That figures," said Cheryl. "He'd always been interested in Eastern philosophy and religion, you know."

"Yeah, I did, but how did you know that?"

"Because he's my father, dorkwad! When I found out he was my dad, I found out everything about him that I could. I don't need to be a pathetic fanboy to know that stuff."

"I'll have you know that I am one of the least pathetic fanboys you'll ever meet."

"Yeah, that's probably true. You're cute, too." The ring increased its RPMs.

"You're looking pretty fine yourself," said Duckie. "Sorry if I screwed up your plans for the evening."

"Nah, it's all good, really," said Cheryl. Duckie noticed a mild flush spread across her face. Was that because of him? "You said that Mickey had told you something that might help you find your friend," she said. "What was it?"

"Yeah, that's what I wanted to ask you about. This is actually pretty weird, in a cool sort of way."

"Wow. Maybe we should get another round first." She gestured with her mostly empty margarita glass.

"Nah, I better take it easy on the booze," said Duckie. "I haven't had time to call around and find a place to crash. I might have to drive Christ knows how many miles. How far is Los Feliz?"

"Too far," she said. "It'll take you at least an hour to get there." The ring was now spinning on her finger like a carnival ride. "Look, you can crash at my place, if you like. We've got a comfortable couch, and it's only a couple of minutes away. Beats the hell out of going all the way to Los Feliz."

"Yeah, sure," said Duckie. "Thanks. I was pretty sure that I'd end up sleeping in my car, anyway."

"Great!" said Cheryl. "Let's get going."

They paid up and split, Duckie following Cheryl's Honda through the anonymous grid of Northridge. She turned into an apartment complex of identical faux-stucco apartment buildings with faux-tile roofs.

They wound and wove for another five minutes before parking in front of a building that was indistinguishable from the others. Duckie followed Cheryl up the covered stairway to the third floor, and into apartment 371-F.

"Sorry about the mess," said Cheryl. The place looked spotless to Duckie, aside from one or two small caches of girl-stuff.

"You live here alone?"

"No, but my roommate's away. Visiting her mom in San Ysidro."

"Oh," said Duckie. "Cool." He tried to suss out how to play things. As an entertainer who had a modicum of social skills and personal hygiene, he'd been in this situation before. Going back to the woman's apartment was an almost certain sign that he was in like Flynn. Almost. He could say or do something to spoil the mood – something that had happened to him more than once. It was something Duckie was eager to avoid right now. He didn't relish the thought of trying to find another place to stay, or crashing in his car.

Besides, he really *liked* Cheryl. He didn't want this to be a greasy one-night stand. Not that there was anything wrong with the occasional greasy one-night stand, but he didn't want this to be *only* that. He decided to focus on being polite, friendly and not getting thrown out in the middle of the night.

"Uh, hope you don't mind," said Cheryl. "I'm gonna go freshen up a bit, get into something more comfortable."

"No prob," said Duckie. "I need to call the airline, figure out how I'm gonna get home."

He flopped down on the couch and called Alaska Airlines. With minimal difficulty, he got on the standby list for a 10 am flight the next day.

Cheryl reappeared in a pair of sweatpants and a short t-shirt. Both were tight enough to accentuate her figure. Duckie had to make a conscious effort to keep from gawking. "Want a beer?" she asked. "I've got some vodka, too, if you'd like a cocktail."

"Beer's fine."

She returned from the kitchen with a pair of bottles of Bud Lite and popped the caps with a Bic lighter that was sitting on the end table. She handed Duckie one and held up the other. "We should drink to something," she said.

"Hmm," he said. "How about to 'finding what we're looking for.'"

She nodded. "Here's to finding what we're looking for." They clinked bottles and drank.

"You said that Mickey thought he knew where your friend Chuck might have gotten to. What was that about?"

"He said that there was a place on Vancouver Island that comics used to go to, y'know, unwind and chill out. Like a secret retreat or something. Said it was called Laughingstock. You ever hear of anything like that?"

Cheryl shrugged. "Nope," she said. "He never mentioned anything like that to me."

"The thing is," Duckie continued, "he made it sound like a secret, but not a *top* secret, you know what I mean? Like it's possible that I would have known about it somehow. I mean, I always thought I was a top-tier comedy geek. I can tell you George Carlin's favorite type of salad dressing – Thousand Island – but I've never heard of a secret comic's retreat. Have you?"

Cheryl shook her head. "No, sorry."

"Shit," said Duckie. "Well, at least I got a place I can start looking."

She took a long sip from her beer and said, "Why do they call you Duckie?"

"Huh?"

"Why do they call you Duckie? That's not your real name, is it?"

"Uh, no, my real name is Wilbert. Don't laugh!"

"I'm not laughing," she said solemnly. "But how did you get from 'Wilbert' to 'Duckie'?"

"You've seen *The Blues Brothers*, right?"

"Yeah, sure. It's a classic."

"Well, the bass player in their band is a guy called Donald 'Duck' Dunn. White guy with a big orange 'fro, smoked a pipe. When Chuck and I first saw that movie, we laughed our asses off. Funny as hell. But I thought that Dunn was cool as toast, just puffin' his pipe and jamming on his bass. Since my last name is Dunne, Chuck started calling me 'Duckie" and the name stuck. I mean, it's not a badass nickname or anything, but it beats the hell out of 'Wilbert.'"

"I dunno, I kinda like it," she said. "'Wilbert' sounds kinda English … y'know, like royalty."

"I'm pretty sure that's what my parents were going for," said Duckie. "An old family name, they said. To me, it sounds like the name of a cartoon dog."

Cheryl sighed. "Yeah, an old family name," she said. "Wilbert. It doesn't sound too bad. Sometimes I wish I had an old family name. Or an old family anything."

"I think Cheryl's a pretty name," said Duckie.

"'Cheryl Watson' – how white-bread can you get?" she said. "Look, if we're gonna talk about my family, I need to get into the right headspace. Do you get high?"

Duckie shrugged. "I can take it or leave it," he said. "I'm doin' okay with the beer." He lifted the bottle. "If you can call Bud Light 'beer.'"

"You don't mind if I smoke, then?" she asked.

"Not at all."

She nodded and went into the kitchen, returning with a small, colorful glass pipe and a tightly rolled baggie. She loaded the pipe, sparked it, and took a delicate puff. When she exhaled, there was almost nothing to see. She took two more ladylike hits, sinking a little further into the couch with each one. "Sure you don't want any?" she asked, holding out the pipe and the lighter.

"Yeah, why not?" said Duckie. He took a small hit, more for hospitality than anything else, and passed it back.

Cheryl took one more hit, and launched into a coughing fit. Duckie gave her a few whacks on the back and offered her his beer. "Thanks," she said. "You don't get off until you cough, so they say."

"So did you get off, then?"

She gave him a long, speculative look and then said, "Enough to talk about my family, I guess. What do you want to know?"

"Well, I guess just how well you know Mickey, for starters. Do you talk to him a lot?"

"First, you gotta remember that I didn't know I was adopted until I was eighteen. I was *so* pissed at my mom and dad. Y'know, the ones who raised me. The white-bread Watsons."

"I bet," said Duckie. "Did they say why they waited to tell you?"

"Yeah, they said they never wanted me to feel like I wasn't a real part of the family. They were so sorry that they had hurt me. I can't blame them entirely. But I was still pissed."

"Okay, then how did you get in touch with Mickey?"

"He got in touch with me, obviously. I didn't believe him at first. Why would I? I was still totally spun out about the whole adoption thing. And then having my dead father, who I'd just learned about, actually call me up…"

"Shit, I'm surprised you didn't just hang up on him."

"I did, a bunch of times. He kept calling, though. Wanting to apologize."

"So what made you decide that he was the real deal?"

"I'll show you," said Cheryl. "Follow me." She got up and led him into the bedroom. "Sit here," she said, indicating the bed. She dug around in the closet and came up with a folded manila envelope. She sat down next to Duckie on the bed and pulled out an 8 x 10 glossy, showing it to him with a flourish. It pictured a middle-aged man with long hair holding a copy of the *American Investigator* with the headline DEAD COMEDIAN'S SECRET LOVE CHILD. Underneath were pictures of Mickey Gross onstage and a high-school yearbook shot of Cheryl. The man holding the newspaper was clearly the same one shown performing. It was Mickey Gross, six months after he had "died."

"Jesus," said Duckie. "What a mindfuck. I'd have a hard time believing it if I hadn't just met the guy and gotten pepper-sprayed by him."

"How do you think I felt?" asked Cheryl. Her voice was thick, and Duckie could see her eyes tearing up. He put his arm around her. She was soft and warm, and leaned into him.

"I can't imagine how you felt," he said. "How you must still feel…" Her shoulders hitched under his arm.

"I … I still feel weirded out about it, kinda," she said. "It took a few more calls after he sent the picture before I finally talked to him. I'm not sure why I did, in the end. Maybe because he seemed genuinely sorry for what had happened, and that he really wanted to connect, as best he could. But he wanted to be cautious. It was a two-way street, do you understand?"

"He was worried you might blow his cover, huh?"

"I thought about it, too, believe me. I was pissed at him, at my parents, at whoever had spilled the beans to *American Investigator*."

"What about your real mom? Did you try to connect with her?"

"Couldn't. She's dead. Breast cancer, ten years ago. The piece in the paper made it clear that her family didn't want anything to do with me. They found the whole thing to be a terrible, terrible embarrassment."

"Buncha assholes," muttered Duckie. "What about Mickey's family? Did you have contact with any of them?"

"Nope."

"Okay, and what about Mickey?" asked Duckie. "Did you ever, like, meet him in person?"

Duckie's arm was still around Cheryl's shoulders. Her shoulders hitched again, then relaxed. She sagged a little and leaned in further. "Yeah, I met him face-to-face twice. Once in San Francisco about four years ago, and again last year in Las Vegas."

"Wow, what was that like, meeting him for the first time?" Duckie was genuinely interested. He thought that *his* family was fucked up, but at least they were a stable sort of fucked up.

"Jesus, what do you want me to say?" asked Cheryl. "It was messed up. It messed *me* up. It still does. Five years later, and I'm still processing it. Christ, and now I've gone and told you all about it, for some unknown fucking reason. And *you've* gone and blown it. He said he'd never talk to me again if I told anyone, and I told you and you just about knocked yourself out running right down there and confronting him. I'll probably never see him again now. You bastard!" She began sobbing.

Well, if you didn't want me to get in touch with him, why did you give me his address? thought Duckie. *What did you think I was gonna do, send him a postcard?* It didn't seem like a good idea to vocalize this. Instead, he wrapped his arm around her a little tighter, and said, "Hey, hey, don't worry. I don't think he'd do something like that. I mean, he was pretty pissed at me, that's for sure. And he knew how I'd found out where he was living. But he wasn't pissed at you. He was actually, y'know, real concerned about you. Wanted to know how you were. Said he thought you looked a little skinny last time he saw you."

"Really?" asked Cheryl. "He said that? What did you tell him?"

"I said he shouldn't worry, 'cause you're big as a house now," said Duckie. He immediately regretted it, but the scene was getting a little heavy for him. He always shot his mouth off when things felt tense.

She glared at him momentarily, but the fury in her eye faded quickly. "Mr. Funnyman," she said to herself. "Just my luck to be surrounded by funny men." She looked him straight in the eye with an expectant gleam and a quarter smile.

Clutch time, thought Duckie. This was where he usually blew it by overthinking. But was he *really* overthinking the situation? Here he had just shown up at short notice and dumped a steaming pile of emotional baggage on Cheryl. Clearly, she had some daddy issues. Who wouldn't, given the circumstances? If he made a move on her now, was he taking advantage of her delicate and vulnerable and complicated feelings about her father? And would she be angry at him for taking advantage of her, after he was the one who had stirred up all those feelings in the first place?

He realized that the silence in the room had drawn out as these thoughts jounced around inside his head. He looked down and Cheryl was still staring at him with those sparkling blue eyes and partial smile.

So he kissed her.

He leaned down and gave her a light buss on the lips, pulled back slightly to make sure she was still onboard with the whole kissing thing, and seeing that she was, leaned in and gave her a real kiss. She turned into him and kissed back, hard.

Duckie found himself being swept away. This was usually the time he liked best, and scared him the worst: the very first time with someone new. Normally, he would be overthinking like mad at this point, but he just went with it, his mind blissfully blank as their kisses become more urgent and passionate. He pulled off his t-shirt and flung it into the corner, then began removing her shirt. It joined his t-shirt in the corner. He slid her bra straps down, kissed down her neck to where it met her shoulders and gave a light bite. She shuddered and half-rolled, wrapping her left leg around his back, pulling him tighter to her. His cock was grandly hard, pulsing against her pelvis. He slid his left hand around her back, felt for the hook.

"Need some help?" she breathed.

"Got it." He thumbed the catch open. It was one of those irritating triple hooks, but he knew how to handle it. He gave the bra a celebratory twirl above his head and tossed it to join the shirts.

She rolled over onto her back, her breasts firm, nipples half erect. She lifted her hips up slightly, and Duckie slipped the sweatpants down and tossed them in the corner. He rolled back into her, kissing hard. His hand moved up and caressed her cheek, slid down and circled her breast, his thumb sliding back and forth across her nipple, feeling it harden under his touch. His hand continued its journey down, following the curve of her waist, the flare of her hip, moved down across her stomach and down onto the front of her panties. They were already very wet, and Duckie moved the side of his thumb up and down against the damp silk. She arched her back and moaned.

He slid his hand inside her panties and gently stroked the moist cleft, then slid his hand back up to stroke her clit. At the same time, he leaned down to that magic junction where her neck and shoulders met and began kissing, licking and sucking. The effects were galvanic.

"Oh, Jesus," she breathed. "Oh, Jesus FUCK! Don't stop! Please don't stop!"

Duckie had no intention of stopping. Instead, he redoubled his efforts, applying more pressure at the top of the key and continuing to kiss her neck. It didn't take long. Her repeated cries of "Don't stop!" became guttural moans. Her breathing came faster and faster. Her back arched and she opened her mouth in an inarticulate cry of pleasure. He gently slowed his rubbing and kissing, then he rolled over while Cheryl caught her breath.

"Holy shit!" she exclaimed. "That was incredible! Where did you learn that?"

"Page sixteen in the Boy Scout Manual."

She sat up, the flush slowly fading from her face and chest. "It appears to me," she said, "that there is a bit of an imbalance in the pants department." She reached down, rubbed the front of his jeans and began fumbling with his belt buckle. It occurred to Duckie that this was probably as big a pain in the ass for women as bra hooks were for men. He lifted up his hips and she slid his jeans and underwear off with a smooth tug. His cock, unbelievably hard, stood almost straight up in its nest of dark hair.

"Well, you really are a stand-up comedian," she said with a wolfish grin. "Got a rubber, Duckie?"

Shit! He had three or four in his shaving kit, but that was still out in the car. "Uh, yeah," he started. "But I gotta go get…"

"Shhh," she said softly, and leaned over and wrapped her mouth around his cock.

Duckie leaned back into the flowery-smelling girl-bedroom pillows and sighed. It had been one hell of a day, and a long one, but this was a great way to wrap it up. Cheryl was quite skilled and enthusiastic. He relaxed and enjoyed the experience.

Cheryl kept pumping away, and Duckie began to worry that he had plateaued. The fellatio felt great, and he was having no trouble maintaining his erection, but it just felt like he didn't have enough to get over the finish line. It happened sometimes, and he hated it. He was always afraid that his partner would feel hurt or inadequate.

Suddenly, Cheryl shifted and Duckie knew that the end was in sight. He looked down and saw that Cheryl had grasped the base of his tool with both hands, and was twisting them back and forth as her head kept pumping.

The orgasm rushed up on him like a highballing freight. He heard himself making a guttural groan, *hhhuunnnghhhh!* His hands scrabbled at the sheets, as if he was trying to keep from flying off the edge of the world, and he could feel his eyeballs bulging out of their sockets. He ejaculated grandly, moaning.

He sunk further into the flowery pillows, trying to catch his breath. Cheryl's grinning face rose up to greet him. "Wow," he panted. "How…?"

"Girl Scout Handbook," she said. "Page fifteen."

Chapter 39

Days went by, and Don Bundy still had no clue as to the whereabouts of Chuck Marshall. He had to make twice-daily reports to Malachi Wolff, who was growing increasingly unhappy. While Don was playing sleuth, he also had to keep things moving on *Chucklefest*. Fortunately, the first season was complete. However, if Marshall wasn't found soon, there would be no second season.

At first, Don was in regular contact with a detective named Julius about the case. At Malachi's insistence, Don called him several times a day for updates. Eventually, Julius stopped returning his messages.

Don tried checking with Marshall's crew. He went for the low-hanging fruit first, and contacted Arthur and Danny from the pilot. Neither knew where he might have gone. Danny got a little mouthy with him, and Don had had to lean on him a bit - but nothing that would be legally objectionable.

He'd tried some of Chuck's other acquaintances, but encountered a similar lack of success. Don began mining Marshall's social media feeds, and learned that he had been romantically associated with a young actress named Caroline Swenson. It had been easy to get in touch with her; aspiring entertainers practically scrawled their own phone numbers on restroom walls.

Finding Caroline hadn't been the only thing that was easy. When she realized that Don was a bigshot at the Wolff Network, she had practically launched herself at his crotch. Don had given her a polite brushoff and stuck with business.

It turned out that Caroline knew next to nothing about Marshall's whereabouts. They had lived together for a short time, but she had moved out before he'd disappeared. She didn't know where he was and apparently didn't care, having taken up with an assistant director who was "more supportive of her career."

Don quizzed her about whether Marshall had ever talked about taking off somewhere to hole up. She said no, the only possibility she could think of was his family in North Carolina. Of course, Don had already thought of that. The family was clearly worried about him, but had no idea where he was.

Disappointed by the lack of results, Don tried calling the general information number of the Missing Persons Unit, hoping for some new scrap of information about the case. He was astonished to learn that the case had been closed. He'd tried working the woman who'd answered the phone for more information, but all she would say was that the case was no longer active. End of story.

Don was glad to have even this tiny toehold of information to report to Malachi.

"You know what this means?" asked Malachi. "That Marshall's okay. Somehow he got hold of the cops and let him know that there was no need to look for him."

"That's good," said Don. "We need to get a copy of that police report, see if there's anything there that can help us locate him."

"You need to do *something*," said Malachi. "He's been gone almost a month."

"I need a foot in the door with the police," said Don. "I don't have any solid contacts."

"Well, neither do I," said Malachi. "But what I *do* have is an entire floor of lawyers, and lawyers have investigators, and investigators know cops."

A few phone calls later, Don spoke with an investigator with the unlikely name of Vic Electro. Electro said he could get Don a copy of the police file for five grand.

Don paid the money and Electro came through as promised. Don pored over the file, which was short. It noted that initial contact had been made by someone claiming to be Marshall's manager, named Simi Cohen. Don knew that Marshall's manager was a twit named Spinoza, but the name Simi Cohen sounded familiar. A quick Google search revealed her to be the owner of a small comedy club in East Hollywood. She almost certainly knew something about Marshall's whereabouts.

Then the question became what to do about Cohen. A direct confrontation was not advisable. She would undoubtedly warn Chuck that Don was closing in on him, and he would jackrabbit to some place even more difficult to find.

Don pulled an all-nighter, finding out as much as he could about Simi. He was able to get basic information starting with the business license for her club, and from there the information came easy. He found out plenty about Simone Louise Cohen, most of it irrelevant or useless. He learned her home address in Pasadena, which might come in useful later if Don decided to pay her a visit. Probably not, though – Pasadena was pretty well-policed, especially the Oak Knoll neighborhood where she lived.

Of greater interest were the rental properties that she owned: an apartment building in Anaheim and a house in Azusa. Don had spent the better part of the weekend skulking around the apartment in Anaheim, hoping to catch a glimpse of Chuck or his car. He'd come up with nothing.

So he shifted his attention to the house in Azusa. The place looked empty, but there were oil stains on the driveway that looked fresh. Also, the lawn looked recently mowed, although that meant nothing. A property manager might have someone come by once a week to mow.

Don decided that he needed to know who, if anyone, was staying in this house. He really had no other options. If this didn't pan out, he was back to square one. He could always try to lean on Simi a little harder, but that was definitely a last resort.

He parked halfway down the block and waited. It was after 11 pm when a car pulled into the driveway of the house. Don perked up when he saw that it was a Prius. No big deal there - they were common as milkweed in Southern California. He couldn't see the license plate from where he was parked.

He grabbed the small pair of binoculars that was sitting on the seat beside him and trained it on the car. The door swung open and the driver got out. Don's heart sank. The driver had hair nearly down to his ass. In fact, he was decked out in full hippie regalia, complete with bell-bottomed jeans, a tie-dyed shirt, a leather headband and tinted granny glasses. It didn't look like Chuck Marshall at all.

He was about to head home – it was a long drive from Azusa to Sylmar. The hippie walked to the front door, and there was something in his stride that gave Don pause. Something looked familiar. The hippie began fumbling with his keys. His long hair kept getting in the way, preventing him from fitting the key in the lock. In frustration, the hippie reached up and pulled off the headband. The hair came off with it.

It was a wig, and without the hair to obscure the shape of the face, Don knew he had found his man. He slumped down in his seat, reached for his phone, and dialed Malachi Wolff's number. "Hello, sir," he said. "It's me. I've found him."

"Finally," said Malachi. "I was beginning to lose faith in you, Don."

"I understand. What do you want me to do now?"

"Nothing. Just watch, and follow if he goes anywhere. Whatever you do, don't scare him off. I'll take care of the rest soon."

Chapter 40

A week after his return to Portland, Duckie sat nursing a Pabst at the Rickety Robot. It was a small club downtown that specialized in local punk bands and comedians. Since his return, he'd picked up as many shifts as he could at the print shop, while punching up his act. Duckie was slated to emcee a run of shows at Hydrogen, the city's premiere comedy club. He wanted to be sharp. There were a number of well-known comics who would be headlining the shows, including Demetri Martin, one of Duckie's favorites. Not that he expected that someone of Martin's caliber would notice him and ask him to tour or anything, but stranger things had happened. Duckie was more focused on looking good for Hydrogen's management, in the hopes that they might tap him for a feature slot sometime soon. It meant more stage time and more money.

Emceeing was a good start, and he had done it once or twice before at Hydrogen, but admittedly he had kind of half-assed it, feeling that the MC slot was beneath a comic of his talent and experience. That had been a mistake, he knew now, and after his last MC gig (almost a year ago!), he'd had trouble even getting on Hydrogen's open mic list.

Tonight Duckie had shown up late because he'd had trouble finding a parking space that wasn't in front of a cluster of homeless tents. Consequently, he was pretty far down on the list, and figured he'd be here another two hours at least before he got his four minutes on stage. Until then, he was content to sit in a dark corner and wait for his time.

He sat in the dark, brooding. He'd tried calling Cheryl the last two nights, with no success. She just wasn't picking up. He'd finally broken down and left a message for her last night. Still nothing from her. Maybe it was a one-night thing after all. He found the thought profoundly disappointing.

He sighed and took a long sip from his beer, then regretted it. Money was tight since he'd gotten back from his extended trip. His boss was more than happy to give him all the shifts he'd wanted, and his schedule was pretty full for the next two weeks. Good enough – he'd need the dough before the end of the month. At least he could spare enough for another cheap draft.

He wandered back to the bar and got another Pabst. A large shape shambled through the gloom. Duckie knew it was the Gooch just by the walk. The Gooch was a regular at most of the open mics Duckie frequented. They weren't best buds, but had spent enough time together in the local comedy scene to have developed a camaraderie. The Gooch was funny and friendly, and didn't have the insecure paranoia typical of the local pro-am comedians. Duckie found himself perking up at the sight of him.

"Yo, Duckster," said the Gooch. "How's it hangin'?"

"Long, lean and in between," replied Duckie with a laugh. "How's by you?"

"Ah, not so bad. Got a new gig hosting a show out in Beavertron."

"No shit? Where in the 'Tron would this be?"

"Little neighborhood pub off of Canyon Road. Shaker's. Specialize in martinis." The Gooch held up his martini glass; he drank nothing else. "You interested?"

"How much time can you give me?" asked Duckie.

"Ah, let's say seven minutes."

"Make it ten. You give me however much time you think you gotta give me. But I'm staying up on that stage for ten minutes, okay? Maybe you forget to light me. You're taking a leak or getting a drink. Or I just ignore you. What difference does it make?"

The Gooch grunted companionably, and they spend the next few minutes watching a rotund woman in a leather vest work through her set.

"Miranda's pretty good," said the Gooch when she got off the stage. "I've heard that bit about stealing pot from her stepdad about a dozen times now. She's getting it pretty tight."

"Oh yeah, her material's good, but Christ, her voice! It's like a bandsaw cutting sheet metal."

"Ah, it's an acquired taste. She also totally exaggerates it onstage. She doesn't sound like that when you just, y'know, talk to her."

"I've never summoned up the courage to try," admitted Duckie. "Why the hell play that up, though?"

The Gooch shrugged. "Part of the stage persona, I guess. Hey, it worked for Bobcat Goldthwaite and Gilbert Gottfried."

"Yeah, I guess so," said Duckie.

"Hey, that reminds me," said the Gooch. "You're a big-time Mickey Gross fan, right? There's been another sighting."

"What? Where?"

"Vancouver, at the airport."

"What, across the river? Didn't know they had an airport."

"No, not Vantuckey," said the Gooch, referring to the city across the Columbia River from Portland. "British Columbia, man. Canada."

Duckie tried to appear uninterested. Ever since his "death," there had been dozens of alleged Mickey Gross sightings. All were improbable, Duckie had thought, but this one might be another story. "So, what was this one? Someone spotted him playing poker with Andy Kaufman, Elvis and Bigfoot?"

"Naw, I just skimmed something on one of the FB groups. There was even a picture, but it was pretty blurry."

"Probably nothing," said Duckie. "Still, I'm always interested in the crazy shit people will believe. Which group?"

"Uh, Laugh Crafters, I think," said the Gooch. "Whoa! Gotta hop, man. I'm almost up. Hey, give me a call about the shows at Shaker's. Wednesday nights at eight. You got my number?"

Duckie checked his phone. The number was listed under "Gooch, The."

"Yeah, I got it," said Duckie. "Lemme check my work schedule. I'll give you a call tomorrow."

"Solid, man," said the Gooch. He shambled off towards the stage.

When Duckie got home that night, he felt like going straight to bed, but knew he had to stay up to get back on his normal 11 pm to 8 am work schedule, which he'd be picking back up tomorrow. He heated some water and dumped in a wad of Folger's, then sat down at his computer.

He used to be active on a number of social media groups devoted to comedy. A lot of the chatter in these groups was genuinely hilarious – there were very funny and talented comedians who contributed. However, most of these hilarious, talented comedians were also frustrated young men with limited social skills. As a result, the commentary in some of these groups could get creepy in a hurry.

Duckie had once been an angry young man on the Internet, but a lot of that venom had mellowed as he had gotten older. Sure, his life sucked in some respects. He had a crummy, unfulfilling job, was engaged in an exhausting struggle to improve his comedy skills and get attention, had a perpetual lack of disposable income, and no girlfriend.

So, yeah, it sometimes seemed like life sucked, but it was all a matter of perspective. From his apartment in the Hollywood District or from his place of employment downtown, you only had to walk two blocks in any given direction to find someone whose life *truly* sucked. Homeless tents were everywhere. Maybe Duckie's life wasn't a romantic comedy, but so what? It could always be a fuck-ton worse.

A lot of people on the comedy-nerd Internet groups didn't share this view, which is why Duckie didn't spend much time there anymore. However, the Laugh Crafters group was aboveboard and aggressively moderated, so it was a lot less icky than some of the other ones. Duckie jumped on to Facebook and clicked through to the Laugh Crafters group. He scrolled down the day's postings. Plenty there, but nothing about a Mickey Gross sighting. He scrolled back a few more days but saw nothing. He did a search. The most recent post about Mickey had been a video of a bit from the '90s about Dan Quayle cheating on his taxes. That one had been posted last year.

Duckie checked in a couple of other FB comedy groups and Mickey Gross fan sites, but came up with nothing that sounded even remotely like the story the Gooch had been talking about. In desperation, he turned to Reddit. He had soured on a lot of the Reddit comedian forums; the reek of frustrated, irresponsible, unlaid jerks was overpowering. He held his nose and dove in. Duckie waded through the conversational miasma, but nothing about a recent Mickey sighting.

In desperation, he started looking through the fan forums, and found a brief mention in the always-lovely r/ComedyNecrophila (383K members) group that pointed him to a subgroup, one he'd never heard of called r/MickeysNotDead. It was a sub-Reddit devoted entirely to Mickey Gross faked-death conspiracy theories and it was here that he found what he was looking for.

According to u/BiteTheHand, Mickey Gross had been seen leaving the Vancouver airport two days ago. BiteTheHand claimed to have spotted him as he was leaving the main terminal, and had known right away that it was the late, much-lamented Mickey Gross. He knew because he was a huge Mickey fan, had seen countless hours of performance footage, TV interviews and still photographs. His one regret in life was that he had had an opportunity to see Mickey Gross perform live, but had missed the show because his wife had been inconsiderate enough to give birth to their first child that night. Duckie thought that this weird little detail gave BiteTheHand a little cred. Most posers would have just claimed to have seen yea number of live performances.

BiteTheHand had included the day and time of the sighting as well as the exit Mickey had used (door D-1). He'd also included a picture that he'd managed to snap with his cell phone. It showed a man with long hair with a black carry-on bag slung over his shoulder. His head was turned three-quarters of the way away from the camera. Duckie squinted at it. It could have been Mickey, but at that angle it could have been almost anybody.

While he was contemplating this, his phone rang. He almost swiped to reject the call without looking at it. He was tired. When he saw it was Cheryl, he snatched the phone up and almost fumbled it in his haste to answer.

"Cheryl, hey, hi!" he said, sounding a little over-eager. "I mean, 'sup?"

Trying to over-compensate.

"Hi, Wilbert, hope it's not too late," she said.

"Wilbert? Really?"

"Sure," she said. "I've decided that I kinda like it."

"Oh, please, no. I'm glad you like my name, but I fuckin' hate it. Please don't call me Wilbert. I'm asking nicely here."

"Okay, fine, Duckie. That better?"

"Christ, yes," sighed Duckie. "What's up? I've been trying to call you."

"Yeah, sorry, work's been a bastard lately."

"What do you do, actually?"

"Actually, I work in an advertising firm. We had a lot of deadlines coming due. Hell, I just got home, earliest I've gotten off work all week. I thought I'd try calling, hoping you were still awake."

"No worries, I'm pretty much a night owl. Sorry to hear your job's so tough." Actually, he wasn't. It was kind of a lame excuse, but he was too glad that she had called to be worked up about it.

"Look, I got this weird call the other day. I wanted to talk to you about it."

"It wasn't me," said Duckie. "I always sign off on my dirty phone calls, 'This audio perversion brought to you by Duckie Dunne.'"

"It was from my Uncle Richard."

"Yeah, so?"

"I don't have an Uncle Richard. At least I didn't know I did 'til yesterday."

"Mickey's brother," said Duckie. "I remember reading about him. He was the only member of the family that really 'got' him, apparently. So what did he want?"

"I don't know," said Cheryl. "The message said that he had some family business to discuss, and that I should call him right away."

"Did you?"

"I tried, but there was no answer, and the voicemail box was full. Couldn't leave a message."

"Did he say where he was calling from?"

"No, but the number he left had a 604 area code."

"Hold on." Duckie typed "604 area code" in his browser. "Holy shit."

"What?"

"That's a Vancouver area code."

"Why did you say 'holy shit' just now?"

"I just found out that someone claims to have spotted Mickey at the Vancouver airport a couple days ago."

"Really? Do you think it was him?"

"Hard to say," said Duckie. "I saw a picture, but it was pretty blurry. Coulda been anyone."

"Never mind that," said Cheryl. "In your gut, do you think it was him?"

"Yeah … yeah, I do," said Duckie.

"Well, what do you think we should do?"

This question stopped him flatfooted. What the hell *should* they do? It seemed inevitable that one or both of them would be going to British Columbia in the very near future. He wondered how he could slot that with his increasingly full schedule here in Portland. He had a seven-day run of shifts at the print shop to make sure he could cover his rent, and that also overlapped with his MC gig at Hydrogen. Was it really worth it to untangle all of that mess to go on what was likely to be a wild goose chase in the Great White North?

"Well, I guess the first thing you need to do is to actually talk to Richard Gross and find out what he wants. After that, we can figure out what to do."

"Okay," said Cheryl. "I'll just keep calling until I get an answer. Do you think this Mickey sighting is going to make the news?"

"Probably not," said Duckie. "I mean, this happens every year or so. It's old news, now. When was the last time you heard about an Elvis sighting?"

"That *is* old news," said Cheryl. "If Elvis was alive, he'd be about a hundred by now, wouldn't he? Now, take Amy Winehouse – there was a fuss about two years ago that she was still alive and had been spotted in Tupelo, Mississippi."

"Yeah, I remember that," said Duckie. "But it turned out to be just a regular person. Who would've thought that there'd be women with beehive hairdos and heavy eye makeup in Tupelo, Mississippi?"

"You got me there, ace. Look, it's been a long day and I'm startin' to fade. I'll keep trying this number in Vancouver and let you know what I find."

"Sounds good. Talk to ya soon."

"Good night, sweet Wilbert," she said, and hung up.

Duckie lingered for a moment, thinking of his night with Cheryl. Then he poured another cuppa, put in a DVD of *Richard Pryor: Live in Concert,* and sat back to enjoy a master at work.

Chapter 41

The next night, Duckie was feeling horny. Really horny. Normally, he'd have no problem at all with taking the matter into his own hands and dealing with it forthwith. However, over the last year he'd found that if he resisted the urge to wallop the weasel and instead focused on writing, he would often come up with really good material. It was as if all of the biological energy that went into creating a load could be repurposed to create something artistic instead.

He sat down at the kitchen table and opened up his spiral-bound joke notebook. Once he'd scribbled the loosely formed ideas down in the notebook, he would slice and dice them into individual gags, which were written down on 3x5 cards. These he arranged and rearranged to form a cohesive bit. The stack of 3x5 cards were then hauled to an open mic, where Duckie would see if they got laughs.

His recent travels had given him an idea about some airline jokes. Of course, Duckie knew that jokes about airlines were hacky as hell. He figured he'd just acknowledge this up front and use it as a launching point for the bit: Orville Wright complaining about his experience on the first airplane flight.

He quickly got in the groove, and the ideas came tumbling out almost as fast as he could slop them down on the page. He really enjoyed when the creative juices got flowing – inspired, apparently, by the other juices that he kept bottled up. In what seemed like no time, he had three pages filled with ideas. He glanced at his phone and was surprised to see that nearly an hour had flown by. He shrugged and kept at it, although he'd have to leave for work pretty soon.

When the phone rang, he was pissed. He was almost done with his airline stuff, in the home stretch. Why would some asshole want to bother him now? He glanced angrily at the phone and saw that it was Cheryl calling. *Fuck the airline bit,* he thought. He dropped his pen and picked up the phone.

"Hey, pretty lady," he said suavely. "I thought I was having an outstanding night, but you just made it better."

"Well, you sound like you're in a good mood," said Cheryl. "What are you up to?"

"Doing some writing. Had an idea for a bit, and the ideas just kept coming."

"Just kept coming, eh?" she said with a seductive timbre in her voice. "You are quite the funnyman, aren't you? Quite a man, indeed, I think."

Immediately, his erection returned full force. "Whoa," he said. "When you talk like that, my pants get shorter."

It took her a second to get the joke, and then she burst out laughing. "Maybe you shouldn't be wearing pants at all," she suggested.

"It's just an expression," he said. "Actually, I haven't worn pants for the better part of the week."

"You paint a vivid picture, Wilbert," said Cheryl. "Look, seriously, how difficult would it be for you to get up to Victoria?"

"Canada?"

"Of course, Canada. British Columbia, Vancouver Island, all that jazz we'd been talking about? I finally managed to get hold of my Uncle Richard."

"Uncle Dick!" exclaimed Duckie. "How's the old bastard doing?"

"I don't know for sure," said Cheryl. "He said that he had some family business to discuss, something about Mickey. He didn't want to talk about it over the phone, but he's going to fly me up to Victoria for a long weekend. Can you make it?"

"When?"

"I'm flying up Saturday. Is that too soon? Sorry for the really short notice, but Uncle Richard made it sound kinda urgent."

It absolutely *was* too soon, but Duckie's desire to see Cheryl again eclipsed any inconvenience of taking another trip. He knew he could beg off at the print shop. His gig at Hydrogen was another story. If he bailed, he would be blackballed from the best comedy club in town. It might soften the blow if he lined up a replacement – but it would still be a black mark against him. Then there was the issue of getting to Victoria. He'd stretched his finances pretty thin already.

"Yeah, sure … I can make it work," said Duckie. *The things we do for lust,* he thought. "But I probably won't be able to make it up until Monday. Any chance of Uncle Dick of coming across with an airline ticket for me?"

"Well, I don't know about that," said Cheryl. "I mean, he was awful generous to offer to bring me up in the first place. I wouldn't want to impose—"

"No, no," said Duckie. "Just kidding. I'll figure out how to get up there. Pretty sure I can drive up to Washington and get a ferry." He carried his phone over to his beat-up Acer laptop and started searching. Sure enough, there was a ferry that ran between Port Angeles, Washington and Victoria. The trip was 90 minutes and the fares were reasonable – certainly much better than an airline ticket. "Yeah, I can pretty much swing that," said Duckie. "What about accommodations?"

"I'll be staying at Uncle Richard's place," said Cheryl. "Maybe once you get up there, I can ask him…"

"Look, don't worry about good ol' Uncle Dick," said Duckie. "I know this is pretty weird for you as it is, without having to factor in … a guest."

"Look, I appreciate you being so cool about this. To be honest, I'm really glad you're going to be able to come up. The whole thing is pretty weird. I mean, I've never even spoken to this guy, and now he's flying me up there to stay with him. I'll be glad to have you … y'know, with me."

"It's cool. Look, I'll find someplace nearby to stay, and if Uncle Dick turns out to be a cool cat, maybe I can come on out. Do you have an address?"

She did, but it was actually in a town called Cobble Hill, about twenty miles outside of Victoria. "Not a problem," Duckie told her. "I'll have my car. I'll just find some cheapie motel or hostel that's convenient to Cobble

Hill. It won't be a problem."

"Oh, thank you!" she gushed. "You're my hee-row! I'll be lucky to have such a strong, smart man to look after little ol' me."

"I'm looking forward to seeing you again," said Duckie. And he was. He really liked the idea of spending some more time with her. And of course, there was that unfinished business…

First, Duckie had some business of his own to attend to. He called his boss and told him he had to leave for a few days next week. Then he called the Gooch and asked him if he'd be willing to fill in for him as MC at Hydrogen. Then he called Hydrogen and gave the booker a cock-and-bull story about a sick uncle in Victoria. The booker was pissed, but calmed down when Duckie told him that the Gooch would cover for him. The Gooch had emceed there before; he had a good rep.

Having tied up those loose ends, he worked through his checkbook, wondering how he was going to finance this trip to the Great White North and still make rent.

Chapter 42

In the depths of the *MV Coho*, Duckie fought to keep from getting seasick. It was dim. The only light came from the bare fluorescent fixtures overhead. He took a look at the crummy coffee he'd bought from the snack bar, set it aside and checked his phone. Still no signal.

He had gotten up at 2 am and hopped in his car to make the first ferry from Port Angeles to Victoria. Unfortunately, the combination of the caustic coffee and the rocking motion of the ferry was not kind to his stomach. But that was a minor concern. He was going to see Cheryl again, in just under an hour if the ferry was on time. She had flown up to Victoria two days before.

Duckie's mind had been awhirl ever since Cheryl had called him from Uncle Dick's apparently palatial estate and told him that it was absolutely okay for him to come up and stay with them. Duckie had eagerly agreed and canceled his reservation at the hostel in Victoria.

Even more important than seeing Cheryl again was that he felt like he was close to finding Chuck. Once they had paid a visit to Uncle Dick, they could get going with tracking down Laughingstock and, presumably, Chuck. Of course, they may spend all week traipsing all over Vancouver Island and come up utterly empty-handed.

But they wouldn't.

Duckie didn't know that, *couldn't* know that, but somehow he did. It felt like Chuck was close. And that he needed help.

A crackling voice came over the loudspeaker, bouncing off the steel walls of the car deck and making it all but impossible to understand. Something about keeping the car engine turned off. They must be getting ready to dock. Duckie checked his phone. No bars, but as he watched, they started to come back. One, two, three bars. The phone started pinging madly, and Duckie could see that he'd missed a number of messages and a phone call from Cheryl. He checked the voicemail first: "Wilbert, dear, it's me. I hoped I could catch you before you left, but I guess I didn't. I wanted to tell you that you could leave your car in Washington. Uncle Richard has a car we can use." There were a string of texts, mostly repeating the same sentiment. With the last one – sent just twenty minutes earlier – reading, *Look 4 the limo when you clear customs.*

The limo? thought Duckie. What was up with that? Cheryl hadn't told him much about her trip so far, other than Richard Gross was rich but nice, and that it was perfectly okay for Duckie to come and stay at his house rather than some grotty hostel in the city.

The *Coho* shuddered to a halt and a loud thump reverberated through the ship. In a few minutes, a klaxon sounded and light spilled into the interior as the bow of the ferry opened and a ramp was lowered. Lighted signs advising people to keep their engines turned off winked out, and the interior of the ship shook with people starting their vehicles.

Even though he was near the front of the ship, it still took Duckie the better part of an hour to exit and go through immigration and customs. When he cleared the final barrier, he saw a long black SUV pulled up to the entry of the Customs building. As he drove slowly by, the back door popped open and Cheryl climbed out, waving frantically. Duckie pulled to the curb and got out of his car.

Cheryl ran to him and gave him a big hug, and an even bigger kiss. "Yeah, I've been looking forward to seeing you, too," said Duckie.

"Oh, I'm so glad you came," said Cheryl. "This whole trip has been really amazing, and my Uncle Richard is a super-nice guy. He says he'll help us find Chuck."

A man in a white polo shirt and chinos had climbed out of the driver's door of the SUV and stood a respectful distance away from their reunion. "That's Doug," said Cheryl. "He's one of Uncle Richard's personal staff."

"*One* of them?" asked Duckie. "How many servants has this guy got?"

"Four that I've met," said Cheryl. "There may be more."

"Jeez, the guy must be loaded."

"You don't know the half of it," said Cheryl. "He flew me from the airport to his house in a *helicopter*. I'll give you all the deets on the way up to the house."

"Would the gentleman care to leave his car in the parking lot?" asked Doug.

"The gentleman paid an extra fifty bucks to bring his car across and he's going to drive it, thanks," said Duckie.

"Very good, Mr. Duckie," said Doug. "You can follow me up whenever you're ready." He turned and climbed back into the SUV. Duckie and Cheryl climbed into Duckie's Toyota. They followed the limo through downtown and onto the highway that led to Cobble Hill.

"So, uh, am I crazy or is Uncle Dick's man Dougie carrying a piece?" asked Duckie.

"I hadn't noticed," said Cheryl.

"I watch a lot of thriller movies," said Duckie. "When rich-guy servants go around with untucked shirts, it usually means there's a gun stashed back there. I could kinda see the handle underneath the shirt."

"Yes, Uncle Richard is apparently worth a lot of money," said Cheryl, nodding at the SUV ahead. "He has what you'd call a comprehensive security setup."

"Rich uncle with armed goons," said Duckie. "Your family is even more interesting than I thought."

"Oh, it gets better," said Cheryl. "Apparently, Mickey showed up a week ago at Uncle Richard's house. Completely unexpected. It kinda blew Uncle Richard's mind. He didn't even *know* that Mickey was still alive."

"I knew it!" said Duckie. "That sighting at the Vancouver airport was legit. Is that why he flew you up here? To tell you that?"

"Oh, there's more," said Cheryl. "Apparently, since Mickey is legally dead, I'm Richard's only heir. He says I'm to inherit a lot of money."

"How much?"

"Fifteen—"

"Eh, not bad," said Duckie. "You could put a down-payment on a pretty decent car for fifteen grand. Or take a nice vacation! How about Jamaica? For that kind of money you could get a really nice place right on the beach."

"Not fifteen thousand, lunkhead," said Cheryl. *Million.* Fifteen million."

Duckie's eyes practically doubled in size. "Holy flerking schnitt! Fifteen *million?* You sure he's not … y'know, yanking your chain?"

"I don't know. But why would he?"

Duckie could think of a number of reasons, but it didn't seem like a good idea to voice them now. Uncle Richard sounded a little too good to be true.

"Is Mickey still there?" asked Duckie.

"No, he didn't stay long. He said he had some business 'up north'"

"At Laughingstock," said Duckie. "It has to be. Did he say anything else?"

"Nope. Not that Uncle Richard said, anyway."

"Something's happening," said Duckie. "I can feel it! We've got to find this Laughingstock place."

"Uncle Richard can help," said Cheryl. "He's already offered the use of his Range Rover. You really didn't need to bring your car."

"Ah, I don't know how comfortable I'd be driving around some rich dude's seventy-thousand-dollar truck. The Ol' Bucket here can manage whatever Vancouver Island can throw at us."

As they rolled through the forested hills, Duckie got more excited. Clearly, Mickey was somewhere on the island, and Duckie was confident that Chuck was too, and that they were both in the same place, or at least heading there.

The limo turned off the main road and went through a large rolling gate that closed as soon as Duckie's car had passed through. They wound through the trees for nearly a quarter mile before pulling up to a large circular driveway in front of an enormous house. The main part of the house was a two-story dark brown Craftsman surrounded by trees. Other wings stuck off at odd angles, as if to accommodate the trees on the property.

As they pulled up to the front porch, a white-haired man dressed in the same white polo/khaki slacks outfit appeared holding a tray with a pitcher of iced tea and a pair of frosted glasses.

"Is that him?" asked Duckie.

"No, that's Guy," said Cheryl. "He's like the chief of staff or whatever. He kinda runs things here."

"Mr. Gross sends his regrets," said Guy. "He is unfortunately tied up with business right now. He will join you for dinner." Guy had a British accent that sounded exactly like Stephen Fry in *Jeeves and Wooster*. "I thought you might enjoy some iced tea after your trip," said Guy. He poured out two glasses and handed them to Cheryl and Duckie, then somehow made the tray and the pitcher disappear. "Mr. Gross wishes me to encourage you to enjoy the amenities until dinnertime."

Duckie took a quick look at the back of Guy's shirt. Sure enough, the grip of a pistol was visible through the fabric. Once again, Duckie thought something was off with Uncle Richard. A huge house in the middle of nowhere, armed servants all over the place. He decided to keep his mouth shut and his eyes open.

"Let's go to the pool," said Cheryl. "It's nice and warm, and I have a new bikini to show you. I'm sure we can scrounge up a pair of trunks for you to wear."

They spent the afternoon at the Olympic-sized pool by the tennis courts. Cheryl was decked out in a red bikini, apparently designed and manufactured in a place suffering from an acute fabric shortage. It was very flattering, and Duckie had a difficult time keeping his eyes off of her.

When she noticed Duckie's gaze, she laughed her tinkly laugh. "Duckie darling, you're not having impure thoughts, are you?"

"Nope, not at all," said Duckie. "Absolutely pure lust, one hundred percent."

She laughed again. "I'm glad to see that you are still interested," she said. She held up a bottle of sunscreen. "Why don't you come over here and do my back?"

"Okey dokey!" agreed Duckie. He took a couple of deep breaths and hopped out of the pool. He looked over at Cheryl, who was eyeing the front of his trunks with obvious satisfaction. She rolled over and let Duckie apply the sunscreen to her back.

"Do you want to take off your top?" he asked. "Just for the sake of, y'know, an even tan and all that."

"Of course not," she said. "I wouldn't want people to get the wrong idea."

"And just what is the *right* idea?"

"That I am a woman who enjoys being admired, but does not want to be objectified."

"Fair enough," said Duckie. It seemed like the safest response. "Would you like me to do your front? I mean that in a totally utilitarian, non-objectifying way, of course."

"No, thanks," she said. "I took care of that already. Maybe this evening, however, I'll be able to find some things you can help with in that area."

"Yeah, that reminds me," said Duckie. "Is there a connecting door between our rooms?"

"Why, now that you mention it, I do believe there is."

"That's good. It's important that we're able to stay in close contact. In case something comes up." He took a deep breath. "Think I'll do a few laps while you work on your tan." He seemed to have a surplus of energy.

Guy put in an appearance with more tea and asked, "Do our guests have any special requests for dinner?" he asked.

"Oh, yes, great!" said Cheryl. "Cook does wonderful dinners! French cuisine is his specialty. Can you think of something special and French you'd like for dinner?"

This question caught Duckie flat-footed. "Uh, how about … duck à l'Orange?" he said.

"Excellent choice, sir," said Guy. He turned and made his way back to the house with stately grace.

"Ooh, you're so smooth," said Cheryl. "I had no idea you were such the international gourmand."

"Man, that was total dumb luck that I thought of that," said Duckie. "I was thinking French fries, French toast, French onion soup. Hell, I've never even had duck à l'Orange."

"Ha!" laughed Cheryl. "Me too! When Uncle Richard asked me last night,

I said beef bourguignon. I'd never had it, either. Turns out it was just fancy beef stew. Really tasty, though."

Richard joined them midway through the main course. He was tall and dignified, with a deeply lined face and suspiciously dark hair. "Mr. Dunne," he said, "welcome to my home. I'm so very glad you could join us. My apologies for not greeting you when you arrived. I've had a fair amount of unexpected business to attend to, I'm afraid."

"Thank you, sir," said Duckie. "It's a great place you have here."

"Thank you," said Richard. "I'm glad the two of you were able to enjoy the pool. I'm afraid I so rarely have time for things like that."

"Cheryl said you were retired," said Duckie. "You sure seem to be busy for a guy who's retired. Or does 'retirement' have a different definition up here in Canada?"

"Oh, it's complicated," sighed Richard. "Unfortunately, I have been unable to shake the work ethic you Americans have that demands you work yourself to death to pay for things you're too busy to enjoy."

"What do you mean, *you* Americans?" asked Duckie. "I thought you were from Long Island."

"That's true," said Richard. "I have dual citizenship, but I've lived here so long that I think of myself as more Canadian than American. I went to school at the University of Toronto and just fell in love with the city. I stayed after I graduated, and founded my own accounting firm, Gross, Gilmore and Sawchuk. We started in a tiny office above a shoe store, but now GG&S is the third-largest accounting firm in Canada.

"And I'm not really retired, *per se*. I'm more of an *emeritus* partner, and have a certain amount of responsibility. Unfortunately, there is a large project with a deadline coming up that requires more attention than I had initially anticipated. Therefore, I haven't been as gracious a host as I should have. My apologies."

"No prob, Uncle Dick," said Duckie. "There's plenty to keep us busy."

Cheryl scowled and dug her elbow into his side. "Don't call him that," she said sotto voce.

"Oh, sorry," said Duckie. "No disrespect, sir."

"It's okay," said Richard. "It's just an unpleasant memory from childhood. My brother Michael used to call me 'Dick' – he knew it really got under my skin. I shouldn't have let it bother me so, but he has a special skill for finding someone's weak spot and just laying into it. He can be quite merciless."

"I bet," said Duckie. He thought of a bootleg he had from a show in Buffalo where Mickey had laid into a heckler with such ferocity that the man had left the theater in tears. Mickey Gross had a rapier wit and no reservations about sticking it right into people's soft parts.

"Well, if we're going to talk about my brother, I suggest that we retire to the den," said Richard. "I suspect that I'm going to need a drink." As if on cue, Guy materialized and began clearing the dishes. Duckie, Cheryl and Richard headed back to the den, where a fire was already blazing in the fireplace.

Drinks were distributed and pleasantries exchanged. Once they had settled in, Richard took a long sip from his cognac and said, "So, you're looking for a friend of yours and you think that my brother might have some idea where he is. Tell me."

"It was just a wild hunch," said Duckie. "You know that there were rumors that Mickey had faked his own death pretty much since he died."

"Oh, yes," said Richard. "You seem to be very familiar with Michael's career, so I'm sure you're aware that he used to talk about faking his own death – well, I wouldn't say frequently – but it was hardly an untrod path for him. Certainly, the family expected him to turn up alive, especially right after his death made the news. But the funeral came and went, and no surprises. It was an open-casket funeral, too. When I see him again, I'd love to find out how he pulled the whole scam off. *If* I see him again."

"What makes you think you won't see him again?" asked Cheryl.

"He's been alive for the last five years, and I just found out a week ago!" said Richard. "It was quite a surprise, and for more than one reason."

"What do you mean?" asked Cheryl.

"Well, first, I had thought my brother was dead. Second, he literally appeared on the front doorstep. Undetected. I don't know if you know this, but this house has a great deal of security systems and so forth."

"Oh, really?" asked Duckie, thinking of the pistol grips sticking out of the back of the staff's pants.

"Yes," said Uncle Richard. "During the course of my career, I got crosswise with some, shall we say, dubious characters. There is, of course, no real risk – you're perfectly safe here – but why take any chances, eh? The point I'm trying to make is that Michael somehow managed to evade several layers of a very sophisticated surveillance and security system. It was rather unnerving."

"Maybe you just have a crummy security system," said Duckie.

"It jolly well better not be, given what I paid for it," said Uncle Richard. "Of course, I had the company send out a technician the very next day. They checked it over, but it was working perfectly."

"Why did Mickey show up, then?" asked Duckie.

"He didn't say, exactly," said Uncle Richard. "He just said that he had some business up north. He was very vague about it. Now let's get down to brass tacks. You think Michael might know where your friend Chuck is, and you want to try and find them both."

"Yes, that's right," said Duckie. "When I saw Mickey, he told me about a place called Laughingstock. It was, like, a retreat for comics to get away from the pressures of the road and just chill out with other comedians. He said that it was on Vancouver Island somewhere north of here."

"Well, that's most of the island," said Richard. "Did he say anything that would help narrow it down?"

"He said that he'd come into Victoria, then it was a car ride for a couple of hours, then finally he had to ride in a boat to get there. He said that the place started out pretty small, but over the years it got built up. Some big-name comedians kicked in major money to improve it. He made it sound more like a resort than a summer camp, y'know?"

"Did he say if the place was still in use?" asked Cheryl.

"He didn't say," replied Duckie. "I kinda got the impression that it wasn't, but I can't say for sure. I was going to ask him a little more about it, but he did a runner on me before I could talk to him."

"Again, sounds familiar," said Richard. "But at least we have a starting point. Let's go to the map room and see if we can't narrow down the search." He got up and led them to another part of the house, into a small case-lined room with dark, rich furnishings. There was a long built-in table in the middle of the room, and a large flatscreen monitor on the wall.

"He's got a map room?" whispered Duckie.

"He's got an *everything* room," whispered Cheryl.

"Yes, and sometimes these flamboyant and superfluous rooms come in handy," said Richard. "Like now. I've always enjoyed the idea of a map room, ever since I visited the one in the Vatican. Now, let's take a look at good old Vancouver Island." He reached into a drawer, pulled out a large map and spread it on the table. "You said it took a couple of hours by car, correct?"

"That's what Mickey told me," said Duckie. "But that doesn't mean that it was accurate or anything. He said he was pretty fuck— uh, messed up. Your sense of time can really get out of whack when your brain is, too."

Richard leaned over the map and pointed to a place on the east coast of the island. "Nanaimo," he said. "It's about an hour and a half by car, so that might fall within the timeframe. It's pretty big – the second-largest city on the island. Also, it's got a big harbor. Lots of boats, ferries, docks et cetera. Also, there are a lot of islands nearby that can't be reached by car. You'd need a boat to get there."

"We should leave soon," said Duckie. "Actually, I'm looking forward to the trip. It's really pretty up here."

"I have a Range Rover that you're welcome to use," said Richard. "It may be useful if you have to do some off-roading or something like that."

"I think I'll pass," said Duckie. "I don't want to seem ungrateful. I'm just worried about driving someone else's expensive car in another country, y'know?"

"I understand," said Richard. "But you might want to consider this: A Range Rover with BC tags is likely to attract less attention from the gendarmerie than an older car with American tags. Not that I'd expect you to get up to anything illegal, of course."

"Of course," said Duckie. "But we would like to avoid any Imperial entanglements."

"Indeed," said Richard. "May the Force be with you."

Duckie and Cheryl shared a look, then cracked up. "Good one, Uncle Di— Uncle Richard," said Duckie.

"I have my moments," said Richard.

"Well, what happens when we get there?" asked Cheryl. "Nanaimo may be a good starting point, but it's only a starting point, right?"

"True enough," said Duckie. "I mean, we can ask around once we get there, of course. That's pretty much how it's going to have to work."

"You're really good at that," said Cheryl. "I mean, you managed to track down Mickey pretty much on your own. Lots of people had tried, but only you succeeded. You missed your calling; you should have been a detective."

"Ha!" snorted Duckie. "The *only* profession less reputable than stand-up comedy. Besides, it was finding Cheryl that was the real achievement. For a number of reasons."

"I'm glad you think so," said Cheryl, blushing.

Richard gave them both a once-over and grinned. "I think that there's more going on here than just looking for a missing friend, eh? Maybe I should have put you in the same room?"

Cheryl and Duckie shared another look, and this time both of them blushed.

"You wouldn't mind?" asked Cheryl.

"No, why would I?" said Richard. "You're consenting adults. You can do as you please."

"Well, in that case…" said Duckie, stretching his arms and yawning theatrically.

Cheryl whapped him in the stomach with the back of her hand. "Easy, hard charger," she said with a grin. "There'll be plenty of time for that later. Let's focus on the matter at hand. Dinner first, then dessert."

"Yes, ma'am," said Duckie. He stepped over to the map table and leaned over to avoid embarrassing himself. *Cold, cold winter wind in Fester,* he thought. *Blowing right off the Black River. Brrr.*

"What are you doing?" asked Cheryl.

Attempting to hide an erection, thought Duckie. "Just wanted to check out the map some more," he said. "See if we can spot some likely islands or something."

"I've got a better idea," said Richard. He produced a remote and turned on the monitor on the wall. A color image of Earth appeared.

"Google Earth," said Duckie. "Great idea!"

"Even better," said Richard. "It's a direct feed to the Maxar database. Much better that Google. Higher resolution and more up to date. Some of those images on Google can be years old." He fiddled with the remote and the image zoomed in to a spot on the island north of Victoria. It showed a waterfront city with streets radiating out from the waterfront like spokes on a wheel. "So, uh, Duckie," continued Richard, "do you remember how long Michael said it took to get by boat to this island?"

"Not exactly sure," said Duckie. "I want to say it was an hour, but I'm not entirely sure."

"Okay, at least that's a starting point," said Richard. "Let's see, a pretty fast ski boat can go up to twenty miles an hour. So that means that the destination can be no more than twenty miles from Nanaimo. Let's see if I can get this bit to work." He fiddled with the remote control some more, and eventually got a red ring to appear that was centered on the city on the screen. A little more fiddling and it expanded outward. "There," said Richard. "That's a twenty-mile radius from Nanaimo."

"Geez," said Cheryl. "That covers a lot of territory. It almost goes back to the mainland!"

"Well, you can just start scanning the images," said Richard. "Look for evidence of buildings or camps on the islands that are supposed to be undeveloped. Here, I'll show you." He spent some time showing Duckie and Cheryl how to zoom in and out on the map, and how to switch between the photographs and the map view. "If you don't mind, I'm going to leave you two to go at it. I've had a long day and am extremely tired." He took his empty cognac glass and left, limping slightly.

"I guess we can go at it now," said Cheryl with a smile.

"Yeah, this thing is pretty neat," said Duckie. "Hey, check this one out. It looks like there are some houses or something on this island. Whassit called? 'Mistaken Island.' Maybe that's it."

"No, Wilbert dear," said Cheryl. She slid up behind him and wrapped her arms around his chest. "That wasn't what I was talking about," she whispered into his ear.

"Oh," said Duckie. "Yes, of course. I must have been mistaken." He squirmed slightly as Cheryl continued to breathe warmly into his ear. He felt conflicted. On one hand, it felt like he was getting really close to finding Chuck, and he wanted to keep looking for likely spots for Laughingstock. On the other hand, there was a very attractive woman wrapped around him who was breathing into – no, now she was sticking her tongue into – his ear. That pretty much ended the debate. The moderator in his pants said so.

He turned around in Cheryl's arms and planted a heavy kiss on her lips – a kiss that went on and on. "Tell you what," he said. "Why don't you go back to your room and change into that little red bikini, and I'll be along shortly."

"Why do you want me to put on the bikini?"

"Because all afternoon I've been thinking about peeling it off of you."

"Okay, then. Good. Don't be late."

She departed, and Duckie thought that he ought to spend at least a little time scanning the satellite photos. Sure, Cheryl was probably stripping down and slipping into that tiny bikini right now, waiting for him to join her. On the other hand, his friend needed him. He couldn't just give up on him for sex, right? But it wasn't really giving up, though, was it? Just taking a break – and a well-deserved one at that. He decided that he'd keep scanning for another ten minutes, then go to Cheryl.

Chapter 43

After Don had discovered Chuck Marshall holed up in Azusa, he spent three days watching the house. Chuck had gone out once during the day for a hike, and twice at night to pick up groceries. After that, Malachi had told Don to call off his surveillance, and that he would personally take care of bringing Chuck "back into the fold." He'd also told Don to prepare for a business trip the following Monday, and that they would be taking Malachi's yacht.

He sent a limo to pick up Don in Sylmar and drive him down to the Long Beach yacht basin. Malachi's yacht was so big that it required its own section of the basin. The thing was enormous. White, with four decks, it looked like a cruise ship. "Holy shit," Don muttered. "It's like the freakin' Queen Mary."

He retrieved his bag and walked away as the limo drove off. The yacht was moored stern-inward so he could read the name: *Glamour.* There was a lot of activity going on: ropes being tied up or cast off, boxes carried on and off, polishing and sweeping. As Don drew closer, he saw Malachi Wolff on the dock, berating a swarthy man in cook's whites. The man nodded furiously as Malachi waved his hands and yelled. The cook bowed and scurried up the gangplank.

"Hey! Don!" said Malachi. "So glad to see you. It's a great day for a cruise, don't you think?"

"Sir, yes, sir," said Don. He wasn't actually looking forward to spending so much time on the water. "What was that all about?" he asked, jerking his chin at the gangplank.

"Ah, good help is so hard to find," sighed Malachi. "I was just impressing on the chef that we need to be properly prepared for our voyage. You like steak, don't you?"

"Love it," said Don.

"That's what I thought. I was just telling Musul there that we needed more steak. Good for muscles, good for iron in the bloodstream, right?"

"Sir, yes, sir," said Don dutifully.

Malachi stood back and beamed at the yacht like he had built it himself. "It's a real beauty, isn't it, Don?"

"Yes, sir, it certainly is. You should be proud."

"I am," said Malachi. "The *Glamour* is 421 feet long. Even bigger than Vladimir Putin's yacht. His is only 417 feet. I made sure mine was a couple of feet longer – it pissed him off to no end. It was built by the famous Bickel und Focke ship works in Kiel. It's faster than Vladimir's, too. This baby will cruise at over sixty knots. We'll get where we're going in about a day!"

"Where are we going, sir?" asked Don. Malachi had not been forthcoming with the details of the voyage. He'd made it sound like an extra-private strategy session, held on his yacht out at sea to avoid surveillance. The destination had seemed irrelevant.

"Oh, you'll see when we get there," said Malachi. "Well, let's get you on board and situated. We're very close to casting off. Follow me." He whistled at one of the uniformed people to come for Don's luggage, but Don waved them away.

"Might as well let them get on with getting ready," he said, shouldering the bag.

"If you insist," said Malachi. "Please, come aboard."

Malachi led Don up the gangplank and gave him the quick tour of the *Glamour*. Actually, it wasn't that quick; the ship was huge. It was like someone had taken an entire luxury resort and crammed it into a fiberglass hull. Outside, there was a swimming pool, a helipad, a number of smaller watercraft hung on davits. The bridge looked like something out of a sci-fi movie. The inside was even more opulent, with huge lounges furnished with expensive furniture. There was a massive kitchen and an equally massive dining room. There was also a spa, a dance floor, an indoor swimming pool and a bowling alley. Don gawked at that one; how the hell did you bowl on a ship at sea?

Finally, Malachi said, "And here's your stateroom." He pushed open the door to a small suite that would not have been out of place at one of L.A.'s finer hotels. A junior suite, to be sure, but impressive nonetheless.

"I'll give you some time to unpack and unwind," said Malachi. "I'll meet you up on deck in an hour, and we can talk more about where we're going and what we're doing. Sound good?"

"Yes, sir."

It took Don about three minutes to unpack and another five to completely explore his suite. Having secured his hooch, he decided to walk the perimeter. The problem was that the perimeter was surrounded by water. This made Don nervous; there was no cover and no escape routes. He had to remind himself that this was a business trip, not a combat mission.

He walked around to the broad expanse of the bow, and encountered Gordie the Guru, who sat cross-legged on the deck, eyes closed, palms up on his knees and wearing a beatific smile. Don felt like belting him one, just to wipe the expression off his face.

Gordie's eyes opened, narrowed for an instant, and then he smiled even wider. "Don Bundy!" he cried happily. "So good to see you again!" He went from his lotus position to standing on the deck without any intervening movement. "Would you care to join me in some yoga exercises?" said Gordie. "I have Mr. Wolff do them three times a day. Wonderful for relaxing the mind, relaxing the body. It is very useful to facilitate the other therapies I have developed for him."

"That's just dandy," said Don. "But I've got my own workout routine, and it serves me just fine, thanks."

"All well and good, Don. You are welcome to join me any time." Gordie collapsed back into his lotus pose so quickly that Don couldn't follow it. He had to hand it to him: the guy was nimble.

Don found a little gym in a nook behind the bowling alley, and spent some time going through his own workout. When he finished, he went back to his suite and showered off, then put on some shorts and deck shoes and headed back up to the main deck. The activity on the dock was frenzied, and uniformed crew members were hustling the last few items onboard. On the dock, others were loosening the lines that held the ship fast. The ship's horn sounded a long blast and the scurrying on the dock reached a crescendo.

Malachi Wolff appeared, with a blue blazer and a captain's hat. "Ready to set sail, Don?"

"Yes, sir. I've been looking forward to it." Actually, what Don was looking forward to was the whole voyage being over. It felt like there was something weird going on here; he just didn't know what.

"Don, I'd like you to join me on the bridge as we set sail," said Malachi. "I thought that with your technical background, you might find it interesting."

"Absolutely, sir, thank you." He followed Malachi up to the bridge. It was a sizable space, with windows that provided a panoramic view of the entire Long Beach basin. The captain was there, dressed very similar to Malachi, the cap just a little less fancy. Two other crewmen were hopping between various consoles and displays.

"Don, this is Captain Jack Padova," said Malachi. "Captain Jack, this is Don Bundy. He was in the Marines." The captain tipped him a two-fingered salute. Don gave him a curt nod.

"Ready to cast off whenever you say the word," said Captain Jack.

"Super!" said Malachi. "Can I blow the horn?"

"It's your vessel, sir," said Captain Jack.

"Great! Let's go!" Malachi was bouncing on the balls of his feet like a kid in line for a rollercoaster.

Captain Jack grabbed a microphone and announced, "This is the captain speaking. Stand by to cast off." On the dock, the ropes mooring the yacht were released. Captain Jack gave Malachi a nod, and he yanked on the rope for the horn, emitting an ear-splitting *whonk* which he evidently found enormously satisfying. Captain Jack eased the throttle up and the *Glamour* began to move away from the dock. Don turned to leave the bridge.

"Don't go too far. As soon as Gordie is done with his yoga, we need to have a meeting. Meet us in the forward lounge."

"Got it."

When he got there, Malachi and Gordie were hunched over a table in the corner, whispering. They looked up when Don walked in.

"Excellent," said Malachi. "The gang's all here. Don, it's time to loop you into the purpose of our voyage."

"I thought it was a secure business meeting," said Don. "We're going out to sea to ensure privacy. No corporate espionage."

"Well, that's mostly true," said Malachi. "Although this isn't strictly Wolff Network business."

"It's about Mr. Wolff's life extension program," said Gordie brightly. "We've reached a breakthrough stage. This is going to be big. Very big."

"If it all goes well," said Malachi, "you may be returning to Los Angeles as the new executive head of the network. How's that sound?"

"That sounds fine to me," said Don. And it did … to some extent. After all, that was his ambition. The problem was that it sounded too easy. He had actually been looking forward to getting his hands dirty, at least a little bit. Just having the keys to the kingdom handed to him wasn't as much fun.

"You said 'if it all goes well,'" said Don. "What is 'it' and what might go wrong?"

"Oh, nothing can go wrong!" said Gordie. "You need to keep a positive attitude."

Don thought that his attitude would be a lot more positive if he could get his hands around Gordie the Guru's neck. *Okay, okay,* he thought. *Just calm down.* This trip was already getting on his nerves. Time to take a few deep breaths and act like a professional.

Malachi stood up. "Okay," he said. "I think it's time to introduce Mr. Bundy to our guest. Follow me, please."

Malachi led Gordie and Don down one level and to the bow of the yacht. They stopped at a large double-door at the end of a wide passageway. "Normally, I would be staying in the master suite here," said Malachi. "However, it is only fitting that the guest of honor should have the nicest cabin." He fished a large keyring from his pocket and unlocked the door, then swung the doors open.

The master suite was, as expected, massive and luxurious. It was dominated by a California king bed at the far end of the room. An unconscious figure sprawled on the bed. There was an IV line running from his arm to a bag suspended from a pole on the corner of the bed.

It was Chuck Marshall.

"Holy shit!" said Don. "What's *he* doing here?"

"He's going to make all of our dreams come true," said Malachi. "Right, Gordie?"

"Absolutely," replied Gordie. "We're sure that the procedure will be a success." He hustled over to the IV drip and checked it, then nodded.

"Procedure?" said Don. "What the fuck are you talking about? This guy's the star of my show. If you do anything to him, the show's a bust. We'll never replace him."

"Oh, Don, Don, Don, Don, Don," said Malachi. "You need to step back and see the big picture. I thought you were a big picture type of guy. You are, aren't you?"

"Yes, sir, but the show—"

"Oh, *fuck* the show!" snapped Malachi. "Shows come and go. Don, we're on the cusp of something that will change the world. Don't you understand that?"

"I'm not sure what having an unconscious comedian with an IV, locked in a boat cabin has to do with it," said Don.

"You will," said Gordie. "Trust us."

"We have some time to fill you in on the details," said Malachi. "That's one of the reasons we're taking the yacht. I had hoped that you would see things our way, Don. If you don't think that you're man enough, well, we're still close to shore. You can take a launch back to the marina and start looking for another job. The time to choose is now. Are you on the boat or off the boat?"

Don's mind spun frantically. Clearly, this was something very strange – even stranger than the other crazy bullshit in Wolff's basement. He had no problem with strange and even wrong. He had done many strange and wrong things when he was in Afghanistan – at least some people thought they were "wrong."

Was kidnapping a TV comic that wrong? Maybe not. Not in the grand scheme of things. Besides, Don stood to gain quite a bit, if Malachi Wolff's promises came to fruition. Quite a lot indeed. Besides, Marshall was still alive, and didn't seem to be in any discomfort. Should some presumably minor inconveniences for a single person preclude Don achieving his goal? It was right here within reach. He'd be a fool to pass it up.

Or would he? It seemed too good to be true – which meant that it probably was. The whole setup was more than a little hinky.

"You're either on the boat or off the boat, Bundy," said Malachi. "I need your answer right now."

Chapter 44

uckie had wanted to spend another ten minutes scanning the maps; he lasted sixty seconds.

He couldn't help thinking of Cheryl. Cheryl lounging by the pool in her barely there bikini; Cheryl laughingly calling him "Wilbert;" Cheryl in bed with him that first night in her apartment. His attention evaporated as these images flashed across his consciousness.

"Out, out, damn spot," he muttered, trying to keep his mind on his search for his friend. He knew that Chuck was close; he couldn't just blow him off for a piece of tail.

Then again, Cheryl wasn't just a "piece of tail." She was really cool, and smart, and Duckie genuinely liked her. She was a friend, too. However, Duckie's persistent distraction was a clear indication that he needed to take care of first things first.

He was almost back to his room when his phone buzzed with a text. With minor difficulty, he levered it out of his pants and saw that it was from Cheryl. It read, "knock 3 times."

With a Tony Orlando earworm ricocheting around his brain, Duckie opened the door to his room. He made enough noise going in that Cheryl would hear him. He eyed the connecting door, and had to resist the temptation to rush in. *Show a little class,* he thought. It had been a long day, and he was worse for the wear. It would be a good idea to try and spruce himself up first. He stripped out of his clothes and went through a quick sink-bath: deodorant, brush teeth, wash face, comb hair. It seemed like there was something else, but he couldn't remember. Then there was the matter of wardrobe. He spotted a heavy terrycloth robe hanging from the back of the bathroom door. Perfect. He threw it on and gave the connecting door three sharp raps.

"Who is it?" came a teasing voice from the other side.

"It's the plumber," said Duckie. "I've come to fix the sink."

"Oooooh, good! I'm in need of a man who knows a thing or two about pipes."

Duckie gave his armpits a final sniff, then pushed open the door. The room was bathed in a low red light – Cheryl had draped a crimson scarf over the reading lamp by the bed. The room seemed steamy.

Cheryl was in bed, with the top sheet pulled up to her chin. Her eyes were large and luminous, and followed Duckie's every move. "I believe there was some unfinished business?" she asked.

Duckie gulped. "Yes, indeed," he said. "Ma'am, you showed me great hospitality at your place a while back. I am in your debt. And I always pay my debts. You can call me Duckie Lannister."

"Well then, Duckie Lannister, I guess it's time for a little payback." She whipped the sheet off, revealing her naked form underneath. "Oh no," she breathed. "I seem to have forgotten my bikini."

Duckie sucked in his breath. She *was* breathtaking. He stepped through the door, dropped the robe and launched himself into the bed. Immediately, they were intertwined, arms, legs, tongues coiling around each other.

They kissed passionately, holding each other tightly. Duckie knew that he was on the verge of losing control. Just one quick thrust and he could be inside her.

He took a deep breath, then pulled away slightly and kissed her neck. Then down where her neck and shoulder met. She moaned as he kissed and bit her there. Then down to her breasts, tongue lingering over one hard nipple, then the other. Onward! He scooched down on the bed and lightly kissed her belly.

"Where are you going?" she asked.

"As you mentioned, I have some unfinished business to take care of downtown."

He arrived downtown to find things already very wet. He slid his tongue up her cleft, reveling in the taste, the texture, the scent. He played his tongue around her clit, then began alphabetizing.

Duckie would *never* tell this to any of the women he'd slept with this, but this was one of his best moves in bed – and he'd gotten it from a Sam Kinison bit. "Lick the alphabet," Sam had advised his audience, and now Duckie did just that. His tongue traced the shapes of the letters around her cunny, spending time wherever possible at the top of the key. He looked up, and she was gazing back at him, her sparkling blue eyes wide.

When he got to Q, he thrust his tongue inside her. She cried out and arched her back.

"Like that, do you?" he asked.

"Mm-hmmm," she said, nodding.

He slid a finger inside her, then two, and continued up through R, S and T.

"Oh, there!" she moaned. "Right there! Don't stop! Please don't stop!"

Duckie didn't. He kept doing what he was doing and Cheryl's cries became intense and guttural. He looked up, but she was no longer looking at him – her eyes were squeezed tight. A deep flush appeared on her cheeks, then down her breasts, and her belly. *Hang on to your hat, boy*, thought Duckie. *We could end up miles from here!*

"Ohhhh … holy … *shit!*" gasped Cheryl. Her back arched again, and she froze for a moment, panting. Duckie was momentarily trapped as Cheryl locked him between her legs. At last she relaxed and lay back, breathing hard. Duckie slid down a bit, trying to reposition himself and catch his breath.

"And where do you think *you're* going?" asked Cheryl. She grabbed his forearm with both hands and hauled him up. His cock was titanium-hard, and slid up inside her with no resistance at all. He knew he had to take it slow, or he'd go off like a firecracker.

"Ohh, Duckie," she moaned. "Ohh, Wilbert!"

"Wilbert" briefly put him off his stride, but it didn't take long to regain it. He was really close now. *Really* close. He didn't want to bust his cookies too soon. He really wanted Cheryl to enjoy the experience. He needed to distract himself to keep from coming too quickly. He tried thinking about baseball. He tried thinking about cold winter nights in Fester. He tried thinking about gross horror movies. It didn't matter. His orgasm was coming like a tidal wave.

"Oh … my … *Gawwwd!*" he cried as his eyes locked with hers. He came like a typhoon, then his arms gave out and he flopped down on top of her. He kissed her gently and rolled off.

"Oh, wow," he said. "I mean that sincerely. Wow!"

"Well, Mister Businessman, you really gave me the business. And you really know your way around downtown."

They lay there, panting and intertwined. "Oh, snap!" said Duckie. "Damn!"

"What's wrong, darling?" Cheryl. asked.

"I just realized I forgot something," said Duckie. "A condom. Oh, crap!"

"Don't make a fuss. You're spoiling the moment."

"Aren't you worried about getting pregnant?"

"Not really. I started taking the pill a couple of weeks ago."

"Well, what about, um, disease?"

"I also got tested," she said. "I'm clean." She gave him a long look, then added, "I hope that doesn't freak you out or anything."

"Why would that freak me out?"

"Ah, I dunno. I was worried you might think that I was, y'know, getting too serious or something."

"I'm not freaked out," said Duckie. "Not with you. In fact, I'm a little flattered."

"Well, I'm really glad to hear that," said Cheryl. "However, I'm a little worried about you, though, Mister Funnyman. God only knows how many chuckle sluts you've been with."

"Not as many as I would've liked," said Duckie. "But look, while we're being all responsible and stuff, I think I ought to get tested, anyway. Until then, I'm perfectly good to wear a condom, um, going forward."

"No, that's okay. If it was a big deal, I would have said something earlier.

And I appreciate that you're willing to be responsible, and that you're not running for the door."

"Run from you? Not a chance!" He rolled over and gave her a deep kiss.

"Besides, I was never really that worried," she said when they broke their liplock. "I *do* know comedians, y'know. If they were actually getting any, they wouldn't be comedians."

"Way to spoil the mood, Cheryl. That's usually *my* job."

She slid her hand down and began massaging his cock, which sprang to attention immediately. "Sorry about that," she purred into his ear. "Although it sure doesn't feel like the mood is spoiled."

"By Jove, I think you're onto something."

"Not yet. But I will be."

Chapter 45

Duckie got up early the next morning. He didn't really want to, but he felt he owed it to Chuck. When he woke at first light the last thing he'd wanted to do was unwrap himself from Cheryl. Still, he felt the same strange twitch that he'd gotten on the ferry ride over from Port Angeles, even stronger now. Somehow he *knew* that Chuck was nearby and needed help. That galvanized Duckie to get up – slowly, as not to disturb Cheryl – and head back to the map room to look for Laughingstock.

He tiptoed to the door and cast a look over his shoulder at Cheryl's sleeping form. It was still dim in the room, but Duckie could see her face relaxed and smiling, with an inner glow. In repose, she looked so perfectly and beautifully human, and Duckie felt a flutter in his chest.

Oh God, I think I'm falling in love with her, he thought. His next thought was that it would be so easy to just climb back in bed, think of an inventive way of waking her up, and have some more awesome sex. He shook his head. He had to find his friend. He tiptoed through the door and closed it gently behind him.

As soon as he had ensconced himself in the map room and fired up the monitor, Guy appeared bearing a tray of fresh coffee. As Duckie sipped his java, he turned to the monitor and continued scanning the islands near Nanaimo.

An hour later, Cheryl wandered in, sleepy-eyed and smiling. "There you are, dear heart," she said. "I thought you'd run out on me."

"Never," he said. "Just looking for more places where Chuck might be.

I've got three more possibilities in addition to Mistaken Island. I'd really like to get going to Nanaimo this morning. I think we're getting close."

"Can we at least have breakfast first?" asked Cheryl. "I've got a hell of an appetite this morning. For some reason."

After a hearty breakfast, Uncle Richard saw Duckie and Cheryl off on the journey to Nanaimo. After a lot of back and forth, they finally decided that they'd take Richard's Range Rover, but Cheryl would do the driving.

It was a sunny morning, cool but warming rapidly, and the drive through the hilly wooded areas of southern Vancouver Island was bright and pleasant.

In the driver's seat, Cheryl shivered and then grinned.

"You okay?" asked Duckie.

"Oh, yeah," said Cheryl. "Just an aftershock from last night, Wilbert dear."

"Oh. Okay. Good."

"Oh, it was *real* good. Don't you think?"

"No, I don't think," said Duckie. "I *know*. That was freakin' awesome, sweetheart. Probably the best I've ever had. No, *definitely* the best I've ever had."

Cheryl giggled and blushed, and Duckie's heart did the same double-tap that it had earlier that morning when he'd watched her sleeping.

"Do you mind if I ask you a question?" she asked.

Talking about the relationship, thought Duckie. *Yay.* Then he bit down on the impulse to say something sarcastic. He had done so many times before when the subject had come up, and it had never gone well. *Yeah, women like to talk about relationships,* he thought. *You want a relationship with this woman, right? Then you better be ready to talk to her about it ... and not be an asshole in the process.* He said, "Sure thing, beautiful. Shoot."

"What do you think's going to happen when this is over? With us and all?"

"Uh," said Duckie. "Wow. I mean, I guess it depends on whether we're still even talking to each other then."

She gave him a scowl. "Why wouldn't we be talking?"

"Hey, hey, don't get me wrong," said Duckie, holding up his hands. "I think you are just the bees' knees, darling. It's just that … well, I'm a comic fer Chrissake. We're all damaged."

"And I'm the daughter of one of the biggest and most damaged comics of all time, right?"

"Yeah, okay," said Duckie. "I see your point. I mean, your dad is my comedy idol, but he's also got a pretty fucked up track record. No offense."

"None taken. That was my point. You gots baggage. I gots baggage."

"Well, at least the baggage seems to match. We should go on a trip together!"

"We are, dear, we are."

"Okay, Cheryl, in all seriousness, I was actually thinking about this, sorta, when I got back home from your place. I really haven't been doing much for myself other than treading water, y'know? Working enough at my slave job to keep the bills paid, keeping up my rounds on the local comedy scene, that's pretty much been it. Maybe I'm due for a change."

"Well, I haven't really been making any major moves myself, lately," said Cheryl. "There was the thing with Nigel, but I let it drag on for nearly a year even after it was obvious that it wasn't going anywhere. He wasn't really bad or abusive or anything. He just got more … neglectful, I guess. Cancel plans at the last minute to hang out with his friends, wouldn't call for long stretches, that sort of thing."

"Jesus, what a bonehead! Shit, with a name like 'Nigel,' whaddaya expect? He's probably gay."

"Jeez, I don't know whether to be flattered or offended."

"Okay, yeah," said Duckie. "That was a dumb thing for me to say. If we're gonna spend time together, I'm afraid you're going to have to get used to it, because I say dumb, insensitive shit all the time. The hell of it is that I don't really mean most of it, I'm just trying to get a cheap laugh. Here's a secret about comedians: We're all 13-year-old boys inside. Even the most suave, sophisticated comedian you ever heard is desperately trying to keep a lid on a volcano of fart jokes. I just think any guy who walked away from you must be a major idiot, that's all I meant. Being gay is the only thing that explains such irrational behavior."

"Okay, I'll go with flattered, with just a little bit of offended for good measure," said Cheryl. "You're just lucky I don't make judgments based on names. Duckie."

"Yeah, okay I don't have a he-man name, but it beats 'Nigel' all to hell."

"It certainly does, Wilbert," said Cheryl, and she leaned over and gave Duckie a peck on the cheek. The Range Rover swerved alarmingly.

"Yarrgh!" said Duckie. "Watch the road!"

"Oh, calm down," said Cheryl. "If the car gets dinged, I'll be the one to deal with it."

"I don't care about the car getting dinged; I'm worried about dying in a fiery wreck."

"Jeez, you sure are highly strung today. It was just a little kiss."

"I'm sorry," said Duckie. "Just getting a little wound up about finding Chuck. It feels like he's close. But it also feels … weird, somehow. The kiss was very nice."

"Good," said Cheryl. "How much longer do you think it will take us to get to Nanaimo?"

"I'll check," said Duckie as he pulled out his phone. He thumbed the screen a number of times and reported, "Uh, looks like there's some traffic up ahead, but we should hit the city limits in about forty-five minutes."

He continued futzing around with his phone, and was struck with a sudden idea. "Shoulda thought of that before," he muttered. He thumbed the screen some more, then stopped. "Oh, holy shit," he said. "This *can't* be a coincidence."

"What? What did you find?"

"I don't know why I didn't think of this before, but I thought I should see if there are any comedy clubs in Nanaimo."

"Well, are there?"

"Mostly, it's bars and restaurants that have a comedy night once a week," said Duckie. "It looks like there's only one dedicated comedy club in town."

"Yeah, what about it?" asked Cheryl.

"It's called Laughingstock."

Chapter 46

They rolled into Nanaimo forty minutes later and checked into a hotel. Uncle Richard had insisted on booking a room for them at a place on the waterfront called the Harbourview Suites & Marina. It sounded fancy, but it wasn't. It was a little cramped, a little old and a little mildewed. However, the staff was friendly, and it did provide a pretty view of the harbor.

"I guess Uncle Richard chose this on the basis of the name alone," said Cheryl.

"Yeah," said Duckie. "I don't know that I'd go so far as to call this a 'suite.' It's more like a run-of-the-mill motel unit with a sitting room in front of the crapper. On the other hand, can't beat the price."

"Yes, it was very generous of him to pay for our accommodations."

"And it's in a good location," said Duckie. "It's only about six blocks from Laughingstock."

"What time does it open?"

"Not until seven," said Duckie. "So we've got some time to kill."

"Great!" said Cheryl. "Let's explore."

"Sure, I just want to stop by the front desk on the way out."

They walked down the stairs because the elevator was out of order. Behind the desk was the large, friendly woman who had checked them in. According to the tag on her rayon blouse, her name was Marge.

"Oh, hi there," said Marge. "Did you get all settled in? I'm so sorry about the elevator. The repairman should be here any time now."

"Well, Marge, we sure are enjoying the stay so far," said Duckie. "There're all sorts of interesting aromas in the room! Very international. I just had a couple of questions for you."

"Oh, sure," said Marge. "What can I do for you?"

"First, there's a comedy club up on Chapel Street called Laughingstock. Have you ever been there?"

"A comedy club?" asked Marge. "Oh, yes, I think I know the place. It just opened last year. No, I've never been there. Me and the husband just keep to ourselves at night. We don't really go out to clubs and such."

"Okay," said Duckie. "A swing and a miss. Have you ever heard of a place called Mistaken Island?"

"Oh yes, that sounds familiar," said Marge. "I think it's up the coast a little ways, up by Parksville."

"Do you know anything about it? Is there anything there? Like maybe a camp or something?"

"Oh, I sure don't know about that," said Marge. "There's all sorts of islands around here, dontcha know."

"We saw satellite photos of some buildings on it," said Cheryl. "We thought it might be a camp or something."

"Well, y'know, a lot of these islands used to have little fishing camps that are abandoned now. Like I said, they're all over the place."

"Oh, okay," said Duckie. He had been afraid of this. In the map room at Uncle Richard's, he'd been amazed by the number of islands and out-of-the-way peninsulas on Vancouver Island. He knew the search wasn't going to be easy, but it was shaping up to be more difficult than he had thought. He hoped like hell that the Laughingstock comedy club was going to provide a solid lead, but the fact that it was only a year or so old was a little disappointing.

"C'mon," said Cheryl. "Let's explore."

"Just call me Magellan," said Duckie. "Let's bop on down to the waterfront."

The Nanaimo waterfront was beautiful. They found a brewpub close to the harbor and had a late lunch. Across the street was a vibrant park packed with people out enjoying the pleasant weather. There were also a number of buskers, jugglers and people selling trinkets spread out on blankets on the ground. Cheryl spent some time browsing the jewelry vendors. Duckie started to get impatient, and looked around for something to occupy his attention.

A few feet away from the jewelry vendors was a man crouched down inside a cardboard box. A square had been cut in the front of the box, and underneath were the words "Reality Television" in black Magic Marker. The man looked to be in his late fifties, with a broad forehead and thinning gray hair. He was talking in a credible imitation of Walter Cronkite, babbling something about French Indo-China.

The setup reminded Duckie of an old Monty Python sketch. He strolled over and said, "Can you do a documentary about mollusks?"

"Depends on the color of your coin, mate," said the man. "Five dollars."

"Five bucks?" said Duckie. "You gotta be kidding."

"Wait – are you American?"

"Yeah."

"In that case, ten bucks."

"Screw you, Jackson," said Duckie.

In a pitch-perfect imitation of John Cleese, the man in the box said, "The mollusk is a randy little fellow whose thoughts scarcely stray from the subject of you-know-what."

"Disgusting!" said Duckie. "But more interesting! Do more."

The man cut his eyes down to a battered metal cup in front of the box. It had a few multi-colored bills and a handful of coins in it. Duckie pulled out his wallet, extracted a fiver, waved it in front of the box and dropped it into the cup. The man in the box continued with the Python routine, with Duckie throwing in the handful of straight lines to keep things moving. When the skit ended, the man in the box froze, his face carefully blank.

"Ha ha ha!" laughed Duckie. "That was awesome. You nailed it. How about Kids in the Hall? You gotta know them – they're Canadian."

The man's face stayed carefully blank, but he cut his eyes to the metal cup again.

"Sorry, dude," said Duckie. "That was my last bill. I need to pick up some more funny money."

The man stayed frozen for a moment longer, then scrunched up his face. "Funny money, huh?" he said. "What do you know from funny, Yank?"

"I know plenty," said Duckie. "I'm a comedian."

The man in the box looked at him long and hard, then rolled his eyes. "Hell, *everybody's* a comedian. Come back when you get some *funny money*."

"Yeah, maybe," said Duckie. "If I need an overpriced imitation of a fifty-year-old comedy bit, I know where to come."

"Oh, I'm sure I'll see you again soon," said the man in the box.

Duckie shrugged and walked back to where Cheryl was finishing up her jewelry transaction. Behind him, the man in the box began talking like Dick Clark, introducing the O'Jays on American Bandstand.

"Didja get something nice?" asked Duckie.

Cheryl nodded and held a gold necklace with large green stones up to her neck.

"And just when I thought it wasn't possible for you to get any prettier," said Duckie.

"You're so sweet," said Cheryl. She leaned over and gave him a kiss. "What's that guy's deal?" she asked, jerking her chin at the man in the box.

"Street performer," said Duckie. "Pretty cool. Does a good Python."

"Oh, cool. I wanna see!"

"Do you have any cash? If not, you'll probably only hear Tom Brokaw talking about the war in Bosnia."

"Nope, just spent my last cash on the necklace."

"Well, I wanted to pick up some more of the local simoleons, anyway," said Duckie. "Let's find an ATM."

After they had secured some Canadian cash, they strolled around downtown, digging the laid-back vibe of the place. After a while, they wandered back close to the hotel. They decided to return to their room for a little afternoon delight, which was followed by a well-deserved nap.

Duckie woke up and looked at his phone; it was quarter to eight. He was starting to get hungry, but more than that, he wanted to go back to the comedy club and hit them up for information. "Tell you what," he said, "I'm gonna shower off, then I'd like to go to the club. Maybe we can get a bite there."

"Oh, a comedy club meal," said Cheryl. "Probably at least as good as a school cafeteria Salisbury steak."

"If we're lucky," said Duckie, thinking about a venue in Portland called the Big Top that featured the worst heat-lamp pizza known to mankind. "We'll find someplace else to eat afterwards. I just want to find out what they know."

They both took a quick turn in the shower. Cheryl wanted to shower together, but Duckie demurred, knowing that they'd likely not leave the hotel room if that happened. Cheryl pouted a little, but soon they were back on the street.

The lights were on at Laughingstock, but it looked dead. There were only a few cars in the parking lot, and no one going into or coming out of the club.

"You sure it's open?" asked Cheryl.

"Looks pretty beat," said Duckie. "Let's find out what's going on." He strode up to the front door and gave it a yank, thinking it would be locked. Instead, it flew open revealing a sparsely populated showroom. The lights had just gone down, and a guy with a rainbow afro wig and a basket of props was taking the stage. Duckie sighed. A prop comic. Only a notch above mime in his estimation.

To the right of the door was a small bar. A young man with a goatee and a nose ring said, "Welcome to Laughingstock. That will be five dollars each, please."

Duckie strolled up to the bar and put down a pair of Canadian fivers, which were bright blue and had a picture of a stuffy-looking priest. "Ten dollars Canadian," he said grandly. "Nice place you've got here."

"Thanks," said the bartender. He stuck out his hand. "I'm Milo."

"Pleased to meetcha, Milo. I'm Duckie and this is Cheryl. Say, is the owner available?"

"You're talking to him, Duckie," said Milo.

"Oh," said Duckie. He had hoped that the owner was some grizzled old-school comedy veteran who knew all the dirt on the local scene. Milo, on the other hand, looked like he was barely old enough to rent a car. "So, Milo, what can you tell me about the history of Laughingstock?"

"Oh, sure," said Milo. "We moved out here last year from Kamloops and opened this place up. We wanted to find a place in Victoria, but rent's too expensive there. I figured we'd get things going here, then maybe move to the big city once it took off."

"That's a great name you came up with – Laughingstock. Really good name for a top-notch chuckle hut such as this. Where'd you get the idea?"

Milo shrugged. "Dunno. It just seemed like a good name. Kinda like Woodstock, but for comedy."

"So it's not, y'know, based on something else?" asked Duckie. "Maybe another place nearby used to be called that? Like a campground or something?"

Milo looked confused. "A campground?" he asked. "Why would a campground be called Laughingstock?"

"I dunno," said Duckie. "Like, maybe there was a campground or place where comics would, like, go to relax and chill out?" He studied Milo for a glimmer of recognition, but could see none. The guy genuinely had no idea what Duckie was talking about.

"Well, I tell you, I've never heard of anything like that," said Milo. "This place is less than two years old, and it isn't really named after anything. Sorry."

"It's okay," said Cheryl. "This is a really nice club you've got. We're sort of comedy historians, and we heard about a place up here that comedians used to go and hang out. We heard it was called Laughingstock, so when we saw the name of your club, we figured there was a connection."

"Just a coincidence, I guess," said Milo. "So you're comedy historians, eh?"

"Well, I'm more of the historian," said Cheryl. "Duckie here is more of a practicing comedian."

"Really?" said Milo. "That's great! Are you famous?"

"Well, I'm pretty well-known in places where they know me," admitted

Duckie. He pulled out his phone and showed Milo his web page, duck-iedunnecomedy.com.

"Wow! A famous USA comedian!" said Milo. "Would you be willing to get up and do a few minutes?"

"Well, I don't know," said Duckie. "This guy looks like he's going to be a hard act to follow." He gestured towards the stage where the guy with the rainbow wig was making balloon animals and telling dick jokes. "Besides, I'm having my leg amputated tomorrow."

"I'm sorry to hear that," said Milo. "Oh, Chet's almost done." He jumped up on stage to introduce the next act: a man who recited bawdy limericks while juggling beanbags. He immediately got big laughs, even though the limericks were chestnuts Duckie had heard on the elementary school playground.

"Sorry I couldn't be more help," said Milo when he returned.

"That's okay," said Duckie. "Right now, I just want to get a steak while I can still walk. Is there some place nearby with good steak?"

"Oh, ayuh," said Milo. "The Chief of Beef. It's down on Cliff Street. I can draw you a map—"

"No worries," said Duckie. "I'm sure we can find it on our own."

"I hope everything goes well with your surgery tomorrow," said Milo.

"Thanks!" said Duckie. "I'll send you what they cut off. You can mount it over the bar!" Without waiting for a reply he pushed through the door, pulling Cheryl behind him.

"Hey! Leggo!" said Cheryl.

"Sorry, babe, sorry," said Duckie.

"What's your problem?" said Cheryl. "And why didn't you perform?"

"Holy Christ, it was that club!" said Duckie. "The vibe in that room was so wrong. Rainbow afro wigs and balloon animals! Holy shit!"

"You'll feel better once you get something to eat."

"Yeah," said Duckie distractedly. He really didn't feel like eating right now. "Do you mind if we just walk for a little? I need to clear my head."

They wandered down by the park they'd visited at lunchtime. In the early evening's glow, the park and the water beyond looked soft, inviting, mysterious. There were fewer people here now, and almost all of the vendors had left. The Reality Television guy was still there, apparently re-enacting an episode of *I Love Lucy*. Cheryl wandered over to watch.

Duckie mulled over the events of the day. They hadn't been good. "Shit!" he said bitterly.

"What's wrong?" asked Cheryl.

"Ah, hell, everything's wrong. The trail's gone cold now. I thought we had it knocked with that club name, that it would be the answer and would lead us right to Chuck. But no. *Goddammit!*"

"Well, I still think we're close," said Cheryl. "Even if it's just a coincidence that the place is called Laughingstock, it could be a meaningful coincidence. Maybe Milo overheard something that inspired the name, and he just forgot."

"Excuse me, sirrah," said the Reality Television guy in perfect Terry-Thomas voice. "If by 'Laughingstock' you are referring to the semi-secret comics' retreat rather than the squalid Jack-in-the-Box comedy club, I may be of some service."

"What?!" said Duckie. "You know about the *real* Laughingstock? Is it nearby? Where is it?"

The Reality Television man bulged his eyes out slightly and cast a meaningful glance at his tin cup.

"Huh?" said Duckie. "Yeah, okay!" He dug out his wallet and pulled out a bill. "Okay, here you go, twenty bucks. And this better be good!"

"I'll level with ya, pal," said the Reality Television guy in an East Coast accent. "I don't know *exactly* where the place is, but I can point you to someone who does. It's up close to Courtenay. Ya gotta go up to Courtenay and find the Bookbinder. He can tell you."

"The bookbinder?" asked Duckie. "What the fuck are you talking about? Who is that?"

"Look, I just told you…" said the Reality Television guy. His head whipped around. Two police officers were quick-walking to where they were talking.

"Goldurnit, Hippo!" said one of the cops. "We told you about a million times: We don't want to see you down here evenings and weekends. We had a deal! And this is about the fifth time we've warned you, too. I think we're going to have to take you down to the station now."

"Oops," said Hippo. "Gotta split." He jumped up, grabbed his cup full of money and took off at a dead run, leaving the cardboard TV box behind him. The cops sprinted after him.

"Remember!" called Hippo over his shoulder. "Courtenay! The Bookbinder!"

"Thanks!" called Duckie, as Hippo disappeared into the bushes at the edge of the park.

"Okay, great," said Cheryl. "The trail is no longer cold. Feel better?"

"A lot," said Duckie. It was interesting how things were falling together. The whole journey had taken on an epic quest quality. "Now we know what the next step is."

Chapter 47

The next morning they were back on the road, headed north towards Courtenay. Cheryl was still behind the wheel and Duckie stared out of the window. There was little conversation in the car. They were getting closer. Duckie could feel it.

"Almost there," said Cheryl. "Where should we go once we get there?"

"To the bookbinder's"

"Yeah, but where's that?"

"I dunno," said Duckie. He pulled out his phone and Googled "bookbinder courtenay bc", but got no hits. "Shit, nothing," he said. "I guess we ought to try to find a place to stay. Y'know, establish a base of operations."

"Try to find a place with a little less mildew," said Cheryl.

Duckie grunted and went back to his phone. "Here's a Best Western. It's a little spendier than the others, but I think we can expect a slightly lower mildew content than the no-name brands."

Cheryl's phone rang. She swiped it and began talking. "Hello, Uncle Richard," she piped. "No, we've left Nanaimo. We're going to a place called Courtenay. Duckie got a tip that there's someone there who can help us. What? No, I don't, but I can give you a call when I find out. Okay, bye."

"Uncle Dick checking up on us?" asked Duckie.

"Yeah, he's really interested in helping to find your friend. He's so sweet."

"Yeah. Good ol' Uncle Dick," muttered Duckie. It seemed like Richard Gross was monitoring them. He didn't like it.

They drove on. In an hour, they were in Courtenay, which seemed a smaller version of Nanaimo. The woman at the Best Western check-in counter was a clone of Marge.

"Hey, do you have a twin sister in Nanaimo?" Duckie asked the woman, whose name badge proclaimed her to be Beatrice.

"No, but I have a couple of brothers in Vancouver," Beatrice said. "They're not twins, though."

"Do you know where we can find the Bookbinder?" asked Duckie.

"Who?"

"The Bookbinder. Some guy in Nanaimo told us to come to Courtenay and find the Bookbinder. The way he said it made it sound like everyone knew who he was."

"I sure don't," said Beatrice. "There's a place up in Black Creek that does art restoration. Maybe they'd know."

"Where's Black Creek?" asked Cheryl.

"Oh, about twenty kilometers up the road," said Beatrice.

"You're sure you've never heard of a bookbinder?" asked Duckie.

"I just told you that I didn't," said Beatrice, with un-Canadian archness. "Who told you about him?"

"The Queen! The Queen of Freakin' England landed in a solid-gold helicopter and offered me a hit off her joint. I politely declined because I had to find my friend who was abducted by a lovesick Sasquatch. When I told Her Majesty that, she said I should go to Courtenay and seek the Bookbinder. Then she smoked the joint down to a nub and ate the roach. You can trust her – she's the Queen! She's on your goofy-colored money! C'mon, Beatrice!"

Beatrice raised one carefully plucked eyebrow. "I'm sure I don't know what you're talking about," she said.

As they walked to the room, Cheryl said, "Why did you say all that stuff about the Queen? It made you sound nuts."

"Ah, I was just screwing with her," said Duckie. "I didn't like her attitude."

"Well, I thought you were mean."

"Mean?" said Duckie. "I was just having some fun with her. She seems to have a dull life. I just thought I'd make her day a little more interesting."

They got to the room and opened it with the key and found that it had twin beds. "Twin beds?" said Duckie. "I specified a king in the reservation. I'm going to go back and see if ol' Beatrice can set us up with a king, like I wanted."

"Don't bother," said Cheryl.

"What? We'll never both fit in one of those twin beds."

"I know."

"What the hell's wrong with you?" asked Duckie. He realized that did not come out sounding good, but knew that at this point he was likely to do little more than cram his foot further into his mouth.

"You're the hell wrong with me," said Cheryl. "You're being a real jerk."

Duckie opened his mouth to say something sarcastic, closed it, opened it again, closed it again. He sat down on the bed opposite her. "Look, honey, I'm sorry if I came off a bit … jerky. I know I do it. It's part of my stage personality, and it's also part of my real personality, too. I try to keep the two separated, but sometimes it's not that easy. Especially now, with all of the running around we've been doing to try to find Chuck. Now it feels like we're really close, and I'm pretty keyed up. Ol' Beatrice there wasn't particularly helpful, and I guess I let it get under my skin. I'm sorry."

Duckie's mouth kept running of its own accord. "Hell, I don't know what I was thinking, expecting a motel clerk in the Canadian boondocks to know anything about books. Hell, it's a rare day when someone like ol' Beatrice picks up any printed matter weightier than *People* magazine. Hold on a minute … I just had an idea."

"Swell."

Duckie pulled out his phone and Googled "rare books courtenay bc." It got one hit, other than the Barnes & Noble at the mall. "Here we go," said Duckie. "Next Chapter Used Books. If there's a place in town that would be able to point us to a bookbinder, that would be it. And it looks like it's only a mile and a half away."

"Great," said Cheryl. "Have fun. Knock yourself out."

"What, you're not coming?"

"No. I have a headache." She fished the car keys from her purse and flung them at Duckie's head. He managed to make a quick grab before they smacked him in the face. Cheryl flopped back onto the bed and stared at the ceiling.

"You know I'm a little uneasy about driving your uncle's…"

"Then walk," said Cheryl. She rolled over, turning her back to him.

He tried to figure out something to say, but he couldn't think of anything that wouldn't get him further into hot water. Something was bothering her, and it had to be more than the few smart-ass remarks he'd made to the motel clerk. It didn't seem like a good idea to pursue the matter right now.

"Um, okay, I'm going to go check out this rare book place, see if they can point me to the Bookbinder. You want me to pick up anything for you while I'm out?"

Cheryl grunted and kept her back turned.

"Okay, fine," he said. "Text me if you change your mind."

This elicited no response. Duckie went out the door, suppressing the urge to slam it behind him. The Range Rover sat just outside their room, engine still ticking from the drive. He grabbed the keys in his pocket, then shook his head. He still felt uncomfortable driving Uncle Dick's fancy ride, and he really wanted to just walk to clear his head. Maybe Cheryl will have come off whatever ledge she was on by the time he got back. Duckie shook his head, shoved the keys back in his pocket, and began walking into town.

Chapter 48

Duckie puzzled over what had gotten Cheryl so upset. Had he really been such an asshole to Beatrice in the motel office? He didn't think so, but he knew that his mouth could get away from him. When he got on a roll, sometimes stuff would come blurting out unfiltered, and it could be caustic.

He couldn't remember saying anything that would have qualified as such, or that could have put Cheryl so out of sorts. *Women,* he thought – half wistfully and half angrily. Well, he'd pick up a gift for her, maybe some flowers, and hope that she wouldn't be in such a bad mood when he got back to the Best Western.

Once he got off the main drag, the walk was a lot more pleasant. Victoria, Nanaimo and Courtenay all seemed like miniature versions of each other – like Russian nesting dolls. All were enjoyable and well laid out, with well-preserved buildings from the late nineteenth and early twentieth centuries.

The thing with Cheryl would blow over pretty quickly, he hoped. Maybe they had rushed into the relationship, but the circumstances had speeded things along. Up until now, there had been no complaints or problems. But at the core of it, they had been total strangers until relatively recently, and now they were spending all of their time together. It wasn't too surprising that there would be some friction. Duckie had noticed a grocery store across the way from the motel. He'd swing by on his way back and see if they had any flowers.

He continued up the street, enjoying the vibe of the place. He almost passed right Next Chapter Books. He wouldn't have noticed it at all if there hadn't been a slate sandwich board on the sidewalk, advertising a "Dickens Blowout." Duckie brought himself up short, turned, and went into the narrow storefront.

It was crammed with floor-to-ceiling bookshelves, and it was suffused with the dry, cinnamony scent of countless printed pages. The smell was so strong that it almost made Duckie's head spin. He took a couple of deep breaths.

"Best smell in the world," said a voice from off to his right.

Duckie looked over and could see the top of a woman's head just peeking above a towering stack of books on a counter. "Oh, sorry," said the voice. A hand appeared and slid the stack to the side so Duckie could see a smiling, round-faced woman with mouse-brown hair pulled back into a ponytail. "Sorry," said the woman. "We just got a huge consignment of Waugh in this morning, and I was sorting through. My name's Sheila." A hand extended though the gap in the books.

"Looks like you've got a wall of Waugh," said Duckie, shaking the hand. "My name's Duckie."

"That's a funny name," said Sheila.

"I'm a funny guy. At least some people think so."

"A 'wall of Waugh.' That *is* pretty clever. Are you a writer?"

"Even better. I'm a comic."

"Who isn't, these days?" said Sheila. "Now what can I do for you, Mr. Duckie?"

"I'm looking for the Bookbinder."

"Oh, well, if you have a rare book that's damaged, there's a place up in Black Creek that restores art—"

"No, no," said Duckie. "I'm not looking for a bookbinder, I'm looking for *the* Bookbinder. I was told he's here in Courtenay. Do you know who I'm talking about?"

Sheila sighed. "Yes, I believe I do," she said. "Although if you have a rare book, I wouldn't get it within a hundred meters of him. His name's Dave, and he's just sort of a tourist attraction, if you know what I mean. He just makes little blank journals and diaries, sometimes copies of public-domain works. None of them very high quality. It's more of a show, if you take my meaning."

"I don't," said Duckie. "Take your meaning."

Sheila sighed again. "It'll be easier if you just see for yourself," she said. "He's not too far away. Just three blocks up and take a left. It will be on your right. Look for the wooden sign above the sidewalk. It's not very well marked."

"Well, thanks for the info," said Duckie. He turned to go.

"Okay, Duckie the Comic. Good luck!"

Duckie nodded and went back outside. Sheila was certainly a lot more helpful than what's-her-name at the motel. He went up three blocks, took a left and stopped dead. The street was entirely empty. In fact, it was more of an alley than a street. There were a handful of blank doors and painted-over windows, all a uniform light gray. Maybe he had miscounted, or this really didn't count as a street. Towards the end of the street, a small wooden sign hung from a bracket above one of the doors. Duckie walked a little closer, squinting at the legend that appeared to have been handwritten in grease pencil: D. Stellaris, Binder of Fine Books.

Duckie yanked the door open, and stepped into a dimly lit room. It took a few moments to for his eyes to adjust to the gloom. The windows were painted over, and the only illumination came from candelabras on a long counter that ran the length of the room.

Behind the counter was a middle-aged man, with long graying hair braided into a plait. He wore a rough linen shirt with laces on the front, and over that a stained leather work apron. He was working with a clay pot of glue and a large brush, gluing blank pages into volume with a bright pink picture of Hello Kitty on the cover.

He peered over his half-spectacles and said, "Greetings, traveler. How may I serve thee today?"

Duckie looked around, took a breath, and said in his best dramatic Gandalf-fighting-the-Balrog voice, "I seek … the Bookbinder!"

"Thou hast found him," came the reply.

"So you're the famous Bookbinder, huh?" asked Duckie. "I've come a long way to find you."

"Pray, I dost not divine the meaning of thine speech. I only understandeth the king's tongue."

"Look, dude, can we just skip this ren-fair bullshit? I'm not a tourist, okay?"

The Bookbinder drew himself up as if to launch forth on a long-winded tirade about the importance of proper speech in the context of medieval-style bookbinders in Canadian tourist towns. Duckie snatched up a large wooden mallet from the counter and smacked its head into his hand in what he hoped was a threatening manner.

"All right, fine," said the Bookbinder. "But if anyone else comes in, I will speak only in the speech of mine sovereign."

"Works for me," said Duckie, and put the mallet back on the desk.

"Whaddaya want, kid?" asked the Bookbinder.

"I need to get to Laughingstock."

"You came too far. It's down the coast in Nanaimo."

"I'm not talking about that lame-ass comedy club," said Duckie. "Been there, saw a guy with a rainbow wig and balloon animals. I wouldn't have performed there on a bet."

"So *you're* a comedian, huh? Shoulda figured that as soon as you came in."

"Yeah, and I don't give a rat's ass about that lame club. I'm looking for the comics' retreat. I heard it was on an island or something nearby here."

"That's what you heard, huh? And who told you about that?"

"A guy in a cardboard box in Nanaimo. I think his name's Hippo. He told me that you could help me find it. He didn't get a chance to say much more because the cops were chasing him."

"Sounds like Hippo, all right. So he said I could lead you to it?"

"He said 'seek the Bookbinder in Courtenay.' Apart from some art restoration house up in Black Creek, you're it."

"How do you know about it in the first place?" asked the Bookbinder. "It's supposed to be a secret."

"Yeah, us comedians are pretty shitty at keeping secrets, okay? Especially the ones that drink and use a lot of drugs. Which is most of us."

"Yeah, but who told you?"

"Someone who's been there."

"Yeah, but *who?*"

Duckie rolled his eyes. He'd promised Mickey that he'd keep his secret, but at this point he didn't care, especially since Mickey had run out on him in Tucson. "It was Mickey Gross who told me."

The Bookbinder scowled. "Mickey Gross?" he scoffed. "He's been dead for years!"

"So I used a fuckin' Ouija board! What difference does it make?"

"I don't know, really," said the Bookbinder. "It just seems that there's been a lot of whispering about that place lately. It's making some people nervous. You come barging in here, asking me about a place that's supposed to be a secret, that you learned about from a dead guy. What the hell am I supposed to think?"

"So you know comedy, huh?" asked Duckie.

"I know funny," said the Bookbinder.

"You heard of Chuck Marshall?"

"Yeah!" said the Bookbinder. "I've seen a couple of episodes of his show. Pretty good stuff. I heard that he got pissed at the network and bailed."

"That's the public story. He disappeared, all right. But nobody knows where he's gone. Look, I've known the guy since sixth grade. We started in comedy together, did our first performances in North Carolina. I've been chasing him down all over the place, and I think he's at Laughingstock. The *real* Laughingstock."

"That you heard about from Mickey Gross."

Duckie hesitated. "Okay, fine," he said. "I promised him that I wouldn't tell anyone, but considering that he pepper-sprayed me and then ran out – fuck it. Yeah, Mickey's still alive."

"Uh-huh," said the Bookbinder. "You, of all people, have solved the mystery of Mickey Gross's death."

"I managed to track down his daughter, and she put me in touch with him."

"Oh, yeah, I remember hearing about that. She didn't know she was adopted until some tabloid weasel spilled the beans."

"Well, she's at the Best Western down the street."

"Really? Cheryl is here in Courtenay? Why didn't she come with you? I'd love to meet her."

"If you help me, maybe you will. She had a headache and needed a nap. Now are you going to help me or not?" Duckie cut his eyes towards the mallet. The Bookbinder saw and snatched it out of Duckie's reach.

"No need for the mallet, okay?" said the Bookbinder. "I'll try to help you, but I make no guarantees. Honestly, I haven't been there in a long while. There's this guy named Shep. He's kind of a caretaker for the place, and he's got a boat. He can take you there … if he decides he wants to."

"Ah, Jesus," said Duckie. "Every damn time I think I'm getting close, there's one more person I have to chase down. Okay, fine. Where do I find him? The North Pole?"

"No, look, I'll talk to him. He's a little, um, prickly sometimes. You can't just roll up on him and start talking about Laughingstock – he'll shut right down. Tell you what, I'll talk to Shep for you and then we can meet later on. There's a pub called the Scotchman's Arms, right around the corner on Fitzgerald Avenue. Meet me there at five. If all goes well, Shep will be with me, and we can see about arranging a trip out there to look for your friend."

"Thanks, man," said Duckie. "Sorry about, y'know, threatening you with a mallet and all."

"Should hope to smile and kiss a duck," said the Bookbinder. "Hey, what's your name, anyway?"

"Duckie. Duckie Dunne."

"Seriously?"

"For the purposes of this conversation, yes."

The bell over the door rang, and a middle-aged couple wandered in.

"Yea, verily," said the Bookbinder. "Our business hath come to a conclusion for the nonce. We shall see each other again at five of the clock!"

"Verily indeed, good sir," said Duckie. To the couple who had wandered in he said, "Thou hast chosen to patronize the finest fake-medieval bindery in all the land. Fare thee well, my lords and lady. Huzzah!"

Duckie walked out of the Bookbinder's shop feeling better than he had since landing in Canada. Finally, he felt like he was getting somewhere, and that he would soon reach his goal and find his friend.

As he walked back towards the hotel, something that the Bookbinder had said came back to him: "Should hope to smile and kiss a duck." What the hell did that even mean? Duckie was sure he had heard that expression before. Even weirder, it seemed like he had heard the *Bookbinder* say it before. How was that possible?

Duckie shrugged and went into the Thrifty Foods to see if he could find a make-up gift for Cheryl. After some debate, he picked out a bunch of red roses. They were expensive, but Duckie felt the situation called for a top-notch gesture. He left the grocery store with a spring in his step.

When he got back to the motel room there was only one problem: Cheryl was gone.

Chapter 49

At first, Duckie thought that Cheryl had just gone for a walk, had gotten bored waiting for him to come back. Then he noticed that her suitcase was gone. He searched the room, thinking that she might have stashed it under the bed or in the closet, but there was no sign of it. He ran to the front door and looked out, but Uncle Dick's Range Rover was still there. He still had the keys in his pocket.

She must have just split. He tried calling her cell, but it went right to voicemail. He fast-walked back to the office. Beatrice was still there.

"Well, if it isn't the funnyman," she said when he walked in.

"Hey, look, I'm sorry I was kind of a jerk earlier," said Duckie. "Y'know, I actually am a comedian. Sometimes my mouth runs away from me. Like I said, I'm sorry."

Beatrice grunted.

"Look, I'm trying to find my, uh, friend," he said. "I went out for a bit, and she wasn't here when I got back."

"Huh," said Beatrice. "It's a wonder that she wouldn't want to spend every waking minute with such a charming companion as you."

"Okay, I guess I had that coming," said Duckie, resisting the urge to lay into Beatrice again. That wouldn't do. He needed her help. "But look, her luggage is gone, but the car's still here. I'm worried."

"Oh, that's not good," said Beatrice. "Did you have a fight or something?"

"Yeah, sorta," admitted Duckie.

"Maybe she just went for a walk to clear her head."

"Maybe. But with her luggage? You didn't see anything, did you?"

"Nope, I was just sitting here reading," she said, indicating a dog-eared soap opera magazine on the counter. "Maybe you should call the police."

Duckie shook his head. He wasn't going to get the police involved. "No," he said. "At least not yet. I'm going to see if I can find her. Please keep an eye out for her. And for what it's worth, I'm sorry I was mean to you earlier."

"That's okay, hon," said Beatrice. "I can call around to some of the other hotels nearby and see if she's checked in."

"Would you? Thanks," said Duckie. He ran his hand through his hair. "Jeez, we came up here to find a friend of mine who's been missing, and now I've got another missing person on my hands."

"You're a regular Blue's Clues, aintcha?" said Beatrice.

"Blue's Clueless is more like it," said Duckie. "I'm gonna hit the streets. I'll stop by soon to see if you've turned up anything. Thanks for helping."

"Oh, I'm not helping you so much as I'm helping her."

Reluctantly, he got into Uncle Dick's Range Rover and started cruising the streets, driving in a widening spiral away from the motel to cover as much territory as possible. There was no sign of her.

After an hour, he pulled into the parking lot of a Tim Horton's donut shop and pulled out his phone. It was clear that she wasn't hauling her suitcase through the streets of Courtenay; maybe she had taken the bus. He found a location for the inter-city bus depot over by the Driftwood Mall. He pulled up, but it was basically just a big bus shelter. No sign of Cheryl. He pulled into the mall parking lot and did a circuit of the mall interior, but still no Cheryl.

In desperation, he Googled ferry depots. There was one in the adjacent town of Comox. When he arrived at the ferry ramp – which was a good ten miles out of Courtenay – it was practically deserted. He tried calling her again. Straight to VM. He sent her another text, but got no reply.

Unsure of what to do next, he went back to the motel. He checked in with Beatrice. She said she'd called a dozen nearby motels, but none of them reported anyone matching Cheryl's description having checked in. Duckie went back to the room and threw himself into the ugly armchair in the corner.

He'd just have to try calling Uncle Dick directly. He pulled out the phone book and called directory assistance. The operator had no listing for a Richard Gross in Cobble Hill.

Duckie hung up and cursed. Maybe he should call the cops in Cobble Hill, explain the situation, and see if they could put him in touch with Uncle Dick. He didn't like the idea, and the more he thought about it, the less he liked it. It seemed that by doing something like that he was just setting himself up for taking the fall if it turned out that something bad had happened to Cheryl.

He tried calling Cheryl again. Straight to voicemail. He sent another text.

None of this made sense. Duckie felt a coil-spring of fear unwinding in his gut. The search for Chuck had seemed like a personal crusade, a task that the rest of the world just didn't have the time to care about. Now, it occurred to Duckie that there may be something seriously sinister going on. Maybe Chuck hadn't just run off because of the pressure of the new show. Perhaps someone had disappeared Chuck. Maybe they had found out that Duckie and Cheryl were getting close to finding him. If Duckie hadn't been out walking the mean streets of Courtenay, he'd be just as gone as his two friends.

"Oh man, I've got to get out of here," he said. "RIGHT FUCKING NOW!"

Okay, okay, slack, slack, he thought. *I'm giving myself the jibblies.* He took a few deep breaths, trying to slow his racing heart. Yeah, it wouldn't be a bad idea to get a new base of operations. He fired up his phone and began looking for cheap motels – the skeezier, the better.

He found one down the street, close to the mall. He decided not to say anything to Beatrice or even take his luggage – he'd just split. He peeked his head out the door. Beatrice sat behind the counter in the office, engrossed in her soap opera magazine. He slipped out the door and around the side of the building before she could look up.

He walked down the street to the mall and made a few purchases: an oversized ball cap and sunglasses, some cheap clothes and gear, and a backpack to tote it around in

He walked to the roach-motel and negotiated a one-night stay, paid in advance with cash. He replaced the sheets on the bed with ones in the closet – you could never trust the housekeepers in these dumps – and sat on the edge of the bed, wondering what to do next. He couldn't just wait here in this dive; he had to keep looking for Cheryl. He thought about calling the Best Western but decided to walk up there first and scope it out. *It pays to be paranoid,* he thought.

This was borne out fifteen minutes later when he emerged from a side street by the Best Western. Two uniformed cops were climbing into a police cruiser in front of the office. Duckie receded back down the side street and slowly tied his shoe until the cruiser left the parking lot. What was that all about? Had Beatrice ratted him out? Or did Uncle Dick have the cops looking for him? Duckie started to feel scared. This could end very badly, he realized.

At this point all he could do was meet the Bookbinder and his pal at the bar and hope they could do something for him. What had it come to? Duckie's only hope and personal safety depended on a man who slapped Hello Kitty diaries together by candlelight, and some paranoid guy named Shep. When this was all over, he was going to get a hell of a routine out of the experience.

This thought made Duckie feel a little better. He pulled his new ballcap down over his eyes and began hotfooting it up England Avenue towards the Scotchman's Arms. He got there a little after four. He found a nice dark corner that gave him a good view of the front door and plate glass window. Then he ordered a beer and a burger.

He waited and watched. The burger came and he chomped it down. It was pretty damn good. With a full belly and the effects of the beer starting to take hold, Duckie was able to relax, a little. It had been a busy, crazy day, and things were still pretty weird, but the sense of panic that had been dwelling in the back of Duckie's head dialed back a few notches.

The pub started to fill up. Duckie tried to scrutinize the people coming in, keeping an eye out for the Bookbinder. He didn't see him.

He ordered another beer and checked his phone. It was now nearly 6 pm;

the Bookbinder had told him to show up at five. Was he being stood up? Then again, maybe the Bookbinder had just forgotten to wind his sundial.

Another half-hour dragged by, and Duckie's anxiety grew with every passing minute. He ordered another beer. Duckie wasn't a heavy drinker, at least compared to most of the comics he knew. However, the later it got and the more anxious he got, the more he wanted to drink.

He was edging into paranoia now. There were two guys at a table in the corner who kept looking over at him. Or were they? It was dark, and Duckie couldn't tell for certain. He squinted, trying to get a better view of the two men. The one facing him was skinny, with shoulder-length graying hair and an equally shaggy beard. The man with his back to him was larger, and he was wearing a faded tie-dyed t-shirt and an old straw cowboy hat.

As he was watching, the guy in the cowboy hat turned around and looked right at him. At least Duckie thought so; the guy was wearing aviator shades. Something looked familiar about him. Duckie squinted some more, and the guy in the cowboy hat lowered the shades. It was the Bookbinder. He made an impatient shrugging gesture and waved at an empty chair at their table.

Duckie gaped. A missing piece fell into place with the sight of the Bookbinder in his aviator shades. It was that weird expression, "*Should hope to smile and kiss a duck.*" Duckie remembered where he'd heard it before: Chelsea's Birthday Monkey's "I Love You But You Kinda Suck." The woman at the bookstore had said his name was Dave. The name in front of the Bookbinder's shop read "D. Stellaris." Dave Stellaris was David Starr, lead singer and guitarist of Chelsea's Birthday Monkey.

Duckie affixed a blank look to his face and hauled his beer mug over to the table. "I didn't recognize you," he lied as he sat down.

"Good," said the Bookbinder. "You weren't supposed to. Shep, this is Dookie."

"That's Duckie, actually," said Duckie. He stuck out his hand to shake.

Shep gave Duckie's hand a dismissive glance and looked Duckie straight in the eye. After a moment, Duckie lowered his hand.

"So you wanna go to the camp, huh?" said Shep, in the same tone of voice he'd use if Duckie had suggested taking a leak on his mother's grave.

"Yeah, I need to get to Laughing—"

"Shhh!" hissed Shep. "Shit, don't say the name out loud, man! What's wrong with you?"

"How long a list do you want?" said Duckie.

"Don't need a list, man," said Shep. "I can *tell*." He turned to the Bookbinder. "Who is this asshole, man? This guy's a narc."

"C'mon, Shep," said the Bookbinder. "I wouldn't have brought him out here if he wasn't legit."

"I'm not a narc, I'm a fuckin' *comedian*," said Duckie. "I've been chasing my tail trying to get to, uh, the camp. My friend has disappeared. I think he might be there."

"Yeah, and what makes you think your friend's there?" scoffed Shep. "Hell, who told you about the camp in the first place?"

"Mickey Gross."

Duckie expected Shep to flip him more shit at this revelation, but instead he just sat back and stared him down.

"Hey, what about Cheryl?" asked the Bookbinder. "I thought you were gonna bring her out."

"So did I," said Duckie. "She's … uh, gone now, too."

"Whaddaya mean?" demanded the Bookbinder.

"I mean that when I went back to the motel, she was gone. Her luggage, too. But her uncle's car is still there. That's how we got up here."

"Her uncle?" asked Shep.

"Yeah, Mickey's brother, Richard. He lives in some little town outside of Victoria. Cobble Hill. We stayed there for a night before we headed up here."

Shep and the Bookbinder exchanged a quick look. "What's been going on since Cheryl split?" asked the Bookbinder.

"I've been looking for her," said Duckie. "No luck. Cruised around a bit, checked the bus station, even drove over to the ferry ramp. Been calling and texting, too. No dice."

"Did you drive up here in Richard Gross's car, then?" asked Shep.

"Nope," said Duckie. "After I got back to the Best Western, I got really paranoid. I went out for a walk, and when I came back, I saw a cop car pulling out of the parking lot. So I found another place to stay."

"Where?" asked the Bookbinder.

"Not the Best Western," said Duckie. He leaned back and crossed his arms.

"Look, uh, Duckie," said the Bookbinder. "You mind giving us a minute?"

"No prob. I gotta take a leak, anyway." He got up and headed towards the men's room. Instead of going in, he hung back in the alcove, watching the Bookbinder and Shep. He half-expected them to get up and leave. If they did, Duckie intended to follow them. These guys were the last link to the mystery. They didn't leave, though. Instead they huddled, having a serious discussion.

When he came back, Shep and the Bookbinder were still there, silently swigging from their beer mugs.

"So, you say you're a comedian, huh?" said Shep. "And you're looking for a friend of yours who's also a comedian?"

"That's what I say," said Duckie. "And I mean it."

"And you say that Mickey Gross – who's been dead for five years – told you about … um, the camp?"

"He's not dead. I saw him about three weeks ago in Arizona. Also, his brother said he showed up at his place in Cobble Hill last week. Gets around pretty good for a dead guy, huh?"

Shep stared into his beer mug. "Yeah, I been hearing his name a lot recently," he said.

"Yeah?" said Duckie. "So tell me, Shep, when was the last time *you* saw Mickey Gross?"

Shep might act like a badass, but he was a terrible liar. He cut his eyes back and forth a few times before saying, "It's been a while, man. Can't really remember."

"Okay, sure," said Duckie. "But what do you mean about hearing his name around lately?"

Shep shrugged. "You know, you hear stuff. This isn't a big town, eh?

It's been a good twenty years since people – comedians – were coming up regularly to visit the camp. It was a big deal then, and a lot of famous faces came to this bar to toss back a few."

"I think what Shep is trying to say," interjected the Bookbinder, "is that it takes a special personality to stand up in front of a room full of strangers and try to make them laugh or feel or think. I think it's based on a fundamental understanding of just how fucked the human condition really is. Most people just build their walls, find ways to ignore it. Some people can't, and they either start playing songs or start telling jokes. Or going crazy."

"Or all three," said Duckie.

"Amen!" exclaimed Shep, loud enough for people at adjacent tables to look over at them.

"You know," said Duckie. "They say that all comics really want to be rock stars, and rock stars want to be comics. Ever want to get laughs, Mr. Dave Stellaris? I think you got the rock star part covered."

"Yeah, you know who I am," said the Bookbinder. "And so what? Think you're going to blackmail me into getting what you want? Don't bother, I couldn't give a shit. I can haul stakes and start doing something new somewhere else. Maybe a coffee shop in Belize or something."

"Hey, I'm not going to blackmail anybody," said Duckie. "I can keep a fuckin' secret."

"You oinked out Mickey's name pretty fast," pointed out Shep.

"That was different." protested Duckie. "It was the only way I could convince David, uh, the Bookbinder here I was the real deal. Also, Mickey pepper-sprayed me."

"Okay, fine," said the Bookbinder. "You don't blow my cover, and I won't mace you."

"And you take me to the camp," said Duckie. "Before the hammer drops on me."

"Yeah, okay," said the Bookbinder. He looked over at Shep, who gave him a nod.

"All right, I'll take you to the camp," said Shep. "Do you know where Marina Park is?"

"Nope," said Duckie.

"Then you better figure it out," said Shep. "There's a little café there, right by that marina. Be there at 6 am sharp. If you're not there at six, the whole thing's off. Got that?"

"Yeah," said Duckie. "Got it. Thanks, man."

"Yeah, okay," said Shep. "That's it, then. I'm outta here. Things are getting kinda heavy. Think I'll lie low tonight. Remember: six sharp."

Duckie thanked him again, and headed back to the men's room. When he came out, the Bookbinder and Shep had gone.

Chapter 50

Duckie didn't see any reason to hang around the Scotchman's Arms. Sticking once again to the side streets, he worked his way back towards his flophouse. Down on the corner by the main drag, he spotted a 7-Eleven. He thought it would be a good idea to stock up on belly-filling junk if he was going to be running around in the wild tomorrow. He sidled down the street, keeping an eye out for police cars, and ducked into the convenience store.

He grabbed an armload of beef jerky and Clud Bars, as well as a couple of liters of water. At the register, he noticed a display stand of disposable cellphones. The cheapest was thirty bucks. It seemed like a decent thing to have. He wanted to try calling Cheryl with an anonymous number. He paid for his purchases and eased back away from Cliffe Street.

When he got to the corner, he busted the burner phone out of its bulletproof plastic packaging. Under a streetlight on the corner, he juggled the burner in one hand and his regular phone in the other while he punched in Cheryl's number on the new phone. It didn't go straight to voicemail, and Duckie's heart speeded up a bit. Maybe she would answer. But it rang and rang. After twenty rings, he hung up.

Next he called the Best Western with the burner. A male voice answered.

"Hello, is Beatrice there?" asked Duckie.

"No, she got off shift at six," said the voice.

"This is Mister Dunne in room 109. I was just calling to see if there were any messages for me."

A pause. "Um, yes, Mr. Dunne. There is a message for you."

"Okay, great," said Duckie. "What is it?"

"I'm afraid I can't tell you," said the voice. "A person left a … um, written note. Handwritten. They said it was for you only. You'll have to come get it in person."

A squirt of fear-acid flooded Duckie's stomach. This did not sound good. He resisted the urge to just hang up. Instead, he said, "Yeah, that's great. I'll be there in ten, fifteen minutes, okay?"

"Very good, Mr. Dunne. We'll be waiting for you."

I bet you will, thought Duckie. The whole thing had the feel of a poorly plotted thriller novel. While he was contemplating this, he kept a wary eye on the Best Western parking lot down the street. In a few minutes, a cop car slid into the lot. Duckie eased behind a tree as the two uniformed officers emerged from the car and went into the office. The sight of the cop car blasted away the last remaining doubts that something supremely fucked-up was going on here, and he was right in the middle of it. There were police looking for him, and it had to do with Laughingstock, Chuck, and Cheryl's disappearance.

He peered around the tree to make sure that the cops were still in the office, then took off at a fast walk, heading for his fleabag motel. He pulled the oversized ball cap down on his face and put the shades on. He thought they might just draw attention to him – it had been dark for hours now – but they gave him a feeling of protection and anonymity. This was good, because Duckie could feel a full-blown freak-out waiting just in the shadows.

He took a deep breath and pushed on, walking fast but not running. He did a button-hook around a KFC and slipped into his room. He kept the lights out, and lay on the bed fully clothed, tossing and turning.

He must have slept, because he had the Porta Potty dream again. This time, Chuck's knocking at the door was more insistent. "Come in, Duckie, come in," said Chuck. "You're almost there!" Duckie awoke sweating, and stared at the ceiling until 5 am.

He shoved all his mall-bought gear and 7-Eleven snacks into his backpack, dropped the key off at the front desk and made his way to the café at the

Marina Park. There were a few picnic tables scattered in front of it, and Duckie sat down at one of them, nervously scanning all around him while trying to look casual. Not that there was anyone around to see him.

There was a sound like a hissing steam radiator coming from bushes about thirty feet away. Duckie looked over and saw that some of the bushes were shaking. As he watched, a hand emerged from the bushes and crooked its finger in a "come here" gesture. Duckie looked around to see if he was being observed, but there were no other people in the vicinity. He hoisted his mall backpack and scurried over to the bushes.

"'Bout damn time," said Shep when Duckie got there. "I been tryin' to get your attention for the last five minutes."

"Sorry, man," said Duckie.

"Okay, let's go, let's go," said Shep. "We're behind schedule now."

"We have a schedule?" asked Duckie. Shep shot him a dirty look, but offered no reply.

"Is the Bookbinder coming?"

"Hell, no," said Shep. "We gotta have somebody backing us up here. We can't put the whole crew in the boat, dum-dum. C'mon!"

Shep led him through the brush, away from the marina. He shortcut through a hole in a chain link fence that surrounded a small airstrip. "Don't worry," said Shep. "Flight operations don't begin until nine." They pushed through another hole in the fence and into a small stand of trees. A faded blue Boston Whaler powerboat was tied to an overhanging branch.

"Get in," said Shep.

"How?"

"Whaddaya mean, 'how'? Climb down the bank and get in the boat! Damn, you're dumb."

Duckie opened his mouth to object, but snapped it closed. He should have counted on getting wet if he was going to be on a clandestine boat mission.

Shep must have read his mind. "You're going on a secret boat trip. What, you thought you wouldn't get wet?"

"Yeah," said Duckie. "I think dumb shit like that all the time." Shep gave him a puzzled/pissed-off look, as if he couldn't figure out if Duckie was making fun of him or not. *Good,* thought Duckie. That was exactly the response he'd been going for.

They splashed into the boat, Duckie getting soaked in the very cold water almost up to his crotch. *Swell,* he thought. *Sun's not even up and I've got the makings of pneumonia.*

Shep untied the line from the branch, pulled out a plastic paddle and shoved off from the bank. The boat began drifting down the river to where it widened out to meet the open water. Shep went from one side of the boat to the other, digging a few strokes of the paddle each time.

"What, you're gonna paddle the whole way there?" asked Duckie.

"No, smart guy. I'm just getting us past the populated area before I start the engine. Jeez."

Duckie plopped down on a cushion at the stern of the boat and stripped off his shoes and socks. He hadn't thought to buy extra socks. He wrung out the socks and put them back on. It was better than nothing – but not by much.

Shep continued paddling for a bit until they were out in the middle of the widening river. He sat down behind the steering column, lit a foul-smelling cigarette, and started the engine. "Hang on," he hollered and pushed on the throttle. The boat jerked forward with a roar and Duckie was thrown back in his seat. Shep laughed. "Toldja to hang on," he said.

The banks on either side receded as the Boston Whaler moved further into the open water. They passed a spit of land on the left, and the water broadened out into the Strait of Georgia. As they got further away from land, Shep seemed to relax. He motioned for Duckie to come up to where he was piloting the boat.

"See that?" Shep asked, waving at a stretch of land that broadened off the starboard bow. "That's Denman Island. Couple people living on it, but it's mostly, y'know, for tourists and stuff."

He swung the boat to port, angling away from Denman Island. In the distance was an island that was smaller, but more mountainous, rising hundreds of feet from the water. "That's Hornby Island," said Shep. "Not as big, but more people living on it. Place we're heading to is off the south of Hornby."

"Is there anything I can do to, y'know, help?" asked Duckie.

"Nope. Just sit back and enjoy the ride."

Duckie did just that, lounging on the bench seat in the back of the boat. The sun was now fully up, rising above Hornby Island as Shep guided the Boston Whaler between Hornby and Denman. The early morning chill was lifting as the sun rose, and Duckie tried to relax. Someone else was doing the navigating and decision-making for a change.

Duckie felt a rising sense of excitement. He had been chasing Chuck for a while and was finally reaching Laughingstock. He would see his friend again and get to the bottom of this strange situation. Of course, Laughingstock could be completely deserted, and Duckie would be back to square one. He doubted it, though. There was too much weirdness going on in Courtenay for this to be a complete bust.

Cheryl wasn't far from his thoughts, either. He hoped that he had just pissed her off enough for her to bolt because that would mean she was safe. Regardless of how pissed she was with him, he just wanted her to be okay.

The reach of water between the two islands narrowed as they went south, then opened up. Ahead, Duckie could see a low, flat island covered with trees. Shep seemed to be scanning the sky, a frown on his grizzled face. "Did you see that?" he asked Duckie angrily.

"No. See what?"

"Something just flew past the boat, 'bout a hundred feet up. Right across the bow!"

Duckie squinted, looking up above the boat, all around. He didn't see anything. Maybe Shep was having some sort of tweaker flashback or something.

"Damn, there it is again!" shouted Shep. He throttled the engine back and killed the ignition. The sudden silence was a shock. Duckie scanned the sky, but still couldn't see anything. However, he could hear a high-pitched whine, like a mechanical mosquito. "There!" said Shep, pointing above the port side of the boat. Duckie squinted and could see a small dot zipping by high in the air.

As he watched, it flew past the boat and circled around the stern, dropping in altitude. It came closer, flying along the starboard side. Duckie could make out a cruciform shape.

"Damn!" said Duckie. "It's a drone!"

"Bull*shit*, Klaus," muttered Shep. He reached into a compartment next to the steering column, and pulled out a long, waterproof case. He opened the end and removed a pump shotgun.

"What are you going to do with that?" asked Duckie, alarmed by the sight of the gun.

"What do you think I'm going to do with it, Einstein?" spat Shep. He jacked a round into the chamber, took aim at the drone – which was now passing low across the bow – and fired. The drone wobbled a little bit but kept going. Shep pumped another round into the chamber, sighted, fired. The drone exploded into a cloud of plastic fragments.

The sound of the shotgun report rolled across the water and died away. The only other sound was the water lapping on the side of the boat, and Duckie's frantic breathing. "Jesus Christ!" exclaimed Shep. "That was some freaky shit! I wonder where the hell it came from. Do you know what kind of range those things have?"

"I dunno," said Duckie. "Couple miles, maybe? I know this architect in Portland. He has one of those drones he likes to fly around the city and take pictures of buildings and stuff. I think he said he could get it to two or three miles."

Shep looked around. "I guess it could have come from Denman or Hornby. But maybe it came from Bowser Island, too."

"Where's Bowser Island?" asked Duckie.

"That little island up ahead," said Shep, pointing. "It's where Laughing-stock is."

"You mean 'the camp'?" asked Duckie.

"Yeah, I mean the camp. We can say Laughingstock out here. Unless there's any more of those fuckin' drones." Shep scanned the sky. It must have looked clear, because he started the engine. "Gonna go slow. Try to keep an eye out for more drones. Or anything else weird. Keep your eyes peeled."

"Aye aye, Captain!" said Duckie. Shep shot him a dark look. Duckie shaded his eyes with his hand and made a show of scanning the horizon.

The boat moved forward at half speed, with Shep and Duckie both looking all around. There were no discernable threats. Duckie began to think that it was just some asshole on one of the big islands, just having fun buzzing the passing boats.

After five minutes of not spotting any suspicious drones, submarines or spy dolphins, Duckie flopped back down on the rear bench seat and pulled a Clud Bar out of his backpack. He hadn't had a chance to eat breakfast, and had been too nervous to think about stopping at a local diner. Maybe he should go easy on Shep – it seemed like paranoia was the flavor of the week in Courtenay. They were now passing between Bowser Island and the mainland, moving closer to the island itself. It wasn't much to look at: small and mostly flat, with a scrubby forest that grew down to the water's edge.

"Old dock on the south side of the island," said Shep. "We'll pull up there." Duckie nodded and closed up his backpack.

They began to round the far end of the island, and then suddenly Shep slowed the boat and turned it 180 degrees.

"What's up?" asked Duckie.

"I think I know where that fuckin' drone came from," said Shep. He pointed beyond the stern of the Boston Whaler. A crooked wooden dock poked out from one end of the island. A mile or so beyond it, a large yacht lay at anchor.

"Jesus!" said Duckie. "That thing's huge! It looks like a cruise ship or something."

"No, it's some rich prick's toy," said Shep. He kept looking over his shoulder as the enormous yacht disappeared from view behind Bowser Island. When it was out of sight, he put it in neutral, but left the engine running. "Okay, I don't think he saw us," he said.

"Whose boat do you think that is?" asked Duckie.

"No clue," said Shep. "Couldn't see the name or the registration. I've heard people talking about some goddamn big yacht cruising around the area the last couple of days."

"So what do we do now? Are you still going to get me to Laughingstock?"

"Shit," said Shep. He took off his ball cap and ran his hand through his long graying hair. "This mission's turning out to be hotter than I thought. Please tell me you're smart enough to have a burner phone."

Duckie rummaged in his backpack and pulled out the phone he'd bought at 7-Eleven. "Will this do?"

"Yeah," said Shep. He snatched the phone and began programming in a number. "I was planning on just tying up at the dock and letting you do your thing, but that's not safe anymore. I'm going to get you as close as I can to this side of the island, and you can wade in from there. You won't have to swim, but you're gonna get wet."

"Swell. I'm getting wet just thinking about it."

"Whatever. I'm going to go back to Hornby and tie up at Ford's Cove. There's a little dock there, and it's only a couple of miles away. If things get hairy and you need extraction, just call the number I put in. I'll haul ass and pick you up at the dock."

Duckie looked at the number that Shep had programmed in under the name "John Doe." "Do cell phones even work out here?" he asked.

"Just when I think you've got a little smarts," said Shep. "Of course they work. There are towers all over the place, and the mainland is only a few miles away. How many bars you got?"

"Three," said Duckie. He hadn't thought to look. He was getting pretty sick of Shep calling him dumb, but it didn't seem like a good idea to flip him any shit about it now. This scrubby sumbitch was his only link to civilization. "Okay," he said. "Let's do this."

Shep nodded and started moving the boat forward. He brought it in close to the island, peering over the side to make sure he wasn't going to run it aground. When they were about ten yards from shore, he cut the engine. "All right, this is as close as we can get."

Duckie stripped down to his drawers, much to Shep's amusement. He stuffed his clothes and shoes into the backpack, and climbed onto the gunwale. "Any words of advice?" he asked.

"There's a bunch of rundown cabins down by the dock. Start there. The cabins are pretty much just for show. The real deal is more towards the center of the island, which can't be seen from the water. There is a path from the cabins to the main complex, although it's pretty overgrown. Find the path, and see what you can see."

"Right," said Duckie, and he hoisted the backpack over his head and hopped off the boat. The water came up past his knees and it was *cold*. He waded to land and sat down on a fallen tree to put his clothes back on.

Shep saw that he was safely ashore, gave Duckie the thumbs-up, started the boat and pulled away. In a minute he was a diminishing dot.

Duckie shrugged his backpack on and started picking his way along the shore to get back around to the ramshackle dock. He was almost there.

Chapter 51

The sound of Shep's boat receded into the distance, then silence. It was peaceful, with the water lapping gently at the shore and the birds chattering in the woods. Duckie followed the shoreline, trying to stay just inside the border of dense trees that came right up to the water's edge. The shoreline turned to the east, and Duckie moved slower. He pushed through a stand of tall grass and saw that the dock was only fifty yards away. He couldn't see the yacht, but his range of vision was limited by the bushes. He crept up to the very edge of the brush. Beyond it was a patch of mostly open dirt. The dock was right in the middle of this patch. At the back of the clearing, away from the water, Duckie could see a tumbledown log cabin, and part of another.

He stuck his head out of the bushes to get a better view. There were four cabins along the tree line at the back of the clearing, all in various stages of decay.

And there was the yacht, now visible off to the east side of the island. Duckie squinted, trying to see if anything was going on there. It looked like there were people moving around on the deck, but the huge vessel was too far away to tell for sure.

Duckie cursed, wishing he'd picked up a cheapie pair of binoculars at the mall, or asked to borrow a pair from Shep. He began working his way around the clearing. There wasn't much to see. Three of the cabins had collapsed roofs. The fourth cabin looked mostly intact, but the door was jammed shut. Duckie tried looking in the window in the back, but it was grimed over with dust.

Duckie began slowly walking along the edge of the clearing behind the cabins. Shep had said that the cabins were just window-dressing and that a path led back to the real Laughingstock closer to the center of the island.

Duckie was no woodsman, but he was no city boy, either. He had actually spent a good portion of his late adolescence skulking around in the woods in rural Pennsylvania. Duckie unfocused his vision, stared into the middle distance and slowly paced along the tree line. He took his time, just slowly putting one foot in front of the other, trying to look about ten feet behind the tree line. Midway between the middle two cabins, there was a barely perceptible lightening of the foliage. Duckie relaxed and stared at it blankly for a moment, then stepped through the tree branches and found himself on a path that led further into the woods.

He had a little trouble following the trail. It was old and very overgrown, and several times Duckie had to stop and hunt around to pick up the path when he'd lost it. It led deeper into the interior of the island. Bowser Island must be larger than it looked, because after a few minutes, Duckie had gone far enough where he couldn't hear any noises from the water at all. The air was still and heavy, and there were only muted insect sounds. The place was too quiet, and it felt like someone was watching him.

He shook his head and pushed forward. That line of thinking wasn't going to result in anything but a serious case of the jibblies. Fortunately, the path seemed wider and better-defined now. There were also some visible footprints, but Duckie couldn't tell how old they were.

Can't be much further, he thought. The whole damn island couldn't be more than a mile long, and he had already gone several hundred yards past the clearing by the dock. The trees seemed to be getting higher and more spread out. There was a clearing about thirty yards ahead. As he got closer, he could make out straight lines and forms through the brush and tree branches. There was definitely something manmade up there. He began moving faster.

He pushed through a small grove of scrubby pines and popped out into a clearing. There was a large wooden lodge, surrounded by a number of smaller bungalows and a handful of outbuildings. The buildings were nicer than the crude ones by the dock. The place looked like a miniature version of Uncle Dick's place, well-designed and solidly built. There were no caved-in roofs or collapsed walls, but it seemed like these buildings had not been used in a long time. He tried the door of one of the bungalows, but it was empty. He then checked out the sheds and outbuildings. Other than a rusty rake and a dirty old hoe in a toolshed, they were all empty.

Duckie went up to the main building. The main portion was L-shaped with a wing sticking off at a 45-degree angle, and other small additions poking out at weird angles. A covered porch ran along the sides of the building that faced the courtyard. Duckie climbed on the porch and tried the nearest door. It was locked. He found another, but it was locked, too. He tried peering in the windows, but they were too dust-grimed to be able to see clearly what was inside: just vague shapes that could have been furniture or piles of garbage.

Having spent all this time to come all this way, Duckie wasn't about to be stopped by a cheapjack door lock. He hopped off the porch and spent a few minutes rooting around in the woods until he came up with a fist-sized rock and a large stick. He heaved the rock through the glass of the front door, and used the stick to clear the rest of the broken glass. He reached in, unlocked the door and stepped inside.

He had finally reached Laughingstock.

He stood in a foyer, with a bathroom off to the side. It looked like someone had been in here relatively recently. There was a patina of dust on the floor, and it looked as if it had been walked on. There were no distinct footprints, but there were disturbed trails through the dust, as if someone had made an attempt to broom over the footprints.

To the left was a large kitchen, with most of the appliances in place. There was a clean spot on the floor where a dishwasher had once stood. He reached out to open the refrigerator to see if the power was still on, but caught himself. Might be a bad idea – there might be something extremely unpleasant in there. Instead, he flipped the light switch. Nothing happened, but that didn't mean there wasn't a generator nearby. In fact, there almost had to be. There couldn't be power lines running from the mainland.

Duckie explored the rest of the building. It was fascinating, with odd little nooks and alcoves in unexpected places. The biggest room in the building was a large auditorium space, with a raised stage and a small bar in the back corner. Three dusty tables and a handful of ratty chairs were arrayed around the room.

There was a small green room to the side of the stage. There were no windows, and it was dark as the devil's armpit. Duckie fired up the flashlight on his phone and looked inside. His jaw dropped. The walls were covered with graffiti and signatures from dozens of comedians. Many of them Duckie knew. A lot were big-name comics: George Carlin, Richard Pryor, Bill Hicks, Robin Williams… Duckie's amazement grew the more he explored. High up in the back corner he found, "Thank the lack of God for Laughingstock! This place has saved my life!" It was signed "Mickey Gross, Esq." in a large curlicued script. Duckie took a picture of that one.

He could have easily spent two hours in the green room, reading and photographing every last scribble and signature. That wasn't what he came here for, although he wasn't sure he was going to find anything at this point. Yacht or not, Bowser Island and Laughingstock seemed like a dead end. Reluctantly, he left the green room and sat down on the edge of the bar in the corner. It was getting on noon and his stomach was growling.

He munched on a Clud Bar and contemplated the stage. How many comedy legends had been on that stage, while others just as famous and not quite so famous watched from this very room? It boggled his mind.

Duckie finished his Clud and tossed the wrapper on the floor. What next? He was fighting a growing sense of despair that his long search for Chuck (and now Cheryl) had hit a wall. He did one more circuit through the main building, then did another walkthrough of the bungalows and outbuildings. He came away with nothing. Briefly, he thought about bushwhacking the other parts of the island to see if there was something else hidden away in the trees, but the idea just seemed exhausting.

Instead, he made his way back to the dock to search there again. He didn't have any problems finding the trail as he could clearly see the way he'd come in. He slowed as he got to the end of the trail, not wanting to come crashing out without knowing who or what might be out there. He peered out of the trees and, seeing nothing, emerged into the clearing. He looked to his left, but could no longer see the yacht. He slowly made his way to the dock. It looked like it was in pretty decent shape.

Duckie sighed. He guessed he'd have to cut his losses and give Shep a call to come take him off this sorry island. There was nothing for him here. He'd figure out his next step once he got back to the mainland.

He sat down on the end of the dock and pulled out his burner phone and dialed the "John Doe" number that Shep had programmed in. It went right to voicemail. Duckie was pissed, but what could he do? He said, "Hey, this is, uh, your passenger. I'm down at the dock. There's nothing and no one here. Even that yacht we saw earlier is gone. Come get me, please. I ain't going anywhere." He hung up, still steamed that Shep hadn't picked up his call.

Steamed, and worried. He was literally stranded on a deserted island. "Just call me Gilligan," he muttered to himself. He'd always thought that Gilligan's Island was kinda stupid, but he might end up having to Professor his way off this island. Off to the west, the shore of Vancouver Island was no more than two miles distant. He was an okay swimmer, but he wasn't sure he could swim two miles. But he could paddle that far. He could probably scrounge enough stuff from the main lodge to put together a raft.

That thought made him feel better. He sat down on the dock and took inventory: a half dozen Clud Bars, two liters of water, a fistful of beef jerky and – thankfully – a bottle of heavy-duty sunblock. There was also a spare t-shirt and a sweatshirt. And finally, his cellphones. He tried calling Cheryl from each. Still no answer, straight to voicemail.

He sat down on the end of the dock to slather himself with sunblock. He heard a scrabbling sound from the direction of the woods. The scrabbling got louder, then came a series of heavy thumps from inside the one intact cabin. There was another loud thump, some more scrabbling, and as Duckie watched in amazement, the door flew open and a buck-naked man staggered out.

Chapter 52

Duckie stood paralyzed as the naked man lurched out of the cabin. Duckie was still at the end of the dock. He was completely exposed, and had absolutely nowhere to run or hide. He was stuck between the devil and the deep blue strait. He hunkered down at the end of the dock, hoping the naked man wouldn't notice him. Of course he would. The guy was practically looking right at him. Duckie glanced at the water. If the man rushed him, he could probably just jump in and swim for it.

The naked man stopped abruptly. He blinked in the sunlight and looked around, confused, shading his eyes with his hand. Duckie squinted. The naked man looked familiar. For some reason, his mind went back to sixth-grade gym class. He remembered the awkwardness of having to undress and shower in front of his classmates, the weird lack of privacy, and the variety of physical characteristics of his peers, most of whom stood and moved hunched over protectively, just like the naked man in the clearing. Then he realized that he actually had *seen* the naked man naked before, in that very same middle school locker room.

It was Chuck Marshall.

"Jesus Christ," said Duckie to himself. Then, louder, he called out, "Chuck! Holy shit, Chuck, is that you?"

Chuck squinted and turned his head to the sound of Duckie's voice. His hands instinctively cupped his junk. "Who … who is that?" he called out. "Where am I?"

Duckie walked quickly to where Chuck stood. "Easy, buddy, just take it easy," he said. "It's me. It's Duckie. You remember me, right?"

"Jesus Christ," said Chuck, still blinking myopically. "Duckie? Is that really you? What's going on? *Where the fuck are we?*"

"Okay, you have a lot of questions," said Duckie. "I'll try to answer them in order: yes, it's me; I really have no fuckin' clue about what's going on; we're on a small island off the coast of Canada."

"Canada? How did I get to *Canada?*"

"That's what I was about to ask you. *I* took a ferry."

"What are you doing here?"

"Lookin' for *you*, dipwad. Jesus! What a fuckin' clusterfuck this has been. Where are your clothes?"

"Don't know," said Chuck. "I woke up and I was kinda tied to this bed. Like a hospital bed. I sorta remember people being there with me before, but they were gone when I woke up. I managed to untie myself and got out of the room."

"Jesus," said Duckie. "Where? In there?" He indicated the cabin.

"Yeah," said Chuck. "No idea how I got there."

"How are you feeling?" asked Duckie.

"Naked," said Chuck. "And freaked out. Also pretty hungover."

"Yeah, of course. Hold on, I got some clothes in here." Duckie dug in his backpack and came up with the sweatshirt and the t-shirt.

"You got any pants?" asked Chuck. "I could really use some pants."

"What you see is what you get, brother. Damn lucky I brought these."

Chuck put on the t-shirt and managed to fashion the sweatshirt into a loincloth.

"Jesus, what's up with your arms?" asked Duckie, eyeing his friend as he put on his makeshift outfit. "You look like a junkie or something."

"Ugh," said Chuck, rubbing his arms. "I feel like a pincushion." There were small needle marks all over the insides of his arms and the backs of his hands. "Jesus. They must have kept me doped up like crazy."

"Who? Who did this?" Duckie demanded. He yanked a bottle of water out of the backpack and thrust it at Chuck, who upended it and downed half the bottle in one go. "Can you eat?" Chuck nodded and Duckie handed him a Clud Bar.

Chuck wiped his mouth with the back of his hand. "I don't know exactly who did this, but I think it was someone from the network."

"What's the last thing you remember?"

"I remember seeing Malachi Wolff, and…"

"Wait, *the* Malachi Wolff?" interrupted Duckie. "Entertainment mogul, zillionaire and asshat extraordinaire?"

"The same," said Chuck. "I was lying low at a friend's house in Azusa. It was the middle of the night, and someone came into my bedroom. I'm sure it was Malachi Wolff, and I think someone else was with him. He said something freaky about having big plans for me, then I felt a sting on the back of my neck. After that, everything gets really, really hazy. I think I was on a boat for a while."

"A big white yacht?" asked Duckie.

"Don't know. I just vaguely remember being laid out on a bed, and the whole room was rocking back and forth. I thought maybe it was the drugs, but I can remember hearing seagulls and the sound of waves. Then I remember being in this room with a hospital bed and some medical equipment. There were people in there with me, I remember that. But then I woke up, mostly, and there was no one there. I opened the door and came out, and there you were."

"Okay, wow," said Duckie. "That's a hell of a lot to unpack, man. First things first, though. We gotta get off this island. I'll call the guy who brought me here. He said he'd be waiting just a couple of miles away."

"Why didn't he just, y'know, hang out?"

"We saw this big-ass yacht as we were coming up to the island, and he got spooked."

"How did you know to come here?" asked Chuck.

"Oh, hell, that's a long story. We've definitely got a lot of catching up to do, but let's get the hell off this island first." He pulled out the burner phone and dialed "John Doe." It rang, which Duckie interpreted as a good sign. But then it kept ringing, then went to voicemail. "Goddammit, Shep, I need to get off this island right fuckin' now! I found my friend, and he's in bad shape. We need evac *now*, dammit!"

"What now?" asked Chuck.

"I'm gonna go check out the cabin you crawled out from," said Duckie.

"Well, count me out," said Chuck. "No way I'm going back there." He shivered.

"I wouldn't expect you to," said Duckie. "Besides, I need you to keep lookout."

Inside the cabin, it looked like a combination of a hospital room and a workshop. One half of the room was dominated by a large hospital bed that showed signs of a hasty departure. The bedclothes were thrown back, and a number of IV lines lay on the sheets like listless snakes. An amber-colored liquid dribbled out from one of them.

The other side of the room had shelves and cabinets that were crammed with exotic-looking medical equipment. A wheeled table held several trays with wicked-looking implements. One of the things was definitely a bone saw, and another looked like a miniature circular saw. There were also a variety of knives, cutters, pokers, scrapers and a couple of small hammers.

Duckie shivered and stepped away. He'd seen enough – it was definitely time to leave. The place was totally fuckin' creepy. He couldn't imagine how Chuck had felt waking up in such a place. He went back on the porch.

"Jesus," he said. "That's a real chamber of horrors in there. How'd you—"

"Hold up," said Chuck. He was peering out towards the dock. "I think your friend's here to get us." In the background the muted growl of a power boat could be heard.

"Thank God," said Duckie. "It's about time. I was starting to think that ol' Shep was gonna turn out to be … wait." He peered out the cabin door. A powerboat circled into view from the east side of the island. It was not Shep's boat. This one was larger and fancier. Also, there were four people on the boat. Duckie had expected one, maybe two, tops, if the Bookbinder had come along for the ride. This was wrong. As he watched, the yacht hove into view from behind the island.

"Oh, man," said Duckie. "We need to get out of here right now."

"But your friend—"

"That ain't my friend. I think those are the people who brought you here."

"Oh shit!" said Chuck. A look of animal fear crossed his eyes. "*Oh shit! We gotta get outta here man, we gotta... Where are we gonna go?* WE'RE TRAPPED!"

"Jesus, calm down!" said Duckie. He felt the tendrils of panic creeping up his spine. Chuck was allowed to panic; he'd just been through fifty-seven flavors of freaky. Duckie had to hold it together for both of them. "Okay, okay, slack, slack. There's another place we can go, in the middle of the island. They're sure to find us there sooner or later, but it will at least buy us some time. C'mon!"

They took off on the trail behind the cabin, but they hadn't gotten more than five feet before Chuck stopped and began hollering.

"What's wrong?" asked Duckie.

"Ow! I stepped on a rock or something! Damn!"

"Oh, fuck," said Duckie. He'd forgotten that his friend had no shoes. He went back to where Chuck stood, turned around and bent over with his hands on his knees. "C'mon," he said. "Let's go."

Chuck looked confused. "What, you want to have butt sex?" he asked. "Look, I'm glad to see you, too, but this doesn't seem like a good time—"

"I'm giving you a piggyback ride, dumbass! Hurry, they're getting closer!" The sound of the motorboat was much louder, and Duckie thought he could hear people shouting.

"Okay," said Chuck. "But you better call me in the morning."

Duckie made an impatient grunt and Chuck climbed up on his back. Duckie was surprised by how little his friend weighed. Maybe it was the adrenaline or maybe Chuck had lost a lot of weight on his journey here. Either way, Duckie was able to stand up and move relatively easily with Chuck on his back. "Watch your head," he said, and soon they were crashing through the underbrush towards the Laughingstock lodge.

Chapter 53

They pounded through the woods. Duckie knew the path now, so he was surer of where he was going. Unfortunately, Chuck's movement kept throwing Duckie's balance off.

"Hey, knock it off with the squirming!" said Duckie. "You almost knocked us over just now!"

"Hey, I'm just trying to keep these tree branches from taking my head off," complained Chuck. "My head's about a foot above yours now."

"S'all good, man," said Duckie. "You ain't heavy. You're my brother."

There was a high-pitched whine overhead. It diminished, then got louder and stayed that way.

"What's that?" asked Chuck, looking around wildly.

"Must be another drone," said Duckie. "They had one scoping us out on the way to the island, but Shep took it out with a shotgun."

"There's a lot of this story that I haven't heard yet, huh?" asked Chuck.

"Oh, man, you don't know the half of it. Hell, you don't know the *tenth* of it. But it's going to have to wait. Besides, we're almost there."

They reached the main lodge building, and Duckie lowered Chuck onto the porch, then bent over to catch his breath.

"What is this place?" asked Chuck.

Duckie took a few wheezing breaths, then stood up. "It's called Laughingstock," he said. "It was a secret comic's retreat back in the '80s and '90s. Doesn't seem like it's been used for a while."

The mechanical whine got louder, and the drone appeared above the clearing in front of the main lodge. Duckie picked up a rock and hucked it at the drone, missing it by a mile. "We need to get inside," Duckie said. "Gimme a sec." He went in the door and kicked enough of the broken glass out of the way for Chuck to come in without getting cut. They rushed inside and slammed the door.

Outside, the whine got louder. The drone dropped into the clearing and began slowly moving along the front of the lodge, its camera pointed towards the inside.

"We should try to find a place with no windows," said Chuck.

"I know just the place," said Duckie. "Follow me." He led Chuck through the twisting hallways and into the show room.

"Wow!" said Chuck. "It's like a comedy club in here. This place is amazing. At least the drone won't be able to see us in here."

"Not that it matters a whole lot," said Duckie. "They'll know where we went. And it's not like we've got other options. They'll find us soon enough." In the front of the lodge, they could hear indistinct voices arguing.

"Shit!" said Chuck. "Now what?"

"Now they catch us, I guess," said Duckie. "After that, I have no idea."

"We gotta do something!" said Chuck. "Isn't there someplace we can hide?"

"Yeah, there is – but it'll take them about four seconds for them to find us there. Still, you should at least have a quick look at this before they catch us." He led Chuck up into the green room, and shone his phone light on the signatures on the walls.

"Oh my God!" said Chuck. "Are these for real?"

"As real as that diaper you're wearing."

"Diaper? This ain't no diaper, you mook—"

"Shhh!" said Duckie and turned off the light. The search noises were getting louder. Duckie and Chuck peered out of the crack between the green room door and the frame. As he watched, a tall man with a buzzcut stepped into the room and took a look around. He picked up the Clud wrapper Duckie had dropped, sniffed it, and left. Chuck whistled between his teeth.

"Do you know that guy?" asked Duckie.

"Yeah. It's my showrunner. His name's Don Bundy. He's a psycho."

"Swell," muttered Duckie.

Don disappeared and Duckie and Chuck relaxed, but only momentarily. Don returned a few moments later with an older man and a younger woman.

"Holy shit!" hissed Duckie. "It's Cheryl!"

"You know her?" asked Chuck.

"Yeah, I came up here with her. She disappeared from the motel room yesterday."

"So, what, she's your girlfriend?"

"Christ, I dunno," said Duckie. "I really have no idea what's going on with anything anymore."

"Well, you're still way ahead of me," said Chuck. "At least you've been conscious for the last week."

"Hold up," said Duckie. "That older dude looks familiar. Where do I know him from?"

"That's Malachi Wolff."

As they watched, another man came into the room. He was bald and wore a saffron-colored robe and sandals. He strode into the show room and stood in the center with his hands on his hips.

"Who's that?" asked Duckie.

Chuck shivered. "I think he's Wolff's 'spiritual advisor,'" he said. "His name's Gordie or something. I'm pretty sure he's the one who dosed me."

"They're here," announced Gordie to his companions. "Comedians will always gravitate to the stage. They can't help themselves, being the attention whores that they are."

"I don't see anyone," said Malachi.

"Oh, they're here, said Gordie. "If they're not on the stage, they must be ... in the green room." He turned and walk purposefully towards the green room door. "C'mon out, boys. You're trapped!"

"Ah, we're boned!" muttered Duckie.

Behind them there was a slight sliding whisper. Hands wrapped around their mouths, and a voice hissed, "Come with me if you want to live."

They turned around to see a dark figure who hadn't been there a few moments earlier. The figure faded back into a dark gap in the back wall and beckoned Duckie and Chuck to follow him. They stepped back into a small passageway concealed behind the green room. The dark figure slid the hidden panel back into place just as Gordie ripped open the door to the green room.

"Ah ha!" exclaimed Gordie. "Got you! SHIT!"

"What's the problem?" came Malachi's voice.

"They're not here," said Gordie. "I was sure they would be here!"

"Maybe they went out a back door or something," said Malachi. "Don, call Captain Jack and have him send up another drone. Find those bastards!"

The dark figure with Chuck and Duckie pressed his eye to a crack in the sliding panel. "Huh," he whispered. "I thought that voice sounded familiar."

"What—" began Duckie, but the dark figure shushed him.

"I'm going to take the girl back down to the dock," said Malachi. "Gordie, check the other buildings. Don, check the woods, see if you can find a trail. They can't have gone far. It's a fucking *island* for Chrissakes!" He grabbed Cheryl by the upper arm and began pulling her towards the entrance.

"Hey, leggo, asshole," she protested. "I'm going, okay? What, I'm gonna run away or something?" They disappeared from the show room, followed closely by Gordie and Don.

After a few moments, the noise had died down, and Chuck and Duckie's rescuer snapped on a tiny LED flashlight. "Follow me," he said. "We need to talk." He shined the light down the passage in which they were standing. At the far end, a wooden ladder led down an earthen shaft. "Watch your step," he said. "There's a larger space underneath the stage. We'll be safer there, and we can talk."

"Okay," said Chuck reluctantly.

They followed the figure down the ladder into a space so dark it seemed to absorb the light from the tiny LED.

"Hold on," said the dark figure. "There's an electric lantern here somewhere." He fumbled around by the base of the ladder, then there was a click and a light flared up, illuminating the dark figure's face.

"Damn!" said Duckie. "It's you!"

"Hello, Ducknuts."

"Wait, you know this guy?" asked Chuck.

"Yes, I do," replied Duckie. "And so do you. Chuck Marshall, may I present Mickey Gross."

Chuck's jaw dropped to his chest. He started to speak, but could only get out a few *whuff* sounds.

"Actually, I go by Karma Zhimay now."

"You might as well go by 'Flat Leaver,'" said Duckie, "after that roadrunner act you pulled on me in Tucson."

"I'm sorry about that, Duckie," said Karma Zhimay. "The whole thing spooked me pretty hard. I felt bad about leaving like I did, but I had to get away, get some perspective on the situation."

"Okay, okay," said Chuck, who had finally regained the power of speech. "You're telling me that this guy is really Mickey Gross, who's obviously still alive. And you met him before? In Tucson?"

"Yeah," said Duckie. "Then he maced me and later ran off."

"Sounds about right," said Chuck. "Don't worry, Mr. Zhimay, we've all wanted to mace Duckie and run away at some point or another."

"Ain't that just fuckin' swell?" said Duckie with mock anger. "I come all the way up here to rescue you, and you're ragging on me! Some friend you are!"

"You might as well just call me 'Mickey' from here on in. 'Mr. Zhimay' – that's just too clunky."

Duckie looked around the space they were in. It looked to have been dug out beneath the stage area. The wood framing of the stage could be seen overhead. Underfoot was just dirt. Cinderblock walls lined the space, at least as far as he could see. The light from the lantern didn't throw very far.

"Can anyone tell me just what the fuck is going on here?" asked Chuck.

"Probably not," said Mickey. "Look, this whole place was designed and mostly built by comics. There are hidden rooms and secret passages all over the place. It's a good thing that they don't know about them."

"Okay, so who the hell's this Gordie guy?" asked Duckie. "You said you recognized his voice."

"His name's Gordon Sawchuk," said Mickey. "He's probably the worst comic I've ever seen."

"Worse than Carrot Top?" asked Duckie.

"*Way* worse than Carrot Top," said Mickey. "He used to hang around here back in the day. He was buddies with the guy that owns the island. We kept him around mostly as a gopher. It made his head swell up to be hanging around so many big-time comedians, but man, he's got the worst sense of timing. When he'd get up on stage, he'd always get laughs … because he was so bad."

"So how did he end up being the spiritual advisor, or whatever, to someone like Malachi Wolff?" asked Chuck.

"I don't know," said Mickey. "But it doesn't surprise me much. Gordie was always a power tripper, if you know what I mean. He liked to play mind games with people, fuck with their heads in little ways. He wasn't a lot of fun to be around, but like I said, he was buddies with Murray – who owned the place – so he was always lurking about. Actually, I heard he was into some weird shit. S&M type stuff. Hurting people, regardless of whether they were into it or not. Also heard some rumors about some illegal shit, run-ins with the cops, stuff like that. All real vague. One thing's for certain though: the guy's a huge fuckin' creep."

"How did he end up whispering in the ear of a high muckety-muck like Wolff?" Duckie said.

"Well, look," said Mickey. "Gordie wanted power. He probably knew he didn't have the chops to accumulate it himself. He certainly wasn't ever going to be a comedy powerhouse, that's for sure. So he went where the power was. Coulda been Washington; coulda been New York; it ended up being L.A. It was a good choice. There's a lot of people in that town with a lot of money and a howling spiritual void inside. It's easy to exploit people like that. He probably started small, glomming on to some B-list names and building up a rep. 'Oh, Gordie the Guru totally helped me get my head together!' Word travels fast, and superficial people will gravitate towards superficial bullshit to make their superficial lives superficially better. He probably worked himself up to Malachi Wolff in just a few years."

"Oh, it took a lot longer than that, Gross," said a voice from the darkness.

Duckie, Mickey and Chuck jumped, and Mickey held up the lantern to reveal Gordie the Guru leaning in the corner.

Chapter 54

T ake off," said Gordie. "Do you have any idea how much effort I put into cultivating Mr. Wolff? How many no-name dimbulbs I had to advise to make a name for myself in the entertainment industry? Hundreds and hundreds. All mindless, self-centered, attention-seeking cretins. Believe me, it wasn't much fun. Okay, it was fun when I advised them to kill themselves and they did. But I couldn't do that very often. I was playing the long game."

Mickey pursed his lips as Gordie stepped closer to the circle of light cast by the struggling lantern. "I knew I recognized that voice," said Mickey. "If it isn't Gordie the Chuckle Saw, the man who could cut the funny away from any joke!"

"Don't call me that!" hissed Gordie. "You bastard! You were always looking down on me! Well, now I've got you right where I want you."

"How's that?" asked Duckie. "There's three of us and only one of you."

"You've got a point," conceded Gordie. "But how many guns do you have?" He reached into his robe and pulled out a flat black Glock pistol.

"Uh, actually, fewer guns that that," said Duckie.

"Okay, then," said Gordie. "So why don't you smart guys just keep your hands in the air and follow every goddamn instruction I give you, eh?"

"How the hell did you get down here?" asked Mickey. "I thought I knew every trick door and hidden passageway in the place. And you… Well, we didn't tell you anything back in the day."

"Don't I know it," said Gordie. "You all treated me like a dog turd."

"Well, I can see now how mistaken we were," said Mickey. "Clearly, you are a kind, sensitive guy who would help kidnap people and then pull a gun on them. I can see now how terribly wrong we had you."

"Sarcasm doesn't become you, Gross," said Gordie. "Never did. Too bad it was the basis of your whole act. C'mon, let's go. The boss is going to be happy that you're here, though." He tittered, a high-pitched, jaw-grinding sound.

"Who's the boss?" asked Mickey.

"Well, seeing as how I'm the guy with the gun, I guess *I* am," said Gordie. "But if you're asking who signs the paychecks, that would be none other than Mr. Malachi Wolff."

"Ah, goodness gracious," said Mickey. "It's Old Nemesis Week. I've got Gordon the Chuckle Saw *and* asshole network bigwig Malachi Wolff. What's next?"

"Uh, Cheryl's here, too," said Duckie.

Mickey looked nonplussed for a moment. "So I saw," he said. "I assume that she's with you."

"Sorta," said Duckie. "Y'see, your brother invited her up to visit him, and I just tagged along for the ride."

"Dick?" said Mickey. "He's mixed up in this somehow?"

"Oh, yes," said Gordie. "Your brother was very cooperative. When he learned that your daughter and her dumbass boyfriend were on their way to look for Laughingstock, he let me know right away. He owes my family a favor or two, you might say."

"That bastard!" said Duckie. "I *knew* he was up to something shady. There was just something off about the guy."

"Oh, don't blame Richard too much," said Gordie. "Y'see, I have him by the short and curlies. My father was one of his business partners, did you know that? No? Well, no matter. Anyway, the firm took on some … um, interesting clients. Clients who paid really well, but whose activities were, shall we say, a bit extralegal. At one point, Richard Gross had the choice to fish or cut bait. He could have walked off with a decent piece of cash and go on, retire, start a new company, play the ponies, whatever. Instead, he decided to keep going with his questionable clients. It gave us a lot of leverage over him. When we knew we'd be coming up here, we contacted him, and told him to let us know if anything unusual happened. And lo and behold, it did! First Mickey put in an unexpected appearance. We definitely wanted to intercept him. It was Malachi's idea to have Richard invite Cheryl up to visit. She was bait, to draw out her father."

"That fuckin' scumbag!" hissed Duckie. Mickey just looked sad and shook his head.

"Just what the fuck is this all about?" demanded Chuck. "Why did you go to all the trouble of drugging me, kidnapping me and taking me all the way to Canada?"

"All will be made clear soon," said Gordie. "For now, we have places to go and people to see." Still waving the gun, Gordie the Guru sidled over to a dark corner of the subterranean room and yanked open a door. Daylight and a run of wooden stairs could be seen beyond it.

"Where the hell did that come from?" said Mickey. "I sure don't remember *that.*"

Gordie shook his head in disgust. "I put it in, Mr. Big Shot. I own this place now. The whole damn island. Bought it from Murray ten years ago."

"You bought Laughingstock?" asked Mickey.

"Fuck yes," said Gordie. "Cost a pretty penny, too. Murray drove a hard bargain. Didn't matter, though. I had plenty of money. Shit, I wasn't providing spiritual advice for those Tinseltown twats pro bono, you know."

"Jesus," said Duckie. "You are one screwed-up hombre. I thought Canadians were supposed to be nice. You're the most fucked-up Canadian I've ever heard of, except maybe Gordon Lightfoot."

"DON'T YOU SAY ANYTHING BAD ABOUT GORDON LIGHT-FOOT!" screamed Gordie. "HE'S A NATIONAL TREASURE!" He waved the gun at Duckie, and for a brief moment, he thought the crazed guru was going to shoot him right there. Then a devious smile spread across Gordie's face. "Up the stairs you go," he said. "Chop-chop!"

Mickey led the way, with Chuck and Duckie close behind. Chuck looked like he was having some trouble keeping his balance, so Duckie grabbed his shoulder to steady him. Gordie the Guru followed them up.

They emerged in a small clearing behind the lodge. "Halt!" commanded Gordie. He pulled a phone from the folds of his robe. "Got 'em, boss," he said into the phone. "And a couple of bonuses. Well, okay – one bonus and one smartass, soon to be fish bait. But trust me, sir, it's a big bonus. I think you're going to be very pleased. Bring the team back to the theater. We'll meet you there." He hung up.

Gordie herded the group around to the front of the lodge, through the front door, and back to the show room. He pushed them into a corner and held the gun on them. After a few minutes, the rest of the contingent from the yacht appeared: Malachi, Don, and a couple of guys in sailor uniforms who were carrying guns.

"Well, well, well," said Malachi. "What have we here?"

"I'd call it three for the price of one, boss," said Gordie with an ingratiating grin.

Malachi strolled over to the corner where the three comics sat at one of the dilapidated tables. "I see that you managed to recover our *Chucklefest* star," said Malachi. "But who are these other two clowns?"

"Well, this one's a nobody," said Gordie, indicating Duckie. "But he claims he's a comic, so he might be of some use.

"The other one, however, is the *pièce de résistance,*" he said. "In fact, he's the entire reason we're here, you might say."

"What?" said Malachi. He squinted, looking Mickey up and down. "Jesus Christ! It can't be! Mickey Goddamn Gross! Well, Gordie, I must say I am impressed. I was very angry with you for letting Mr. Marshall get loose, but to bring back this prize… Well, you've more than redeemed yourself. It's so nice to see you again, Mickey. And so fitting that you're here to be a part of our activity!"

Mickey stared back impassively, saying nothing.

"What about Cheryl?" said Duckie. "Where's Cheryl?"

"Oh, yes," said Malachi. "Darling Cheryl is on her way back to the yacht. She's quite safe … for now. I'll be honest: I'm not entirely sure what is going to become of her. Perhaps she'll just go to Cobble Hill and stay with her loving uncle. That shouldn't worry you too much, though. I'd say that you have more immediate concerns." He threw back his head and laughed.

"First, we have some logistics issues to take care of," announced Gordie. "How are we going to, uh, process three people?"

"Well, first we should restrain them, so they don't get away," said Malachi. "Captain Jack, you got any zip ties on the launch?"

The man in the fanciest uniform looked uneasily at the other two sailors. One of them shrugged and nodded. "Yeah, I guess so," said Captain Jack.

"Well, what are you waiting for?" demanded Malachi. "Go get them and tie these bastards up!"

"I don't want to be disrespectful or anything, Mr. Wolff," said Captain Jack. "But all of this is more than we signed on for. I mean, tying people up? Kidnapping? That's pretty messed up. We could land in a lot of trouble."

"Um, Captain Jack?" said Mickey calmly. "Look, we're all in a … ah, treacherous situation here, one that could wind up being very dangerous and *costly* for everyone involved. Wouldn't it be best if we just sort of stopped things right here, before they really get out of hand?"

Captain Jack looked worried, the sailor behind him even more so. They looked at each other nervously.

"Ah, hey, none of that bullshit," said Gordie, who quickstepped over from where he was conferring with Malachi. "You have to watch this one. He lies very, very well and will cloud your mind."

"Ignore him!" said Malachi. "What the hell am I paying you people for? Okay, okay – I know there's been some mission creep here, especially with our two new arrivals. How about this, Captain Jack: I will triple – no, *quadruple* – the bonus pay we agreed on. Fair enough?"

"Cash?" asked Captain Jack.

"Of course," said Malachi.

"Aye aye, sir!" said Captain Jack as he snapped off a smart salute. "Stratton, go back to the launch and bring back some zip ties and some half-inch nylon line." One of the sailors sketched a lazy salute and disappeared out the door.

In the corner, Duckie, Chuck and Mickey eyed their captors, saying nothing. Malachi and Gordie stood in the corner, engaging in an intense whispered conversation.

The sailor returned, bearing a coil of orange nylon rope and a bag of large plastic zip-ties. Captain Jack and the other sailor looked relieved to see him. "Got the rope and the zip ties, boss," said Captain Jack.

"Good, good," said Malachi. "Gordie informs me that we can perform the procedure right here. No need for fancy hospital beds and the like."

"What?" cried Duckie. "Procedure? What kind of fucking *procedure* are you talking about, Wolff?"

"Don't worry about it," tittered Gordie. "You won't feel a thing … after, of course, the initial thirty seconds of mind-bending agony."

"Jesus, Gordie, quite the charm-school graduate, aintcha?" said Mickey. "As for a 'procedure,' I doubt it. You couldn't pick your nose without written instructions and at least three YouTube videos!"

"We'll see who's laughing soon, Gross," snarled Gordie.

Malachi clapped his hands like a bitchy stage director. "Okay!" he said. "Let's get everything squared away! I want these three up there on stage, tied to their chairs."

"Hey, fuck you, man!" shouted Duckie.

Malachi nodded at Gordie, who pulled the gun out of his robe and immediately fired into the floor by Duckie's feet.

"Whoa, now," said Mickey soothingly. "Let's just take it easy. We'll do as you say. Okay, guys?"

Duckie and Chuck nodded dumbly, and the three hauled their chairs up onto the small stage. Malachi instructed the sailors to zip-tie their hands behind their backs, their ankles to the chair legs and to tie them to their chairs with the rope. Soon they were trussed up like Thanksgiving turkeys.

"Okay, you guys go to the cabin by the dock," said Gordie to Captain Jack and the sailors. "Haul up all of the equipment that's sitting on the counter by the back wall. And don't forget the power drill!"

Mickey seemed supremely unconcerned. He gazed serenely around the room, whistling the theme song from "Jeopardy."

Ten minutes later, the sailors came back and dropped off a couple of milk crates filled with creepy-looking medical gear and a power drill. Malachi sent them back to the yacht to wait for further instructions.

When they'd left, Malachi stepped to the front of the stage and looked up at his captives. He smacked his hands together and rubbed them in anticipation. "So, my friends, it has finally come down to this," he said. "I'm so glad that you are here to help me – and Gordie – in this little project. I am, in fact, very, very grateful for your participation. You, gentlemen, are about to help us make history. Your names will live forever. So will mine, for that matter, but that's not so important, because after today, *I* will live forever!"

The three comics on the stage just looked at him blankly. After a moment, Mickey said, "Oh for Christ's sake, Wolff, is that what this is about? That night at the Comedy Shoppe? Jesus Christ, that was, what, like ten years ago? Fifteen? It was a *joke,* you egotistical baboon!"

Malachi's face reddened and he seemed to deflate. "You … you … nincompoop!" he sputtered. "It may have been a joke to you, but it was serious to me! Deadly serious! You might say it changed my life!"

Up on stage, Mickey nodded. "Okay, I see it pretty clear, Wolff. I guess I really rubbed you the wrong way that night, if you've been stewing over it for the last fifteen years."

"You know what this is all about?" said Chuck.

"Well, I don't know what these two jackoffs have planned for us," said Mickey, jerking his chin at the boxes of sinister equipment. "Although it sure doesn't look pleasant. I can tell you how it started, though. It was 2005, and a hotshot network executive was trying to make a name for himself. Let me tell you what happened."

Chapter 55

Los Angeles, September 2005

Mickey didn't remember how he'd gotten to the club. He was pretty sure he hadn't driven, though. He'd been drunk and coked up for the last day and a half, and he was barely capable of operating a urinal, much less an automobile. He had just come out of a mini-blackout, and he was standing outside of the Comedy Shoppe on a Saturday night. He wasn't sure how he knew it was Saturday; he was barely certain of his own name. One thing he did know was that he'd just been royally screwed by the Wolff Network.

He looked around to see if Abby was in the crowd. It seemed likely that Abby had brought him. She was his roommate/personal assistant/fuck buddy/chauffeur/enabler. He couldn't see her, but that didn't mean anything; the crowd was heavy and Abby was short. *Fuck it,* he thought. He staggered towards the thickest part of the crowd jammed in front of the Sunset entrance to the Comedy Shoppe, figuring that was where the door was most likely to be located. The crowd was starting to get to him, and all he really wanted was a booth in a dark corner and a strong drink.

"'Scuse me, pardon me," he said as he lowered his shoulder and pushed rudely through the throng. He could see Julio, the huge, bald bouncer up ahead, and redoubled his efforts. He shoved his way through a knot of indignant lingerie models and pulled up in front of the door. "'Lo, Julio," he mumbled. "Need a drink."

"Hello, Mr. G," said Julio. He lifted the velvet rope and let Mickey pass through the doors. Behind him, a muttered mixture of awe and indignance: "That wasted guy was Mickey Gross!" "Yeah, well, he's still a dick. He stepped on my new cha-cha pumps!"

Once inside, he made a beeline for the bar. Missy materialized in front of him with his drink. Missy Bloomington was the owner of the Comedy Shoppe and the grande dame of Hollywood stand-up. She and Mickey were thick as thieves.

"Figured we'd see you here tonight," said Missy. "Heard the news. Tough break. Sorry to hear it, Mickey."

"Ah, shit, itsa blessing in disguise," said Mickey. He picked up the tumbler of iced gin and downed it in one go. "It was a doomed idea from the start. Me'n a buncha puppets? Fuckin' ridiculous."

"Well," said Missy, "if anyone could make a puppet show about outer-space monkeys funny, it's you." She refilled Mickey's drink.

"You're a doll, Missy," said Mickey. "Yeah, it was a stupid show. Still, I could use the money."

That part was certainly true. Mickey was in serious debt to two coke dealers and three lawyers. They were all vicious, but on the whole, Mickey preferred the coke dealers. At least they knew how to have a good time.

Missy nodded sympathetically and topped off Mickey's drink.

"All they do at Wolff is rip off tried-and-true ideas," said Mickey. "Not a single original thought in the whole damn network. Just a buncha yes-men. Hell, even that stupid cartoon. What's it called?"

"Boscoville?"

"Yeah, that's it. Boscoville. Just a rip-off of Happy Days. Stupid fuckin' show."

"Well, what about your show?" asked Missy. "Why'd it go south?"

"Other than the fact that it was a stupid concept from the outset? You've seen it. These monkeys from outer space fly down and kidnap some regular schmoe – me – and fly him off so they can study our planet, and of course get into yea number of wacky-ass adventures."

"That doesn't sound too bad," said Missy. "What went wrong?"

"I don't know. Just found out today that the network canceled the show.

Not gonna order any more episodes."

"That's tough, Mickey."

"Shit, yeah."

"Well, I got something that'll make you feel better," said Missy, tapping her nose. "If you'll follow me into the office…"

Mickey came out about twenty minutes later, feeling much more buoyant and rather thirsty. He worked through the crowded showroom. He had gotten nearly to the back of the room when he saw something incredible: Malachi Wolff was sitting at a table in front of the stage. Mickey rubbed his eyes – this had to be a hallucination – but Wolff stayed right where he was. Mickey grimaced and staggered back to the bar. "Where's Missy?" he asked the bartender. "I gotta talk to Missy."

Missy materialized like a genie at the mention of her name. "What say, Mickey?"

"That bastard Wolff is here. I want some stage time!"

"Sorry, man, no can do. Roster's full. Tell you what, why don't I call you a cab?"

"Fuck cabs," spat Mickey. "Fuck everybody! C'mon, Missy, just five minutes. That's all I need."

"Nothing doing, Mickey," said Missy. "I'm doing you a favor, man. You get up on that stage tonight, the whole town's going to be talking about it tomorrow. And not in a good way. You don't want that, do you?"

"The only thing worse than being talked about is not being talked about," said Mickey in a slurred British accent.

"Yeah, well, Oscar Wilde didn't have the Hollywood tabloid press to contend with," said Missy. "You'll regret it once you sober up, trust me."

"Not gonna sober up," muttered Mickey. "Look, why don't you just throw the fucker out, huh? He's just here to fuck with me! You know that!"

"You must think I'm all sorts of stupid, Mickey. I can't just throw Malachi Wolff out for no reason. Now, if he was as fucked up as you are, I might consider it. But he's just sitting at a table by the stage, sipping a club soda and lime. Says he wants to scout some new talent. Nothing wrong with that."

"So you're turning on me too, huh? Well, thanks a lot!"

"Just let me call you that cab, okay? Hell, I'll drive you home myself if you want. You know something bad's gonna happen if you hang around here."

"I know nothing of the sort!"

"Look," said Missy. "I don't want to have to set Julio after you, but I will. You've done some really stupid shit in my club before, but I've always tolerated it. However, everybody's got a limit, and I have a feeling that you're approaching mine."

"Okay, okay, fine," said Mickey. "I'll behave, Missy. You've been real good to me. I ain't gonna crap where I sleep." He shoved the G-sans-T back towards the bartender. "Gimme a Diet Coke," he said. "I'm gonna try and find Abby and go the fuck home."

"Okay, good," said Missy. "If you can't find her, let me know. I'll make sure you get home, no problem."

"Thanks, Missy," said Mickey. "You're the best!"

He swept up the fizzing soft drink and lurched away from the bar. He tried to walk carefully, but failed miserably. Mickey caromed from table to table, making pointless chit-chat. He took a sip of his Diet Coke and immediately regretted it. It tasted like battery acid and saccharine. His stomach took a wild lurch, and he spun on his heel and made a beeline for the men's room.

He just made it, sliding on his knees and coming to rest in front of a urinal before letting go. It was an epic upchuck, seemingly going on forever. People came and went, and Mickey just kept heaving. No one seemed to care; this wasn't really an unusual sight on a Saturday night in the Comedy Shoppe men's room.

Eventually, the spasms subsided, and Mickey rose shakily to his feet. He felt … not bad. Certainly a lot better than he had any right to feel, given his heroic consumption of cocaine and ethanol. The ill effects of the alcohol were almost entirely gone: no shakes, no balance problems, no nausea. He could still feel the coke in his system, but instead of feeling cranked up and paranoid, he felt loose and energized. It was like his psyche had been given an enema.

He strolled back to the bar and ordered a Shirley Temple. "You probably ought to send someone with a mop into the men's room," he told the bartender. "Some foul peon filled one of the urinals with puke." He took a sip of his Shirley Temple. It tasted wonderful.

There was one more thing to do, then he could get out of here. He strode up to the stage, where a frizzy-haired comic was complaining that her boyfriend was afraid of commitment. Mickey walked up to the table where Malachi Wolff sat – alone – and planted himself directly between Malachi and the stage.

Malachi looked up at him. He was dressed in the standard Hollywood douchebag style: black Armani suit, black bespoke silk dress shirt, dark gray silk tie. His hair was slicked back with some sort of greasy kid stuff that probably cost $300 an ounce. He seemed confused: his eyes were unfocused, and the pupils dilated. It looked like he was tripping on something. Mickey laughed.

Malachi snapped back into focus. "Think of something funny?" he asked. "That would be a first. Maybe you should consider working it into your act."

"Fuck you very much," said Mickey politely. "Although I don't know how you reached that conclusion. You wouldn't know funny if it bit you on the ass."

Malachi sighed theatrically. "Oh, is this about that damn monkey show?" he asked. "You don't have to be a talent scout to know that wasn't funny. Phew, what was I thinking on that one?"

"Yeah, it was a goofy premise, but we were making it work. *I* was making it work."

Malachi sketched an eye roll that would have made Jack Benny proud. "Oh, spare me," he said. "The great Mickey Gross lost his TV show and now he's throwing a sulk."

"Not sulking," said Mickey. "I just want to know why you pulled the plug on the show. It had production problems, but it was tight. We were getting decent reviews and ratings. Why'd you give it the axe, Wolff? That's all I want to know."

"Why did I deep-six your show?" asked Malachi. "Simple. Because I could. That's all."

"What?" said Mickey. He had expected some razzmatazz about focus groups and advertising revenue projections. The last thing he'd expected from Malachi Wolff was the truth.

"You heard me," said Malachi. "I was in a bad mood that morning. I don't even remember why, not that it matters now. I was in a shitty mood so I killed the show. So what?"

"So what? A lot of people worked really hard on that show. I worked really hard on it. Yeah, it was ridiculous, but so what? It was no goofier than that damn Boscoville cartoon. I mean, seriously? That thing is sillier than a hatful of assholes."

Malachi shrugged. "I'll make money with or without your space monkey show. I'll make money regardless of how well Boscoville does."

"It's not about the money, Wolff. Don't you understand that?"

Malachi made a whining sound and tilted his head to the side, like a dog being shown a magic trick. Finally, he said, "Shows what you know. Although I'll give you this: It isn't about the money. It's about the power. Money is just the most common vehicle for the power. That's what you don't understand."

"Maybe I understand it better than you think," said Mickey. He didn't have a network executive amount of money, true. But he could stand up on stage in front of thousands of strangers and make them laugh. Make them feel what he wanted them to feel, and *that* was real power. He liked to think that he used that power for good. Unlike Malachi Wolff who used his power for … what, really? Self-aggrandizement? Accumulating more wealth than he could spend in a hundred lifetimes? Why fucking bother?

"Let me ask you something, Wolff," said Mickey. "Sure, you've got money tumbling out of your asshole. You've got power, yeah. You can make and break people like that." He snapped his fingers. "But riddle me this, asshat, does anybody love you? Anybody?"

Malachi opened his mouth and closed it. His eyes darted around the room in confusion. The people at the adjacent tables had stopped paying attention to the frizzy-haired comic and were keenly watching the interchange between Mickey and Malachi. *This* was an amazing show.

Mickey grinned. He had really gotten under Malachi's skin now. But his triumph was tempered by an unfamiliar emotion. It took him a moment to recognize it: pity. For all his trappings of success and glamour, Malachi Wolff was just another regular person like everyone on Earth. He got up in the morning with bad breath and messy hair and took a dump with his pajama bottoms around his ankles.

Malachi was breathing deeply now, almost hyperventilating. "Sure people love me!" he shouted. "Thousands of people! Millions! I bring them quality entertainment around the clock. And the people who work for me. They love me too! They know I put food on their family's table and keep a roof over their heads. They know if they didn't love me, then they'll be out of a job and on the streets!"

"Doesn't sound much like love to me," said Mickey. "Sounds like fear. Any cheap thug with a twenty-dollar pistol can get that." He looked around. All eyes in the club were on them now; even the frizzy-haired comic had halted her bit and was watching them in open-mouthed wonder.

"Love, fear, what's the difference?" asked Malachi. His eyes glittered wickedly, and Mickey thought he could see a slight tremor in his hands. "It doesn't matter as long as I have power. I can do things that no one else can. Certainly not you, Gross. Not anyone! I AM ABOVE ALL OF YOU PEOPLE!" The last came out as a shout, and the entire room went quiet.

"Oh, man," said Mickey, shaking his head. "You just don't get it. You are one confused motherfucker, Wolff. You think you're that much better than everyone else in the room?"

"Don't just think it," Malachi said through clenched teeth. "I know it!"

"Well, here's something to consider, Mr. Superior: In a hundred years, you'll be dead. For all your money and power and over-priced hair goo, you'll be dead as a doornail. Just like me and everyone else in this room. In that respect, you are one of us. And there's nothing you can do about it."

Malachi's eyes opened so wide that Mickey thought they might fall out of his head. He had clearly touched a nerve. Again, the howling contempt he held for this man was tempered by pity and – could it be? – compassion. With a large amount of luck, Malachi might actually take something away from this exchange, possibly be a better person who makes the world a better place.

Or maybe not.

Malachi huffed and puffed, his pupils now dilated to the point where his eyes looked like ebony, only a thin ring of white showing around the edges. "BULLSHIT!" he roared. "I am not like you! I am NOT LIKE ANY OF YOU!"

Mickey threw back his head and laughed. He felt cruel doing so, but Malachi Wolff was clearly beyond redemption, not worthy of pity or compassion. "Yet you are mortal. You will still die. You *are* one of us."

"NO!" said Malachi. "Never!"

"One of us!" repeated Mickey. "One of us!" He looked around the room and flapped his hands at the crowd, encouraging them. They picked it up quickly.

"One of us!" The chant filled the room. "One of us!"

Malachi looked around in confusion. Up on stage, the frizzy-haired comic took up the chant. She swallowed the mic, and her voice, now artificially deeper, boomed around the room. "ONE OF US! ONE OF US! ONE OF US!"

Malachi pushed back from his table and rose unsteadily, his chair toppling behind him. Two very large men in sunglasses and dark suits materialized behind him, taking him by the arms. One whispered to him, and Malachi nodded. The other looked directly at Mickey and stuck his arm under his suitcoat. Mickey jutted his chin at him, effectively saying, *Just try it, asshole.* Around them, the chant continued: "ONE OF US! ONE OF US!"

The bodyguard paused and removed his hand from his suit. He and his companion began hustling Malachi towards the door, bulling people out of the way.

Mickey followed, still bellowing, "ONE OF US! ONE OF US!" He watched as Malachi and his bodyguards hustled out the front door and into a waiting limousine. A large contingent of the crowd followed them outside, still chanting. The chant faded as the limo pulled out with a screech of rubber and disappeared down Sunset Boulevard.

Mickey looked down to see Abby standing there, giving him a look that was mixed amusement and disgust. "Ah, there you are!" said Mickey. "I'm really hungry all of a sudden. Let's go hit up IHOP."

Chapter 56

Laughingstock, June 2019

Y'know," said Mickey from the stage. "I'd almost forgotten about that. I always wondered why it never made the tabloids."

"I made sure it didn't," said Malachi. "Had to pull some strings, and call in a lot of favors. It was worth it though. I couldn't have my name become a … a laughingstock!"

"I couldn't ever figure out why you even showed up at the Comedy Shoppe in the first place," said Mickey. "You must have known that it was my turf, that you would be seen as the interloper. What made you… Wait. You were fucked up on something that night, weren't you?"

Malachi's face pinched and reddened. "Well, what the hell. I might as well tell you now. It's not going to make any difference. I was seeing a therapist at the time, a man named McIver. You see, Dr. McIver was a protégé of Dr. Mortimer Hartman." He paused, as if expecting a reaction.

"Who?" asked Chuck.

Malachi shook his head. "Kids these days," he said. "Dr. Hartman was a proponent of LSD therapy in the late '50s and early '60s. He had a clinic in Beverly Hills and worked with a number of famous people, using LSD to help reconnect the broken parts of their minds. His most famous patient was Cary Grant.

"McIver took it even further. After LSD was outlawed, he continued working with it, even making his own and tinkering with the formula. I had engaged in a therapy session that afternoon, in fact. A new experimental variation of LSD that Dr. McIver had just developed."

"Well, I'd say the experiment was a failure," said Mickey. "You were a bigger prick than usual, which was something I hadn't thought possible."

Malachi's face pinched even further and he flushed red. "You don't know what you're talking about," he said tightly. "And pretty soon you'll know nothing at all, and neither will your foolish friends." He paused and rubbed his chin. "And while I'm thinking of it – Bundy!"

"Yes, boss!" said Don, who had been observing the entire exchange from his perch by the bar.

"Get down to the launch before they take off. Bring the girl back here. I want her to be part of this too."

"Really?" asked Don.

"Yes, really!" snapped Malachi. "Don't question me, Bundy. Just follow orders. Now go!"

"Sir, yes, sir!" Don snapped off a brisk salute and took off at a run.

"You son of a bitch!" said Mickey. "You leave her out of this." He struggled against his bonds and cursed, his cool now totally blown.

"Nothing doing, funnyman," said Malachi. "Might as well make it a family affair." Behind him, Gordie the Guru snickered.

"So, Gordie," said Malachi. "Will this work with four, ah, subjects? Will it be four times as effective?"

"Well, it will certainly be more effective," said Gordie. "I can't make any guarantees as to the quantity, though. I think you'll find that the results will be amazing. Consider this: We have the primary subject." He nodded at Chuck. "In addition, we have Mr. Gross, who is definitely of the phenotype we need, and we have his offspring, so genetically that's at least another fifty percent."

"You motherfuckers!" yelled Mickey. "I'm gonna make you pay for this!"

Gordie ignored him. "Finally, we have this guy," he said, waving at Duckie. "I don't know anything about him, but I guess he styles himself a comedian, so what the hell. The icing on the cake, eh? At the very least, it's one less witness."

"You're a fucking maniac!" said Mickey. "Christ, Wolff! Is this really what you're about? Kidnap and murder? Torturing innocent people to death?"

Malachi Wolff faltered, and a look of confusion crossed his face. Gordie stepped up to him and clapped him on the shoulder. "Don't listen to him," he said. "He can cloud your mind. It's all that mystical Eastern stuff he's studied."

"Oh, yes," said Mickey. "I almost forgot." He clammed up and stared off in the middle distance, smiling mildly.

"Well," said Malachi. "While we're waiting, I might as well let you know what's in store for you."

"Hold up," said Duckie. "Shouldn't you be sitting in a swivel chair and stroking a cat while you're telling us this?"

"Oh, you are a real comedian," said Gordie.

"Better than anything you ever came up with," said Mickey.

Gordie ground his teeth. "You won't be laughing soon, Mr. Big Shot."

"I don't recall having *ever* laughed at anything while you were in the room, Chuckle Saw."

Gordie took a deep breath to respond, but now it was Malachi's turn to intervene. "Well, let's just get this out on the table, and I think our friends will see that this is dead serious."

"How did I get mixed up in all this?" said Chuck. "I can't help but feel that I started all this."

"Not really," said Malachi. "You were just in the right place at the right time. Actually, it all comes down to a matter of brain chemistry. As Mr. Gross related, on the night when he mocked and humiliated me in public, I was indeed in what you might call an enhanced state of consciousness. It affected me very deeply. At first, I was quite upset – and deeply depressed – for quite a while after that evening. Dr. McIver tried to help me work through the experience, but he never really understood the effects of his own chemical formulation. Perhaps if he'd tried it himself, it might have been different, but he ended up scrapping the formula shortly after my encounter at the Comedy Shoppe."

"Probably because he saw that it turned you into a first-class fruitcake," said Duckie.

"No, you slob," said Malachi. "It was because he lacked the vision to see that I really *could* live forever. Not metaphorically, through endowing a scholarship or a college building, but to literally never die. Ever!"

"Fucking bonkers," said Duckie. Mickey sighed and shook his head. Chuck just looked scared and confused.

"So, once I realized that I could become immortal," Malachi continued, "it was just a matter of figuring out how. Of course, I started with the obvious routes: diet and exercise. Special trainers, dieticians and such."

"What about this Dr. McIver?" asked Duckie. "He didn't want to help you in this quest for immortality?"

"Ah, sadly not," said Malachi. "As I said, the man lacked vision. Shortly after I ended our professional relationship, he took his own life. As time went on, I resorted to more, ah, esoteric means to achieve the goal that I knew was so eminently achievable."

"Drinking the blood of virgins?" sneered Duckie.

"No," said Malachi. "At least, not right away." This remark elicited another series of titters from Gordie. "I started looking into historical precedents and examples. The rituals of Aleister Crowley, Dr. John Dee, Abramelin the Mage—"

"Yeah, 'cause those guys are still alive," said Duckie. "Hell, I saw Aleister Crowley just last week working the fryer at the In-and-Out Burger. Of course, it might have just been some fat bald guy."

"Either is possible," said Malachi. "I believe that the ancient seekers of wisdom were on to something. Perhaps they actually achieved their goal, but in the process had achieved the wisdom to keep quiet about it. For all you know, that might actually have been Aleister Crowley working at the In-and-Out."

"You never know," said Mickey. "At the height of his fame, Andy Kaufman worked as a busboy. He got a kick out of it when people told him that he looked just like Andy Kaufman. He'd tell them, 'Yeah, I get that a lot.' He thought it was hilarious."

"Is that what you're going to do, Mr. Wolff?" asked Chuck. "Become immortal, then keep a low profile and work at a fast food restaurant?"

"Why are we having this conversation?" said Duckie. "This is insane! First, there's no such thing as biological immortality. Second, even if there were, this egomaniac would shout it from the rooftops and try to take over the world!"

"It doesn't matter, because it's impossible," said Chuck.

"That is where you're wrong," said Malachi. "You see, my studies in modern biotechnology techniques seemed to dovetail with the ancient wisdom recorded by the likes of Dee and Crowley. Gordie the Guru provided the last piece of the puzzle. It involved finding the right subject, and performing the procedure during the solstice at a location close to the 55th parallel. Astrological reasons, you see. And now all of the circumstances have aligned rather nicely. Don't worry. I expect things will go very smoothly. There were some problems with our, ah, initial trial subject, but I think we've learned from our mistakes there, eh, Gordie?"

"That one was too feisty," grumbled Gordie. "It would have worked too, if she hadn't fought back so hard. Damn near shot me with that candy-ass pistol."

Chuck's head snapped up. "Farrah!" he said. "You were the ones who killed her! As a test run for your psychotic experiment! You fucking murderous scumbags!"

"Don't you see?" asked Malachi. "You're helping change the future of mankind. You and Ortega will be venerated as the ones who helped bring about my godhead."

"I think I'm starting to see now," said Mickey.

"I doubt it," sneered Gordie. "Might as well start getting ready." He dragged one of the larger tables into the middle of the room and began setting up the lab equipment. "I think the generator should be online." He found a wall outlet and plugged in a centrifuge. He flipped it on and it whirred to life. He gave Malachi a thumbs-up and said, "Just give me a few minutes to set this up and we can begin the extraction process."

"Extraction process?" said Duckie. "What extraction process? What are you going to extract?"

"Not much," tittered Gordie. "Just your pineal gland."

Chapter 57

ordie held up a battery-powered drill with a long, tubular bit and squeezed the trigger. It made a horrible grinding sound. It sounded remarkably like his tittering laugh. "Special drill bit, you see," said Gordie. "It's like a tiny little test core drill they use for rock samples. Just go in through the ear and get right to the center and pull out the pineal gland. Sure, it's a little mashed up, but we're going to pulverize it anyway. Don't need the gland intact."

Duckie and Chuck shouted in alarm, but Mickey just looked rueful and shook his head.

Malachi continued with his Bond-villain explanation. He seemed very proud of himself. "I discovered through my research that the human pineal gland was the key to the Elixir of Life. The Ancients thought of the pineal gland as being the seat of the human soul. Even modern science doesn't really understand what it does."

"But you do?" asked Chuck.

"We're about to find out," said Gordie. He continued rummaging in boxes and setting up equipment on the table. "Where are the books?" he asked Malachi.

"I think they're in that box in the corner," Malachi responded, indicating a black plastic storage tub. Gordie opened it and began hauling out ancient-looking books.

"What are those?" asked Duckie. "Your high-school yearbooks?"

"Tomes of ancient lore," said Gordie. He consulted one of the old books, then took a can of spray paint from the box. He painted a circle surrounding the three hostages on the floor of the stage, with strange letters and sigils around the perimeter. He then set up nine candles at regular spaces around the circle. "The ritual space has been defined," he said. "Now, where's the notebook?" He pulled a black three-ring binder from the box, flipped it open and began reading.

"Why do you need to go to all this bother?" asked Chuck. "I mean, why can't you just get a pineal gland from a cadaver or something?"

"Good question," said Malachi. "First, it's long been known that the pineal gland had to be extracted from a living human donor."

"Donor?" asked Duckie. "Who's donating? I wouldn't donate a cup of piss to you, you fuckin' psycho. This is criminal. Grand theft pineal!"

"Furthermore," continued Malachi, "not just any donor would do, as it turns out. This is the last part of the puzzle that dear Gordon here was able to provide."

Gordie the Guru looked up from his notebook. "Oh, yes," he said. "It can't be just some schmoe off the street, otherwise we would have just pulled some schmoe off the street. Plenty of those in L.A. No, it has to be a comedian. There's something about the brain chemistry of a person willing to stand up in front of a room full of strangers and talk about their private parts that gives the pineal gland that certain special something."

"Nor is it just any comedian," said Malachi. "We know; we tried. Gordie determined that the proper subject would have to have a certain type of outlook, a certain comedic style. They had to be funny but also empathetic. No dick-joke merchants allowed!"

"Well, that rules me out," said Duckie. "You pretty much just described the basis for my entire act."

"But it doesn't rule out your friend here," said Malachi. "In fact, he was the perfect comedian for the program. That's why we green-lighted your show for midseason," Malachi said, turning to Chuck. "I wanted you near me. The fact that the show took off and was successful was just dumb luck."

"And even better," said Gordie. "We have Mr. Big Shot Mickey Gross here. He is – or was – a pretty good match, too. At least in his younger days, before he got all coked-out and jaded."

"What about me?" asked Duckie. "You said no dick jokes, right? Hey, what's the difference between a dick and a bonus check? You can always find someone who's willing to blow your bonus check!"

Gordie shrugged. "Nah, I just don't like you," he said. "Hell, I think I'm going to do you first, just for practice." He snapped the notebook closed and continued setting up the equipment on the table. It looked like a junior mad scientist rig: the centrifuge, a laptop computer, a thing that looked like a miniature microwave, and a small array of test tubes and beakers. When he finished, he looked up and said "Showtime!" He squeezed the drill's trigger a few times and tittered.

Duckie and Chuck looked around in a panic. Mickey watched Gordie impassively. "I'm sure we'd all like to know how Mr. Gordon Sawchuk went from being Gordie the Chuckle Saw to Gordie the Guru," he said.

"Pfft," said Gordie. "I've studied knowledge that you can't possibly begin to fathom. I learned. I grew."

"Well, try me," said Mickey. "I've studied what you might call esoteric teachings. Tibetan Buddhism is, after all, essentially a study of the human mind. I am also familiar with the teachings of Bön, which has a little bit more of a mystical component, you might say."

"Hogwash!" spat Gordie. "A bunch of sweetness and light bullcrap, suitable only for weaklings and old ladies. I know the real truth. I have experienced the human soul. I've seen and studied things that make your Buddha stuff seem like weak tea indeed."

"You mean like those poor women in Winnipeg that you tortured and killed?" asked Mickey.

Gordie the Guru froze and his eyes grew wide. "What... H-how?" he stuttered.

"You thought no one would ever know," said Mickey calmly. "You can't hide your deeds from the universe, man. Anyone with the right eyes can see what you did. Preying on the weak and marginalized. Performing your sadistic 'experiments' on them, then raping and killing them. Although not necessarily in that order."

Duckie and Chuck stared in open-mouthed horror. Gordie the Guru went beet-red and started huffing out nonsense syllables: "Buh … duh …"

Even Malachi seemed momentarily taken aback. It didn't last long. "Don't let him rattle you, old friend," he said. "You said yourself that he could cloud minds. Don't let him derail us when we're so close."

"Right, right," said Gordie. He picked up the drill. "And I've changed my mind. I think I'll start with you." He nodded towards Mickey.

"Whatever's right," said Mickey.

Gordie took a stainless-steel tray and the drill and mounted the stage. Mickey sighed loudly. "Poor Gordie," he said. "All this suffering because you couldn't ever get a laugh. I've got a good one, too. I was going to give it to Duckie here, to make up for running out on him in Tucson. Now it'll never get used. Hate to say it, Gordie, but since you're the only comedian who looks like he's going to get out of this alive, I should probably give it to you. Do you want it?"

"What?" said Gordie, eyeing Mickey suspiciously. "What are you talking about?"

"You always wanted to get a good laugh," repeated Mickey. "I've got a good one, guaranteed to kill. You tell this joke and it will bring down any room. You want it, it's yours."

"Bullshit," said Gordie. "You never gave away any jokes."

"Not true," said Mickey. "I gave Robin Williams the gag about the platypus being proof of God getting stoned."

"You're lying," said Gordie, although he looked thoughtful.

"Okay, you're right," said Mickey. "I actually traded him two grams of coke for it. Hey, it was the '80s. And I *did* give Eddie Murphy that 'goonie goo-goo' gag for nothing. I knew he'd make it work better than I could."

Gordie lowered the drill, fascinated. "Really? That was yours?"

Mickey nodded. "Whatcha got to lose, Gordie? You get this gag; you'll bring down the house anywhere you tell it. If you don't like it, you still get my pineal gland."

"Fine," said Gordie. "Let's have it."

"Naw," said Mickey. "Best if I just whisper it. Don't want anyone else running off with it."

"Who cares?" said Gordie. "The only one left will be Mr. Wolff, and I trust him."

"That's sweet," said Mickey. "But can you be sure the room's not bugged?"

Gordie cast a suspicious glance at Malachi, who flapped his hand at him. "Whatever, whatever," he said. "Just get on with it."

"Great," said Gordie. "You whisper in my ear, then I'll whisper in yours." He gave the trigger of the drill a quick squeeze.

Gordie the Guru bent his head so his ear was hovering a few inches from Mickey's mouth. Mickey whispered quietly into the ear. It didn't take long, maybe fifteen seconds. When Mickey had finished, Gordie stepped back. He dropped the drill and clasped his hands at his chest. His face bore a comically prissy look of surprise.

For a moment, nothing happened.

Then Gordie began laughing. "Oh, holy shit!" he wheezed. "That's gotta…" He laughed harder, cutting off the words. He guffawed heartily, tears streaming from his eyes. His chest heaved as the laughter poured out of him like a thunderstorm. His face turned red, then purple. His eyes bulged from his head. Still, the torrent of mirth rolled forth. He went down on his knees and rolled over on his back. His heels drummed the worn wooden boards of the stage and kicked over one of the candles. His laughter devolved to harsh, choking gasps. He struggled to take in air, yet despite the bugging eyes and eggplant-colored skin, there was still a wide smile on his face.

Finally, there was a harsh, choked cry – CAW! – and Gordie the Guru lay dead on the stage.

"No!" cried Malachi. "No, no, no, NO!" He rushed over to Gordie's body and felt for a pulse. "You bastard!" he screamed at Mickey. "My guru! You've murdered him!"

"Wow," said Duckie. "Some people just can't take a joke."

Chapter 58

There was a commotion in the hallway outside the showroom. Cheryl stumbled through the door, closely followed by Don Bundy. Her hands were bound in front of her with a zip tie, and her mascara ran down her cheeks in dark streaks. Don gave her a shove, propelling her towards a corner of the room. He stopped to survey the scene. "What the hell happened in here?" he asked.

"That … that bastard killed Gordie!" said Malachi, waving a furious finger at Mickey. "Where the hell have you been?"

"There were some problems with the boat," said Don. "All good now."

"Hardly," said Malachi. "Gordie's dead, and that sonofabitch did it, somehow. You've fucked with me for the last time, Gross. I swear it!"

"What happens next?" asked Don.

"We proceed," said Malachi. "I can carry out the procedure, just not as well as Gordie could. My hands might be a little unsteady, and it's bound to be significantly more painful for the subjects." He gave the three comics on stage a dark look.

"You mean more painful that when someone usually shoves a power drill in your ear?" said Duckie.

"But first," Malachi continued, "as punishment for what he did to Gordie, I want you to eliminate the girl in front of Mr. Gross, Don. Make it slow, make it messy. Use a knife."

Mickey's Zen-like calm evaporated. "NO! NO!" he cried. "Leave her out of this! She has nothing to do with this. NOTHING AT ALL!" He struggled in his chair, fell over backwards, and continued to struggle and flop.

Don unsheathed a combat knife with a matte-black blade and brutal serrations along one edge. He advanced on Cheryl, who sank into the corner, whimpering and rigid with terror.

"Sorry about this," Don told her. "Just following the boss's orders. It's nothing personal."

Don reached where Cheryl was curled up, raised the knife, and with a swift stroke brought the blade down and neatly severed the zip tie binding her hands. Then he turned on his heel and threw the knife. It spun across the room and buried itself in Malachi Wolff's thigh halfway to the hilt.

Malachi fell over sideways, screeching with rage and pain. Mickey – who couldn't see the rest of the room from his position on the stage – cried "Cheryl! No! CHERYL!"

"It's okay, man," soothed Chuck. "She's fine. She's fine."

"Maybe you better give me that, sweetheart," said Don to Cheryl. "Looks like we're not going to need it after all."

Cheryl held a small automatic pistol which was shaking wildly. With relief, she carefully put it down on the floor, then turned back to the corner and threw up.

Don quick-stepped to where Malachi was writhing on the floor. He examined the wound and bound Malachi's hands behind him with a zip tie.

"Help me, you bastard!" demanded Malachi. "You're supposed to be my right-hand man. Untie me this instant! Help me! I'm dying."

"You're fine," said Don. "Don't be such a pussy. As for being your right-hand man…" He reached down and extracted the knife from Malachi's leg. "I've just tendered my resignation." Delicately handling the blade, he held the hilt of the knife up in front of Malachi's face. The words "I QUIT" were written there in Magic Marker.

"Let's see about this guy," said Don. He climbed the stage and knelt down by Gordie's body, feeling for a pulse. "This guy's deader than dinosaur shit. Looks like an embolism or something. What the hell happened?"

"Mickey told him a joke," said Chuck. "It killed him."

"Wow, must have been a hell of a joke," said Don. "What was it?"

"'Why did the chicken cross the road?'" said Mickey.

On the floor of the show room, Malachi writhed and squealed. "Help me, you bastard! I'm bleeding out here."

"It's only a flesh wound," said Don. "First things first." He wiped the knife off on his pant leg and deftly freed Mickey, Chuck and Duckie from their chairs. Duckie staggered down from the stage and ran to where Cheryl stood shaking in the corner, and gathered her in his arms.

"Don't hug me," she said. "I smell like puke."

"You smell like rainbows and unicorn farts," said Duckie.

"You're such a romantic," she said. Mickey got down from the stage and also rushed over to hug his daughter.

Overhead, the thudding pulse of a helicopter could be heard getting louder by the second.

"Just what the hell just happened here?" asked Chuck. "Don?"

"Long story, Chuck-O," said Don. "Look, I'm an ambitious guy, but I will not stoop to cold-blooded murder. Unlike *some* people." He turned and gave Malachi a light kick in the stomach. Malachi screeched.

"Don't you think you ought to do something?" asked Chuck. "There does seem to be a lot of blood."

"Oh, okay," sighed Don. He extracted a small first-aid kit from his cargo pants and knelt down by Malachi. "Stop squirming," he told Malachi, "or I'll bop you." Malachi stayed still as Don wound a bandage around his wounded leg.

"When I found out that Malachi and that dingbat were planning on killing you for your pineal gland, I knew I couldn't go along. Just too fuckin' macabre."

"Why didn't you go to the cops?" asked Chuck.

"I didn't have any proof," said Don. He finished binding Malachi's wound and stood up. "Besides, Chuck, I am not a good person. But I'm not as bad as this jerk." He gave Malachi another light kick. "I didn't want to upset the apple cart until I knew for sure what was going on."

"But you let them drug me and kidnap me to another country!" said Chuck.

"I didn't know that," said Don. "I wasn't there when you were drugged.

Hell, I didn't even find out you were on the yacht until we were well into international waters."

"You still could have done something!"

"I did do something! I called the Mounties." He waved at the ceiling, where the sound of the helicopter was right overhead. "There's a Canadian Coast Guard cutter boarding the yacht right now. That's an RCMP helo overhead."

"You sure waited long enough," said Chuck. "I guess you needed to make sure that you were going to get what you wanted."

"Sorry," shrugged Don. "Show business is a bitch. I think Hedy Lamarr said that."

"Look," said Duckie. "Are we about done? I'd really like to get the ever-loving hell out of here!"

"Yes, by all means," said Mickey. "I had some good memories of this place, but they've all been spoiled now."

"Yes, let's move out," said Don. "Time to meet our new Canadian friends. I'm sure they're going to have a lot of questions."

"What do you think is going to happen to Laughingstock?" asked Cheryl.

"It would suit me just fine if they burned it flat," said Duckie.

"Me too," said Chuck. "This place is a joke."

Chapter 59

Los Angeles, February 2020

The audience in Studio 9 of the Wolff Network studio complex was eagerly awaiting showtime. The Wolff Network had been promoting this episode hard, promising an unforgettable evening and an unbelievable secret guest star. Studio 9 was the largest in the facility. The show usually taped in the much smaller Studio 17; however, this was such a big event that it had been moved to this venue, which was normally reserved for the Wolff Network's most lavish productions.

It wouldn't be the Wolff Network for much longer. A rebranding effort was well under way following the sudden and surprising retirement of Malachi Wolff. It was rumored that he was spending his days on his own personal island in the Maldives.

Actually, Malachi Wolff was right there in southern California, in a structure built especially for him. It was a private sanitarium outside the tiny town of Palomar Mountain. He was going to reside there until he died. That might not be much longer, as his health – mental and physical – had declined drastically since the "Bowser Island Incident."

That was what the local papers had called it at first, and then they had stopped mentioning it at all. The Wolff Board of Directors had moved heaven and earth to make sure any information regarding the Bowser Island Incident stayed as obscure as possible. They'd had a great deal of help from the U.S. State Department, along with the FBI, the Canadian Coast Guard, the Royal Canadian Mounted Police and the Los Angeles

County Sheriff's Department. The Wolff board had spread a lot of grease around to ensure that everyone was in agreement that the matter was best consigned to oblivion.

Part of the agreement entailed Malachi Wolff's perpetual confinement in his own personal nut hatch. Right around the same time, there was a massive fire at Wolff's residence in Holmby Hills. The entire complex was considered a loss, and Wolff's heirs – after a lot of legal haggling – had had the charred remains of the structures bulldozed, and donated the land to the city to be used as a public park. A similarly destructive fire occurred on Bowser Island about a month later, but it went largely unnoticed.

The LASD had announced that the murder of Farrah Ortega had been linked to one Gordon Sawchuk, a Canadian national, now deceased. The RCMP was investigating Sawchuk in connection to a series of disappearances and murders of indigenous women in Manitoba that stretched back to the 1990s.

The sudden departure of Malachi Wolff had thrown the network into chaos. When the dust had finally settled, Don Bundy was named the new CEO. There was a lot of hue and cry at first, given that Bundy was an obscure showrunner whose limited experience was mostly in the engineering department. The board had quickly made it clear that anyone who didn't like it was free to seek other employment.

In the green room, Chuck and Duckie nervously sipped sparkling water. They were dressed to the nines, with brand-new bespoke tuxedos. Their show had been running for three months and was moderately successful. Tonight was going to blow it wide open.

"You ready, brother?" asked Chuck.

"As ready as I'm gonna get, man," said Duckie. "I can't believe how fuckin' nervous I am."

"It's gonna be great!" said Chuck. "We are going to make show business history. People are gonna talk about this show like they did with the last episode of *The Sopranos*."

There was a knock on the door and a PA with a headset and a clipboard poked her head in. "Five minutes, guys," she said, and disappeared.

Chuck clapped his hands together. "Let's do this," he said.

In Studio 9, the house lights went down. Even as the crowd quieted, the tension in the studio ratcheted up an order of magnitude.

A booming kettledrum roll thundered from the PA system. From offstage, the show's announcer said, "Ladies and gentlemen! Welcome to *Mic Drop* with Chuck Marshall and Duckie Dunne!"

A tsunami of applause rolled forth from the audience as Chuck and Duckie entered from either side of the stage and met in the middle. Looking natty in their tuxes, the two bowed modestly and waited for the applause to die down. Once the crowd had settled, Chuck began speaking. "Folks, thanks so much for coming out tonight," he said. "I know we've really hyped this show and our special surprise guest, and I know you're probably going crazy with anticipation. Well, now the waiting is over."

"And it's a good thing, too," said Duckie. "We gotta get these tuxes back to the rental place by midnight." A burst of nervous laughter came from the audience.

"We've promised you a special guest," said Chuck. "And that's exactly what you're going to get. For this special show, our only act is going to be our special guest. You'll see why soon."

"Jesus, I can't stand it," said Duckie with genuine emotion. "Let's just get it over with. Just go ahead and introduce him, Chuck, before I lose it!"

"No way, my friend," said Chuck. "That honor is all yours."

"Okay, then," said Duckie. "I'll dispense with the showbiz bullshit. Tonight we welcome back to the stage a comedy legend who we haven't seen for too long. He's also my future father-in-law! Ladies and gentlemen, please give it up for MISTER MICKEY GROSS!"

The audience went dead silent. A few mutterings of *bullshit* could be heard from the crowd over a kettledrum roll.

The stage lights went down, replaced by a spot on the curtain at the back. Chuck and Duckie hustled back to the wings as Mickey stepped through the curtain. Unlike the hosts, he was modestly dressed, in a pair of fresh jeans and a t-shirt featuring the face of a smiling man smoking a pipe. As he approached the mic, the noise from the crowd swelled and swelled, with a few more *bullshits* riding the crest. Mickey stepped to the stand and removed the mic.

The crowd went insane.

An atom bomb of applause, laughter and hoots exploded from the audience. Despite the lines of age around his face and the modest haircut, this was clearly the legendary Mickey Gross, back from the dead! The entire audience was on its feet.

The tumult might have gone on for half an hour, but Mickey managed to get them to settle down. "C'mon, c'mon," he said. "You couldn't have missed me that much!" This elicited another burst of raucous applause.

When the audience had settled down, Mickey said, "Yeah, the rumors of my death were greatly exaggerated. It sure feels good to be back up here. We got a lot of catching up to do. I feel that I owe you an apology and an explanation.

"But first, I want to tell you the *second* funniest joke I ever told."

THE END

Please Leave a Review!

If you liked what you read, I'd appreciate it if you'd take the time to leave a reviews. Heck, even if you didn't particularly like what you read, please leave a review. Reviews help drive readers to my books, and help me become a better writer. Please take a few moments to review this book.

Review on Amazon

Review on Goodreads

Review on Bookbub

About the Author

Crawford Smith rises every morning at 4:30 to meditate, exercise and eat a breakfast of oat bran husks.

Or so he would have us believe.

He also claims to have mastered both engineering and architecture, and says he has documentation to prove it, but few have seen it.

What *is* known is that he can quote an unsettling amount of material from Monty Python and *The Simpsons.* He is also the author of *Jackrabbit* (2019), a speculative retelling of the career of gangster John Dillinger. This was followed by *Powwows* (2021) and *Fester* (2021) – tales of the strange and hilarious goings-on in the town of Fester, Pennsylvania. In 2024, he released *Laughingstock*, a story of the weird underbelly of standup comedy.

He hangs out in Portland, Oregon.

You can connect with me on:

🌐 http://sweetweaselwords.com

 https://www.facebook.com/CrawfordSmithAuthor

Subscribe to my newsletter:

✉ http://sweetweaselwords.com/contact

Also by Crawford Smith

Fester

Inspector Martin Prieboy has a lot on his plate, and when two high-profile cases land on his desk, he soon finds himself entangled in an ancient mystery that Fester's leading citizens want to keep buried. Soon, a chance discovery in the woods unleashes a volatile mixture of history, mystery and greed, threatening the future of Fester. Will Martin stop the absurd dark forces that have been unleashed and keep the town from being torn apart?

Powwows

Deep in the woods lives a wizard called the Professor. In the depths of the Depression, the residents of Fester, Pennsylvania call on "powwowers" such as the Professor to heal ailments, tell fortunes . . . and exact revenge. When an upstart powwower threatens to horn in on the Professor's business, he starts making plans for his own revenge. The sinister forces he sets in motion spiral out of control, and soon threaten to consume the leading citizens of the town.

Jackrabbit

What really happened to John Dillinger? It's 1934, and America is in the middle of a crime wave. John Dillinger, a.k.a. the Jackrabbit, has become America's first celebrity criminal. Now desperate to escape the perilous life that he's created, the Jackrabbit concocts a daring plan to disappear. As the FBI draws the noose tighter, the Jackrabbit knows that time is running out. Will his audacious scheme work, or will he go down in a thunderstorm of lead?

www.ingramcontent.com/pod-product-compliance
Lightning Source LLC
Chambersburg PA
CBHW011125190726
48289CB00012B/2912